COLORS *of*
TRUTH

Center Point
Large Print

Also by Tamera Alexander and available from
Center Point Large Print:

A Note Yet Unsung
Christmas at Carnton
With This Pledge

**This Large Print Book carries the
Seal of Approval of N.A.V.H.**

COLORS *of* TRUTH

A Carnton Novel • Book 2

TAMERA ALEXANDER

CENTER POINT LARGE PRINT
THORNDIKE, MAINE

This Center Point Large Print edition is published in the year 2021 by arrangement with the author.

Copyright © 2020 by Tamera Alexander.

The text of this Large Print edition is unabridged. In other aspects, this book may vary from the original edition. Printed in the United States of America on permanent paper. Set in 16-point Times New Roman type.

ISBN: 978-1-64358-732-5

The Library of Congress has cataloged this record under Library of Congress Control Number: 2020943882

DEDICATION

To all those who, like me,
are drawn to cemeteries
and the secrets they hold

$\mathscr{A}$ Note from the Author

Dear Reader,

I love a love story. Even better, I love a love story steeped in real history, which aptly describes the novel you're holding now.

The journey you're about to embark on in *Colors of Truth* is drawn heavily from the pages of American history and from the lives of the real people who lived and worked at Carnton in Franklin, Tennessee, in the nineteenth century. As you read this novel, I invite you to step back in time into a world vastly different from ours today. Yet even with all those differences, some of the issues that nearly tore this young nation apart then, still reverberate today.

Slavery is an abhorrent evil. It was in the past and remains so in the present. We as individuals, and as nations, have an obligation to do all we can to eradicate it. For one human being to own another is immoral. Because the ground at the foot of the cross of Christ is level. Every human being is created in God's image, and the Word of God clearly states that "*every* tribe, nation, people, and tongue" will be represented in the Kingdom of God. That's been God's plan from the very beginning, and that eternal truth should shape not only our perspective in this world but should guide how we view—and treat—one another.

The years following the American Civil War were rife with chaos, heartache, and struggle, yet they also showcase the incredible strength and resiliency of the human spirit—and of how God intervenes during such times in amazing ways. To glorify himself, as he alone is worthy, but also to lift up the brokenhearted in a nation on the brink of bankruptcy. In more ways than one.

On April 14, 1865, President Abraham Lincoln signed a piece of legislation authorizing a government agency that would one day be responsible for protecting the president of the United States. But Lincoln's authorization of the United States Secret Service empowered ten men—ten special operatives—to track down counterfeiters and bring them to justice. The legislation for the United States Secret Service was the last official act of President Lincoln before he left for a showing of *Our American Cousin* at Ford's Theatre in Washington, DC.

I live a short distance from Carnton and travel almost daily over the once blood-stained battlefield of the Harpeth Valley from the Battle of Franklin on November 30, 1864. If you've not visited Carnton—or if it's been a while—I'd be honored to give you a brief tour. Join me on my website: TameraAlexander.com, click BONUS FEATURES, then WATCH VIDEOS, and I'll show you the home and grounds and share the significance of this estate in American history.

Once you've read Wade and Catriona's story, I'd love to hear from you. You can write me at TameraAlexander@gmail.com.

Thank you for entrusting your time to me. It's a gift I treasure and never take for granted.

Every blessing in Christ,
Tamera

EPIGRAPH

I, the LORD, search all hearts
  and examine secret motives.
I give all people their due rewards,
  according to what their actions deserve.
                    JEREMIAH 17:10 NLT

CHAPTER 1

March 16, 1866
Franklin, Tennessee
21 miles south of Nashville

Catriona held tight to her younger sister's arm, knowing better than to loosen her grip when surrounded by such tempting delights. For once, she could buy Nora almost anything a mercantile might offer to satisfy the desires of a seven-year-old girl's heart. But as she'd spent the bulk of her life skimping and doing without, rarely knowing the contentment of a full belly, much less a full cupboard, not even the thick wad of bills Ryan had mailed back to the family in Ireland could persuade her cautious nature to yield to extravagance. Not with so uncertain a future.

"Let go of me cape, Cattie!" Nora pulled hard, her frown more severe than usual. "I'm only pinin' to take a keener look at her."

"A keener look, you say!" Catriona kept her voice low, mindful of the busy mercantile but especially of one man's scrutiny from behind the counter up front. The proprietor, she guessed, based on his close interest and the air of authority he wore. Apparently store owners in the town of Franklin held the same low opinion of the Irish

11

their counterparts in Nashville did. They hung the same shingles above their entryways too—No Irish Need Apply. But the sign just above that one outside—No Freedmen Allowed—bothered her far more. The word *freedmen* had been crossed off, and another word, a vile word she'd learned upon disembarking in New York City, had been scratched into the wood.

So much for a warm welcome to America. And to Franklin, Tennessee.

She tugged her sister closer, aware of other patrons looking their way. "Child, you're forgettin' that I know what a *keener look* from you is akin to." She shook her head. "Nay. You no more want to take a keener look at that doll than I want to travel in soot and cinder for another three days goin'."

Nora again yanked hard in response and lunged for the porcelain doll propped against a vase atop a much-too-low shelf. The determined little scamp was surprisingly strong for one so wee, and the heat of her temper rivaled the flaming red of her hair. But Catriona held fast. While she didn't share the fiery Irish kiss of her sister's curls, her own hair a darker shade, she did share her temper and matched it full on.

"Nora Emmaline O'Toole, quit your olagonin'," she whispered through clenched teeth. "You'll mind yeself, or we'll be havin' more than words when we get back outside. Are you hearin' me?"

Nora glared up, her slender jaw set like granite.

12

Not for the first time, Catriona felt more like the mam than the older sister, and with seventeen years between them, no wonder. That feeling scared the starch right out of her wits. Because she was no mother. A sister? Aye, she knew that role well enough. But she strongly suspected that Nora needed far more than she could give. And the girl deserved it. But one thing Catriona knew for certain: experience had taught her to hold tight to her sister lest the cute little rapscallion take to doing what *she* wanted to do instead of what she'd been told, much as she'd behaved on the voyage from Ireland.

Recalling what could have happened brought Catriona a shudder. She'd crushed Nora to her that night, so grateful nothing worse had befallen her young sister in that dark corridor aboard the ship— and so thankful that Ryan had insisted on teaching her how to handle the dagger he'd given her before he left for America with his three closest friends. Yet even as relieved as she'd been once they'd made it safely back to their cabin, she'd also wanted to throttle Nora within an inch of her life for giving her such a fright.

The mere recollection of the memory stoked her ire and sickened her stomach, and Catriona doggedly continued in the direction of the dry goods, half dragging her sister behind her. But the mercantile was packed with patrons, and progress was slow.

She would make the scant purchases they

needed, then leave the crowded store before Nora could do any harm. Not that she was eager to face their next undertaking here in Franklin. Far from it. Every day since they'd boarded that ship more than a month ago, she'd felt this particular dread growing inside her. If there were any way to avoid calling upon Colonel John McGavock, she would do it.

But in Ryan's last letter, her twin brother, so full of family honor, wrote of his determination to confront the man whose grandfather had cheated the O'Tooles out of their ancestral land years ago. Why he felt such a compulsion to settle that score after all these years, she didn't know. Yet if Ryan *had* found his way to John McGavock's home, the man might at least possess some information regarding her brother's whereabouts, and that was information she desperately needed. Because Ryan's last letter, the envelope dated the twenty-ninth of November 1864, well over a year gone now, was the last they'd received from him. And that had taken more than five months to find its way to Ireland, arriving ahead of the wrapped bundle of bills by only a handful of weeks. *This money will be enough to bring the family here, and to let us start fresh,* Ryan had scribbled on a scrap of paper tucked inside the currency. *Keep it from Da. Don't let him spend it on drink, and come as soon as you can. So me heart can feel whole again. Believe me ever to be your loving brother . . .*

Catriona couldn't wait to see him, her *baby*

brother—born five minutes later—who stood a head taller than her and had shoulders as broad as a doorway. And she *had* come to America as soon as she could. But how would she find the words to tell him the cruel twists and turns life had taken in recent months? Da had been the first to succumb to dysentery, which she'd written to Ryan about last summer with little emotion other than relief. But the events that followed were too painful to put to the page. A month after Da's death, when they'd been set to sail for America, Mam, Bridget, and Alma all took ill with the same ravaging disease. Bridget and Alma had walked a hasty path through the veil. Only eighteen days. But Mam . . .

Mam had lingered for weeks, wasting away despite Catriona's caregiving and repeated prayers. Bridget and Alma, scarcely twelve and ten, had passed on the very same day, as close in death as they'd been in life. For that reason, she chose to bury them together, and half of her heart had lowered into the earth with them. The rest of it had been buried along with Mam. In the days following, she'd taken to bed herself, weak and exhausted from caretaking and grief. But Nora, youngest and strongest of them all, had never shown a hint of sickness. And now, finally, here she and Nora were. In America. But where was Ryan?

Had he ever received her last letter telling him about Da's passing? If so, he'd never responded. Perhaps he'd written a separate note with instructions on where to meet him over here. Only, she'd never received such a letter. Maybe it arrived *after* she and Nora had sailed from Dublin. Whatever the case, how would they ever find each other in this endless sea of a war-torn country without help? So like it or not—and she didn't— Colonel John McGavock seemed to be her only hope.

Strong-arming the fear inside her, she pushed it away, as she did the question that plagued her day and night: Was Ryan still alive? She'd heard of mothers sensing when their children had died, but she'd never heard of a sister able to feel the death of a brother. Even a twin. But if it could be done, she was certain she would have felt that moment *if* Ryan had breathed his last. They'd been inseparable growing up, bonded in a way that even she couldn't explain after twenty-four years. She'd loved him all her life, and from the moment Da had started beating on him, she would have given her life for his. So surely if Ryan was gone, she would know it. She would feel it in her bones. But she didn't. Which had to mean he was still alive.

And once she located him—and she *would*— the three of them would find a way to move on. Together. She would fulfill her promise to Mam to find her "baby boy," and they would make a new start here, just as Ryan said. Things would be better then. He had such a way with Nora. He, of all people, could bring their little sister back to the land of the living. Nora had never made any secret

16

of the fact that Ryan was her favorite. So despite the theft of their ancestral land by the McGavock family, if lowering herself to prevail upon them would assist in finding her brother, then she would—

Somehow Nora broke free. Catriona spun to lay claim of the girl again, but she couldn't, and the next few seconds seemed to stretch forever.

Nora turned and lunged for the doll, and this time managed to grab the hem of its skirt. But she also bumped the shelf. For a heartbeat, both the vase and the porcelain Southern beauty teetered, the doll's stylish blonde curls bobbing as though she were debating whether to remain where she was or take a headlong plunge to her certain demise. The weight of the vase proved more substantial than Catriona would have first imagined, and she hoped that perhaps—

But no.

The vase pitched forward and brought the blonde-headed beauty along with it. Catriona braced herself for the impact.

The crash of glass on hardwood silenced the thrum of patron conversation, and the subsequent absence of noise was deafening. Catriona's face burned as curious onlookers turned to stare. She looked at Nora. Gone was her little sister's former bravado, her creamy white complexion now pale. Though not as pale as that of the porcelain-faced doll, now lying in a most unladylike heap at their feet, her silk skirts in disarray, her once-lovely painted countenance and even her demure porcelain hands strewn in pieces across the floor.

Nora looked up, eyes wide, and Catriona bit back the harsh words begging to be let loose—especially when she spotted the proprietor barreling down the aisle toward them, his face all manner of red.

"You're gonna have to pay for what that daughter of yours just did! That doll was special-ordered from Paris, France. And the vase was *pure Flint glass!*"

The accusation in his tone only deepened her embarrassment, and she didn't bother correcting his misassumption. "Aye, sir, I'll be payin' for the damages. We're at fault."

"You bet you are." His eyes slid from her to Nora, then to the damage done, then to her again. "First, your kind comes in here trying to steal me blind, taking what don't belong to you. Then you waltz in and start breaking everything in sight. Problem is you all got no respect for others' property. So like I told you, you'll be paying for *every* last penny of what that cost me. Plus what I stood to make before your little urchin went and—"

"I've already given you me word, sir. I'll be payin' what we owe." His anger scalded her pride, but his arrogant contempt prodded her temper. Catriona nudged Nora to stand behind her, wanting to shield her from the man but also to shield him from her. Her sister looked as sweet as Mam's

18

butterscotch pie, but the girl was ornery with a capital *O*. And yet Nora *was* her sister.

"One question does come to me mind, sir. Somethin' I find a wee bit curious." Catriona managed a partial smile. *"Why* would you be placin' so precious a doll on so low a shelf? And beside a vase made of *pure Flint glass* and all." She purposefully pronounced the phrase with the same hoity-toity inflection he'd used—and judging by the crimson creeping up his beefy neck, her insinuation wasn't lost on him.

He took a step toward her, but she didn't shrink away. From a young age, she'd learned to stand her ground when pitted against a man's anger, and this man wasn't five pints full of whiskey and rum, which always made the situation more precarious. That said, her father had never taken a hand to her or her three sisters when deep into his liquor. He'd saved that for when he was sober. As though he wanted to remember the feel of the back of his hand striking them across the face. Yet Mam and Ryan had borne the brunt of his rage, his being sober or not. Catriona had tried to protect them both, but Mam had known how to draw Da's attention away. And Ryan, God bless him, had come into this world with a sense of chivalry that wouldn't allow him to stand aside. He'd considered the duty of protecting the women as his alone. Through the years, their father had made certain Ryan paid for that decision. Again and again.

Ryan had struggled with the decision of going

19

to America, not wanting to leave the rest of them vulnerable to Da's wrath. But when he'd been faced with either starving to death or bearing the brunt of their father's abusive nature, the decision had been clear enough. And, along with Mam, Catriona had managed to protect the younger ones.

She never realized how much she hated their father until she saw him lying in that pine box, his hands folded over his chest so easy and gentle-like. Such a contrast to the hand raised in rage. She'd sworn then never to waste another tear on the man, and she was finding that an easy pledge to keep.

"The doll was displayed where patrons could see it!" The proprietor's tone, tough as steel, matched the glint in his eyes. "And if you'd read the sign right there—the one written in good *American* English—you would've known the doll was fragile. And anyone with half a brain would know the vase was too." The smirk curving his mouth darkened his eyes as well.

Sure enough, a handwritten placard stared mockingly from the shelf, affirming his claim, which only fueled Catriona's irritation. "How much am I owin' you, sir? For the doll and the vase?"

His eyes narrowed. "Sixteen dollars and fifty cents."

Soft gasps rose from onlookers standing nearby, and Catriona had to quell a gasp of her own. The amount was far more than she'd wagered. She had that much—and considerably more—thanks to Ryan, though it pained her to part with such a sum under the circumstances.

"So will you be paying what you owe? Or should I fetch the authorities?"

Clear challenge lined the man's ultimatum, and Catriona caught a hint of pleasure in his tone as though he hoped he'd be called on to do the latter. "Aye, sir. I'll be payin' you. As I said I would."

Disbelief furrowed his brow.

"But I'll be needin' a bit of"—she softly cleared her throat—"privacy to retrieve the funds."

His gaze moved over her, though not in a lewd manner. More as though she were some wretched pup wandered in from the fields covered in muck and mire.

She sighed. "Could I make use of a storeroom, perhaps?"

"I'm not letting you go in there by yourself. You'll rob me blind, then take your leave out the side door, and that's the last I'll ever see of you and your little girl."

"Me name is Nora!" Nora pushed past Catriona, tiny fists on her hips. "And I'm her sister, you nasty oaf, not her daughter."

Catriona yanked Nora's arm and sent her a scolding glance. But the bravado in Nora's eyes had returned. *This child . . .*

"Sir," Catriona continued quickly, eager to see the situation resolved, "I'm not a person who shirks her debts. But since you're not trustin' me,

21

enlist your clerk there, the girl behind the counter, to be goin' with us."

Begrudgingly, the proprietor made the arrangements. But Catriona felt his gaze on her and Nora every step of the way as they followed the young clerk into the storeroom. Catriona gestured for Nora to precede her and gave her another look, daring her to do anything other than stand statue-still and hold her tongue.

She had to find a way to get Nora under control. The child had grown up without proper constraints. How many times had she warned their mother about that? *"But Nora's me youngest, Cattie, and me last,"* Mam had whispered in her final weeks. *"One day you'll understand, when you're havin' bairns of your own. You're goin' to have to be both sister and mam to her. But I know you can. I've seen you with her. Go to America, find Ryan, and make a good home . . . the three of you. But please, let me Nora be a child for as long as she can. This world thieves away youth so swiftly. Much as it did for you. Much as it's still doing, me sweet, stubborn Cattie. Remember what I've been tellin' you time and again—God's help is nearer than the door. Don't let life harden you, dearest. There's still much good in this world despite all the bad. Sometimes it's just hard to see for all the nettles."*

Recalling her last conversations with her mother and the promises she'd made against her better judgment caused her throat to tighten. Mam had endured such a difficult life, thanks mostly to Da.

22

Catriona swallowed hard. Never did she want to be yoked to a man like her mother had been. Life was challenging enough without willingly taking on that added burden. Best to go through life alone. She had Nora and Ryan, after all. That would be enough.

Aware of the clerk's somewhat shy attention, Catriona turned to the side and discreetly lifted her skirt. When she'd sewn herself a new reticule, she'd also fashioned a money pouch with laces that tied snuggly around her upper thigh. She didn't trust stashing the money in their trunk as they traveled, and she for sure wasn't about to carry it around on her wrist in a reticule.

She untied the money pouch, then retrieved the additional cash she needed. *Sixteen dollars and fifty cents.* Such a sum for a silly blunder. What would she have done if she *hadn't* had the money? Ryan must have saved every last dollar he'd earned after being conscripted into the Confederate Army before sending it all back home. She'd read about the wealth and prosperity that could be found in America, but she'd had no idea a soldier in the recent war could earn so generous a wage. Especially a soldier on the losing side.

Yet even knowing that, she found the claims of this country's bounty unaligned with what she'd witnessed upon arriving in Nashville late yesterday afternoon. If it were possible for a city to mourn itself, that's how she would describe the Nashville she'd seen. Buildings boarded up, the faded names of businesses lingering in ghostlike letters on dilapidated brick walls. Streets largely deserted save the contingents of armed, blue-clad Federal soldiers on nearly every corner. Women draped in black and brown—much like her and Nora—their heads bowed, most of them with ragamuffins in tow. But the clusters of men in tattered trousers and coats, former Confederate soldiers from the looks of it—the outcome of the war written in their stooped shoulders, in the lostness in their gazes—reached deepest inside her and tugged hard. She'd searched each of their faces, hoping to see Ryan's.

She counted the bills she'd withdrawn a second time and slipped the rest into her reticule, then secured the pouch again to her thigh and adjusted her skirt. With the pouch facing outward, the folds of fabric hid it well enough.

"That was very brave," the young clerk whispered.

Catriona turned and looked at her.

"What you did out there. Standing up to *old Mr. Pritchard.* That's what people call him behind his back." The girl glanced toward the door leading into the mercantile.

Hearing admiration in her tone, Catriona shook her head. "I've no patience a'tall for people who treat others with such disdain. 'Specially someone they don't even know. Some people look at a person and see what they've *decided* to see instead of what's truly there. But I have to be tellin'

24

you"—she lowered her voice—"it did feel right good to stand up to the ol' tyrant."

The girl laughed, and Nora did too.

"What's your name, dear?" Catriona asked.

"Braxie."

Catriona smiled. "Now there's a name with a story comin' behind it, to be sure." She guessed the girl was around eleven or twelve. Bridget's age. She was pretty in an understated way, and her brown eyes had a cleverness about them that issued a warning. Anyone wise enough to see it would do well not to underestimate her.

"My papa named me after a boy he grew up with back in North Carolina. A friend of his. Turns out, that friend became a general in the war. General Braxton Bragg."

She'd stated it with pride, and Catriona nodded for her to continue, sensing there was more.

"I shortened it to Braxie some time back, though. Me and Mama figured that sounded more like a girl."

"I agree. And I'm likin' the name. It suits you. Have you ever met your esteemed namesake?"

"No, ma'am. But I hope to one day." Braxie's eyes brightened. "General Bragg commanded the Army of Tennessee for a while."

"The Army of Tennessee?" Catriona found her interest piqued. "Me brother was in the—"

"*Our* brother!" Nora peered up, her expression obstinate as she fiddled with a ball of string she'd found who knew where.

Catriona confiscated the string and placed it on a nearby shelf, countering her sister's mulishness with a sharp look. Nora responded by turning up her nose and stuffing her hand into the pocket of her cloak. Even before the girl withdrew its contents, Catriona narrowed her eyes. She'd warned Nora to stop picking up those blasted stones. But everywhere they went, she insisted on gathering them. She'd even hidden a sack of them from home in their trunk. With defiance glittering in her blue eyes, Nora held out a handful of rocks, and Catriona took a deep breath, determined not to take the bait. She turned back to Braxie.

"*Our* brother was in the Army of Tennessee," Catriona continued, her voice determinedly even.

"He fought in the war here?" Braxie looked back and forth between them.

"Aye, he did. He and three of his mates came here from Ireland in spring of '62, and straightaway they were conscripted into the Confederate Army." In the space of a blink, the vivid image of Ryan, Liam, Brody, and Ferris—friends since childhood—leaving to board the ship in Dublin rose to mind. Dear Ferris had been killed early on in the war, Ryan had written. A bullet to the heart. Ryan penned that when Ferris had stumbled beside him, he'd leaned down to help him up only to discover his friend already gone. Catriona couldn't fathom. "So," she continued, pulling her thoughts close again, "we've come to Franklin to—"

"*Braxie!* Aren't y'all done back there yet?"

Irritation sharpened the proprietor's voice, and Braxie moved to open the door, though none too hastily. Catriona silently applauded the girl's gumption.

"All is fine . . . Uncle." Braxie gave Catriona a pointed look, and a smile tipped her mouth.

"He's your uncle?" Catriona whispered, cringing at how she'd described the girl's relative a moment earlier.

Braxie's smile gave way to laughter. "I took no offense to what you said. He may be my uncle, but he's an *ol' tyrant* too." With a reassuring look, Braxie led the way back to the front.

Catriona followed, grateful for the girl's understanding and to discover the mess in the middle of the aisle cleaned up. To her relief, most of the patrons who'd witnessed the debacle were nowhere to be seen. With Braxie's assistance, she located the items she'd come for and proceeded to pay.

Braxie blew out a breath, fingering the bill in her hand. "I haven't seen a fifty-dollar greenback in *forever.*"

Catriona smiled, slightly uncomfortable at the attention Braxie's comment drew from patrons close by but even more so beneath *Uncle* Pritchard's close attention. He stood only feet away, silently auditing the transaction, no doubt making certain she paid for her transgressions.

Beside her, Nora had grown sullen, which was more customary than not these days. These dark clouds usually descended in late evening, closer to bedtime, and most always they portended a bout of silent sobs. Hearing her sister weep like that broke her heart. Once, shortly after dysentery finished its cruel work and Mam had passed, she tried pulling Nora close to comfort her. But Nora pushed away. Only after she'd finally surrendered to sleep could Catriona coax her little body close and attempt to soothe the hurt. The same hurt breaking her own heart.

Braxie counted out her change, then held out the cloth sack containing their purchases. "You and your sister please come back anytime," she said in a friendly yet overtly conspiratorial tone.

Grateful, Catriona accepted the sack and glanced over to see if Mr. Pritchard had noticed, but he'd already moved on to help another customer. "Thank you again for your help, Braxie. Maybe we'll see you again while we're in town."

"I hope so." Braxie glanced to Nora, then looked at Catriona again. "I just realized I don't even know your names."

"Oh, forgive me. I'm Catriona O'Toole, and this is me sister Nora."

"Well, it's a pleasure to meet you both."

"Likewise, to be sure." Catriona peered down to see if Braxie's comment might have drawn her sister out a bit, but the dark frown remained. With Nora's hand securely in hers, she'd just started for the door when she spotted Mr. Pritchard carrying the porcelain doll to the storeroom. He was meticulously brushing the dust from the doll's skirt when it occurred to her that . . .

"Beggin' your pardon, sir!" she called out.

He didn't respond.

She tried again. "Mr. Pritchard!"

He paused, and then gradually, almost begrudgingly, he turned. His eyes narrowed. She waited, but apparently a hateful expression was all the response she merited.

"We'll be takin' that doll with us, please." She gestured, closing the distance between them.

He looked at the doll, then at her. "But it's ruined. Worthless."

She couldn't be certain, but she would've bet all the money in her reticule that he didn't believe that. "She's broken, not ruined. And not beyond some form of repair, I think. So we'll be takin' her, thank you kindly." Catriona held out her hand.

He made no move to comply.

"I've paid good money for that doll, sir. Far more than she's worth, in me good opinion. And I'm not of the mind to be leavin' her behind. I'll take the vase too." The expensive glass was broken to bits, but some pieces were larger, and she wouldn't risk him working those into something else and getting one cent of value—or satisfaction—from the item she'd paid for so dearly.

"The vase is already in the rubbish bin."

She cocked her head. "Then it won't be difficult to be pourin' the pieces into a sack, now will it?"

The tightening in his jaw told her he'd about

reached his limit. He glanced around them, then back at her. "You'd best watch your tongue, girl," he said low. "A lot of folk around here don't take kindly to you people moving in, trying to settle in our town."

She widened her eyes. "Who's sayin' I'm movin' in? Although seein' as how *kind* everyone's been to us, this might not be a bad place to be puttin' down roots."

Meanness slid in behind his eyes, and while she didn't fear him acting on his anger here, in the middle of a mercantile with onlookers, the slight weight of the dagger hidden up her sleeve gave her courage. She'd used the blade only once before, in self-defense in that corridor on the ship, but the outcome had been quite effective despite how her hands had shaken. She'd vowed then to always keep the weapon with her. Because she knew men. Knew the wrath, and wrong, they were capable of.

Pritchard retrieved the broken shards and thrust the bag at her, then held out the doll before letting go prematurely. Catriona managed to catch her, sparing the now faceless and handless beauty a second trauma for the day. She flashed Pritchard a triumphant if not a tad gloating smile. "Nice doin' business with you, sir."

She didn't waste another look at him as she and Nora left the store.

Outside, a cruel March wind snaked a chilling hand inside their woolen cloaks, and Catriona pulled the hood of her cloak up over her head. She reached down to do the same for Nora, but her sister batted her hand away. *Fine, then.* Once those little ears turned to ice, she'd think differently.

They walked in silence down the muddy street. She spotted a church on the corner a short distance ahead and squinted. Franklin Presbyterian Church. Constructed of brick, the building was fancy enough with its stained glass windows as tall as two doors placed end to end and with a steeple as high as heaven itself. A person could probably see the church from miles away. Not that she planned on darkening the doors of that building anytime soon. She'd given up on the feeble promises such places had to offer. But the lovely grove of walnut trees bordering the church . . . Now, *that* she would welcome anytime, along with a lazy summer afternoon.

They continued on for a piece until they passed the Williford Hotel they'd visited earlier, the hotel the porter at the train station recommended. She'd already secured a room for them for the night. Then, depending on what she learned from John McGavock today, if she learned anything at all, they'd move on from Franklin to . . . somewhere.

Her eyes filled unexpectedly with the flood of weariness and grief she'd coerced into submission for weeks, nay, months now. But the long-denied emotions fought back with a vengeance and near stole her breath away. It wasn't that she didn't believe the Almighty saw people's plights and worked on their behalf. She did. She simply no longer believed he would do that for *her*.

"I'm hungry, Cattie!"

Catriona breathed deep, struggling to find her voice—and the tiniest thread of hope. "Finally, you're speakin' again."

Nora's scowl grew fierce. "I'm not likin' this place. And I'm *not* wantin' to be here."

"Truth be told, I don't like it much either. But rarely do we get to be choosin' our path in this life. We talked about that. Do you remember?"

Nora said nothing, but her eyes narrowed to slits.

Catriona sighed. "We're here because it's the last place we know for certain our dear Ryan said he was goin' to be. *Franklin, Tennessee.* He wrote that in his last letter. I read that part to you again on the train. So we're goin' to walk some distance from town to make inquiry of a man I'm hopin' can help us find our brother." Catriona reached into the cloth sack and withdrew a box of crackers, then held them out. With Braxie's help, she'd stealthily purchased a special treat for her sister as well, but she was saving it for later that night, at bedtime when Nora would need it most.

Without a word, Nora grabbed the box, then opened it and began shoving the salty bits into her mouth.

Catriona waited, then pointedly eyed her sister. "I'm beggin' your pardon?"

Nora peered up sweetly. Too sweetly. "Thank you, Catriona . . . for the *dry* crackers."

Catriona heaved a sigh, tempted to snatch the box away. After all, Nora couldn't be that hungry. They'd shared a generous plate of hotcakes, eggs, and bacon in Nashville before boarding the train earlier—and a cinnamon bun too. They both adored confections of any kind, one of the few things they could agree on these days.

But if she took the crackers away from her sister now, she'd have to deal with tears or rants or worse, and she had neither the patience nor the will for any of that at the moment. So she walked on, attention trained ahead and intent on her task, all while the ache for home and family carved an even deeper hole inside her.

She looked at the field spreading out to their right, all wintry gray and lonely feeling. How she missed the brilliant blues and greens of home, standing on the edge of the cliffs in County Antrim and staring out to sea, the spray of the ocean chilling her face even as it kindled memories of what she and Ryan had dreamed America would be like for their family. How different that dream was turning out to be.

The road leading south from town narrowed as they went, and to avoid the worst of the wagon ruts clawed deep into the center, she edged her way to the right-hand side and gestured for Nora to do the same. The clerk at the hotel had given her directions to the McGavocks' home. "It's about a mile or so southeast of town, along Lewisburg Pike. The Harpeth River will be on your left, Carnton on your right."

Carnton. So the McGavocks had taken a bit of the homeland with them when they left Ireland behind all those years ago. Despite the grip of British rule, Gaelic was still common enough in County Antrim, but she found it odd that the McGavocks would choose to describe their home in America with such a word. *Cairn.* A pile of stones. A memorial. To honor the dead, no less. Like a cemetery. A macabre choice to name a home, in her opinion. For as long as she could remember, she'd loathed cemeteries. Hated the finality they represented and the images they conjured from childhood. Images she determined to let stay buried back in Ireland.

Something the hotel clerk added still rang uneasily within her. *"You can't miss the place."*

That sounded as though John McGavock had done more than a little all right for himself—by treading on the backs of the O'Tooles, of course. Printers by trade for generations, her family had never been wealthy, but they'd done well enough—especially since Ryan possessed a special talent for illustrations and decorations. He had an astounding eye for detail and a deft drawing hand. Wealthy people paid a goodly sum for such things.

She shook her head. How different her own family's legacy might have been if John McGavock's grandfather hadn't cheated her great-grandfather out of their land. Without land, a family was nothing. And that's what hers had become. Nothing. She laid a weighty measure of the blame at her father's feet. He'd squandered what inheritance he'd been given, little though it was, on drink and wagers. But maybe if he'd been given everything due him, he'd have been a different man. A better one.

Gray clouds billowing overhead finally made good on their threat, and soft sheets of drizzle, fine as the fanciest lace, fell without a sound, soaking everything that moved and didn't.

"I'm thirsty, Cattie!" Nora whined, several steps behind her.

"Then tip your head back and open up that gob o' yours. You'll be findin' your thirst slaked soon enough."

A moment passed.

"Me feet are achin'! *Och!* These boots you bought me are good for nothin'."

"They're a far sight better than the wafer-thin slippers we had before we left home, so hush up and keep to walkin'. We'll be to where we're goin' soon enough, then you can rest yeself."

An exasperated sigh was all the comment Catriona got, and she offered no response. She focused instead on what she'd rehearsed to say to John McGavock. Right at the outset, she planned to state who she was, and admittedly, she was eager to see if a flash of remembrance lit the man's eyes at the name O'Toole. A bundle of years and more had passed since her family's land had been

35

thieved away, long before she was born. Her father himself had been only a wee lad. But she'd heard Da recount the story so many times that she could recite the woeful tale herself.

Next, she'd ask McGavock about Ryan, her real reason for coming here, and whether her brother had ever called upon Carnton to speak with him. If Ryan had made it there, hopefully he hadn't left social relations with McGavock on so poor a footing that the man would intentionally withhold information from her for spite. She hoped against hope to be leaving Franklin on the morrow with some scrap of detail about—

A curdled scream rose behind her.

Catriona nearly turned around before she caught herself, knowing better. "Nora, I know you're tired," she called out. "But I've no more time or patience for your theatrics today. So hush your whinin' and keep movin'. We'll be there soon."

"Cattie! Help me!"

Anger flared hot in her chest, and Catriona quickened her pace, throwing the words over her shoulder like stones. "Nora Emmaline O'Toole, I am weary to the bone of your—"

"H-help me, C-Cattie. *Please!*"

Catriona slowed. It wasn't in her sister's nature to beg. She turned around, but as soon as she spotted Nora perched atop an old tree stump, taking a rest, her anger spiked again—until she read the look of terror on her face. Catriona dropped the two cloth sacks and ran.

She'd scarcely raced fifteen paces off the road when she saw it, like something from Dante's *Inferno*. At the base of the stump upon which Nora sat huddled, face buried in her knees, was a hand protruding from the earth, its fingers stiff and twisted, reaching up as though to grab hold and drag you under. Time and nature had eaten away most of the flesh, and Catriona swallowed a scream of her own. Especially when her foot sank into the mud and met with something solid beneath. She looked around and sucked in a breath. Not six inches behind her was a skull. But what shook her to the core was that it appeared to still be attached to a body. The one beneath her boots.

She lifted Nora into her arms and ran, tripping over what appeared to be a crudely made head marker that bore a name and other markings she didn't stop to inspect. When they reached the road, Nora's vise-like grip around her neck grew fierce, making it even more difficult to breathe.

"Nora . . ." Catriona gasped for air. "I've got you, dearest. I've got you."

But Nora kept her face buried in the curve of her neck. Her little body convulsed, whether from fright or cold or both, Catriona couldn't be sure. She held her sister tighter and smoothed the bright red curls down her back while whispering over and over, "It'll be all right, it'll be all right," just as their mam had done before she died. Yet even as the promise left Catriona's lips, she tasted its hollowness.

She squinted and stared across the field that stretched for a good mile or more, and she spotted countless other protrusions from the earth that, from a distance, had lent the appearance of a furrowed field in early spring. But now she suspected differently. At that moment, the wind shifted, and she put her hand to her nose, her suspicions confirmed.

Nora's arms tightened around her neck, and Catriona kissed her and cradled her close, pondering what sort of fiendish hell had visited the sleepy little town of Franklin—and hoping with everything in her that their dear Ryan hadn't been part of it.

CHAPTER 2

"The name's Wade Cunningham, Colonel McGavock. I'm obliged to you for meeting with me this afternoon on such short notice, sir." Satisfied that his tone sounded cordial enough, Wade took McGavock's welcoming expression as further confirmation.

"It's my pleasure to speak with you, Mr. Cunningham. Please take a seat."

Wade eased into the Grecian rocking chair opposite the man seated behind the desk, a man he'd been investigating for the past several weeks.

McGavock had ushered him into what appeared to be the office, or perhaps study, of the well-appointed mansion. Lingering aromas of pipe tobacco and well-oiled leather reminded Wade of his own father's "study"—a room off one side of their barn where he'd helped his father mend saddles and farm equipment. And where, on occasion, once the day's work was *done enough, even if not fully done,"* as his father used to say, Pa would throw open the side door and invite his boys to join him. Then they'd all sit and admire the sunset as his father smoked his pipe. Wade still cherished that pipe. And the memories.

McGavock glanced out the window. "I see the

39

weather's turning disagreeable again. I'd hoped all this cold and rain would have moved on by now."

Wade raised a brow. "Seems nobody informed March that spring should be upon us."

"March in these parts can be as wet and cold as December. But spring in Franklin is a most beautiful sight. I don't know whether the business that brings you to Carnton will allow it, but I hope you're able to stay long enough to experience it."

Wade nodded. "As do I, sir." Engaging in cordial conversation with Colonel McGavock was like a burr in his saddle. The man himself, whose military rank had been bestowed, not earned, was everything he'd imagined a Confederate plantation owner to be. Well-bred, in the Southern sense at least, with an air of wealth and confidence about him. But that air held a putrid stench Wade had fought a war to subdue. No, not subdue. Eradicate. Yet what troubled him far more was being back here in Franklin, Tennessee, a corner of the world he'd sworn never to return to.

When he joined the newly formed United States Secret Service last spring, he understood that, as a government operative, he could be assigned anywhere in the country. Anywhere with counterfeiters. And where counterfeiting was endemic. With over a third of the money currently in circulation counterfeit—and this still-fragile nation on the brink of bankruptcy—*coney men,* as the agency called them, were setting up shop everywhere. The Nashville area was rife with them, and their enterprises were prospering while also bedeviling the Federal Government and posing a serious threat to the nation's banking system.

Yet when Chief Wood informed him he'd been assigned to Franklin specifically, he'd strongly objected. But it quickly became clear that Wood wasn't going to budge, so Wade had determined to get in here, get the case solved, and leave this place behind him. For good. He'd figured he would need a month, at the most, to solve this case. But now, sitting here only a mile away from where it all happened, he felt a lot less confident, his gut churning with memories of what he'd seen and what he'd done the last time he was here. He wished he'd pushed the chief a lot harder.

McGavock gestured. "That rocking chair you're sitting in was a gift to my father from a most distinguished friend. The late president Andrew Jackson."

Working to re-center his thoughts, Wade heard admiration in the man's tone and ran a hand over the curved wood and leather arm of the chair as though impressed. "It's a fine piece of furniture, Colonel. And holds a treasure of memories for you and your family, I'm sure."

"Indeed, it does. And those memories grow only dearer with time's passing. Once, when I was a young man, President Jackson joined us for dinner, and afterward, he sat in that very chair and regaled us with stories about the wars he'd been in and all the . . ."

41

Wade did his best to appear interested. In preliminary investigations, he'd unearthed the association between the McGavock family and the late president. Jackson and Randal McGavock, John's father, had been close associates. And from a young age, John McGavock himself had been known to be a "great favorite" of Jackson's. Helped along by that distinction had been an appointment facilitated by Felix Grundy, John's uncle and an influential lawyer and politician. Grundy had personally arranged for John to be the aide-de-camp for the late president James K. Polk, then governor of Tennessee. And this with John only twenty-five years old. To say the owner of Carnton had enjoyed a privileged upbringing was putting it mildly.

Wade wasn't about to admit it in present company, but President Jackson wasn't a man he'd ever choose to emulate. The country's seventh president had been a slave owner, for starters. And a staunch Democrat, like McGavock. But Jackson had possessed one trait Wade found worthy of respect. According to older colleagues in Washington, DC, who'd known Jackson personally, the president had been fiercely jealous of his honor. That had led him to engage in occasional brawls, and Jackson had even killed a man in a duel for casting an unjustified slur upon his wife. Wade had to admire that depth of honor. Because a man without honor wasn't a man.

Integrity. Uprightness. Fairness. All traits he

strove to build his life upon. Sometimes his position with the agency mandated secrecy and deception, and while he never liked lying to people, he did what had to be done. Much like the late president Lincoln, he ranked the Bible, the Declaration of Independence, and the Constitution as the guiding principles of his life. Granted, he didn't read the first of those three as often as he probably should. But he was well-versed in the Declaration and the Constitution, and he'd memorized large sections of each. Integrity, uprightness, and fairness were woven throughout those documents. And in his estimation, they were traits greatly lacking in men like John McGavock. These men were traitors to their country, short and simple.

So it hadn't surprised him at all when, during his preliminary investigation, John McGavock's name rose to the top of the list of those under suspicion of counterfeiting. So many of these large plantations were facing financial ruin after the war   and with good reason. That world was part of the old South, not the new. Yet Carnton was still prospering, and he aimed to find out how.

It had been Chief Wood's idea for him to keep his affiliation with the agency undisclosed. Not that operatives didn't routinely keep a low profile. They did. Sometimes trusted leaders in the community were notified of the agency's presence. But this time several of those "trusted leaders" were suspects. No, with nearly fifty thousand dollars of counterfeit money issued from this part of the country, too much was at stake, and they didn't know who their allies were.

Only two people in town knew who he was and why he was here. A contact at the local bank and one at the post office, two of the three favorite "business venues" for counterfeiters—the third shops and mercantiles, for obvious reasons. The employees at the bank and at the post office had each been subjected to a thorough evaluation. They were clean and eager to lend assistance to the agency. One of them even held strong, albeit secret, Northern sympathies, which was good to know. Still, Wade had to be careful, as evidenced by the recent murder of a fellow operative. Injustice tightened his chest.

Anson Bern's body had been found floating in the Cumberland near Nashville, his throat slit. A former police officer, Bern had been an excellent investigator—and friend. They'd worked together on several cases. Always affable and quick to laugh, Bern had feverishly pursued justice and the upholding of the Constitution. He'd been a formidable force, too, both in his commitment to the agency and in life itself. Over six feet tall and resembling a tree trunk, Bern hadn't been easy to take down. Wade had managed it only once, and that right hook had been merely lucky. Besides, it had all been in fun, a way to blow off some steam. He could still remember the look of surprise on Bern's face, though. *"Didn't know you had that in you, Cunningham!"*

Wade swallowed. Bern's body was discovered nearly two months ago, and he still had trouble believing his friend and fellow operative was gone. Over the past several months, the Secret Service had dismantled nearly one hundred counterfeiting rings, and Wade felt a sense of pride that nineteen of those could be credited to his efforts. His and Bern's. Given time and patience, and with the agency's far-reaching connections, the Secret Service could locate and apprehend almost anyone.

But after a brief surfacing of counterfeit money in Nashville and New York last year, this particular group of counterfeiters had eluded them completely—until a tip they'd received from New York directed them once again to Nashville, then here, to Franklin. Now, along with John McGavock, several of the men with whom McGavock conducted business were in the crosshairs. The foremost being Woodrow Cockrill, a former Confederate officer and, of all things, an accountant in Franklin. *McGavock's* accountant. It wasn't difficult to imagine, considering the devastation the war had wrought upon Nashville and the surrounding area, that an accountant would feel pressure to seek an additional line of income.

Wade needed to quietly investigate all the suspects. So when the chief saw the position of Carnton overseer advertised in the Nashville newspaper, the man recognized the opportunity for what it was and insisted Wade apply. While Wade understood the advantage that being overseer would give him, the memories of what had happened here still haunted his waking and sleeping hours.

But John McGavock's position in this town, his social connections, and the interest Carnton's business dealings drew from outlying areas would prove of great worth to his investigation. The very meeting Wade had witnessed taking place in the parlor across the hallway when he arrived confirmed that fact. He just didn't know the nature of the gathering—yet.

At first glance, though, several prominent men of the community appeared to be in attendance, and that alone sparked his interest. Perhaps they were plotting another Southern subversion, following the South's first catastrophic—and failed—attempt in the recent war. Even now, pockets of resistance against the Federal Government still permeated the South. Post-war rebellions remained plentiful, some more passive than others.

He'd learned that McGavock had a brother-in-law, a General William Giles Harding who lived near Nashville on an estate called Belle Meade. The man had vowed not to cut his beard again until he saw the South resurrected. As far as Wade was concerned, General Harding could die with that beard puddled around his ankles.

An assault of a much more serious nature was materializing in a town on the southern border of Tennessee in the guise of a secret "society" of white-robed, hooded ex-Confederate soldiers.

They were assaulting and terrorizing Negroes, sometimes lynching them. All for no reason other than hatred and a continued antagonism toward the North and the freedmen in general. There'd been rumors that the "white-robed membership" was expanding to Franklin, and one of the suspects already on Wade's list for suspicion of counterfeiting had been linked to those murmurs. That made sense, because societies, even immoral ones draped in white robes, had to be funded.

Outside, the rain and wind picked up, and the branches of a newly bloomed redbud waged protest against the window pane and directed Wade's full focus back to McGavock's voice.

"Jackson's men marched in agony, as you might imagine." McGavock continued with his story, shaking his head. Wistfulness filled his eyes. "Many took ill; even more died. Jackson bought provisions for them out of his own pocket. After all that happened, his men started calling him 'Old Hickory' because he was so tough. And he was that, let me assure you."

Wade gave an acknowledging tilt of his head. "I believe you might have learned a thing or two from Old Hickory, sir. You're a mighty fine storyteller."

McGavock laughed. The sound came across as easy-natured, relaxed, and Wade knew he was well on his way to winning the man's trust, which he had to do to pull this off. If McGavock somehow found out who he really was—not only a US Secret Service operative investigating him and his peers but a former Federal officer of the United States Army, the latter of the two being the most offensive to any good Southerner—he was done for. He'd never get the information he needed. But after he'd identified the counterfeiters? He didn't give a lick if McGavock found out about him. In fact, when the time came, revealing who he was to this staunch supporter of the Southern cause might be enjoyable.

"Now, Mr. Cunningham, to the matter that's brought you here today . . . You said you wanted to speak to me about Carnton. But you haven't yet revealed what—"

"Forgive me, sir." Wade leaned forward. "But are you certain you have the time to spare? When you granted me entrance, I couldn't help but notice that I called you away from other business at hand. Perhaps I should take my leave and return later this afternoon when—"

McGavock waved off the comment. "Not at all. The men and I were finished with our discussion. We were merely reviewing details about a community matter that's needed to be dealt with for some time now."

Wade nodded tentatively as though not fully convinced, while silently congratulating himself on reviving the Southern accent he'd worked so diligently to rid from his speech years earlier. Growing up in southern Kentucky had afforded him many advantages, but the slight drawl hadn't been one of them. As part of preparing for this assignment, he'd nurtured the abandoned drawl until it was more than passable now. Whatever the job demanded.

The silence lengthened, but Wade only leaned back in the rocker. A longtime student of human behavior, he'd learned that reticence in conversation wasn't necessarily a bad thing. Some people were rattled by the silence, and in their discomfort, they attempted to fill the space, revealing more than what they might have otherwise. Other people merely enjoyed the opportunity to talk about themselves. Both types served his purposes.

"Sometimes with community matters," McGavock continued, looking at him over steepled hands, "the greater number of opinions gathered equates to less progress being made. However, in this instance, my neighbors and I find ourselves of like mind. Especially considering the current state of affairs since the war. And what the Federal Government is doing to us. Or, in this case, is *refusing* to do."

Wade offered what he hoped was a commiserating look. "The Federal Government can be . . . cumbersome to deal with at times."

McGavock gave a quick laugh. "That, Mr. Cunningham, is one of the truest statements I've heard of late." Gradually, his expression sobered. "You came down Lewisburg Pike on your way here."

It wasn't a question, and Wade shifted in his chair. "I did."

49

"And may I assume you're familiar with what happened here in Franklin toward the end of the war? And that you saw the condition of the field today off to your right?"

Wade hesitated. It had taken all his resolve not to look across that field as he'd passed it earlier, and memories that only moments earlier had churned his gut suddenly pushed their way to the surface. Images from that brutal night fifteen months ago rose as clear and ghastly in his mind as when he'd stood atop the Federal breastworks with the 104th Ohio Volunteer Infantry that Indian Summer day and stared across the Harpeth Valley. As long as he lived, he'd never forget that burnt-orange sun sinking low on the western horizon as he and twenty thousand fellow Federal soldiers watched the grisly spectacle of Confederate death unfold.

As daylight faded and Federal cannon fire began to rain down, he'd searched the endless sea of butternut and gray marching steadily forward, row after row, column after neat column, all while hoping he wouldn't see his brother's face, praying that perhaps Wesley's regiment had been summoned elsewhere. Temperatures swiftly plummeted that night, and a bitter wind ushered in freezing rain and sleet. Still, Wade had searched every face. But the single wish he'd carried within him for months during the war—to see his little brother again—never came. He never spotted Wesley on the vast battlefield that day. Never got to make things right between them. And never would. Which only made the recent sale of the farm in Kentucky at auction feel even more like a betrayal.

He'd held on to the family land and home for more than a year, knowing he'd never return to live there. It wasn't home anymore. Not with his parents and Wesley gone. He still had his sister, Evelyn, but she was seven years younger and married with children. She hadn't wanted the place either. Her life was in Chicago with her family. His was in Washington, DC, and anywhere else his duties for the agency took him. He'd received a fair amount of money for the farm. And even after giving Evelyn her share of the proceeds, coupled with what he'd already saved, he had enough to purchase land and build a house elsewhere.

He knew he'd done the right thing in selling. Even though at times like this it sure didn't feel like it. Problem was, no other place felt like home either. He wondered if any place ever would.

Sensing McGavock's close attention, Wade swallowed against the tightening in his throat. "I'm aware of what happened here, sir. And of what's in that field."

McGavock's slow sigh held a weight of fatigue. "A group of us petitioned the government to help exhume and properly bury the nearly two thousand men lying in the Harpeth Valley and in the yards of homes and businesses in town where the fallen soldiers were buried after the battle. We especially must remove the remains of all those buried in the fields, exposed to the plowshare. But the government has refused to give aid. They consider those men traitors to their country." He shook his head. "Men who were willing to give their lives for the Confederacy, same as those who were willing to die for the Union. We were a nation of brothers fighting brothers. Don't they know that? But now that war is over. Should we not strive to put the division behind us and move forward as one?"

It took everything within him to even try to appear sympathetic. *"A nation of brothers fighting brothers . . ."* McGavock stated it with such conviction, as though he really understood what that meant. And this from a man who hadn't even fought in the war. Who had never looked down the barrel of a Springfield aimed dead-on at another man's chest before pulling the trigger. As for the exhumations, what McGavock told him wasn't news. Wade had been made privy to the town of Franklin's request that the government pay for reburying the Rebel soldiers. And he wholeheartedly agreed with their decision not to. After all, the South chose to secede. To very nearly tear this country apart. All to maintain a livelihood built on the belief that one race was superior to another.

"What's worse," McGavock continued, "is that they've already exhumed the Federal soldiers buried here. This past fall, all those bodies were removed and shipped to Stones River National Cemetery in Murfreesboro. So while they're at rest, our boys are still lying out there in the cold earth, their honor slowly being stripped away with every day that passes. They deserve so much better." He leaned forward. "Hence, a group of us have formed a burial committee with the aim of seeing every last one of those Confederate soldiers properly buried. I've spoken to my wife, and Mrs. McGavock is in full agreement that we donate two acres of land in our backyard for that very purpose."

"You'd bury them all here? Hundreds of soldiers? On your own land?" The question was out before Wade had properly thought through the delivery. He heard the disbelief in his tone and silently chastised himself for not being more guarded. "What I meant to say, sir, is—"

"I know it may seem odd to some. But we got to know many of those boys personally. Carnton was designated to be a field hospital that night. And you saw the condition of that field today. I daresay you wouldn't be able to leave the men you'd fought with for nearly four years, the men who'd died beside you, in such a state."

A muscle tightened in Wade's jaw. "No, sir. I wouldn't."

McGavock studied him for a moment, and Wade felt certain the man was sizing him up.

"What division did you serve in during the war?"

Having anticipated this question, Wade was prepared for it. But he wasn't prepared for the prick of guilt needling his conscience. Recalling the oath he'd taken upon being sworn in as a government operative of the United States Treasury Department helped him push past it. "The Army of Northern Virginia."

"So you were with Lee? In Richmond? At the end?" McGavock's voice had quieted. Faint nostalgia swept his expression.

"I was."

He'd had to choose the Army of Northern Virginia. Outside of General Lee's army, only one other Confederate force had been left in the western theater in the winter of 1864—General John Bell Hood's here at the battle in Franklin, which Colonel McGavock was far more familiar with. "Grant had Lee in a most difficult situation up in Virginia, sir. But I believe General Lee handled himself with the greatest of decorum. And that he did what was best for the Confederacy. One might even say he did what was best for the country." The lie came out smoothly, as though he believed it was God's honest truth.

McGavock eyed him. "My feelings align with yours to a great degree, though I hold that the outcome of that battle was tragic. Given a handful of strategic decisions, the situation might have turned out very differently. General Lee was one of the greatest militarists of our time. Perhaps . . . of all time."

Movement through the window caught Wade's attention, and he spotted a little redheaded girl hurrying up the brick pathway to the house, her head bent, shoulders stooped against the wind and rain. She couldn't have been more than six or seven years old, and she appeared to be alone. Perhaps she was McGavock's daughter.

"So . . ." McGavock straightened. "Enough about the war and days past. We must turn our faces to the future. You stated at the outset that you're interested in speaking with me about Carnton."

"That's correct, sir. About a position, actually. I read an advertisement in the *Nashville Daily Union* stating that Carnton needs an overseer. Someone to run things. I was raised on a small farm in southern Kentucky. I learned the business from my father. So there's not much I don't know in that regard. And as is the case with so many former soldiers these days, I need a job."

McGavock regarded him. "And what business brought you to Nashville?"

Wade detected distrust in the man's demeanor—or at least apprehension. "As I said, I need a job. The family farm is gone now. My folks are too." He looked down and away, the mournful expression required in the moment coming more easily than he would've liked. "Kentucky doesn't hold anything for me now."

McGavock gave a slow nod. "And what do you know of Carnton?"

Wade looked back. "I know it's not just any farm. Carnton has quite the reputation. But surely you know that. From what I hear, not too many years ago you garnered an award for Carnton being the

55

best farming estate in the county." Another tidbit Wade had unearthed in his digging.

Satisfaction colored McGavock's expression, and Wade could tell his comment had hit its mark. One foolproof way to get on a man's good side was to compliment what he considered his life's work. It never failed.

"Yes, Carnton's reputation has quite a reach. Which is not due solely to my own efforts, of course. My own good father, God rest his soul, laid Carnton's foundation. Literally and otherwise. We all stand on the shoulders of those who've come before us, wouldn't you agree?"

Thinking of the countless slaves who were no doubt responsible for laying the foundation of this house, this estate, McGavock's wealth, and the once-burgeoning, now-collapsing Southern economy, Wade chose to treat the question as rhetorical. Because Randal McGavock wasn't the primary person John needed to thank. Not by far.

McGavock picked up a fountain pen. "Do you have references with you?"

Wade pulled a single piece of folded paper from his coat pocket. "Just the one, sir." He handed it over and then watched as McGavock read it.

The man finally looked up. "This is a military commendation from your commanding officer, *Lieutenant* Cunningham."

"Yes, sir. The only farm I've ever worked is the one I was raised on. My father and mother have passed, as I said. My only brother too. So unless you want my younger sister to put her opinions to the page, that's what I've got to offer."

McGavock looked from Wade to the letter and back. Wade held his stare. The letter was authentic. The only thing the secretary in Washington, DC, had changed when copying it was the name, rank, and signature of the reporting officer.

"You know livestock, Lieutenant?" McGavock finally asked. "That's primarily what I'm dealing in now."

"Yes, Colonel, I do. From cattle to pigs to horses to chickens." At least that wasn't a lie. His father had taught him everything there was to know about working a farm. Not that theirs had been anything like Carnton.

"A while back I had a few Ayrshire cattle imported from Scotland. Have you had occasion to work with that breed?"

"No, sir. But I've heard they're hardier than Guernseys and have an easier time birthing."

McGavock nodded. "One of my heifers is set to birth soon, so we'll see."

The sound of a door opening in the entrance hall brought McGavock to his feet. "Well . . . thank you, Lieutenant Cunningham, for—"

"Please, sir. *Mr.* Cunningham is fine. Like you said, best turn our faces to the future." And better for him personally if the two of them avoided anything that might spawn future discussions about the war.

"I agree. Thank you for coming to see me today. You're staying in town, I assume?"

"Yes, sir. At the Williford Hotel."

"Very good. Mrs. Williford and her manager run a clean place, nothing fancy. Fairly simple, in fact. But she has the best food around, next to what you'd get here, of course. I'll get word to you within a few days at most."

Wade followed him into the entrance hall, where they discovered the meeting across the way dispersing. Wade took mental notes on the various men, listening to their conversations, evaluating them. But what drew his attention most was the little girl loitering in the corner by the door, clutching a tattered-looking doll to her chest, her red curls seemingly impervious to the inclement weather. Her impish features were downright charming, downcast though her countenance appeared to be.

"Is that your daughter, sir?" Wade asked, gesturing.

McGavock trailed his gaze. "No, it's not. In fact, I don't know who the child belongs to. Perhaps she's a friend of my daughter's. But . . . before you leave, I have one last question. I'm curious as to whether you've—"

"Colonel John McGavock?" A confident voice of the feminine persuasion came from behind them.

Wade turned along with McGavock to see a woman staring up at their host with a spark of fire in her eyes. And though her auburn hair wasn't quite as curly as the little girl's, the similarities in their features—maturity only having deepened their beauty in hers—made any denial of kinship untenable. Even the drab brown color of her dress beneath her cloak did nothing to diminish her loveliness.

McGavock inclined his head. "Yes, ma'am. I am Colonel McGavock. How may I be of service?"

"Me name is Catriona O'Toole. And I hail from County Antrim. Our homeland."

The lilt of her Irish accent was thick, but Wade didn't think he'd imagined the emphasis she'd placed on her last name. And he was certain her mention of County Antrim and *our* homeland was meant to hold weight. Sure enough, when he looked at McGavock again, he knew for certain the young woman had struck a chord.

And she knew it too. The slightest lift in her chin confirmed it, as did McGavock's unmistakable backstep.

CHAPTER 3

"County Antrim, you say, ma'am?"

Wade caught uncertainty in McGavock's tone, as though the man didn't trust what he'd heard.

The young woman nodded. "That's right, sir. And I'd appreciate a moment to speak with you. Preferably without an audience listenin' in."

She glanced first toward the group of men, then in Wade's general direction. While she didn't directly meet Wade's gaze, he caught her meaning loud and clear and curbed a smile. Judging by the woman's directness, she wasn't intimidated by McGavock, nor by the man's home or his wealth. Knowing little more about her than this, save first impressions, which couldn't always be trusted, he found his interest piqued and his estimation of her increasing by the second.

McGavock glanced at the tall case clock on the opposite wall, then gave a tilt of his head. "Of course, ma'am—"

"Catriona *O'Toole,*" she supplied, a slight frown revealing her irritation—perhaps over McGavock's quick glance at the clock, or maybe at having to repeat her name, which she'd already offered. Wade had made note. What he hadn't heard was an accompanying Miss or Mrs. He guessed the latter based on the child she had with her. That was one lucky husband and father. Something he hoped to be—someday. Not that the path he'd chosen with the agency allowed for such.

She looked over at the girl and mouthed something he didn't catch. Yet the forefinger she aimed pointedly at the child's boots communicated a firm *stay put.* In a blink, the girl's countenance went from disheartened to out-and-out annoyed. And again, Wade worked to mask his amusement. Though not swiftly enough, he realized, when the child flashed her blue eyes in his direction. With a single look, the little pixie told him she found his enjoyment at her expense unacceptable. Which only encouraged the smile he already knew he wasn't hiding well enough.

"Please, ma'am, remove your damp cloak"— McGavock pointed to where a couple of men's coats hung on a mahogany coat rack—"then step inside the farm office here." He gestured to the room he and Wade had just exited. "Have a seat, if you would, and I'll be in to see you after I bid my guests good day."

She did as he requested, removing the child's cloak as well. Wade watched her as she stared past him at McGavock and the men who were leaving. If he were a betting man, which he wasn't, he'd wager a hard-earned dollar that she and her daughter were just recently off the boat. Based on the traces of soot and cinders still clinging to her travel clothes, even a little in her dark reddish curls, he guessed they'd disembarked not more than a day ago. Two at most. But even weary from the long trip, Catriona O'Toole could turn a man's head, as was evidenced by several of the men glancing in her direction even now. They were careful not to stare overly long or inappropriately, Wade noted. But with unmistakable appreciation. Which he shared.

"A word with you, John?" A man approached McGavock, tall and lean and with interesting facial features. Sloped eyes half hidden by bushy brows, a deep cleft in his chin, and highly pronounced cheekbones. Taken as whole, they lent a quite melancholy look. Studying him, Wade couldn't shake the feeling he'd seen him somewhere before. Yet he'd been to Franklin only that once. Still, something about the man sent him scouring his memory. Even the way his shoulders stooped forward as though bowing beneath an unseen weight seemed familiar.

"John, I appreciate you and your wife accepting this responsibility." Southern heritage deepened the cadence of the man's voice. "Don't think for a moment that I am unaware of what this will cost you, friend. Not only in a pecuniary sense but also in living with the constant reminder of that night, of all that we've lost. And in your backyard to boot."

McGavock shook his head, then glanced at Wade as though to say, *Excuse me for a moment.* Wade

63

nodded and stepped off to the side, though not too far off.

"In a sense," McGavock said in a low voice, "what we're pledging to do here, Fount, is no more than what *you've* done for all these long months. Those are your fields they're buried in, after all. And as we discussed earlier, we'll find various ways to raise funds from the community. An idea I failed to mention to the burial committee is also petitioning the states represented by each regiment of soldiers buried out there. We can write them, asking them to assist with this effort. I believe we can influence them to help since their fathers, sons, brothers, and uncles are among those to be reinterred."

The man nodded. "That's an exceptional idea."

"For which I cannot take credit. Mrs. McGavock contributed that insightful suggestion. And as we both know, my wife is a woman most comfortable in speaking her mind."

"Yes, she is. And she does it so graciously. She is a most practical, and good, woman, John."

McGavock's expression turned earnest. "As was your dear wife, Polly. May she rest in peace."

The men continued speaking, and Wade listened, in no hurry to leave. McGavock had been about to question him on something. And considering it could be about the position of overseer, he was content to wait. If McGavock liked his answer, he might just leave here today with that job, which would greatly aid his investigation. Beyond that,

Catriona O'Toole had fueled his curiosity. He wanted to know more about her business here at Carnton, and what, if anything, that business might reveal about McGavock.

Wade glanced toward the little girl and had to smile. Contrary to clearly issued orders, she had moved several feet in the direction of the parlor. And she was working hard at scraping something from the plank wood with the heel of her boot. Intent on her task, she'd tucked her bottom lip beneath her front teeth, and determination scrunched her brow. *Spunky* came to mind as he watched her. *Handful* too.

She glanced up and caught him watching her—and stilled. Her gaze grew wary, and she took hasty steps back toward the front door. He could clearly read her thoughts. Was he going to tattle on her? Tell that she'd moved when she shouldn't have? Innocence swept her expression, and it might have looked convincing if not for the slight, defiant tilt of her chin. Like mother, like daughter. Wade didn't even try to hide his grin this time, and her eyes narrowed in response.

"Mr. Cunningham . . ."

He turned to see McGavock waving him over.

"Join us, please. And allow me to introduce you to Mr. Fountain Branch Carter, a neighbor of Carnton's whose property is about a mile due northwest from here."

Carter.

The last name hit Wade like a blow to the chest,

65

and the tucked-away memory from a moment earlier suddenly jarred loose. His regiment had confiscated the Carter farm before dawn that fateful morning on November thirtieth over a year ago. Brigadier General Cox had momentarily debated whether to take command of the house straightaway or wait until sunrise. Deciding that time outweighed inconveniencing a family, the general had ordered a detail to the Carters' front door. Wade had led that detail.

Fighting the urge to turn and run, or at least duck his head, Wade met Carter's gaze steady on and held out his hand. With any luck, the older man's memory had begun to brittle with time and age. And there *had* been a dozen men in that pre-dawn detail, not to mention the twenty thousand Federal soldiers who'd overrun the man's house and grounds. Upheaval best described the scenario in Wade's memory. Waking everyone in the house as US soldiers flooded every room, eventually relegating the family to the cellar, where they, their slaves, and neighbors took refuge once the battle started. Surely a man wouldn't remember one soldier's face out of so many. Looking at it from that perspective, Wade took hope and calmed—until the sharpness in Fountain Branch Carter's gaze took that hope by the throat and squeezed.

"Mr. Cunningham." Carter's grip was firm. "You were with us here in Franklin, weren't you, son."

It wasn't a question, and Wade felt the weeks of

preliminary work he'd done for this case begin to crumble. He opened his mouth to respond.

"No," McGavock answered, beating him to it. "*Lieutenant* Cunningham had the honor of serving with General Lee himself up in Richmond."

A shadow eclipsed Carter's expression, as though he was certain he'd seen something only to look back a second time and find it gone. "Richmond," he repeated, rumination still coloring his tone.

Wade merely nodded, his pulse creeping up a notch.

Carter's eyes narrowed. "I bet you saw yourself some sights there, son."

Still sensing doubt in the man's bearing, Wade embraced the accent he'd cast off so willingly. "Yes, sir. I did. None of them are sights I care to recall, though. Hard enough to live through it once, much less live it again every day in your memory." Wade knew the images coming to his mind were vastly different from those of these two men. His were inspired by the celebrated field reports he'd reviewed during Grant's successful siege on the former Confederate capital. Reports detailing how the Rebel troops were starving, their supplies depleted on nearly every front. He'd read those reports and tasted victory and freedom. These men had digested that same news and tasted defeat and subjugation. Ironic, considering both of them had owned slaves.

"Come now, my old friend." McGavock gripped Carter's shoulder, his tone effectively sweeping away the cobweb of memories. "Mr. Cunningham and I agreed only moments ago not to go down that dark path again. Let's focus instead on the task ahead of us. On moving forward. To that end . . ." McGavock accompanied Carter to the double front doors and onto the sheltered but windy front porch, the two men conversing as they went.

Wade let out a held breath, shaking his head to himself. If Carter had truly recognized him—though he felt certain now that the man hadn't—this whole case could've been compromised. He could only imagine how irate Chief Wood would have been if that had—

Sensing someone watching him, Wade looked up to discover that now *he* was the object of attention. A mischievous smile spread across the little girl's face, but the way she looked at him—like a matronly schoolmarm peering over eyeglasses at half-mast—told him better than to think the gesture was kindly meant. If he was reading her right, and he bet he was, she was letting him know she thought he'd told a fib a moment earlier. That little urchin . . .

Feeling foolish at the possibility of being found out by a child, Wade quickly replayed his conversation with the two men and decided that his imagination was getting the best of him. He'd done his own share of bluffing in his life, and he was good at it. To that end, he aimed a well-crafted stare at the little girl with the sole intent of nipping in the bud any speculation she might be entertaining. The look did its work, too, judging by her fading smile. Yet despite his efforts, the spark of defiance in those little blue eyes still smoldered.

"Now, what I was going to ask you earlier, Mr. Cunningham . . ."

Wade hadn't heard McGavock return. "Yes, sir?"

"It regards working with the freedmen who are sharecropping my land now. No injury is meant by this comment, I assure you. But I gather by what you shared earlier—you said you were raised on a small family farm—that your family was not in a position to have slaves."

Wade shook his head. "No, sir, we were not."

"And yet you would consider yourself well equipped to supervise freedmen? To manage the contracts I've made with them and to ensure they'll meet the obligations to which they've agreed?"

Wade stared steadily, wondering how McGavock would react if he told the man about his experience with commanding a regiment of colored troops about fifteen months into the war. And about how those men were some of the finest, bravest, and most loyal soldiers he'd ever had the honor of serving with. When his own commanding officer had told him what regiment he was being assigned to lead, Wade had reservations. Not because the men were colored but because they hadn't been properly trained. How did you send untrained men into war? You didn't. Not unless you wanted them to be slaughtered. So he'd worked hard. They all had. He'd shared an analogy with his men, one he'd heard as a young boy from a "traveling man of God," as his father had called him.

The preacher said that even though life was far from perfect and anger and despair abounded, each person had a choice, like every other person who'd ever drawn breath. *"You have to find a way to move forward! To make a better life. For yourselves, and for others. Life isn't fair, plain and simple. You can either scuttle,"* the preacher had said, looking out across the small gathering, *"or you can sail the seas."* A deeply satisfied smile had swept the man's face. *"Navigare necesse est,"* he'd finished, looking directly at Wade. Even now, recalling that moment, he felt his heart beat a little faster.

The men under his command had adopted the Latin phrase, and it became their regiment's motto, of sorts. Navigare necesse est. *One must chart his course and sail.* And so they had. Each of them in his own way. And the phrase had grown only more meaningful to them when Wade shared that the traveling preacher was a freedman.

Natural leaders gradually rose from among the regiment of United States Colored Troops—Isham Pender, Samuel Cabble, Louis Martin—and they eventually assumed command. So Wade was transferred to another unit. But he still thought about them. Especially Isham, a fellow captain and good friend. Cabble and Martin had been killed in the war, he'd learned. But there'd been no record of Isham's death or current whereabouts when Wade checked last summer. Sometimes soldiers just *disappeared,* especially following a brutal battle that involved heavy artillery. Often, too little was left of a man to know who he'd been. At other times, soldiers deserted and fled west, leaving no trail. No way would Isham do the latter. So Wade hoped, and had even prayed, that his friend had made it through.

But since sharing all this with McGavock would fail to get him any closer to gaining the position of overseer . . .

"I have managed men before, Colonel, and I've worked with freedmen on many occasions. I believe if you treat people with respect, most will reciprocate with the same."

McGavock nodded slowly. "And how would you manage those who do not . . . reciprocate, as you call it?"

Wade shifted his weight, wanting to respond more bluntly than his circumstances allowed. He knew only too well what atrocities many plantation owners had committed under the guise of *managing* their slaves. And he knew better than to think that behavior had ceased once the Emancipation Proclamation had been issued into law during the war or even when the North had finally claimed victory. The war was officially over, but battles were still being waged. Even now, standing in this finely appointed entrance hall, face-to-face with McGavock, he sensed the burden of a deep-seated past shaking a begrudging fist at the future. He wished he knew what kind of slave

71

owner McGavock had been. Either way, it didn't change the depravity of owning human beings. And clearly, the man standing before him was still on the wrong side of the war.

"I believe leadership must be rooted in integrity. A leader without integrity is a tyrant in the making. And frankly"—Wade weighed the cost of speaking so openly and chose his words with care—"I think freedmen are like any other men. They want an honest day's wage for an honest day's work. They want the chance to make their lives better. Same for the lives of the people they care about. They want what, I imagine, you and I both want, sir. A chance to chart their course . . . and sail."

McGavock didn't answer immediately, but when he finally did, his expression was inscrutable. "If you'll excuse me, I have a guest waiting. I'd appreciate it if you'd see yourself out. Good day, Mr. Cunningham."

Feeling put in his place by the man and resenting it, especially since McGavock stood for everything the Federal Army had fought to conquer, Wade nodded.

McGavock left the door to the farm office partially open—for propriety's sake, Wade assumed. And Wade begrudgingly gave him credit for it. He caught the exchange of pleasantries coming from within, McGavock's sounding far more pleasant than Mrs. O'Toole's. What could the woman possibly have against John McGavock? She'd only recently arrived from Ireland, after all—if his guess was right. And it was obvious they hadn't known each other before today.

McGavock's voice softened, and Wade stepped closer to the door, attempting to make out the words. He was careful not to look in the little one's direction, knowing she was likely giving him the evil eye for lingering. But he wanted to know what business her mother had here at Carnton.

Bracing himself for the girl's reprimanding stare, he finally turned toward the front door—to find her not the least interested in him. Her dark frown was aimed squarely at a well-dressed, brown-haired boy who stood considerably taller than her. McGavock's son, he assumed.

But the tiny aproned servant glaring at him from the parlor across the hall, hands on hips, told Wade lingering was out of the question.

CHAPTER 4

Still trying to keep up with the conversation between McGavock and Mrs. O'Toole, Wade nodded to the elderly colored woman scrutinizing him, a shock of gray hair caught up in a kerchief on her head. "Good day, ma'am." He mustered a tone he hoped would invoke trust, which was doubtful, seeing as she'd just caught him eavesdropping.

Her eyes narrowed. "You ain't part of the mess o' men who just met with the colonel 'bout reburyin' all them young boys." Not a hint of doubt colored her tone.

Young boys. Interesting she would phrase it that way. Most of the Rebs he'd watched marching valiantly toward the Federal breastworks that November afternoon *had* been young. Too young. Just like Wesley. "No, ma'am. I met with him following that meeting. About the position of overseer."

She said nothing, simply continued to stare, and Wade read the clear question in her eyes.

He thought quickly. "I was about to take my leave, ma'am, when . . . I remembered something else I needed to ask him."

"Well, I get him back for you. Most likely he's right here in the—"

75

"Farm office," Wade supplied. "Yes, ma'am, he is. But he's meeting with someone. A Mrs. O'Toole."

"Missus *O'Toole?*" Her brow furrowed. "I don't know nobody by that name." She peered past him as though contemplating who the woman might be.

Weighing options for how to proceed, Wade caught snatches of the conversation beyond the door and heard what sounded like desperation in Mrs. O'Toole's voice.

"But are you *certain,* Colonel? I know you're a busy man, but he wrote sayin' he was comin' here. Maybe if you—"

The distinct clearing of a throat brought Wade's attention back to the servant whose gaze was now boring a hole through him. The conversation in the farm office lost to him, he took a step toward her, mindful of the children by the door trading stares. From his vantage point, the little girl was winning—and then some. "My name is Wade Cunningham, ma'am."

The woman gave the slightest tilt of her head. "I'm Tempy, Colonel and Missus McGavock's cook. So you say you's here 'bout bein' the new overseer."

"I am. I reckon quite a few men have applied for the position already."

Her gaze held steady. "And I reckon the colonel could tell you hisself just how many they's been."

Wade curbed the urge to take a deep breath. She

didn't trust him, that was evident. As was the fact that if he landed this job, he sorely needed her to. Cooks knew everything about these families—what went on in the house, who came and went, what deliveries arrived, and which employees held grudges, including whom they held them against and why. And there were *always* grudges. He'd gotten off on the wrong foot with the woman. Now, how to make it right?

"How long have you been at Carnton, Tempy?"

"Longer than you been alive, sir."

He cracked the slightest smile. "Oh, I don't know about that. I'm older than I look."

She didn't bat an eye, and he knew then what he had to do.

"Tempy, a moment ago I'm afraid you caught me—"

"What's in that sack there?"

Wade glanced at the boy to see his eyes wide with curiosity, then looked down. Sure enough, a cloth sack lay at the girl's feet.

She quickly snatched it up. "It's me own special sack! And what's in it is belongin' to me and me alone!"

Her haughty little voice was thick with the Irish and spunk, but Wade noticed the little boy didn't seem to be backing down.

"I never said it wasn't yours. I just asked what you've got—"

"Master Winder." Tempy crossed the distance and laid a gentle hand on the boy's shoulder. "We

77

got no cause to ask what's in the young lady's sack, now do we?"

Master Winder. He'd guessed correctly.

The boy's brow knit tight.

Meanwhile, Tempy eyed the girl. "Who you be, child?"

"Me name is Nora Emmaline O'Toole. I'm hungry and I'm tired, and I'd like to be goin' back to town now."

Wade mentally added *bossy* to the list he'd started for the girl earlier. But her name, Nora, fit her somehow.

Tempy laughed, the warmth spreading across her face as genuine as any Wade had seen. Oh yes, he needed to win this woman's trust, whatever the cost. Because whether or not he gained the job of overseer, she'd been at Carnton long enough to know McGavock's business—and this town's—inside and out. She'd be a definite asset.

"Well, ain't you somethin', child." Tempy shook her head. "Just sayin' what you mean right out loud and clear. Not worryin' 'bout what anybody gonna say or think."

Nora's countenance tensed, and Tempy held up a hand.

"I ain't sayin' that's wrong, little miss. But you's in Master Winder's house now. And since you's standin' in his front hall while it's stormin' and rainin' out yonder, I'm thinkin' you might stew on speakin' your mind with a little more kindness."

Nora's jaw firmed. But Tempy merely raised a

78

brow in response, her expression one of patience and experience with negotiation. Wade watched, intrigued, as the woman's gentle benevolence effectually dismantled the girl's defenses.

Nora sighed, then partially rolled her eyes. "If you must be knowin', *Master* Winder, me sack is full of glass. And it's *expensive* glass. Me sister broke a fancy vase when we were shoppin' in town. She's mighty clumsy that way."

Wade frowned and glanced outside. She had a sister?

"She smashed wee Virginia's comely face too." Nora cast a mournful look at the doll now cradled in her arms, and only then did Wade notice it was faceless. Only strands of frayed thread and shreds of fabric remained where her face had once been.

Nora's bottom lip pudged, and she sniffled. Wade felt a stirring in his chest, sorry for her—until he caught the girl's not-so-furtive glance up at Tempy and Winder, her eyes dry as a bone. She added a heavy sigh as though for good measure, then looked back at the floor. Wade stared, partly impressed, partly dumbfounded. What a little conniver . . . Spunky, handful, bossy, *and* manipulative. An accumulation of traits customarily not mastered by one so young, at least in his experience. Not that he'd been around many children.

"Why are your floors so dirty here?" Nora scuffed the heel of her boot along a dark stain on the planked wood beneath her feet. "Don't you have anyone to be cleanin' 'em for you?"

"Of course we have people to clean them!" Winder answered hurriedly. "And our floors aren't dirty. That's blood. From the war. We had us soldiers all over this house, and they bled something mighty fierce. Isn't that right, Tempy?"

The compassion Wade had glimpsed in the servant's expression a second earlier deepened tenfold. "That's exactly right, Master Winder." Tempy looked thoughtfully at the wooden planks. "I done helped to scrub these floors till my hands was raw and my knees swollen. But the wood just won't give up the blood. It's like it wants us to remember. To not forget what happened here." She shook her head. "As if a body could ever forget that night."

Myriad images filled Wade's mind, and once again he could see the endless wave of Confederate troops pressing toward the earthworks he and other Federal soldiers had hastily constructed per General Schofield's orders. An ache fanned out from his chest. No matter how many Rebs fell, more kept coming, pushing forward as if they feared the war would be over if they didn't stop the Federal Army from defeating the "Mighty Army of Tennessee" that afternoon in Franklin. As it turned out, their fears had proven valid.

More than seven thousand Rebels were killed or wounded that night, Wade learned afterward. That hadn't been difficult to believe. Even before his regiment pushed on for Nashville around nine o'clock that evening, bodies lay thick on the smoke-veiled field, piled six or seven deep. Yet those Johnny Rebs hadn't let up, literally clambering over the bodies of comrades in an effort to breach the Federal earthworks, only to be cut down by the unrelenting barrage of cannon and rifle fire. He could still smell the smoke and blood, could still hear their cries rising through the noise of battle.

"Well, Miss Nora . . ."

Tempy's voice tore through the thickness of memory, and Wade blinked, grateful when the images faded from his vision. But the imagined smells and sounds still lingered inside him, as they always did.

"Why don't you fetch your sister, child, wherever she is, and the two of you can join Master Winder and me down in the kitchen for some cookies and milk. *If* y'all are partial to cookies, that is." Tempy reached out and tugged a red curl.

Wade would've sworn he heard Nora's stomach growl from where he stood. His own responded as well, and he hoped the Williford Hotel served a substantial dinner.

"Oh, me sister won't want to be comin'," Nora said a little too brightly. "She's not carin' that much for sweets. Besides, she's in there meetin' with that man."

Tempy glanced toward the farm office, mild surprise in her expression, and Wade trailed her gaze, Nora's comment sinking in. Catriona O'Toole was this girl's *sister?* Not her mother? For reasons

81

clear only to him—and for that he was glad—the discovery brought far more pleasure than it should have.

"I take it you'll be leavin' now, Mister Cunningham?"

Wade looked over to find Tempy eyeing him even as she ushered the children toward a door a few feet down from the farm office. Wariness lingered in her expression, and he needed to act fast.

"Tempy"—he lowered his voice in hopes the children wouldn't hear—"as I was saying earlier, you caught me attempting to eavesdrop on the colonel and Miss O'Toole's conversation. Which was wrong, I realize. But I do have a good reason for doing it."

Her expression said she doubted that. Still, she wasn't turning him out on his ear. That was something.

"Run on to the kitchen, children," she said quietly. "Just through the dinin' room there, little miss. Master Winder, you know where them cookies are. And remember, Miss Nora's your guest."

Wade caught implicit command in the simple reminder, and apparently Winder did, too, based on the serious nod he gave the woman. But the tiniest smile tipped the boy's mouth before he made a beeline for the door. That the boy respected Tempy was apparent. That he felt affection for her was too. Nora followed in his wake, faceless doll in one hand, sack full of glass in the other. Neither child looked back. Wade wondered again what the two sisters' story was and what had brought them to the States. And to Carnton.

"So you're tellin' me, sir, that you're *not* guilty of what happened?" Catriona O'Toole's decidedly sharper tone sliced through the sudden silence.

"What I'm attempting to explain to you, ma'am, if you'll allow me"—McGavock's voice sounded tender by comparison—"is that what you're accusing me of is—"

"If you got somethin' to say, Mister Cunningham—"

Once again, Tempy's voice jerked Wade back, but this time his attention came begrudgingly.

"—then you best say it, sir, and be done. Then be on your way."

Wade's mind raced. "Yes, ma'am." He needed a reason for his eavesdropping. Any reason. And one suddenly came to him. Out of the blue. It was even partially based in truth, which always served him best. He reached for what he hoped looked like a somewhat embarrassed grin. "One might say I could actually lay the blame at Miss O'Toole's feet." He shook his head as though chagrined. "I met her briefly before she went inside there, and . . . I guess I just wanted to know more about her. Maybe even have the chance to walk her back to town, if she'd allow me that honor."

To his complete and utter surprise, the sweetest smile turned the elderly woman's mouth.

"Why, Mister Cunningham, you got the look of a schoolboy come spring, sir. I think you goin' a little spoony over that woman."

Wade laughed, more relieved than amused. "I guess I might be at that."

"And it's so sudden like too. You said you just met her, after all. So you ain't even knowin' her yet."

Wade shrugged. "Sometimes it happens that way, I guess."

A glint lit the woman's gaze. "Which is what makes it so surprisin' to me, seein' as you called her *Missus* O'Toole back there at the first." She gestured in the direction of the parlor where she'd stood moments earlier, the traces of sweetness leaching from her expression. "You thought she was married. It was little Miss Nora who told us different. I saw the look on your face when she said that woman in there is her *sister.* You was surprised. I doubt you was even hopin' she might be a widow woman."

The air left his lungs. If Chief Wood needed any additional agents, he knew where his superior could find a good one. "Listen, Tempy, if—"

"No, Mister Cunningham. I's done listenin'. And now's the time for you to take your leave, sir."

Feeling put in his place for the second time that day, Wade found this dressing-down easier to stomach. Under the circumstances—false though they were—this reprimand was well deserved. A man seemingly setting his cap for a married woman? What kind of cad must he seem in Tempy's eyes? Her dressing-down also served as a warning, which he heeded. If he did get this job, he had an uphill battle before him just to win this woman's trust. And he already had an inkling that, even if he'd started with a clean slate, she wasn't the kind to trust easily.

Knowing when he was beaten, at least for the moment, Wade gave a brief tip of his head. "It was a pleasure to meet you, Tempy. I hope our paths cross again. Soon."

"Mmm-hmm" was all he heard behind him as he strode out the front door and into the storm.

CHAPTER 5

Defeat pressing in hard, Catriona unlocked the door to their hotel room, wet to the bone and shivering. Same for Nora, who'd scarcely uttered a word since they'd left Carnton. The only semblance of a truce between them had come as they'd passed the field of shallow graves earlier. Nora had scooted considerably closer, yet she hadn't said a thing. But they had no way to avoid that field. Catriona had looked as they'd returned to town. Lewisburg Turnpike was the only road from Franklin that led to and from Carnton.

She deposited the room key and the cloth sacks containing their purchases from the mercantile on a side table, relieved to see that their trunk had been delivered as promised. Thankfully, one of Mrs. Williford's employees had laid a fire in the hearth, and the logs burned low, the coals glowing white hot. She grabbed a poker and prodded them to life, then added another log.

"Take off your cloak, Nora, and hang it on the back of the chair by the fire."

"I know what to do, Cattie! I'm not a child!"

Catriona huffed a laugh. Hearing a seven-year-old say that should have sounded humorous to her. Instead, it sounded sad. Nora had faced more death and heartache in her seven years than most children twice her age. *"Let me Nora be a child for as long as she can . . . This world thieves away youth so swiftly. Much as it did for you."* Perhaps it was the crackle of the fire or the darkness of the room, similar to the feel of her family's small three-room stone cottage they'd left behind, but what crowded Catriona's thoughts most was the hushed desperation in her mother's disease-weakened voice. She squeezed her eyes tight. *I miss you, Mam . . . So very much. And Bridget and Alma too.*

She hoped her mother and two younger sisters were at peace now. That God had ushered them into whatever place awaited people who had lived lives good enough to warrant his approval and—when the appointed time came, according to the priest at Mam's gravesite—would receive a welcome into a peaceful afterlife. Mam had always taught them that believers would be in the presence of Christ after breathing their last here on earth. But the young priest who'd taken Father Mulcahy's place when the older man died had adamantly disagreed, saying he was certain Mam and the girls would spend a good amount of time in purgatory. Being refined by suffering, he'd said. Catriona stared into the crackling fire, her jaw tight. Had Mam and her sisters not suffered enough already? Did the Almighty truly need to inflict more pain?

At twelve and ten, Bridget and Alma had scarcely begun to live when sickness snatched them from this world. They'd been girls through and through, the both of them, so full of innocence and dreams. But her mother . . . At two months shy of forty-four years and having buried as many babes in infancy as those who had lived, Mam had endured many lifetimes in one, it seemed. And it had been an especially hard life, too, thanks to Da.

In Catriona's opinion—not that the Almighty cared about that—if anyone had lived a life worthy of his welcome and rest, it was her mother. Giving to others had been the hallmark of Mam's life. Catriona only wished she'd shown her greater appreciation in that regard. How many times in recent weeks had she tried to lay aside that weighty regret only to pick it up again? She wanted to believe the priest was wrong. But she didn't know her way around the Bible like Mam had, and it felt wrong to question a priest too strongly. A point the young priest had hastened to point out to her as well.

Lighting an oil lamp, she let out a sigh she'd been holding since the colonel had closed Carnton's fancy front doors behind them over half an hour ago. Such a frustrating meeting. And man. So . . . pious in his own eyes. And that long beard he wore. It reached at least the fourth button of his elegant coat. She'd never cared for scraggly beards on old men or young. And why were the McGavocks apparently so well accepted in this town while *her kind* wasn't? John McGavock hailed from County Antrim same as her. Granted, the McGavock family had been in America for decades now. And while she hadn't met John McGavock's wife, so she had no idea whether she was Irish born, McGavock himself had not a trace of the homeland in his speech.

Perhaps that was the secret behind the towns-people's acceptance of them. People weren't nearly as afraid of differences they couldn't see. Or hear. Then again, how could a person miss the last name McGavock? It screamed its heritage loudly enough, did it not? She exhaled. It made no sense. But what could she expect from a country that, up until the end of the recent war, had held an entire Negro population in chains? And if there was one thing an Irishman—or woman—knew about, it was being forcibly yoked to another. She had to admit, though . . . America had successfully managed to shrug off England's yoke while Ireland was still shackled in royal chains.

It had bothered her greatly, at first, to learn Ryan was fighting for the "slave states," as some newspapers called them. But having arrived on American soil in South Carolina, he'd had no choice. The Confederate States of America passed a law mandating that all white males ages eighteen to thirty-five be drafted into the Confederate Army. Immigrants included. So for Ryan and his friends, it was either fight for the Confederacy or return to Ireland to starve with their families. And joining the army meant consistent pay and potential bounties. Ryan had also shared his hope that, with Irishmen choosing to fight for their new country, perhaps the Irish would be seen in a better light. Certain occupations had been exempted from conscription, he'd confided. One of them being that of a printer. But he'd insisted that his friends would not go to war without him. *If they go, I go,* he'd written.

The gist of it, though, was that once Ryan O'Toole had grabbed hold of the dream this "land of opportunity" promised, he'd forged his will of iron into making a new life for his family, and nothing could stop him. There was no letting go. They had that stubbornness in common, the two of them, brother and sister. Twins in so many ways. She only hoped the freedom this war had bought would be a strong and lasting one.

She shed her own cloak and draped it over the chair, careful to spread out the hem so it would dry. She did the same to the hem of Nora's cloak, then rose, the muscles in her back and neck screaming with pain. Her left forearm ached, too, from carrying the sack of mercantile goods to and from Carnton.

It was scarcely half past six, but the exhausting journey over the last month was catching up with them both, so the time felt much later than it was. Her stomach grumbled, and she wished again they could have taken dinner downstairs with the other hotel guests. It didn't help that when they'd arrived at the hotel, the meal had already been well underway and every table appeared full. She'd suggested to Nora they stop by the kitchen for a plate, but the child had pitched a fit, insisting that she wanted to go to bed and wasn't hungry. Full because of all those cookies the wee glutton had stuffed down at Carnton, no doubt. Catriona's mouth watered at the thought. She loved cookies, and Nora knew it.

There'd been a time when her sister would've squirreled away one or two in her pocket to share with her. But that Nora was gone. As was the bond they'd shared. Catriona only hoped it wasn't gone for good.

She massaged her shoulders, the conversation with McGavock hanging like a millstone around her neck. It hadn't helped that he'd kept checking the time, first by looking at the tall case clock in the hall when she arrived, then the mantel clock in his office. As though he were bent on pointing out what a bother she was.

"I'm sorry," he'd said. "But I'm afraid I don't remember any such meeting with your brother."

"But are you certain, Colonel? I know you're a busy man, but he wrote sayin' he was comin' here. Maybe if you were to think back. After all, no wee bit of time has passed since then."

"Miss O'Toole." He'd stood and made his way toward the door. "My apologies, ma'am, but it's nearing the dinner hour, and I have responsibilities to which I need to attend. I wish I could help you in this regard, I sincerely do. But again, I'm sorry. To my knowledge, I have never made acquaintance with your brother, nor was he here at Carnton."

Knowing in that moment, as well as she did in this one, that she should have followed his lead and bid him good day, she hadn't been able to make herself do it. Not when intuition shouted that she'd never be given another opportunity to make these inquiries.

"I need to be puttin' one more question to you, sir."

The hint of impatience in his expression had been warning enough, though she still hadn't heeded it. Instead, she'd laid out her case at length—and thought she'd done a rather fine job. Up until the moment his mouth formed a thin, taut line.

"What you're accusing my family of, Miss O'Toole, is simply unfounded. I'm completely unaware of any evidence, nor have you presented any that substantiates your claim, that the McGavocks thieved the O'Toole family land. I most assuredly did not. Nor did my father or, I firmly believe, my grandfather, for that matter. Again, at least that I am aware. And let me hastily add that for either of those men to have done such a thing—and I'm not at all admitting that they did—would have been grossly out of character. They were both men of honor who—"

"And you're sayin' me great-grandfather Tomás was not?"

Catriona could still taste the bitterness of his accusation. But it was the patient look he'd given her in response, like a father would give a recalcitrant child, that had whipped her ire into a full froth.

"I'm saying no such thing, ma'am. What I am saying is that you have presented no evidence of your claim. Indeed, this is the first I've ever heard this charge. However—" He'd held up a hand when she opened her mouth to continue. "I do still have some of my father's and grandfather's farming records stored in the attic. If it would help put your mind to rest, I would be most willing to comb through those files to see if I can find any record of our family's having transacted business in our homeland of County Antrim. Long ago as it's been, I can offer no assurance that I'll find anything, of course. Only that I will look as thoroughly as possible."

Standing by the hearth, Catriona gripped the back of the rocker, still shivering from the cold. His offer had seemed like a practical one at the time. He'd made note of where she was staying here in town and vowed to contact her again in the next few days. But even *if* John McGavock reached out to her again, which was doubtful, what if he told her he'd found no mention of her great-grandfather Tomás O'Toole in those records? What assurance did she have that the man was being truthful with her?

And Ryan . . .

She ran her hands through her damp curls, a steadily increasing throb in her temples. McGavock had answered her question about Ryan so swiftly. Had the man searched his memory thoroughly enough? She didn't believe he had. Yet Ryan O'Toole was not a man easily forgotten. With heredity clearly stated in his deep auburn curls and eyes the watery blue of the Irish Sea itself, her brother was her twin in male form. Only, he had a gift for befriending people that she'd never possessed. From the day he could speak, he'd never met a stranger. Catriona bowed her head. Her sensibilities told her Ryan had not been to Carnton, but her heart simply wouldn't accept it. This was the only place she knew to look for him. If she didn't find direction here in Franklin, she didn't know where else to look.

Nora let out a low growl, struggling to unbutton her skirt. Her face pinched in frustration. Catriona made effort to help, but Nora shrugged her off and turned her back.

Too weary to protest, Catriona ignored her sister's rudeness and readied herself for bed. She hung her jacket and skirt on a peg inside the wardrobe, then untied the money pouch from around her thigh. But where to put it for safekeeping? She glanced around and bypassed several options until she spotted a vase on the mantel. Sure enough, its mouth was wide enough to get her hand in and out. Content with that choice, she stuffed the pouch inside and then returned the vase to its place.

She set the dagger on the hearth, then quickly shed her shirtwaist and underthings and slipped into her nightgown. She laced the ties to keep

95

out the chill. She should have insisted that John McGavock allow *her* to look through those records. That would have been the fairer arrangement. Yet he'd claimed that today was the first time he'd heard of this charge being levied against his family, and the man's audacity and frustration— not to mention the veins bulging in his neck—had seemed authentic enough. When the servant girl knocked on the door announcing dinner was about to be served, the colonel had swiftly bidden her good day. Knowing she'd taxed the man's gentility, Catriona had collected Nora from the kitchen and left.

She released a long, slow breath. So many questions and no answers to fit them. She would simply have to wait on Colonel McGavock. And if he didn't follow up with her soon as promised, she would have to decide then what to do next. Until that time, she and Nora would stay put here in Franklin because this place was the last known connection they had to their brother. Besides, they had nowhere else to go. But visiting Carnton today made her certain of one thing—John McGavock was a powerful man. He held influence in this town, as was evidenced by the meeting taking place in his home. The town elders, she assumed. All older men, about the colonel's age, except for one man who was considerably younger. She remembered him only too well.

Of taller than average height, he had a commanding presence about him that made a woman want to look twice. But she hadn't. Not because she hadn't considered him handsome. She had. And did. Handsome as the devil, some might say. Handsome like her da. Dark-haired, broad-shouldered, an easy, intoxicating smile, chiseled features. And light, bluish-gray eyes that said you could trust him with anything, which was precisely how she knew she couldn't. *That* was what had kept her from looking twice.

Making certain Nora wasn't watching, Catriona stashed the dagger in the drawer of the bedside table. Her sister had seen the blade before and knew what it was. But the girl was more than a little enamored with its decorative grip and sharp edge, so Catriona always took care to store it out of sight.

She paused in closing the drawer and quickly pulled the dagger from its leather scabbard. She ran a finger from the pommel up the stag horn grip, remembering the hours Ryan had spent teaching her how to handle the blade. She'd been so nervous at first, even to hold the thing. But gradually, she'd taken to it. *"Work with it, Cattie, until it feels like part of your arm instead of somethin' you're holdin'."* But she was most proud of the trick Ryan had taught her, which she'd mastered with time. How many times had he made her practice holding the—

"Och!" Nora bit out as she stomped a foot.

Catriona hastily replaced the dagger in the scabbard, then pushed the drawer closed as she glanced behind her, not about to offer her sister help after she'd refused it so soundly. Still chilly, Catriona moved to the fire and stretched out her hands to warm them, then turned around and scooted closer to the flames, warming her backside.

The porter who'd recommended Mrs. Williford's hotel had bragged about how its proprietor set a delicious breakfast for her patrons and brewed the best cup of tea "this side of the Mississippi." Catriona hadn't fully grasped his terminology, but she'd understood his meaning well enough. What she wouldn't do for a cup of that hot tea right now. But at least she'd had the foresight to buy crackers earlier when they were at the—

Catriona stared into the empty box. "You ate all the crackers?"

Nora scowled, still wrestling with her skirt. "I was hungry. And *you* gave them to me!"

"Aye . . . aye, I did," Catriona said beneath her breath, recalling how her mother used to tease that an O'Toole girl could outeat any boy. Catriona imagined that might be true, if there'd ever been food bountiful enough to prove the point. "Are you needin' help with your skirt, little sister?"

Nora's impish features screwed tight as she tugged hard on the button, trying to work it through the buttonhole.

"Careful, Nora, or you're going to rip the cloth. Either that or pop the button clean off."

"Well, you sewed it too tight!"

"I sewed it well so that your buttons wouldn't be comin' undone."

"Or so I could never be sheddin' me clothes and gettin' into the bed!"

Nora glared, but a glisten of tears brightened her eyes before she jerked her head away. Catriona knew better than to try to play the rescuer. Best to act as though helping her youngest sister were a bother, rather than something that, at the moment, she would very much like to do. She summoned a frown that Nora more than matched.

"If you're wantin' me to help you, child, fine. I will. But let's be quick about it. I'm worn and weary meself and ready for bed."

Nora lifted her chin a mite. "Since you sewed it wrong, it's only fair you should be fixin' it!"

Catriona made a show of rolling her eyes, then bent down and gently worked the button through the hole. She *had* sewn it a tad too tightly, she realized, but she wasn't about to admit that now.

Nora donned her bedclothes without assistance, then climbed onto the mattress and slipped beneath the covers. She scooted toward the side closest to the wall, the spot she'd preferred since she could voice an opinion. Which had been moments following birth, as Catriona remembered with clarity. The thought prodded her nearly forgotten sense of amusement. She'd been seventeen years old when Mam gave birth to Nora. Such a cute little bundle the girl had been too—until she'd opened her tiny slit of a mouth. There was no escaping a wee one's wails in a three-room cottage. And Nora had wailed loudly enough to wake the dead.

Catriona looked at that "little bundle" now, all curled onto her side, covers pulled up, covering most of her head. Then she remembered . . . *The special treat.*

She hurried to the side table and dug in the cloth sack past the bar of soap, the two pairs of boot laces, the bottle of leather oil, and other sundry items she'd bought until she found the two soft caramels wrapped in wax paper. Tempted to pop one into her own mouth, she couldn't bring herself to do it. Mam had spoiled her youngest daughter near to rotten—always having a treat for each hand—and Catriona couldn't bring herself to break with tradition. Not considering the promise she'd made. And not even as hungry as she was.

As she crossed back to the bed on her bare feet, she stepped on something sharp and winced. She looked down, then gritted her teeth. Another of Nora's confounded rocks. The girl would be the death of her, she was certain of it. Yet as Catriona leaned over the mattress, she felt the tremors from her sister's silent sobs, and a good measure of her frustration melted away.

"Dearest?" she whispered, then waited.

"What?" Nora finally ground out, her voice surprisingly controlled.

"Hold out your hand."

Nora hiccupped, then, still facing the wall, slowly reached behind her. Catriona pressed an unwrapped caramel into her palm. With a shuddering sigh, the precious, stubborn girl stretched out her other hand, and Catriona slipped the second caramel into her grasp.

Not bothering to wait for a thank-you she knew wasn't forthcoming, Catriona fetched the extra blanket from the bench at the foot of the bed and sank into one of the wooden rockers by the hearth. She drew the blanket close, soaking up the warmth of the fire and relishing the glow of the flame— and the occasional sound of soft chewing. As she rocked to and fro, fading sunlight reached through the floral curtains draping the windows and cast mottled shadows on the floor.

Thinking it might help Nora to fall asleep, she quietly hummed the hymn Mam had sung to all her girls since they'd been bairns. The lyrics came readily enough to her mind, but Catriona tried to block them out, the words like salt in a wound when considering their current circumstances. Because there had been no cleft in any rock where she and Nora could hide in the past weeks and months. The only hiding she'd done was from the Almighty himself. Though despite his stony silence, she sorely suspected he knew every step she'd taken since she and Nora climbed the ship's gangplank in Dublin.

Moments passed, and soon deep, rhythmic sighs from the bed confirmed what she'd been waiting for. Catriona leaned her head back and closed her eyes. She let the grief come then, loosening the knot tied deep inside her, and she didn't wipe away the tears. They trailed down her temples and into her hairline. Before she'd left Ireland, she'd thought she understood what it meant to be alone. To be left behind. But she hadn't. Until now.

Being alone in a place not your home carved a deeper valley inside the heart. Deeper to hold more grief. And grief was a frightening emotion. It stole her breath, taking assurances of the future with it, and made her feel as though she were hugging the edge of a precipice with nothing but air between her and certain doom.

She sat for a handful of moments and allowed the hurt she'd stuffed down deep to rise up just enough to where a portion could escape, like steam billowing from a pot of water set to boiling. If you didn't occasionally remove the lid, the water would boil over. And she couldn't have that happening. Not when it was up to her to hold their world together. To maintain control. So occasionally, like now, she would lift the lid ever so slightly, then just as swiftly replace it for fear that if she fully gave in to the pain, her tears might never cease.

She gradually relaxed and drifted, consciousness easing away from her like an untethered skiff on a glassy pond. She slipped farther from shore and soon was back in Ireland, in her family's cottage. She could smell Mam's boxty frying hot in the skillet, could hear the sizzle of the butter and taste the homey comfort of those tender potato pancakes on her tongue. Then she heard laughter. Bridget and Alma. She couldn't see her younger sisters' faces, but she recognized their giggles, and the lightness of their exchange encouraged a lightness in her. Then she saw him. Ryan. Coming through the door with a smile that seemed to glow from within, and a rush of warmth filled her chest. She ran to him, eager to wrap him in a hug and tell him how much she'd—

From somewhere in the distance, a clock chimed, and Catriona came awake. She blinked, the dream's tide still so full and deep, and she willed herself to surrender to it, to let the pull of memory drag her back out to sea. She wanted to see Ryan again, even if only this way. But her undeniable surroundings pressed close, thieving that wish, and darkness now framed the curtains where, earlier, light had shone through. The clock on the mantel showed half past eight. She leaned forward in the rocker and rubbed the base of her neck, the muscles tight.

With resolution, she stood. Eager for bed, she'd sleep better if she washed away the layer of grime and dirt from their travels. She retrieved the bar of soap from the sack. Washing her hair would be welcome, but that luxury would have to wait. She lifted the pitcher from the stand to pour the water into the—

The pitcher was empty. Grimacing, she stared at the door. The clerk at the front desk downstairs had said if she needed anything she shouldn't hesitate to ask. But asking meant a visit to the front desk.

She glanced down at her gown, then looked at the door again. She sorely wanted to clean up before going to bed, so only one thing to do . . .

She pulled on her boots, minus her stockings, and didn't bother hooking up the laces to the top. She wasn't going far. She shrugged into her still-damp cloak and inspected her reflection in the mirror on the door of the wardrobe. Holding her cloak closed in the front, she decided that unless they looked closely, more closely than they should, no one passing her in the hallway would notice her lack of dress. She retrieved the room key and slowly pulled open the door. The hinges squealed in protest, and she stilled, wincing as she looked behind her.

But Nora didn't stir.

Catriona opened the door wide enough to glance both ways down the corridor. Not a person in sight. She stepped into the hallway, then closed the door noiselessly behind her and slowly turned the knob until the mechanism caught. She locked the door, then headed down the narrow switchback stair-case. No sooner had she reached the lobby than she discovered the front desk unattended. On the desk was a calendar, and she realized what tomorrow was—the seventeenth of March, Saint Patrick's Day. But there was little to no chance that the people in Franklin would celebrate the holiday, not with how most people here felt about the Irish.

The clang of pots and pans drew her attention, and she figured the kitchen was her best chance for assistance. To get there, she had to cross in front of the dining room. But only a handful of patrons lingered following dinner, and they were all seated at a table in a far corner and never looked her way.

She quietly opened the door leading to the kitchen and peered inside. "Hello?"

No answer, so she called out again. This time someone responded, and a moment later a portly older gentleman appeared around the corner.

"How can I help you, ma'am?"

Catriona quickly explained about the empty pitcher.

"Don't you worry, ma'am. I'll have water sent right up. Can we get you anything else?"

She hesitated. "Would it be too much trouble to ask for a cup of hot tea as well?"

"Not at all." He smiled. "We're known for our hot tea."

"So I've heard." She gave him a smile of her own.

"How about I throw a slice of blackberry pie onto the tray too? I believe we have some left over from dinner."

Her eyes watered. "Pie would be lovely, thank you," she managed, touched by the man's kindness and the prospect of easing her hunger.

She thanked him again, then hurried across the lobby and up the switchback staircase. As she turned the corner and started up the second flight of stairs, she heard footfalls behind her. Not at all eager to interact with another hotel guest, especially dressed as she was, she gathered her nightgown and cloak and quickened her pace, eager to reach the haven of her room. Two steps from the second-floor landing, she spotted room 206 and bet herself she could make it before—

Falling forward, she grabbed for the stair rail. And missed.

Her right shin took the brunt of the fall, and she sucked in a breath as pain shot up and down her leg. She gritted her teeth. These blasted boots! She'd tripped over the untied laces. Kneeling awkwardly on the top step, she ran a gentle hand over her shin, already feeling a knot forming beneath the skin. Even more eager now to return to her room, she struggled to rise—when the creak of a door drew her attention.

Only feet away, a man exited the washroom, towel in hand, hair still damp, and with his shirt only half buttoned. Her body went hot, then cold. It was *him*. The man she'd seen at Carnton. Handsome as the devil himself. The man she'd determined not to look at twice. And he was staring straight at her.

CHAPTER 6

Wade recognized her instantly. "Miss O'Toole!"

Her face flushed, the young woman braced herself against the wall, half-kneeling on the top stair. She scarcely met his gaze. Was she ill? Or . . . maybe a little tipsy? Although from what he knew about her, however limited that knowledge, he couldn't quite imagine that last possibility. Maybe she'd simply tripped and fallen. Wade quickly closed the distance and offered his hand. But as though eager to deny him any prospect of gallantry, she hurriedly rose on her own.

He took the hint—and a step back. "Are you all right, ma'am?"

"I'm fine. Thank you, sir." The flatness of her tone and the way her gaze darted from him to a door down the hallway—her room, he presumed—conveyed her lack of interest in conversation. Yet the faint recognition in her eyes when her gaze did meet his said she remembered him well enough. That was something, at least. So was her choice of attire.

Wade didn't allow his gaze to linger, but her cloak had fallen open to reveal she wore only a thin nightgown beneath. A nightgown with blue lace ties. His peripheral vision wasn't the best, but it was good enough to make not looking a second time a real effort.

As though reading his thoughts, she glanced down, and her mouth slipped open. She pulled her cloak tightly about her chest, then pinned him with an accusatory stare as though blaming him for her decision to leave her room in such a state. Similar to earlier that day, Wade had trouble curbing a smile. But Catriona O'Toole was no child, and her pained expression told him she was embarrassed. The flash of warning in her eyes told him he would pay for it too. Guilty or not.

"If you'll excuse me, *sir,* I need to return to me room." She attempted to skirt past him.

"Wade Cunningham," he offered softly, attempting to extend an olive branch. Apparently it worked, because she paused beside him and looked up. Keenly aware of her proximity, he didn't miss how her gaze dropped to his unbuttoned shirt—and lingered. Now, how on earth was *that* fair? "I have the advantage of knowing your name, ma'am," he continued. "So it only seems fitting I should offer you mine."

"How generous of you, Mr. *Wade Cunningham.*" Her mouth turned in a sweet curve, yet her voice held not a trace of cordiality. Which, oddly enough, amused him. Polite mockery. Another trait she apparently shared with her younger sister, Nora. They were quite skilled in it too.

The woman's desire to be rid of his company was evident. But what he couldn't figure was why.

108

She didn't even know him. It occurred to him that some might consider that a prideful thought on his part, but that wasn't his intent. Past experience had simply proven that, in general, women were usually receptive to his attention. Not that he'd given any one woman more attention than another recently. For the past six years, either war or family duty or the agency had consumed his focus. Yet at this very moment, all he could see was her. And that quickly fading smile.

"Good evenin', Mr. Cunningham."

He tipped an imaginary hat. "Evening, Miss O'Toole."

Wade watched her walk away, her stride determined. Her step stuttered once, as though her boot caught briefly on the hem of her nightgown, but he was certain she wouldn't look back at him. And she didn't.

He smiled to himself. Hadn't Nora said something about her older sister being clumsy? The firm flick of the lock on Miss O'Toole's door spoke loudly enough. But it was the memory of the gentle sway of her hips that accompanied him into his own room, directly across the hall from hers.

Closing the door behind him, he shook his head and tossed the damp towel over the rocker by the hearth. Just his luck, he finally met a woman who piqued his interest, but she wouldn't give him the time of day. He sighed. Her obvious dispassion was for the best. He planned to be in Franklin only long enough to solve this case, then he'd be on to the next assignment, wherever the agency sent him.

He raked a hand through his hair. It felt good to be clean, but he was overdue for a haircut. A shave would be nice too. He rubbed his stubbled jaw-line. Maybe Miss O'Toole liked the cleaner-cut, more gentlemanly type. Or someone with scads of money. He fit neither of those criteria.

Judging from the scraps of conversation he'd overheard between her and McGavock earlier that day, Miss O'Toole had inquired about someone—a "he"—having come to Carnton. Or at least she'd been under the impression that *he* had. Then she accused McGavock of something. What, Wade didn't know—thanks to Tempy. He pulled off his boots and stashed the knife he kept in each under the edge of the mattress by his head, then tugged off his shirt and pants. He was aware the servant had only been doing her duty. But whatever McGavock had done, or whatever Catriona O'Toole *thought* he'd done, it sounded serious. Serious enough that Wade wanted to know more. But first, he needed to secure the position of overseer.

He fell into bed, the sheets crisp and cool against his bare back. He closed his eyes, and in the self-imposed darkness his family farm slowly came into view, murky at first, then gaining clarity, like the morning sun burning the shroud of fog off the hills. He could see it all—the white frame farmhouse wearing the passage of years, the barn still sound but sagging in a few places. The corral where he'd

110

broken his first horse. The fields he and Wesley had helped their father turn and plant almost since they could walk. His mother's beloved garden, not untended and gone to seed as it really was after all this time, no doubt, but flourishing with summer bounty. His father's "study" off one side of the barn. And finally, the family cemetery on the upper ridge overlooking the valley where both sets of his grandparents and his own parents rested. *And Wesley too.* But his brother was there thanks only to their sister.

After the war, Evelyn insisted that Wesley's body be located, exhumed, and brought home to Kentucky. So she and her husband had traveled from Chicago to Franklin to do just that. And they'd laid Wesley to rest on the upper ridge.

Wade sighed and opened his eyes. He'd still been so angry with his brother—and bitter toward him—for choosing the wrong side of the war. Then angry with him for dying too. But then the telegram that arrived just before Christmas of '64, informing him of his father's death scarcely a month after Wesley was killed, had all but emptied him of the anger and bitterness. Grief mingled with insurmountable regret had a way of usurping all else.

He swallowed the emotion knotting his throat and reached into the front pocket of his satchel on the floor beside the bed. He withdrew the pipe and held it to his nose. He breathed deeply, relishing the faint aroma of tobacco and dreading the day when that tangible memory, one that could be held and

111

cherished, would fade to nothing. How different life was turning out from what he'd imagined in earlier years. How different *he* was.

Most of the time his work kept him busy enough that the demons lurking at arm's length could be kept there. But in the quiet, in the still moments of evening when shadows loomed in every corner and memories of the war, specifically those from that dreadful night here in Franklin, crowded close, they all but leached the air from his lungs as they troubled the waters of his memory. He didn't like it, being this close to that battlefield again. He took a deep breath, telling himself the tremor he felt inside was only imagined.

Needing a distraction, he turned up the oil lamp and reached for the newspaper he'd picked up downstairs in the lobby following dinner. Reading always helped to slow the throttle of his thoughts. His hand brushed a Bible placed prominently on the bedside table—*For Guests of the Williford Hotel* engraved on the front—and he paused for a heartbeat, then stuck with his original choice. He needed to stay abreast of all that was happening around him, needed to be as prepared as he could be.

His gaze roamed the front page, then snagged on a headline in bolded capital letters. ROBBERY OF THE CLAY COUNTY SAVINGS ASSOCIATION. Two men had robbed a bank in Liberty, Missouri, in broad daylight. The first daylight armed robbery in the United States in peacetime, the reporter said.

Two brothers, from the sound of things. A Jesse and Frank James, two ex-Confederate guerrillas. Wade shook his head. No surprise there. Would the South *ever* finally accept defeat? Another headline caught his attention. FISK UNIVERSITY SEEKS TO RAISE ADDITIONAL FUNDING IN NASHVILLE. The first school for freed men and women had opened earlier that year. He'd heard about the university and applauded the institution from afar. The article was brief, only a mention, really. A perfunctory gesture on the newspaper's part, he guessed. Other schools like it were scheduled to open in other Southern cities. Change was happening, but too slowly for his taste. His gaze dropped to the next column, and he sat up in bed.

WASHINGTON NEWS. RECONSTRUCTION AMENDMENT FACING STRONG OPPOSITION. Wade devoured every word of the article, recognizing names of members of the House who'd fought so hard to get the amendment this far. He knew the opening words of the proposed amendment, the fourteenth, by heart but still read it aloud. " 'All persons born or naturalized in the United States and subject to the jurisdiction thereof, are citizens of the United States and of the State wherein they reside. No State shall make or enforce any law which shall abridge the privileges or immunities of citizens of the United States; nor shall any State deprive any person of life, liberty, or property, without due process of the law, nor deny to any person within its jurisdiction the equal protection of the laws.' "

His grip tightened on the newspaper. How much blood had been shed for these words to be added to the Constitution of the United States? Words that would overturn the decision in the Dred Scott case of '57, which had been immoral, excluding slaves and their descendants from possessing constitutional rights. The House had the votes to pass the amendment, he was certain. They simply needed to get the legislation to the floor of Congress and get it ratified. Representatives from the Southern states would resist, but with Congress requiring them to ratify the thirteenth and fourteenth amendments as a condition of regaining their representation in Congress, they would eventually comply. And the ongoing presence of Federal soldiers in the former Confederate states guaranteed that compliance. He sighed. Hopefully, the ratification would happen by summer. The wheels of progress were indeed moving slowly.

He scanned the next few pages of the newspaper and read until his eyelids began to grow heavy. As he reached over to turn down the lamp, he saw an envelope someone had slid beneath the door. He rose, certain it hadn't been there moments earlier. He would have seen it, even with the mental image of that *gentle sway* still occupying his thoughts.

He crossed the room and leaned close to the door, listening, then slowly drew it open. He peered

114

down the hallway. No one. He glanced across at Miss O'Toole's room, then pushed the door closed.

Chief Wood had told him the courier would be in contact, not saying who or how, which was part of the extra caution being taken this time. The chief had said only that Wade could *"trust this man without reservation."* Wade only hoped that proved true. According to the final briefing, Wade hadn't expected to be contacted for another week or more. He slid a finger beneath the seal. Apparently something important had turned up, maybe a piece of information that would prove useful in his surveillance. Or perhaps information pertaining to Carnton. He withdrew a single sheet of paper. And stared.

Only two words, the handwriting succinct, without any hint of distinction. *Anson Bern.*

Following a restless night, Wade awakened before sunup. He grabbed a quick breakfast in the hotel dining room, and before dawn's pale-pink hues had faded from the eastern horizon, he was situated on a bench off to one side of a main thoroughfare in town. He pulled out his pocketknife and a small piece of white pine, then waited for the community of Franklin to awaken.

A sparrow perched above on a low-hanging pine branch trilled its lyrical song, and a chill cut the early morning air. Wade turned up his coat collar. Against the cloudless sky, a golden sun slowly edged a path over the hills in the distance, promising that the day would be lovely. Spring was indeed on its way.

The anonymous note he'd received still burned a hole through him. Not that it had him running scared or worried. He was always cautious. That came with the territory. And he was good at what he did. But worried? No. Anger was what bored into him now. Anger that whoever had killed Anson Bern was using the murder of a fellow operative— and his friend—to play games with him, to try to intimidate him. Perhaps even hoping to intimidate the agency, which only hardened his resolve to uncover who was behind the unsigned threat. And when he found that person, he would find the counterfeiters. He was certain of it. He was on the right track, being here in Franklin. Otherwise they wouldn't be contacting him. Only people scared of being caught issued threats. Still . . .

That didn't change the fact that someone in this town besides his two contacts at the bank and post office knew who he was. Someone had discovered he worked for the Secret Service, because the agency was the only link between him and Anson Bern. They'd not known each other until shortly before taking their oaths with the agency last year, and they'd made certain never to be seen together in public. So whoever it was had somehow learned the truth about him.

And the question wasn't *whether* they would act on what they knew but *when*. And would they simply make his association to the agency known to all? Or would they try to silence him as they'd silenced Bern?

Workers began arriving at the various shops and businesses, and Wade made note of the individuals unlocking doors and lifting shades. You could tell a lot about people by how they carried themselves and how they went about their daily duties, especially duties often considered mundane. Did someone merely lift the shade on the door and turn away? Or did they lift the shade, then pause to rub the smudge from the lower window before tipping the shingle just so on one side until it hung straight? The former was a hired worker. The latter, an owner. Different levels of pride and responsibility, and to see it, all you had to do was observe. Truth was in the details.

As he whittled and watched, he silently reviewed the short list of suspects. First, John McGavock. He'd already made inroads on that lead. Now if he could only secure the job of overseer, every door in Franklin would be open to him. Next on the list, Woodrow Cockrill, McGavock's accountant. Wade had yet to meet Cockrill, but even on paper the man looked shady.

Leonard Bishop, owner of a local haberdashery just down the street, had enjoyed an exceptionally profitable past year. Especially for a town the size of Franklin, which—owing to the recent war— had far fewer men now than five years ago. So Wade found it interesting that those remaining men had apparently spent a sizable amount of income toward being finely dressed. And this with declining wages and a fragile economy.

Fourth on the list, Whitley Jacobs, owner of what had once been a small farm on the edge of town—until six months ago when that farm doubled in size. Jacobs had not only built bigger barns but built himself a brand-new house. Again, how did a small farmer prosper so quickly in the current post-war climate? Last on the list, Laban Pritchard, owner of a mercantile. Pritchard was the odd one out of the bunch. He wasn't on the list because he'd prospered inordinately over the past year or two. His name was there because he'd been linked to the white supremacist group down south.

Racism was rampant, and just as racism required hate to fuel it, the "hooded ex-Confederates" required money to fund their vile society. A shop owner lacking in morals meant ripe pickings for a counterfeiter. Filtering money through a mercantile was standard fare.

A coney man would enter the store, purchase several low-cost items, pay for them with a large denomination counterfeit greenback—most times a twenty- or fifty-dollar bill—then pocket the change. The *real* money. Then he'd walk down the street and do the same at numerous other shops. Last fall in New York City, Peter McCartney, a well-known and recognizable coney man on the verge of being caught, struck a deal with a mercantile owner. McCartney agreed to give the proprietor a return of whatever portion of fake bills the store owner managed to successfully deposit through the bank. The pair cleared almost fifteen thousand dollars in authentic US currency before Wade and Anson Bern, working hand in hand with the bank, uncovered the deception.

Deceit had no shortage of creativity. But the Treasury Department had a long arm, and a person could hide in few, if any, places once the Secret Service had them in their sights. But Peter McCartney . . . The name brought a familiar bitterness.

After arresting McCartney, Wade had handcuffed the infamous Indianapolis counterfeiter and put him on the train himself. A train bound for Washington, DC—and for justice against the man who'd forged upward of one hundred thousand dollars. McCartney's arms and legs had been shackled, and guards stood sentry. Wade shook his head, still trying to imagine how the scene had played out. The train was moving along at a fast clip, at least thirty-five miles per hour, when McCartney bolted from the bench seat and somehow managed to make it to the back of the train before leaping into the darkness. The train stopped and the guards searched for his body, believing he was dead. But his body had never been recovered. And Wade knew the truth.

Peter McCartney was still alive, somewhere out there, and he was still playing at his game. Was he responsible for Anson Bern's death? Wade paused from whittling and studied the form slowly taking shape at the tip of his knife. His gut told him no. Peter McCartney was many things—an expert engraver and counterfeiter, a charmer who could pull the wool over almost anyone's eyes. But a murderer? It didn't fit what Wade knew about the man. Still, if McCartney was desperate enough . . .

An hour slid by, and the streets began to fill. People passed without even a glance in Wade's direction. So busy in their comings and goings, they paid little attention to the man seated on a bench, head bowed, whittling. And watching.

Being an operative for the Secret Service of the Treasury Department meant long hours of tedious surveillance and careful questioning of locals, most found in the town's more questionable locales. Years back, he'd frequented those places often enough. But no more. The only time he darkened those doors now was when the job demanded it. But he'd come to know that if you wanted to learn the seedier side of a town, those were the places to go. People down on their luck would do almost anything to get it back, including running counterfeit money.

Working for the Secret Service also meant breaking the law on occasion, such as by entering premises without permission. Only it wasn't viewed by the agency as breaking the law. It was viewed as a necessary intrusion on a civilian's privacy to make sure *they* weren't breaking the law. And while Wade was aware that some fellow operatives stretched this allowance to a questionable degree, he had never—and would never—invade someone's privacy without just cause. But given just cause, he'd do it without blinking. Chief Wood approved of almost anything that would help win the war against counterfeiting, including hiring former criminals who'd served time and those still behind bars.

"Lock picking is more art than science," a prison inmate had once told him. *"The more you do it, the better you'll get at it."* The inmate had trained him and the other nine operatives in the art of lock picking in exchange for special amenities behind bars. The inmate had been very good at what he did, too, as evidenced by the list of convictions against him.

Wade stood, needing to move. He pocketed his knife and the piece of wood that, at this stage, bore only the faintest resemblance to a sparrow perched on a tree branch. And that was only if a person employed a good imagination. But he could already see the little fledgling in the wood. He simply had to carve away the excess, which he'd become fairly good at in recent months.

He made his way down the street, his .44 caliber Colt holstered at his hip beneath his jacket. The Secret Service supplied handcuffs, but each operative was responsible for his own firearm, and he'd carried this gun with him throughout the war. The Colt, standard issue for a Federal officer of the United States Army, had served him well. Maybe too well. He fisted his right hand as haunting

121

images from that night in the field a short distance away returned unbidden, forcing their way into his thoughts.

He grimaced, once again seeing the blurred shadows of butternut and gray charging toward him from beyond the breastworks, the thick haze of fire and smoke lending the shadows an almost phantom-like appearance. Fierce determination had hardened some of their faces, hatred had twisted others, and he'd just kept reloading and firing, reloading and firing, unleashing volleys of hot lead. Just as swiftly, it had seemed, the shadows pitched headlong into the smoky haze, their features twisted in pain, the life fading from their eyes. That night was forever emblazoned in his memory, as was the deep muscle ache in his right hand for days following.

Wade took a breath and slowed his steps, praying again that God would forgive all the killing he'd done. He believed the Almighty would—and had. It had been war, after all, and a cause Wade believed in. The ground at the foot of the cross of Christ was level. He'd been willing to die for that belief, and he'd expected to many times over. Looking back, he didn't know how he'd made it through. Then again, he did. Because of God's great mercy. That was all there was to it, and he was grateful to still have breath in his lungs.

But the accountability that came with taking another man's life, even when justified in war, weighed heavy on a soul. Especially when the combat grew brutal and close at hand. In certain moments, like this one, when he looked down at his hands, he could still see the blood that had slicked his palms and stained his uniform.

A stately brick building up ahead drew his gaze, and having thoroughly scouted the town yesterday, he slowed his pace. The words Cockrill & Associates Accounting Services were etched in decorative letters into the plateglass window, and he casually glanced inside as he passed. The three secretaries he could see sat at desks, heads bent over their work, and several offices lay beyond them. Fine furnishings, plush rugs, and expensive-looking oil lamps bespoke wealth and success, communicating without an ounce of uncertainty that this was a firm people could trust. Odd how such an ostentatious display of wealth prompted that conclusion from most people. For him, it usually did the opposite.

A man exited one of the offices, and Wade's attention went to the name placard on the wall—Woodrow Cockrill, President. The man was shorter, not as portly as Wade had imagined but well on his way to getting there. He spoke to one of the secretaries, who immediately grabbed a stack of cut paper and a writing implement and followed him back into the office. The man, Cockrill, Wade presumed, motioned for her to precede him and then made no effort to hide his appreciation of her womanly assets.

Wade continued on past. The time for making

contact with the suspects would come soon enough. After establishing their identities, he would familiarize himself with their daily routines. That way, he could detect any deviations. After all, rats scattered at the first sign of light. Having a legitimate reason to transact business with these men would make all the difference. Again his thoughts turned to Carnton. He had to convince McGavock to hire him. If he were overseer of Carnton, not one of the men on his list would question his inquiries or label his interest curious. He would simply be acting on Colonel McGavock's behest and protecting Carnton's interests.

Spotting a dry goods store ahead, he continued in that direction, needing to purchase a few items. No sooner did he reach for the door handle than the door opened and a patron exited, wooden crate in her arms, her face turned away as though she were speaking to someone behind her. She plowed headlong into him. The box slipped, and its contents went flying. The young woman tried to regain her balance, but in doing so, she over-compensated and nearly fell backward. Reflexes well honed, Wade caught her easily and held her steady, his arm around her waist. Even before she could look up at him, he chuckled, the unmistakable copper curls giving her away.

"Why, Miss O'Toole . . . We meet again, ma'am."

Her head whipped around, and her face promptly turned the color of her hair. "Mr. Cunningham!" She quickly stepped free of his hold, tiny wrinkles pinching the bridge of her nose. She huffed. "Do you not go lookin' before you walk through a door, sir?"

"Cattie, 'twas your own fault!" Nora said behind her. "You were payin' no mind to—"

"You'll be hushin' your mouth, wee one. I was not addressin' you!"

"I know you weren't, but that doesn't mean . . ."

Miss O'Toole turned to face him again, having regained her footing in more ways than the obvious one. Her eyes flashed, and he was certain she was reliving last night when he'd found her, apparently having fallen as she'd come up the stairs. Whatever else Nora was mumbling was lost to him as Catriona opened her mouth to respond. But he quickly beat her to it.

"Don't worry, Miss O'Toole. I wasn't hurt. A little bruised, maybe. But I'll be fine." He winked, anticipating the deepening blue of her eyes. He wasn't disappointed. "Let me help you pick up your items."

He grabbed the crate and reached for a sack of crackers, but she snatched the bag first. "I can be takin' that box, please. And I can pick up me own items. That *you* made me drop." Her smile was sugar itself, though her tone was laced with something a good deal less sweet.

Wade paid her no mind and continued picking up her purchases and placing them in the crate. Besides the crackers, she had a loaf of bread, a cloth-wrapped bundle of what he guessed was

125

butter, and another bundle that, judging from the smell of it, was either smoked ham or bacon. Some raisins and a bottle of molasses rounded out her shopping, along with two green apples that had rolled across the boardwalk. He fetched them both and wiped them clean on his shirt before handing them back to her.

"Thank you kindly," she said with begrudging politeness.

"It's my pleasure, Miss O'Toole."

She quickly took the apples from him and stashed them in the crate, glancing back at Nora as though not wanting the girl to see them. But Nora's attention was transfixed on the peppermint stick she alternately swirled between her forefingers and now-red lips.

Wade found his mood improving greatly just being in this duo's company, and he gestured. "Would you allow me to carry that back to the hotel for you? I'm headed in that direction anyway."

Miss O'Toole gave a shake of her head. "Nay, but thank you. We're not goin' back to the hotel just yet."

"Aye, we are!" Nora smacked her lips. "You were just sayin' that you're—"

"Mind yeself and eat your candy, child!" Miss O'Toole squared her shoulders and her smile. "We have another errand we need to be runnin'. So if you'll be excusin' us, Mr. Cunningham . . ."

Wade stood aside and waved an arm as though granting them formal passage. Nora giggled, candy

126

in her mouth, and skipped past him. Her sister gave him only the thinnest smile. But Wade carried the quick glance she cast back at him when she reached the corner like a picture in his pocket.

CHAPTER 7

"Hurry up and finish your breakfast, Nora. We need to be makin' our way over there." Catriona drained her coffee cup and tucked her folded napkin beside her empty plate. The hotel dining room was abuzz with patrons, and the clock on the fireplace mantel behind her read half past eight.

Three days had passed since they'd visited Carnton and still no word from Colonel McGavock. She'd checked with the front desk at regular intervals, and with every "You've received no correspondence, ma'am," the listlessness inside her grew, which only deepened her despondency. So last night before bed she'd made a brief list of items on which she could take action. Though it wasn't the control over her life she would have liked, it was something.

Ever mindful of the pouch fastened snuggly around her upper thigh, she planned to ferret out a bank this morning. Carrying the small fortune with her while they were traveling was one thing. Keeping it with her all the time—or stashed in the vase in their hotel room at night—was another. She couldn't risk something happening to it.

She'd not deposited money into a bank before, never possessing enough to require doing so. But surely the amount Ryan had managed to send would meet whatever requirements a bank might demand. Her only concern was having ready access to the funds once they found Ryan and could leave Franklin.

Once they found Ryan . . .

The word *if* bullied its way into that thought, and she did her best to vanquish it. She could not and would not lose hope. They'd come this far. They *would* find him.

Patrons filled well over half the tables in the hotel dining room this morning, and she scanned their faces. Thankfully, none of them belonged to Wade Cunningham. So far she'd managed to avoid seeing him again. Perhaps he'd checked out of the hotel. If only she could be so lucky.

When she'd stumbled on the stairs the other night only to look up and find him staring at her . . . *Och.* Reliving that moment caused her face to heat. Her cloak had fallen open to reveal her nightgown, and she *knew* he'd seen that. The man's sly half smile left no doubt. Then she'd run smack into him coming out of the dry goods store! He had to have seen her exiting the store, yet he still allowed her to nearly take them both down. Recalling the solid feel of his chest and the strength of his arms told her that last thought was just an imagining. No way was either of them going down, not with him holding her close. Suddenly feeling a tad overwarm, she fingered the collar of her shirtwaist.

To say that Wade Cunningham lacked in confidence was like saying springtime in Franklin lacked for moisture. The man's self-confidence oozed, same as Da's. Mam used to say Da could charm the skin off a snake. A fitting analogy, as it were. Da had possessed the uncanny ability to make people like him. People who didn't know him, that was. People *not* his family. He always seemed to save the worst of himself for them.

She wasn't blind. She didn't have to wonder what it was about Mr. Cunningham that she didn't like—and whether the comparison was fair didn't matter to her. She'd learned long ago to pay attention to that internal voice of warning. And when it came to Wade Cunningham, warning was all she could hear. Something else bothered her about him. Did the man not own a razor? Always the stubbled jawline as though he'd just rolled out of bed.

Movement from the hallway drew her attention, and when she looked up, she went still inside. A man was facing away from her, but he was tall, broad-shouldered, had dark hair, and—

The man turned, and Catriona let out her breath. Not Wade Cunningham. Still, the sooner they got on their way, the better.

She glanced beside her and would've sworn Nora intentionally chewed even more slowly. She sighed. "Nora, I said to—"

"I'm hurryin'!" Using her fork and knife, Nora meticulously cut her second pancake into eight, uniform pie-shaped bites, then slowly speared three of them with the tines of her fork, working at a snail's pace to make sure each one lined up with its syrupy predecessor.

Catriona fought the urge to take away her plate and be done with it. "Five minutes, then we're leavin'."

Nora's fork clanked onto the plate. "But I don't want to go!"

Aware of hotel patrons looking their way, Catriona discreetly placed a hand on her sister's forearm and lowered her voice. "What you want in this regard is of no concern to me. You *are* goin'. It shouldn't take long, and then we'll—"

"You go on by yeself," Nora said, interrupting with her chin jutting. "I'll wait here."

Her little sister spoke the words with such authority, as though her opinion provided the final say on the matter. Hearing one so young speak with such certainty might have sounded humorous to some, but not to Catriona. Not when images from that near-disastrous night on the ship crowded close. Nora had said something similar to her that night, about waiting for her in their cabin, and the recollection of what could have happened brought a bolt of anger that stoked Catriona's sorely tried patience. It proved a volatile mix.

Catriona peered down at her sister's plate. "Three . . . minutes," she whispered, then watched the storm build behind Nora's eyes.

The girl speared bites of pancake, egg, and sausage and defiantly shoved them into her mouth until her cheeks bulged and she could scarcely chew. Yet Catriona said nothing, knowing the little imp's actions were only a ploy to rile her. The ploy worked. But Catriona didn't dare let it show.

Her patience worn to a nub, she once again found herself itching to take a firmer hand with Nora. But Nora was her sister, not her child. And besides, Da's "firm hand of discipline," as he'd often called it, had only sewn bitterness toward him in her and her siblings. The sting of the back of his hand . . . She could still feel it across her cheek. But when he'd started to take his belt to Nora, she'd managed to block the first blow. Then Ryan intervened and had taken the rest. Nay, she would not discipline her sister as their father had done. She would find another way. But what? Every time she tried being more of a parent to Nora, her efforts ended with Nora either throwing a tantrum or collapsing in sobs. Which only increased her own guilt and made her feel even more of a failure.

She wasn't good at this, at being a mother. Yet Mam had made her wish that Catriona be both sister and parent to Nora more than clear. So on the chance that loved ones gone on before might somehow peer through heaven's veil, even briefly, and see what was happening in the world they'd left behind, she didn't dare risk that her mother would see her breaking her promise.

As Nora gulped the remainder of her milk, Catriona used the privacy the floor-length table-cloth afforded and retrieved the money pouch from beneath her skirt. She slipped it into her skirt pocket. Then, with a hand on Nora's shoulder, she guided her sister from the dining room. She only wished Nora wouldn't insist on lugging around that broken doll with her every time they left the hotel room. Inevitably, while they were out and about, someone would comment on the doll's missing face, and Nora would launch into a fanciful tale about what happened to it. No matter the tale, it was never the full truth—and never Nora's fault. But Catriona figured she had bigger battles to fight at the moment.

It was sprinkling again, the low-hanging gray clouds persistent in their duty, and when she stepped off the boardwalk and into the street, her boots sank in the mud. Nora walked beside her and nearly lost her footing, yet somehow she managed to stay upright. Catriona reached out her hand to help, but Nora turned away. So they continued on, Catriona pretending her sister's reaction hadn't stung.

The hotel concierge's directions to the town's only bank were succinct, and they located the business with ease. Franklin wasn't that large a town, after all. Some seven hundred and fifty residents, the overtalkative server had informed her at breakfast two mornings ago.

The bank lobby was crowded for so early in the day, and Catriona waited in line to speak with one of the clerks seated behind the counter. When it came her turn, she stepped up.

134

"How may I help you, ma'am?" The male clerk looked roughly twice her age and had a brooding, almost sour look about him.

"I'd like to be openin' an account with your bank, please."

He looked from her to Nora, then somewhere beyond them, and Catriona sensed an underlying friction, much as she'd felt during her initial exchange with Mr. Pritchard at the mercantile.

The clerk's brow furrowed. "And do you have funds with which to open this account, ma'am?"

Catriona frowned. What a question. "Aye, I'm havin' the funds. Why would I be needin' an account if I didn't have such?"

His expression fermented further. "What I should have asked"—he pointed to a printed sign on the counter—"is whether you have the *appropriate* funds. We require a minimum of fifteen dollars to secure a demand deposit account with our institution, ma'am. So if you'll kindly step aside, then I can help the next—"

Catriona shook her head. "But I do have the—"

"Is there a problem here, Mr. Wilcox?" A man appeared beside her, impeccably dressed in a suit and one of those funny little bows she'd seen fancy men wearing around their necks. Not very manly, in her opinion. But this man had an air of authority about him, and though his tone leaned toward cordial, it fell shy of convincing.

"Mr. Grissom, sir," the clerk continued, "this woman says she might be interested in opening

135

an account. But as I was attempting to explain—"

"I *am* interested in openin' an account," Catriona said, correcting him. "And I have the *appropriate* funds."

The clerk smiled at her as though she were Nora's age. "Miss, the stipulation means you must maintain that balance in your account. Not merely have that amount to deposit. We are a state-regulated bank and therefore must meet certain—"

Catriona pulled her money pouch from her pocket, then untied it and withdrew the wad of cash. "I believe you'll find that I have that amount and more, *sirs*. But if you'd prefer not to be helpin' me, perhaps I'll take me business to a bank in Nashville and—"

"Oh, no, ma'am!" The clerk's expression smoothed instantly, his focus glued to the stack of bills. A smile she wouldn't have imagined possible spread across his face. "I'm certain we'll be able to help you. If you'll simply—"

"If you will allow me, Mr. Wilcox . . ." Mr. Grissom stepped closer, his attention solely on Catriona now. "It will be my pleasure to assist you personally in opening your account, ma'am."

Feeling as though they were finally getting somewhere, Catriona returned the stack of bills to her money pouch. "Thank you, Mr. Grissom. I would appreciate that very much."

"Follow me, please, Miss . . ." He paused, question in his expression.

"O'Toole. Miss Catriona O'Toole."

"Miss O'Toole. This way, if you would."

Aware of Nora's watchfulness, Catriona gestured for her to follow. They trailed his path to a spacious office adjacent to the front door, where a placard on the wall read Bank Manager. Catriona felt herself stretching a little taller as she entered the office and took a seat in one of two upholstered chairs positioned in front of Mr. Grissom's gleaming mahogany desk. This furniture was almost as nice as what she'd seen in the McGavock home, which was saying something.

Nora followed suit, blessedly quiet for a change and taking it all in. Catriona only wished Ryan were here to appreciate the service they were receiving. Because it was all due to him. She looked forward to telling him about it, and she told herself that one day very soon she would do just that.

"Miss O'Toole, am I correct in assuming you would like to open a demand deposit account with us?"

Catriona stared. She'd caught that phrase in passing when the clerk said something about it, but she didn't know what it meant, and she wasn't eager to admit that to this man.

"Why don't I review the various kinds of accounts we have available," he continued, "and then you can decide."

"Aye, I'd be appreciatin' that very much, sir."

She listened and quickly realized which one best

137

fit her needs. "The demand deposit account, Mr. Grissom. That's the one I want."

"Very good, Miss O'Toole. I simply need to secure some information from you."

She answered his questions without a hitch until they came to residence, then she hesitated. "We're currently stayin' at the Williford Hotel. But I'm honestly not certain how long we'll be stayin' there. Or in Franklin." She wondered how much to share with him, whether to tell him about her trying to find Ryan. Not that she had anything to hide, but she'd always considered it safer to share less than more when it came to items of a personal nature. Especially with a stranger. "But for certain, you can reach me at the hotel, if needed."

He stared for a beat, pen poised, then nodded. "Very well." He completed the paperwork, then placed it before her and handed her the pen. "If you'll sign right here, please."

She did as he indicated.

"How much would you like to deposit with us today, Miss O'Toole?"

"Six hundred and fifty-six dollars."

His eyes widened. "Very good, ma'am."

She withdrew the money from the pouch. She'd counted it before leaving their room for break-fast and had held out enough to cover another two weeks at the hotel, if needed, and more for necessities. Which shouldn't be much, considering that over the past three days they'd ventured out to a butcher for jerky, to a notions shop for needle, thread, and buttons to repair clothing, and finally to the dry goods store across town to purchase staple food items to keep in the room. The same store Wade Cunningham had happened upon.

She stifled a sigh, determined not to let her thoughts take her there again. Although she would've welcomed the chance to see young Braxie for a second time, she'd chosen *not* to return to the mercantile they'd visited their first day in town. She didn't want to risk another run-in with the ol' tyrant, as Nora had taken to calling the man. Which was a lesson in itself, Catriona reminded herself. She needed to be more careful with what she said. Little ears were listening.

She held the stack of bills out to Mr. Grissom, but then something within prompted her to pull them back. She knew a bank was the safest place to keep this money. But Ryan had handled these very bills before mailing them across an ocean to his family. To bring them to America, the "New World" as she'd heard it called. And no telling how hard he'd worked to earn this amount. So though it made no sense, it almost felt as though she were giving away a part of him. A part she might never get back. A thought occurred, and she looked up. "Will I be gettin' this same stack of money back when I take it out of the bank again?"

A slow, kind smile touched Mr. Grissom's face. "No, ma'am, you won't. I'm afraid it doesn't work that way. But you *will* receive the exact amount you're depositing with us today, minus any withdrawals you may make between now and then."

She looked at the money one last time—*thank you, dear brother*—and handed it to Mr. Grissom.

"I'll return momentarily with your deposit receipt, Miss O'Toole."

No sooner had he left than Nora jumped down from her chair.

"I'm hungry." She started for the door.

But Catriona grabbed her by the arm. "We just ate breakfast. Now, sit down until he returns. We have some food back in the room. You can eat somethin' there."

Nora huffed and leaned against the chair, making no effort to sit. She looked around the office as though scouting for mischief.

"I said to sit down, Nora. And I won't be sayin' it—"

"Stop tryin' to be *Mam!*" Nora yelled, her tone unexpectedly bitter. "You're *not* her, and you never will be!"

Catriona stared. Emotion burned her eyes, much as she saw in her sister's. She glanced at the door, hoping Nora's voice hadn't carried into the lobby and that Mr. Grissom wouldn't return before she could get this under control. "I know I'm not Mam. And I'm not tryin' to be her. But"—her voice broke—"I miss her too, Nora, just like you do. And yet we must—"

140

"Nay, you don't. You don't miss her like me, 'cause you didn't love her like me. Else you wouldn't have let her die!"

Catriona stared. "I did not *let* her die, Nora. Mam was sick. I did all I could for her, but then she died anyway. There was nothin' I could do. Nothin' anyone could do."

"You're lyin', Cattie! I heard you that night. Talkin' to ol' Miss Maeve."

Catriona frowned, but Nora's gaze sparked with fresh fire.

"I heard you tellin' her you wished Mam would go ahead and die. And then she did!" Nora sucked in a breath, the tendons in her slender throat corded tight. "It's all your fault!"

Catriona didn't have to reach back far into her memory. She remembered the conversation with Maeve only too well, but she'd thought Nora was fast asleep. She searched her sister's expression. So all this time Nora had been carrying this untruth around inside her. Catriona briefly closed her eyes, the shards of her already broken heart fracturing yet again. "Oh, dearest, I didn't want Mam to die. I was only—"

"You said the words, Cattie! I heard 'em meself!"

Catriona swallowed. "I know what you heard, Nora. Or what you *think* you heard. And I know how it must have sounded. But I said that only after Miss Maeve told me there'd be no gettin' any better for Mam. That she'd be hurtin' and strugglin' to breathe until she passed. That's the only reason

141

I said I wished Mam would go on. I never would have—"

"You're lyin', Cattie," Nora spat. "Just like Da used to do! You're just like him!"

A creak by the door drew both their stares.

"Your . . . receipt, Miss O'Toole," Mr. Grissom said quietly, looking back and forth between them and holding out a slip of paper.

Her chest aching, Catriona rose, unable to keep the unshed tears in their place. She quickly wiped her cheeks and took the receipt from him. "Thank you, Mr. Grissom, for your assistance today. We'll be on our way." She took firm hold of Nora's hand and held tight when her sister attempted to tug away, as she knew she would. But once they were on the street, Catriona let go. Nora glared up at her, the hurt and betrayal thick between them. And no wonder. Little ears had been listening.

Back at the hotel, they'd started up the staircase when Catriona heard her name. She turned around, but Nora didn't. Her sister continued to climb, each stomp of her little boots a none-too-subtle accusation. Tempted to call her back, Catriona knew it would be for nothing. Nora wouldn't obey. And since that staircase was the only way to and from the second floor, and to exit the hotel, Catriona let her go.

She returned to the front desk as the clerk reached behind him.

"This arrived for you while you were out, Miss O'Toole."

Catriona accepted the envelope from him. She read the name in the upper left-hand corner and felt a flush of fresh promise. She only hoped that her second meeting with John McGavock would prove more enlightening than her first.

CHAPTER 8

Wade strode up the herringbone brick walkway leading to Carnton's front portico, the Colt holstered at his side. His jacket hid the precise definition of the gun well enough that anyone not looking for it likely wouldn't notice it. It wasn't that he thought McGavock would disapprove of him carrying a gun. He was more concerned that the man might recognize the .44 caliber revolver as having been the Federal officer's standard issue as well as the envy of every Confederate soldier. Wade didn't want to do anything that might raise the man's suspicions or prevent him from attaining the position of overseer. Which he now more than ever determined to secure.

Wade climbed the steps to the porch and gave three solid raps on the double doors, hoping the brief note he'd received from John McGavock earlier this morning boded well. He also hoped that Tempy, the McGavocks' cook, wouldn't be the one to answer the door—

"Tempy!" He gave the woman his best smile. "Nice to see you again, ma'am."

Standing in the open doorway, she looked him up and down as if he were a skunk who'd just let loose his stink. "Mister Cunningham." She said

145

his name slowly, her disapproval almost palpable.

"Yes, ma'am. I'm here to see Colonel McGavock. At his request," he added and then pulled the envelope from his coat pocket on the likely chance she'd want proof.

She studied the front of the envelope. No, not just studied it. Her eyes moved over the words and comprehension deepened her expression. The woman could read. Tempy, a former slave, had somehow learned to read. No doubt not that long ago, and at her age, that was something. Wade hoped he got the chance to hear that story. And hoped, although he doubted it, that John McGavock had been behind that accomplishment somehow.

Tempy finally moved to one side, then, preparing for what he knew would be an uphill climb—with her at least—Wade stepped into the front entrance hall. The door to the fancy parlor on his left was closed, yet he heard voices coming from within the room. He took caution not to appear as if he were listening or even the least interested, though. Not with Tempy watching his every move.

"I'll tell the colonel you're here."

Though she didn't say it outright, Wade heard a definite *You wait here* in her tone, and he did as she desired. She entered the farm office to his right and closed the door behind her. He glanced toward the parlor. Definitely all feminine voices, which made sense if McGavock was in his office. Probably a ladies' gathering of some sort.

What type of woman was Mrs. John McGavock? Or Caroline Winder McGavock, as he'd learned in recent weeks. She apparently preferred the name Carrie, because that was the name journalists frequently used in the slew of newspaper articles they'd written about her in recent months. Articles referencing her kindness and compassion as she'd cared for the Confederate soldiers in her home during and following the Battle of Franklin. According to several accounts, nearly three dozen of the most seriously wounded men had convalesced here for months.

From habit, he scanned the front hallway, his gaze trailing up the staircase leading to the second floor. Everything looked as it had the other day with the exception of a crate sitting off to one side. A stately mahogany coat rack stood to his right, various side tables and seats occupied available wall space, and expensive-looking wallpaper tempted the eye upward. In the center of the room, anchoring the home's spacious entryway, sat a finely carved mahogany table that held what he presumed was an heirloom vase. But yet again, the floor was what drew his attention.

Dark stains were everywhere. So many of them. He recalled what Tempy said about having tried in vain to scrub them out. Once aged wood got ahold of blood, it didn't let go. Even sanding didn't work. Why hadn't the McGavocks replaced the floor covering in this space? And in the office, too, come to think of it. Yet he didn't recall seeing such prominent stains in there. Then again, a lot of furniture occupied that room. Still, wealthy families like the McGavocks never left wooden floors bare when finely woven carpet or floor cloths were readily available to them.

He could guess why the carpet had been removed. The wounds of the soldiers who'd been brought here following the battle that night would've seen to that. But that had been well over a year ago now. Surely the McGavocks possessed the funds to replace it, to at least cover up the visible memories of that slaughter. "Did you see them Johnny Rebs?" a fellow officer from the 104th Ohio had asked that night after the battle, laughing as their unit pulled out of Franklin, headed for Nashville. "Like lambs to a slaughter, they just kept on coming. Ignorant, backwoods fools. They should know when they're beat. Should know when to tuck tail and run." It had been difficult enough to stomach the young officer's mouth, but when he'd come at one of the surrendered Confederate prisoners—a brigadier general—with the aim of bashing in the man's head with the butt of his rifle, Wade had intervened. And even now he could feel the pain in his right hand as it smashed into the fellow's iron jaw.

Within military rule, he could've been written up for disciplinary action, and he probably would have been if not for his superior officer having witnessed the scene. Shortly before they reached Nashville later that same night, Colonel Withers pulled him aside. "Any man who believes those

Johnny Rebs were fools only proves himself to be one. To march straight into the hell we had waiting to unleash on them . . . Those men weren't fools, Captain Cunningham. They were men who loved their country, just like you and I do, however misguided their reasons for fighting. I've witnessed some of the hardest-fought battles of this war, and never have I seen a more desperate fight. You were right to spare Brigadier General Gordon that assault. He and his men had surrendered." Withers glanced down at Wade's already-bruising right hand, a trace of respect in the gesture. "So thank you for doing what I wanted to do back there but couldn't."

Wade knelt on one knee and ran a finger along the edge of one of the darkest blotches marring the floor, wondering if one of his bullets had caused this particular stain. If so, he didn't regret it. It had been war. If he hadn't wounded or killed the soldiers he'd faced in battle, they would have shot or killed him. But the Confederates who'd fought here at Franklin had been among the bravest, most courageous he'd come up against. His own unit had joined others to form the bulk of the defensive line around the Carter family's cotton gin when the enemy charged forward, two divisions strong. One of the divisions, Confederate general Patrick Cleburne's. The other, Wade couldn't remember now.

But Cleburne's he would never forget. Cleburne, an Irishman who'd come to America, had from all accounts been revered by his men. Wade had heard about Cleburne's fighting qualities, his reliability and coolness under pressure. But to see it played out . . . Even now he could envision the Irish general's division beginning their advance across the open field, two oblique lines moving in splendid form as Federal artillery poured shells into their ranks. Yet still they came.

One of the Federal divisions positioned about a quarter mile in front of the breastworks—a grievous mistake, as it turned out—had nearly been overrun by the Confederates' swift advance, and they'd come rushing back toward the Federal line yelling at their brothers not to shoot them. Cleburne's men had been right on their heels, taking advantage of the cover while firing at them at the same time. Confusion ensued, and Wade recalled struggling to see through the haze of smoke and fire, trying to decipher who to kill and who to let across the line. Finally, seeing no more blue coats in the fray, the 104th Ohio had opened up on Cleburne's division, mowing them down by the scores, while the 6th Ohio Battery poured grapeshot and canister into their ranks without mercy. At last the Rebels fell back about a hundred yards into a ravine, where they reformed and came at the Federal line yet again. This time steady as clockwork. Wade had never seen anything like it.

They charged right up to the ditch, many of them even jumping over the Federal boys' heads.

Some of Cleburne's division were shot while still standing on the breastworks, others while trying to rip down the Federal colors. Wade blinked, the memories thick. Not a man in his own company flinched, though every company to their right fell back. The fighting was brutal, the most savage he'd ever been in. Men shot, bludgeoned, bayonetted, and gouged one another with knives and axes . . . even hoes and shovels. Whatever they could find became a weapon. And the Confederates nearly took the line. Then somehow the Federals rallied and poured in to reinforce the works.

After the firing slackened, he and some others ventured out in front of the breastworks to help any of their own boys who were still lying in the field. But few wounded lay outside of the works. The ditch was strewn with corpses and mutilated men, and as far as he could see in the murky night, a person couldn't walk the field without stepping on bodies. Or what remained of them. The Federal artillery had done its work—and then some—on Cleburne's division.

Wade took a steadying breath. Would memories from this battle always haunt him? He woke up at night sometimes, his body slick with sweat, his heart ricocheting off his ribs. Would he, in those dreams, always be searching for Wesley's face in the ranks? He sighed. So much blood had been spilled in the course to victory. If the South had won, this nation would've had yet another war to fight, battling all over again. And he would've fought that one, too, with everything he had. Until the North claimed victory. Because no matter the debate among his own countrymen, he could not, and would not, abide living in a nation where fellow human beings were bought and sold like cattle.

The squeak of hinges drew his focus upward, and he quickly stood, trying for a more relaxed expression than his current state of emotion dictated. Tempy closed the farm office door behind her and stared at him for a beat, long enough for him to wonder if she'd seen him kneeling. But her guarded countenance revealed nothing.

"Might be a few minutes, Colonel McGavock says. But he'll be with you directly." She nodded to a settee. "You can sit down over there, if you want."

"Thank you, Tempy. But I'm fine to stand."

She only looked at him, then crossed the hall to pick up the crate he'd noticed earlier. He beat her to it, surprised at its weight.

"I'll carry it for you. Just tell me where it goes."

She stared up at him, her expression flat. "I been carryin' crates all my life. Guess I can carry this one, too, same as the rest."

She reached out to take it, but Wade shook his head. "It's downright heavy, and I don't mind. Just lead the way and I'll follow you."

She pinned him with a stare that said she thought she knew exactly what he was doing and that he'd better think again if he thought she would be so easily manipulated. "I said I carry my own crates, Mr. Cunningham."

Wade matched her gaze, but she'd bested him. Yet again. He gave a quick nod. "Yes, ma'am." He handed over the crate, careful to make sure she had a good grip on it before he let go. Her jaw tensed, under the weight of the crate's contents, he assumed. Which appeared to be cooking supplies if his quick perusal of the writing on the crate was accurate.

"Mr. Cunningham, thank you for coming out a second time."

Wade turned and accepted McGavock's out-stretched hand, once again having to force a sense of cordiality he did not feel. "Colonel McGavock, I appreciated receiving your note." A man Wade didn't recognize exited the farm office and wasted no time in leaving through the front doors. Wade was certain he hadn't been part of the meeting about the cemetery days earlier. And the stranger didn't look behind him as he closed the front door.

McGavock gestured toward a back entryway adjacent to the staircase. "I have a few more questions for you, Cunningham. But I prefer to walk and talk. Shall we?"

"Fine by me, sir." Wade followed. But ever aware of Tempy's watchful eye, at the door he turned back. Sure enough, the woman was still eyeing him. On a whim, he dared to toss her a quick wink,

153

then swiftly closed the door before she could shoot him full of daggers.

Outside, Wade caught up with McGavock and matched his pace, choosing to take the invitation to "walk and talk" as a good sign. Same as he did the direction McGavock was headed—toward the barn.

"What was the mainstay of your family farm, Cunningham?"

The farm fresh in his mind's eye, Wade could visualize it all. "Livestock. Cattle, pigs, chickens, some sheep. We grew crops, too, of course. Corn, grain, sweet potatoes, greens, and such. But only enough to feed us and the animals. The bulk of our livelihood came from livestock. My mother also sewed for some of the more well-to-do women in town."

Seconds passed, then McGavock looked at him. "It sounds like your parents were fine people."

Wade kept his attention forward, his throat constricting unexpectedly. "Yes, sir. They were the finest."

Silence settled between them, and Wade let it. He hadn't expected to share such personal details about his life with McGavock. And even now, a small part of him regretted it. John McGavock was not a friend, nor would he ever be. And yet it felt good to talk about his parents, his home. Or what had been his home.

Overhead, a pale but persistent sun cut through the gray clouds and sent shafts of light streaming downward. Wade had a feeling that what this man said about spring in Franklin would prove true. The war had brought him to Tennessee before, but only in winter. Tennessee in spring had an altogether different feel.

McGavock paused outside the barn. "We spoke the other day about the sharecroppers working my land. You said you could handle that, but I also have a sawmill. Back before the war, I purchased two skilled sawyers to operate it. Paid twenty-five hundred dollars for each of those men." He shook his head. "Then I lost them, of course, after the war ended. By chance, do you have any knowledge about working a sawmill?"

Feeling not an ounce of pity for McGavock's supposed loss, Wade at least tried to appear as though he commiserated with him. "What kind of mill is it? Sash-type? Muley saw? Circular?"

McGavock's expression hinted at satisfaction. "Water-powered sash-type, with a long saw."

"An up-down mill, then. With a single straight blade?"

McGavock nodded. "You know it?"

"It's the only one I do know. A neighbor of ours had one back home. I used to work for him some during the spring and summer for extra money. I was mainly muscle to move the logs, then the cut lumber, but I watched the sawyers well enough to know how the mill worked. And how productive it could be."

McGavock gestured northwest toward a line

155

of trees beyond the barn. "The mill's in that direction, alongside our creek just before it crosses Lewisburg and joins the Harpeth River. Presently, I've got two freedmen working it. The last overseer hired them in the fall. The mill had been sitting idle since shortly after the war started. They've repaired it, but it still breaks down more than it should, which is costing me money. Is overseeing a mill something you think you could manage?"

"I don't see why not. A sash mill is pretty straightforward. If memory serves, one of the biggest issues we had was with the handwheel that opens and closes the lower gate in the pond. Either that or the water turbine. And since I was the best swimmer, they always sent me down first. I always hated that part of it."

McGavock eyed him. "Can you still swim?"

Wade didn't have to feign a sigh. "Unfortunately, yes, I can."

McGavock gave him a fatherly pat on the shoulder, then opened the barn door and indicated for Wade to precede him. Bristling at the familiarity of the gesture, Wade stepped inside, feeling his chances of securing the position of overseer improving by the minute despite his animosity for the man. John McGavock represented every-thing he'd fought against in the war. And while fraternizing with the enemy was part of solving this case, he didn't have to like it.

His eyes quickly adjusted to the dimmer light in the barn, and it didn't take long for him to ascertain another of McGavock's prized investments. Wade approached one of the stalls, still keeping a respectable distance while admiring its tenant, a stallion, as well as several mares in stalls on down the line. "You've got some fine horseflesh, sir."

McGavock gave a soft laugh. "That I do. And most of it hails from right here in Nashville. From my brother-in-law, in fact. General William Giles Harding. You might've heard of him?"

Wade nodded, recalling what he'd read about Harding. "I have. General Harding's reputation, and Belle Meade's, are . . . far-reaching."

"Indeed, they are. The general has a freedman who's been with him for years now," McGavock continued. "As gifted with horses as any man I've ever seen. His name's Robert Green. Uncle Bob, everybody calls him. He's the head hostler at Belle Meade. If you're in the market for a thoroughbred, you won't find any better than what they've got there."

Wade forced a laugh. "Thoroughbreds are a bit above this former lieutenant's pay. But these sure are fine animals." With a look, he asked if he could get closer to the stallion.

McGavock nodded, his expression saying to do so with care.

Wade took a step to the left, allowing for the horse's blind spot, speaking softly as he approached. "Hey there, fellow. You're a good boy. Strong and sure of yourself, aren't you?" The stallion, iron gray with black points, snorted and pawed the ground. Wade paused for a moment, then continued forward. When he got close enough, he reached out, nice and slow, the horse watching his every move. He gently stroked the thoroughbred's shoulder, appreciating its beauty and strength while also respectful of its high-spirited nature—and its teeth. He'd once seen a stallion take a chunk out of a man's shoulder, so his regard for hot-blooded horses ran deep.

The stallion's proportions boasted its champion ancestry, standing at least sixteen hands high. A moment passed, and Wade gradually moved his hand to the stallion's head, in awe of the power rippling beneath his fingertips.

"You know your way around a stallion." McGavock spoke softly. "Traveller's well trained, but he can be skittish at times, even with me."

Wade's focus never leaving the thoroughbred, he gave a small laugh, not at all surprised at the name McGavock had given the animal. "You named him after General Lee's horse."

"I did. I'm assuming you've seen him. The *real* Traveller?"

"I have," Wade answered honestly, having glimpsed General Lee astride his famed gray stallion from a distance sometime in '62.

"I imagine that was a sight to behold."

"Oh yes." Wade remembered how the Federals had routed Lee's army that particular day and the gratification he'd taken from it. "It was a sight, for sure."

He gave Traveller one last rub, then followed McGavock past the row of stalls where a line of pretty thoroughbred mares nickered and vied for attention. Bays, chestnuts, blacks, and browns, all with high withers, lean bodies, and long legs. Animals born to run. But it was the quiet little sorrel down on the end that drew his eye. Obviously not a thoroughbred, but a beauty all the same.

McGavock paused by her stall. "I acquired her a couple of weeks ago. She's a quarter horse and comes from excellent stock. I haven't even had a chance to take her out yet. She's harness broke, the breeder said. But she still balks at taking a saddle."

Wade approached her from the side as he had the stallion, and the sorrel backed up a step, tossing her head. He held out his hands, palms up, and spoke softly. "It's all right, girl. I won't hurt you." He started to take another step, but she reared, and he stopped midstride. "Okay," he whispered. "I'll wait for you to come to me, then."

"You might be waiting a long time," McGavock said quietly beside him, amusement in the comment.

But Wade held his ground, watching her, waiting, silently working to earn her trust. She snorted and tossed her head again, but he didn't move, just kept his hands outstretched, gaze steady. She whinnied, and he smiled. "You want to talk some?" he whispered, and her brown eyes flashed. She lunged at the stall door, testing him, but Wade didn't flinch. Smaller than the thoroughbreds, she was well muscled, and her compact body would be well suited to reining, cutting, and working cattle. No doubt she could run like the wind.

Sunlight slanted through the rafters overhead and hit her copper-red coat, turning it a burnished gold. Power *and* beauty. With the right guidance and patient hand, she would more than meet her potential. Yet she was also capable of doing a man ample harm. Judging by her fiery temperament, she knew it too.

"What's her name, Colonel?" Wade asked.

"The breeder called her Cassandra's Legacy. That's what's listed on her papers."

"That's a mouthful."

McGavock shifted his weight. "I haven't come up with a more fitting name yet. Haven't spent enough time with her to know what might suit her."

A thought entered Wade's mind, and he smiled. This pretty little mare reminded him of another feisty redhead he'd met recently. He'd kept an eye out for Miss O'Toole at the hotel in recent days, but he hadn't seen her. He wouldn't put it past the woman to be avoiding him. If she was still in town, which he hoped she was.

The sorrel blew out a breath and shook her head from side to side, watching him the entire time. She was sizing him up, letting him know *she* was in control—and that if she decided to come closer, it would be because she deigned it, not because of anything he'd done. Wade nodded, hands still outstretched.

A moment crept past.

"Well I'll be," the colonel whispered beside him.

The mare took one cautious step forward, then another, toward the stall door.

"Come on," Wade whispered, keeping his promise to stay put. "I'm waiting right here for you, girl."

Though close enough to touch her, he didn't. She batted his hand with her muzzle, and he knew full well that one chomp from those strong jaws would mean he'd be bruised for weeks, if not absent some fingers. But everything within him told him she wouldn't do that. Finally, she stilled. Her ears flicked, and the look in her eyes changed. Ever so slowly, Wade brought his hand closer, and with a featherlight touch, he stroked her long, sleek neck, the weight of the honor not lost on him.

"That's a good girl," he whispered, still seeing traces of uncertainty in those brown eyes. "You're strong. You know who you are. Never mind these other gals with their fancy pedigrees and papers. You're as fine as any of them. Don't you forget that."

She lowered her head, and he gave her a good rub behind the ears.

"Are you as good with cattle, pigs, and sheep as you are with horses, Cunningham?"

Wade laughed softly. "I've not met a cow, pig,

161

or sheep quite as intuitive as this little beauty. But I know my way around most any farm animal. My father taught me everything he knew—or he tried to. I did my best to learn it all." Wade could picture his father's face so clearly. "I only wish I'd known how quickly those years would go by."

A moment passed. Wade sensed McGavock regarding him and finally turned back.

McGavock said nothing, only nodded. "Why don't we head on back to the farm office? Along the way, we'll discuss when you can start your new duties as overseer."

Wade stilled, feeling one major hurdle all but cleared behind him. "Sounds good to me, sir. And I can start immediately."

McGavock extended his hand. "Then welcome to Carnton."

They shook on the deal, and Wade gave the sorrel one last rub. He walked with McGavock toward the house, the colonel discussing compensation and other details about the job as they went. Wade listened and nodded, already contemplating how he could approach the suspects on his list.

Nearly to the back door, someone from behind them called the colonel's name, and McGavock turned. Wade followed suit and suddenly felt time turning back on itself. He blinked, staring at the man walking toward them. It couldn't be. But it was.

What was Isham Pender doing back in the South following the war? And here at Carnton?

"Colonel, I need to talk to you about—" Isham's gaze locked with Wade's.

And Wade knew he'd better act fast or all would be lost. For himself, most assuredly. But likely for his former fellow captain in the United States Colored Troops too.

CHAPTER 9

Wade stuck out his hand. "Wade Cunningham. I'm the new overseer here at Carnton as of about . . . five minutes ago."

Scarcely missing a beat, Isham accepted, and Wade gripped his hand firmly, trusting his friend to follow his lead.

"Isham Pender," Isham responded, returning the tight grip. "I'm one of the sawyers here, Mr. Cunningham. Good to meet you. And welcome to Carnton. I've been here for about four months myself. The colonel's a fine man to work for."

It took effort for Wade not to wince, hearing those words from his friend. Not that working as a sawyer was beneath a man. Working lumber took strength and skill. But as Wade remembered, Isham Pender had dreamed of doing so much more, and was capable of so much more too. An educated man who'd worked hard to improve himself, Pender didn't speak in the vernacular common to those less schooled, yet his accent was still Southern through and through. "I appreciate the welcome, Pender. And the chance the colonel's giving me."

A shadow crossed Isham's face, there and gone faster than anyone who didn't know him could've detected. But Wade saw it, and he knew the two of them were destined for a conversation as soon as opportunity allowed.

On their way to Carnton, as they neared the edge of town, Catriona grew aware of Nora scooting closer to her on the road. Closer than their exchange in Mr. Grissom's office at the bank an hour earlier warranted. Catriona peered down at her, her thoughts still mired in what Nora had revealed.

Those last days of Mam's life were a haze of grief and dread, but she should have taken greater care when she and Miss Maeve had talked things through. No wonder her little sister was acting the way she was. She'd misconstrued what she over- heard. And under the circumstances, Catriona couldn't blame her.

She'd had to practically drag Nora from the hotel room a while ago. Regardless, Nora—toting the faceless Virginia yet again—now matched her almost step for step. Then Catriona smelled it. Could feel its silent warning like goose prickles on her flesh. *Death.* And all other thoughts fell away as the field rose steadily on the horizon. She glanced down at her little sister, wanting to offer to carry her in that moment, to cradle her close as she'd done before. But she knew Nora's pride would never permit it.

As they passed row after row of deteriorating graves, Nora kept her gaze arrow straight. Not once did her focus wander toward the fields off to their right. Catriona didn't let hers either. Still, a shiver skittered up her spine. What if Ryan's body was out there somewhere? As soon as the question came, she banished it, just as she did every other time fear tempted her to question his well-being.

He *was* alive. She repeated that wordlessly several times until confidence finally silenced the fear. Yet she wasn't naive. Those graves *had* to be from the recent war. What she didn't know was whether Ryan had been involved in whatever conflict had taken place here and whether Major General Patrick Cleburne's division had been part of it. That was the division Ryan told them he'd been assigned to. He'd sounded so proud of it in his letters. Because, he'd written, Cleburne was an Irishman like him. And apparently he was held in highest esteem by his men, judging by Ryan's choice of wording.

Catriona hoped to meet this General Patrick Cleburne. She wanted to look into the face of the man her brother had pledged to *follow into battle anytime, anywhere, under any circumstances.* Of course, even though Ryan had written about Cleburne's division being bound for Franklin in his last letter, it didn't mean they'd actually made it here. Military orders were frequently changed. Ryan had confirmed as much in his letters. And besides, the package containing the money and the note had been postmarked a good length *after* the family had received his last correspondence.

Which had to mean that even if Ryan had been involved in whatever battle had been fought here, he'd survived it.

Catriona followed that trail of logic through a second time, wishing it had a bit firmer footing. Still, she chose to believe it.

They reached the turnoff leading to the McGavock estate, and she angled her head from side to side, working to ease the tightness in her neck muscles. Then she smoothed the sides of her hair—glad that she'd taken the time to put it up that morning—and felt the weight of the dagger up her fitted left sleeve. She'd almost left the blade behind in the room, considering their business at hand. Yet she'd promised Ryan she'd always keep it with her, so with her it was.

Both her and Nora's hems and boots were caked in mud, but at least the temperature was warming. The sun had finally succeeded in poking through the clouds, and the tree-covered hills bordering the town of Franklin shone a deep emerald green. Sunlight danced off their still-wet leaves, and a symphony of birdsong—various pitches of warbling and twittering drifting down from overhead—somehow made the sunshine feel even warmer.

They turned the corner, and the large two-story brick house came into view up ahead. Catriona took in her surroundings, her senses more attuned to detail than the first time she'd visited here. A spacious garden lay to the left of the home, anchored by a large Osage orange tree and hemmed in by a welcoming white picket fence.

The garden, still drowsy with winter, had been well laid out with cedar-lined crushed stone and shell paths and neat, orderly plots resembling a patchwork quilt. Roughly half the area served for growing flowers—judging by the dormant rose-bushes, shrubs, and naked trellises, as well as a few brave tulips daring to venture from their hiding places—while the other half of the garden appeared to be designated for raising vegetables.

She'd always loved gardening, flowers especially, and she didn't doubt that Mrs. McGavock's roses and tulips would be lovely. But her favorite flower would always be Ireland's own Spring Squill with its beautiful star-like, lilac-blue petals. It was the first flower she'd ever planted that had lived. And not just lived but thrived. She'd brought a cloth bag full of bulbs with her from the small flower garden she'd planted by the front door of their cottage years earlier. An extravagance her father had called foolishness and a waste of time. Coming home drunk one night, he'd trampled the fledgling spring plants. But like a faithful friend, strong and determined, the pretty blue flowers had returned, as they'd done every year since. Resilient, despite their delicate appearance.

A cool breeze stirred and brought with it the aroma of smoked meat. She looked around and spotted a brick structure adjacent to the kitchen where Nora had enjoyed cookies with young

169

Master Winder. A smokehouse, she assumed, likely full of pork based on the few pigs she'd glimpsed in pens behind the barn the other day. A hefty stone's throw away stood a barn. A grander barn than she'd ever seen. The structure sat proudly a short distance beyond the house, and it wasn't difficult to envision that, come summer, the hundreds of acres encompassing the estate would provide food stores enough to fill it to the rafters. And the house . . .

A two-story gallery porch jutted off to one side, and judging from what she could see, it likely extended the full length of the back of the home. What beautiful views that vantage point must offer. Everything she saw bespoke affluence. Same as the finery she'd observed inside the house— the elegant furniture, fancy wallpaper, fine dishes, exquisitely framed family portraits. All signs of wealth acquired, at least in part, by the taking of the O'Toole family's ancestral land.

Nora stopped abruptly at the gate leading to the front portico. "I'm not wantin' to go inside."

"Don't worry, we won't be long. And you'll be stayin' with me this time."

Nora looked up and shook her head, her red curls bouncing. "*Nay.* I'm not goin'!"

Catriona felt her brows shoot up even as a line of heat inched up the back of her neck. She narrowed her eyes, and the only thing that held her temper in check was knowing what a tender spot Nora was in. The girl honestly believed Catriona had wanted their mother to die? That explained so much, and yet Catriona had no idea how to undo the damage that had been done or how to make it right. And no time at present to sort it out.

She pushed open the gate. "You're goin' with me. *Now!*"

Her lips a thin line, Nora huffed and trudged up the brick walkway. She climbed the front steps, dragging Virginia with her, whacking the doll's head on each step as she went.

Catriona gestured to a worn rug off to the side. "Give your boots a fair wipin' before we go inside." Catriona removed as much of the caked mud from hers as she could, but Nora's effort was perfunctory at best.

As she stared at the front double doors, Catriona's stomach tightened with nerves. What if the colonel had nothing to tell her about the land? What if he'd found nothing in those files? Or what if he *had* found something yet planned to say he hadn't? How many lies had she heard Da tell a patron when they came to the shop to claim their order? *"The press broke down, so it'll be another day or two before we're done."* Or *"We had the detail work nearly finished when a bottle of ink spilled all over the desk, ruinin' everything."* Da would throw in a curse word beneath his breath as if to validate the falsehood.

But the lie that galled her most was the one he told when patrons weren't pleased with his finished work due to the increasing unsteadiness of his hand. *"I thought me son, Ryan, could handle the job. But the fool boy, he botched it up. Don't you worry none, though. I'll do it meself this time."* Such a spiteful lie. Her father had been a right good printer in his day, but Ryan was the artist. Request the most detailed filigree in the fore pages of a Bible, or a legal document, or an engraving—or better yet a completely unique font for a family crest—and Ryan could not only create it but do so masterfully. Da had taught him the basics of illustrating and engraving, but the rest Ryan had simply *known.* Artistry was in his blood. There was no illustration he couldn't draw. She'd thought for a time that she might have had a similar gift. Ryan had even said so. But Da had been right. The gift had skipped her.

Raising her hand to knock on the door, a phrase Colonel McGavock used in his note returned, and she wondered again at its meaning. *"I implore you to visit Carnton again today so we may discuss the charges you have alleged against my family name."* The wording wasn't an admission of guilt nor a defense of innocence. So what was it, exactly? She bit her lower lip and knocked twice. Whatever happened, she must mind her tongue this time. Because more than anything—even restoring lost honor to her family, or what was left of it—she wanted, needed, answers about Ryan and his whereabouts.

One of the double front doors opened, and a handsome woman with dark hair and a mantle of authority about her met Catriona's gaze straight on. "Good day," the woman offered.

Catriona instinctively dipped her head. "Good day, ma'am. Me name is Catriona O'Toole, and this here is me sister, Nora. I'm here to speak with Colonel McGavock. Please," she added, telling herself to stop fidgeting with her reticule. "The colonel sent me a note this mornin' askin' me to come."

Recognition flickered in the woman's expression. "Ah, yes . . . Miss O'Toole. I'm Mrs. John McGavock, the colonel's wife. We've been expecting you. Please, would you both come inside?"

"Aye, ma'am. Thank you." Catriona stepped across the threshold, noting that the woman's voice held not a hint of the homeland, as she'd suspected, but was Southern through and through. Mrs. McGavock stared at something behind her, and Catriona turned to see Nora still perched on the portico, sulking, her customary scowl in place. A blush burned Catriona's cheeks, and she grabbed Nora's hand and pulled her inside. "Beggin' your pardon, Mrs. McGavock. Me wee sister's a bit out of sorts today."

Catriona slid Nora a censoring look, which, to Catriona's chagrin, Nora openly returned.

"Do not fret yourself, Miss O'Toole. I have a son about your sister's age, I believe. And I understand what it's like to have days when we simply do not feel up to our best." Mrs. McGavock

173

leaned down and garnered Nora's attention, then smiled. "And yet," she continued, her tone gentle yet unmistakably firm, "as I tell my own son and daughter, we must not allow our circumstances— or our moods—to dictate our actions. Challenging though that may be at times, I know. At least it is for me."

Mrs. McGavock laughed softly, and though her efforts didn't completely dissolve Nora's frown, Catriona watched as her little sister stood a bit straighter and her puckered brow smoothed by half, which was a marked improvement. And all from a softly worded reprimand. How did Mrs. McGavock manage it? A twinge of something akin to jealousy lit a spark inside her. How many times had she used that identical tone with Nora yet never come close to achieving the same result?

"Let's continue into the parlor, ladies. I'm certain the colonel will be in shortly. He's conducting farm business this morning. But until then, we can get acquainted. You must tell me, though, Nora, what happened to your doll's face? Did she take a bad fall?"

"Aye, ma'am, that she did. Fell flat on her nose and busted her face to nothin'. I tried to mend it, but"—Nora sighed and shook her head—"'twas no use. We'd been havin' us a fine picnic that day and . . ."

Nora followed Mrs. McGavock, jabbering on, fabricating yet another tale about Virginia's injuries—and stepping gingerly as she went, doing her best to avoid the stains that spotted the floor of the entrance hall. The deep blotches were reminiscent of the plank flooring in the print shop back home, stained from all the ink spills through the years. But Catriona very much doubted the McGavocks were running a printing press in their home.

Mrs. McGavock gestured for them to be seated on a sofa so fine Catriona didn't know whether to sit on it or kneel beside it. Nora, however, plunked right down. So Catriona did likewise, tucking her reticule beside her, ever mindful of the mud stains on her hem and also of her posture in Mrs. McGavock's presence. By no means was she Mrs. McGavock's equal, socially speaking. But neither did she want the woman to think of her as some unrefined sapskull.

Everywhere she looked, she found beauty. The sofa, covered in blue damask upholstery, had a carved wooden back and perfectly matched the chairs in the room. An elegant piano resided in one corner by the window, and she wondered if Mrs. McGavock could play it. She'd heard a piano before, of course. Mostly from a barkeep pounding out tunes in a pub while drunken voices poured out the open front door as she walked by. Only a handful of times had she heard the ethereal beauty such an instrument was capable of producing. And that when she'd delivered orders from the print shop to the Crawfords on Paxton Hill. Mrs. Crawford was skilled in playing and could—

"In the interest of easing any trepidation you may have, Miss O'Toole . . ."

Catriona looked over to find Mrs. McGavock watching her.

"I wish to tell you that the colonel shared with me what you spoke to him about last week. And I assure you that my husband has reviewed the matter most thoroughly. Well, as thoroughly as one can when so many years have passed and with only entries in a farm register to serve as witnesses." Her eyes shone with what appeared to be sincerity.

Catriona returned a pleasant smile—or tried to. "Entries in a farm register *and* the solemn word of both me parents." After all, Mam had always nodded in agreement as Da recounted the story, his speech often slurred from the attempt to drown out whatever demons plagued him. So Catriona knew the account of family history was true.

Mrs. McGavock's smile faded, though the supposed kindness in her eyes did not. "If you'll excuse me, I'll ask our cook to bring us refreshment while we wait."

As soon as their hostess's footsteps faded in the hallway, Nora hopped down from her seat. She reached for one of the tiny framed pictures on the table in front of the sofa.

"Nora, don't be touchin' anything. This is not our home."

Nora made a *pfft* sound and reached for the frame anyway.

Catriona grabbed her arm. "I said not to be touchin' things!"

Nora tried to wrench away, but Catriona had a good hold on her this time and pulled her close. "You *will* listen to me and do as I say. I'm your elder sister, wee one, and while I wish Da and Mam were still here"—Catriona paused, knowing that statement wasn't entirely true—"they're both gone. Along with Bridget and Alma. It's just us now. And Ryan," she added quickly, certain that Nora had been about to make the same correction. "We're orphans. We're alone. And that makes me your guardian. The one who has to take care of you. So you *must* obey me."

Contrary to the angry outburst Catriona expected from her sister, Nora simply stared, her ever-constant glower faltering for a beat, her blue eyes, so much like Mam's, wide and fathomless. Searching, almost. But for what, Catriona didn't know. Nora's chin trembled the slightest bit, and Catriona leaned in. Then just like that, in a blink, the momentary truce was gone. In its place returned the hardness Catriona knew only too well.

"I hope you're both hungry. Tempy will be bringing tea and cake directly."

Catriona looked up to see Mrs. McGavock seating herself across from them. Catriona hadn't even heard her enter the room. Nora attempted to tug her arm free, and Catriona let her go.

"The colonel will be joining us as well," Mrs. McGavock continued, the lightness of her tone revealing her awareness of the sisterly rift. "He's concluding a conversation with the new overseer now. But he's eager to speak with you."

"Aye. I'm eager to speak with him as well," Catriona responded, the promise of refreshment having little appeal under the circumstances.

A moment later, the tread of footsteps on the wooden floor in the entrance hall signaled more than one individual, and as conversation drifted toward them, Catriona recognized the colonel's voice. But she nearly came off the sofa when Wade Cunningham walked by the parlor door.

CHAPTER 10

Wade Cunningham was Carnton's new overseer? At the last moment, he turned to look into the parlor, and Catriona swiftly looked down and away, hoping he wouldn't recognize her.

"Miss O'Toole?"

Head bowed, Catriona briefly clenched her teeth, then looked up smiling. "Mr. Cunningham."

Mrs. McGavock looked back and forth between them. "You two know each other?"

"Yes, ma'am," he answered before Catriona could say otherwise. "Miss O'Toole and I met the first day I was here at Carnton. And since then, we've crossed paths a couple of times."

Catriona didn't miss the almost imperceptible look he gave her, as though the two of them shared some intimate secret. He made it sound as though they were more than merely acquainted.

"Actually"—Catriona sat forward, nodding a greeting toward the colonel, who appeared in the doorway—"Mr. Cunningham and I haven't exchanged that many words. So the two of us aren't really knowin' each other well a'tall."

"I see." Colonel McGavock motioned the man into the room, then stepped forward. "So the only formal introduction required then, Cunningham, is with my wife." As the colonel presented Mrs. McGavock, Catriona ignored the way Wade Cunningham's gaze kept returning to hers. The same way she ignored how well his muscular shoulders filled out the coat he wore and how he seemed to be taking everything in at once. He even glanced at Nora and winked, a smile in his eyes. Catriona slipped a protective arm around her sister, only to have Nora shove her away.

"It is my pleasure, Mr. Cunningham, to make your acquaintance, I assure you." Mrs. McGavock extended her right hand, and Mr. Cunningham brought it to his lips and bestowed a light kiss.

For reasons Catriona couldn't explain, and found mildly annoying, she felt a slight shiver at the sight and quickly looked elsewhere.

"Please, Mr. Cunningham," Mrs. McGavock continued, "you're welcome to join us for tea, if you have the time. Tempy is bringing a cake too. And knowing her, we'll have plenty for all."

To Catriona's dismay, he accepted, and even worse, he chose the chair closest to her. She didn't look in his direction.

Conversation centering around "the farm" filled the next several minutes, and Catriona tried to appear interested while the *tick-tick-tick* of a clock in the room reminded her of each passing moment. Above the fireplace hung a large portrait that clearly bore a more youthful likeness of Mrs. McGavock. The young woman captured in oil on canvas wore an off-the-shoulder dark dress trimmed in delicate dark lace. Perched serenely in a red chair, hands clasped loosely in her lap, she held a pair of white gloves. The tiniest smile curved her mouth, and the light in her eyes held the promise of a secure and happy future. A promise Catriona couldn't even remotely relate to.

"Did you have a productive meeting with the ladies earlier?" Colonel McGavock asked his wife during a brief lull in conversation.

"Yes, we did. We confirmed which ideas we're pursuing for fundraisers within the community. Now we simply need to get those underway. Mrs. Parsons agreed to visit the newspaper office today to list an advertisement as soon as possible."

The colonel gave an affirming nod. "By chance, did any of them recommend someone to replace Mr. Lamb?"

Mrs. McGavock sighed. "Unfortunately, no, and it's high time the garden is cleaned up and planted. Hopefully, someone will— Ah, here we are."

A servant appeared in the doorway carrying a silver tray, and Catriona recognized her as the woman she'd met in the kitchen days earlier.

"Thank you, Tempy." On the table directly in front of the sofa, Mrs. McGavock made room for the tray laden with china cups and saucers, plates, a pot of tea, and, as promised, a cake. But a cake unlike any Catriona had baked. The wondrous confection was lofty with at least two layers slathered in white frosting. Catriona caught a whiff of cinnamon and cloves, and her mouth watered.

"Anything else y'all needin', Missus McGavock?" Tempy asked, her attention moving from person to person but holding a little too long on Wade Cunningham.

Catriona shook her head to herself. Even the cook was smitten by the man? How did no one else seem to see him the way she did?

Tempy took her leave, and Mrs. McGavock served each of them tea, then cut the cake, giving generous slices.

The colonel added milk to his tea, along with sugar. "My dear, you should have seen Mr. Cunningham with my new quarter horse. And with Traveller too. Our new overseer has quite a way with horses."

"Is that so?" Mrs. McGavock tossed Mr. Cunningham a smile, then handed Catriona a plate, also with a generous serving of cake.

Catriona had planned to politely decline, not wanting to be beholden to this family in even the smallest way. But the dessert looked and smelled so good, and breakfast seemed a long time ago now. "Thank you kindly, ma'am." Catriona glanced down at Nora, who accepted as well and whispered a soft "thank you" in an unusually subdued voice.

"I hope this admission doesn't frighten you away, Mr. Cunningham"—Mrs. McGavock's expression held mischief—"but I'm most pleased you've agreed to assume this responsibility. My husband has been working sunup to sundown with the details of managing this farm."

182

Mr. Cunningham gave their hostess a smile that Catriona would have sworn was rehearsed. Da used to have those kinds of smiles. Smiles for certain occasions. Like when women would turn and stare at him on the street. They got their own special smile. She didn't remember him having a special smile for Mam.

"Thank you, Mrs. McGavock," he responded. "And I assure you, I'm grateful for the confidence your husband's showing in me and for the opportunity to work. As we were just discussing outside, good positions aren't easy to come by these days."

Mrs. McGavock paused in serving, her countenance softening. "No," she answered. "I would imagine not, since the war. The colonel tells me you were at Richmond. With General Lee."

"Yes, ma'am," Mr. Cunningham replied, his gaze going to the floor.

Mrs. McGavock's eyes glistened with emotion. "Thank you most sincerely, Mr. Cunningham, for your loyal service to the Confederacy."

Mr. Cunningham looked up, and this time it was his countenance that faltered. His jaw tightened. He offered a quick nod. "Just doing my duty, ma'am."

Catriona looked from one to the next—the colonel, his wife, and Mr. Cunningham—and felt as though she were on the outside looking in. On the one hand, she was thankful. She didn't know an overabundance of details about what had happened in the war here. She knew what little Ryan had shared in his letters, of course, and the facts she'd managed to garner from the newspapers in Ireland. But she was familiar enough with violence, with what people were capable of doing to one another in desperate times.

She'd been only a girl when the famine swept through her homeland, wiping out potato crops all across the country. She would never forget seeing adults—fathers, mothers, shop owners, priests even, people she'd known all her life—trample one another, including children, over the mere prospect of a scrap of food. The famine claimed her paternal grandparents first, then her mother's parents. People died by the hundreds in their town, which, in comparison to others, had been spared the worst. Thousands perished in County Antrim. Hundreds of thousands across the country. The bodies of the dead—so emaciated, so deprived of food in life—had swiftly bloated and blackened in death. And the stench that hovered over the village became so foul that—

"Miss O'Toole, are you feeling poorly?"

Catriona blinked as Mrs. McGavock's face, awash with concern, came into focus. Lowering her hand from her throat, Catriona took a deep breath and struggled to break free from the stranglehold of childhood memories—and from those more recent from a field a hefty stone's throw away from where she sat. "Yes, ma'am. I'm quite well, I assure you."

Mr. Cunningham looked over. "Are you certain? Because I'd be happy to accompany you and your—"

"I said I'm well, and I am!" Hearing the edge to her voice, Catriona attempted to soften it with a smile. But the lack of certainty in Mr. Cunningham's expression said she hadn't succeeded. "I believe I'm a touch weary, is all," she offered, directing the statement to the colonel and his wife. "Perhaps the journey from Ireland took a greater toll on me strength than I thought."

Mrs. McGavock offered an acknowledging tilt of her head. "Well, I'm certain that's true. A voyage like that is difficult enough, not to mention the days of travel by train. It's more than exhausting, I'm sure."

Catriona nodded, grateful when the conversation resumed, the attention shifting from her. She took a bite of her cake, and the sweetness of the frosting and comforting tastes of warm spices worked like a tonic, helping her relax. Spice cake for certain, she decided, and every bite more delicious than the last. Nora apparently agreed, because her plate was already clean. Her empty cup and saucer, however, were perched precariously close to the edge of the table. Catriona scooted them toward the center, only to have Nora promptly move them back.

Again, Catriona nudged the china cup and saucer to a safer distance, then leaned down, her voice a whisper. "I don't want you droppin' it, dearest."

"I'm not goin' to drop it, *Cattie!*" Nora

responded in her version of a whisper, which wasn't a whisper at all.

Catriona's face heated. A quick look at the McGavocks found them wholly intent on whatever Mr. Cunningham was explaining without the slightest pause, which told her that all three of them had heard their quarreling but were trying to let her save face. Which only deepened her feelings of inadequacy and made the situation worse.

"And what about the burial committee?" Mr. Cunningham asked. "Has anything been decided since your meeting last week, Colonel?"

"Burial committee?" The words were out before Catriona could call them back. But based on the surprise in their expressions—and what she interpreted to be disapproval—she sincerely wished she could. For a moment, no one spoke, and Catriona desperately reached for something else to say to fill the void. Nothing came.

John McGavock leaned forward in his chair. "Yes, the burial committee has to do with a . . . situation here in Franklin." He fingered his beard, his tone somber. "Something the town has been needing to address for several months now."

Movement at the parlor door drew Catriona's attention. Tempy peered inside and exchanged a look with Mrs. McGavock, who nodded in return. The cook slipped in and began gathering empty dishes and stacking them on the tray.

"As I'm certain you're aware, Miss O'Toole," the colonel continued, "as is everyone who travels to and from Franklin on Lewisburg Turnpike, numerous graves are in the field west of the road." He paused, seeming to weigh his words, his gaze flickering to Nora. But she was busy braiding her doll's hair. "Those graves belong to soldiers who died here in a battle toward the end of the war." He shook his head. "Or *the* end of the war as I view it now, looking back. The Confederacy was dealt a severe blow that day. More than two thousand of our boys lost their lives. Many of them right here in this house."

Grief cast a shadow across his face, and Catriona felt the weight of it in her chest.

"Two thousand?" she whispered, and the question that had been wearing her hope thin for months as to Ryan's well-being suddenly grew talons. "About those graves, Colonel, do you know whether the—" She caught herself and looked down beside her. Nora had gone completely still. Little ears were listening. Catriona wanted answers, but she wanted to protect her sister far more. She looked back at the colonel and gave a tiny shake of her head, hoping he would understand her meaning.

The cook picked up the tray from the table and turned to leave, then suddenly set it back down again. " 'Fore I go, Missus McGavock, there's somethin' I sure could use help with in the kitchen, ma'am."

Catriona didn't miss the look that passed between the two women.

"I got me a puddin' warm on the stove," Tempy continued. "And land sakes if I can't remember puttin' in sugar. You think one of you might come down and taste check it for me?"

Mrs. McGavock glanced at Catriona, who swiftly gathered their intent and nodded.

"Why yes, Tempy," Mrs. McGavock exclaimed. "I'm *certain* one of us would be willing to help you taste that delicious pudding."

Nora's head inched up a bit.

"I'd be willing to help," Mr. Cunningham offered, and all eyes turned to him, his overenthusiastic expression saying he was in on the secret. "I love pudding," he continued and started to stand.

"I love puddin' *too!*" Nora said, a pout still bruising her tone.

Already halfway out of his chair, Mr. Cunningham paused, a worried look coming over his face. "But do you love it more than I do, is the question, Miss Nora."

Nora stared at him, and Catriona could see her sister trying to sort out the question.

"Tell you what." Mr. Cunningham eased back into his seat. "You go on and taste the pudding first. If it's good, you run back here and tell me, then I'll come and eat it all. Do we have ourselves a deal?" He held out his hand as though waiting for her to shake on the agreement, and to Catriona's surprise, Nora hopped off the sofa and did just that.

Watching her little sister's arm pump up and down, she felt a tightening in her chest, and she missed Ryan more in that moment than she had in all the time since he'd left for America. Because Mr. Cunningham's antic was precisely like something Ryan would have done to help distract his youngest sister. Nora adored the way only Ryan could make her giggle. Catriona did too. Even more, she adored Ryan's devotion to his family. He'd always been his sisters' champion. Mam's too. Especially when it came to making them all laugh. And yet glimpsing a similar sense of humor in Mr. Cunningham had quite the opposite effect. On her, anyway.

Tempy lifted the tray and turned to go. "Well, come on with me, then, Miss Nora. But you got to promise to tell me the truth now, you hear?"

Nora nodded, smiling, Virginia in tow. "I will."

"And if that puddin' needs more sweetenin' up, you're gonna have to taste it twice so we can be sure to . . ."

Their voices faded in the hallway, and the silence in the parlor lengthened. It didn't take Catriona long to realize the others were waiting for her to continue. But where did she begin? And with Mr. Cunningham here too. She preferred to keep her personal business precisely that where he was concerned. But seeing the opportunity for what it was, she directed her attention to the colonel. And she felt as though she was about to get answers to the questions that had haunted her for so long. Only she wasn't certain anymore that she really wanted them.

CHAPTER 11

Even though she was sitting still, Catriona's heart raced. "What I was goin' to ask, Colonel, is . . . Was the Army of Tennessee part of that battle? The one you described?"

The colonel's eyes narrowed slightly. "Yes, it was. Why do you ask?"

Catriona briefly closed her eyes as the talons sank deep. *Oh Ryan* . . . Was her twin brother buried somewhere out there in that field after all? His body among the hundreds in shallow graves? Was *that* why she hadn't heard from him all this time?

"Miss O'Toole, do you know someone who fought in the Army of Tennessee?" Mrs. McGavock's voice was gentle, but even in the gentleness Catriona detected an underlying dread.

"Aye," she whispered, lowering her gaze. "Me twin brother, Ryan." Her throat tightened, and she found it difficult to swallow. "He came here, to America, in the spring of '62. The Confederates drafted him and his friends into service. It was either fight or return to Ireland. And returnin' wasn't an option." She pressed her lips tight, slowly looking up. "The last letter we got from him bore the date November twenty-ninth on

191

the envelope, which took until April of last year to make its way to County Antrim. The war was all but over by then. We knew from readin' the newspapers. But Ryan had written that his division was headed here. To Franklin. Which is why we've come. Me and me sister. To find him. So . . ." She consciously unclenched her hands knotted in her lap. "When exactly was that battle, Colonel? The one you're referrin' to?"

"The thirtieth of November," Mr. Cunningham answered instead, his voice oddly quiet. But it was the subtle severity behind his eyes, like the calm before a storm, that fueled her fear.

"Miss O'Toole . . ."

Catriona tore her gaze from Wade Cunningham's, only to be confronted with the apprehension in the colonel's.

"Do you know what division your brother served in? Who his commanding officer was?"

Catriona looked back and forth between the three of them, all of them watching her, waiting so intently that she almost didn't want to answer the question. As if not answering might bring a more favorable outcome. "Ryan was with Major General Patrick Cleburne."

The heartache in Mrs. McGavock's expression expelled the breath from Catriona's lungs. The couple looked at each other as though wanting the other to respond first.

But it was the slow way Wade Cunningham leaned forward, resting his arms on his thighs, his gaze fixed to the floor, that all but stripped away any remaining hope Catriona had of ever seeing her brother again.

"W-what?" she managed to say, finding it difficult to breathe. "What is it that you know?"

The seconds dragged on, and each one felt like another nail in Ryan's coffin. Catriona sought the colonel's gaze, terrified of the truth but wanting to know it just the same. "Please, sir, tell me what you're knowin'. It can't be any worse than what I'm imaginin' right now."

The bracing look in his eyes told her otherwise, and a sharp pain started somewhere near her heart. She sensed a keening rising up from inside, but she forced it back down. She would not give in to her grief here. Not now. Not in front of these people. The McGavocks, who had wronged her family in such a dishonorable way. And certainly not in front of a man the likes of Wade Cunningham. And especially not when she still didn't know for certain of Ryan's fate.

"I will tell you all I know, Miss O'Toole." The colonel looked at his wife. "*We* will tell you. But before we do, may I ask you a question?"

She nodded.

"Am I correct in understanding that you have not heard from your brother since that last letter?"

Catriona hesitated. She wasn't eager to tell them about the package Ryan sent containing the money. But she also wanted to do all she could to help find her brother. That was why she was sitting here in the first place. "We did receive one more note, sir. About four or five weeks after that letter. But it was only a few scribbled lines. Nothin' that told us anything about his goings-on or where he was."

The colonel's thoughtful nod indicated perhaps he'd hoped for something more promising. "General Cleburne's division was, indeed, here at the battle. The division was part of General Cheatham's corps. In fact, Cleburne's men were known far and wide for their courage and toughness. Maybe that's why General Hood positioned them where he did on the field not far from here."

Unbidden, an image of the field rose in Catriona's mind.

"Cleburne's division was assigned to attack an especially well-fortified part of the Federal line," the colonel continued. "The area around our neighbor Fountain Carter's cotton gin. According to the men who fought there, and who survived, that's where the most vicious fighting took place. Which would explain"—he hesitated briefly— "why Cleburne's division suffered among the highest losses that day. But that's also the only place where the Army of Tennessee managed to break through the Federal breastworks. Which is something, considering the 104th Ohio is who they came up against."

"The 104th Ohio?" Catriona asked.

Wade Cunningham shifted in his chair, and she

looked at him, wondering if he would add something. But he remained silent, his gaze stony, fastened to the floor.

"Yes. Just as Cleburne's division was known for their courage and skill, so was the 104th Ohio Volunteer Infantry. So I don't believe it was at all fortuitous that the two regiments met on the battlefield."

Catriona exhaled sharply. "I'd hardly call the scene you've described as a 'meetin'' on the battlefield, Colonel. Seein' as how the 104th Ohio was protected behind breastworks, as you're callin' 'em. But be that as it may, just how many of General Cleburne's men survived?"

Again, the McGavocks exchanged looks, and Catriona's gut twisted.

"Everything was so chaotic that night," the colonel said, his tone clearly hedging the truth. "And in the days following. The number of soldiers involved in this battle alone was staggering. Twenty thousand for each the North and the South. So I'm afraid we don't yet have a full accounting of the number of men who were killed here or of all their names. But let me hasten to say that your brother being part of General Cleburne's division does *not* mean he died that night. Some of Cleburne's men lived. Most who did were—"

"Some of them lived?" It was all Catriona could do to stay seated. "Do we know who? And where they were taken? Can I be knowin' if Ryan was one of them?"

Compassion filled the colonel's gaze. "The wounded were treated in homes and businesses all over Franklin. Carnton included. To our knowledge, none of Cleburne's division was brought here. They were taken to other various locations. Unfortunately, record keeping suffered greatly in the final weeks and months of the Confederacy, so that is why there's no final accounting of all the soldiers who died here. But I can tell you that the men in Cleburne's division who did survive were severely wounded. The important thing, though, is that some of them *survived*. General Cleburne, it pains me to say, did not. He died on the battlefield that night."

Tears filled Mrs. McGavock's eyes, and her husband covered her hand on the arm of her chair. But Catriona could scarcely see straight for the questions roiling inside her—the foremost being how she could learn if Ryan had been one of those who lived.

"They did bring General Cleburne's body here." Mrs. McGavock's voice came out shaky. "They laid it on the gallery porch in the back, along with three other generals who also fell during the battle. Our boys fought so bravely, Miss O'Toole. The wounded were brought here shortly after the battle began. Every room quickly filled until the house couldn't hold any more. So they filled the yards and outbuildings. There were so many injured, and they were *so* young. Too young."

The woman's gaze moved about the parlor as

though she were seeing with her eyes what only her heart could truly see. "We cared for them as best we could. I remember wondering that night if the scream of cannon fire and rifle blasts would ever end. But it did . . . finally. By then, however, the world had been altered. And life as it had been was gone." Mrs. McGavock wiped away a tear. "Not a day goes by that I don't think about the men who were in this house, both those who died here and those who lived, and about how much they each gave for the Confederacy." She fell silent then, and her gaze settled on the floor by Catriona's feet. With purpose, it seemed.

So Catriona leaned forward and followed Mrs. McGavock's line of sight to one of the largest of the dark stains covering the wood floor, and Catriona's breath quickened as truth took hold. She quickly moved her feet, yet knew full well she'd already walked over that stain and so many others like it while in this house. Her eyes stung, and she blinked back tears. But they fell anyway. As though a veil had been snatched away, she could all but see the scene in the house as Mrs. McGavock had described it. The brutality of it nearly pushed her sensibilities beyond their limit and only fueled the urgency within her to gain answers to her questions.

"Colonel," she continued, then cleared her throat. "You said—"

Wade Cunningham suddenly came to his feet, his chair scraping the floor. The sound was overloud in the silence. "My apologies to you, Miss O'Toole, for interrupting. And to you, Colonel and Mrs. McGavock. But if you'll excuse me, I need to . . ." He swallowed, the muscles in his jaw cording tight. Catriona thought she caught a sheen in his eyes. Had he been in the battle here at Franklin too? Judging by the remorse lining his expression, she guessed the answer.

"Thank you, Mrs. McGavock, for your hospitality," he finally said. "And now with your permission, Colonel, I believe I'll explore the farm, as you suggested earlier. Get acquainted with things. Meet your workers."

McGavock stood. "Of course. Take one of the horses. Cassandra's Legacy, if you like. It appears as though you already have a way with her. If it suits you, as the overseer she can be yours. And take the liberty of giving her a name that's less of a mouthful."

Cunningham smiled—or tried to. The gesture fell flat. "Thank you, Colonel. But I believe that particular challenge would best be saved for another day. I will take one of the thoroughbreds, though, with your consent."

"Mr. Cunningham, you are now overseer of Carnton. The management of this estate—the sawmill, the smithy, all the crops and livestock, including the thoroughbreds—now rests in your hands and under your care. I trust you'll supervise my farm as you would your own."

For a heartbeat, Cunningham only stared, then

198

he gave a quick nod. "Of course. I give you my word."

"Take a wagon back to town with you tonight," the colonel added. "You can pick up the supplies we discussed earlier, as well as anything else you deem necessary based on your findings this afternoon. Charge them to my account."

"Will do, sir."

The two men shook hands, then Mrs. McGavock extended hers as well. And for a second time, Wade Cunningham bestowed a brief kiss. He turned to Catriona as the colonel once again claimed his seat. She hesitated, then finally offered her hand, seeing no way around it. He grasped it lightly, his own warm and strong around hers.

"Miss O'Toole . . ." For a moment he simply held her gaze, his expression absent the overly confident air she'd begun to expect from him. "It is my earnest prayer that you find your brother, ma'am. And that your search for him . . . ends in joy."

Taken aback by his sincerity, much less kindness, Catriona nodded, tears threatening again. "Thank you, Mr. Cunningham," she whispered, scarcely able to find her voice.

He brushed a kiss to the crown of her hand and squeezed her fingers ever so slightly before relinquishing hold. She watched him leave, grateful to see him go. Now she could speak more freely to the McGavocks, about both Ryan and the business about the family land. And yet why, even after Wade Cunningham left the room, did she still feel the warmth of his hand around hers along with a stirring deep inside her, one she'd never felt before now? Yet in the same breath, she reminded herself that such feelings were fleeting and not to be trusted. Mam had once shared with her about how, early on, her heart had fluttered at the mere sight of Da. And look how that ended.

Somewhere behind her shelf in the next room, chimes sounded, and Catriona glanced at the clock on the mantel above the hearth. Nearly noon. She'd already been here far longer than expected— and longer than she'd wanted to be. But answers were yet to be had, and she wasn't leaving without them.

"Colonel, a moment ago you said you don't *yet* know the number of men who died here in Franklin or have a list of their names. What was your meanin' by *yet?*"

He nodded. "I was referring to the burial committee I mentioned before. The graves in that field are in extremely poor condition. Hence, this committee has been formed, of which I am part. And our primary purpose is to rectify that situation. We hope to begin the process very soon. Within the month, in fact."

As his meaning gradually took shape, an icy finger traced a path up Catriona's spine. She grimaced. "You and your committee will do this? Exhume the bodies?"

A semblance of a smile touched his face. It

carried a hint of apology. "No, ma'am. The committee is currently accepting bids from workers who are willing to manage such a project. *They* will conduct the actual exhumations."

Catriona nodded, a little numb and also sickened by the imagery forming in her mind. She couldn't imagine any job worse than what those workers would hire on to do.

Something caught her eye outside the window, beyond where the McGavocks sat, and she squinted, making sure she was seeing correctly. The window gave view to the front yard, and there was Nora walking by outside, sweet as you please, headed in the direction of the garden. The girl suddenly bent down, picked up something, and stuffed it into her skirt pocket. Catriona inwardly shook her head. Oh, that girl. Could she not just stay put?

Catriona started to rise but then spotted Master Winder in tow. Along with Wade Cunningham. She frowned. This was what he meant by exploring the estate? While she didn't care for the man, surely Nora couldn't get into too much trouble in his company. And with Master Winder there too. Still, she determined to finish here quickly and retrieve her sister.

"The exhumation team will keep a list of every soldier who is exhumed and reburied," the colonel continued, his tone reverent, and Catriona refocused. "Along with any information they may find about each soldier during that process. They will have a most arduous task ahead of them, I fear. Because while some of the graves still bear wooden markers of some sort, many do not. The past two winters were bitter cold, and many of those markers simply disappeared. Wayfarers needing fuel for a fire, we assume. But that's going to make the process of identifying some of the deceased even more difficult. That is what I meant when I said we don't yet know that information. But we hope to, very soon."

"And how soon is very soon?" Catriona asked.

He thought for a moment. "We've already received several bids from teams willing to do the job. One applicant in particular, a man from Texas, appears to be the most promising. He believes that, working with his two brothers, they could see the task completed inside three months. Four at most."

Catriona rubbed her left temple, a dull ache beginning to form. "Understandin' that these . . . exhumations will take time, is there someone I could write to about Ryan until then? One of his officers, perhaps, who might know what happened to him or where he is now."

"Making an inquiry to the War Department would be a very good place to start. I, of course, don't know who your brother's officers were. But they would have record of that, and hopefully they can provide assistance."

Mrs. McGavock rose. "I have the address to the War Department in my journal. I'll fetch it for you now."

Feeling the door closing on the subject, Catriona experienced a rush of despair and reached for one last tattered thread on which to tug. "I know this may be far-fetched, but . . ."

Mrs. McGavock paused, then sat again.

"Perhaps Ryan *was* brought here to Carnton that night, but you both have no way of knowin' it was him because he never gave his name. If I describe him to you . . ."

Mrs. McGavock's expression softened, as did the colonel's. Catriona could tell they thought she was reaching beyond reason, but she had to ask. It was Ryan, after all.

"Me brother's very handsome. And tall. With hair the color of me own, of course, bein' that we're twins. And Ryan's eyes—" She smiled. "His eyes are full of kindness. You'd swear 'twas an angel lookin' out at you. 'Specially when he smiles. He has a tattoo as well. A Celtic cross. About here on his upper right arm." She pointed. "Mam was never fond of it, but I favored it well enough."

She watched, waiting for the slightest flicker of recognition to show in their features, but none came. She lowered her gaze.

Mrs. McGavock lightly touched her arm. "I'm sorry, Miss O'Toole. Ryan sounds like a wonderful young man. But I'm afraid many Irish soldiers were here that night, so I cannot say conclusively whether your brother was here. I do sincerely hope, though, that the colonel and I have the opportunity to meet him one day soon. As well as the rest of your family."

"You've already met the rest," Catriona responded, then instantly regretted it. She was breaking her own rule—the less shared with strangers, the better.

"So it's only you and Nora, then?" Mrs. McGavock asked.

"Aye, ma'am. Our two sisters died last fall, and Mam in December. Our da before them."

Mrs. McGavock gave her arm a tight squeeze. "Please accept our deepest condolences for your losses, Miss O'Toole."

"Yes, indeed," the colonel echoed.

Catriona nodded her thanks. From all appearances, the McGavocks were turning out to be kinder than she'd imagined. Though appearances could be deceiving.

Mrs. McGavock stood. "If you'll both excuse me for a moment, I'll fetch that address for the War Department."

"While she goes to get that . . ." The colonel reached behind his wife's chair and lifted a wooden crate, then he placed it on the table before them and raised the lid.

From somewhere in the entrance hall, the squeak of door hinges sounded.

"Oh, we meet again, Mr. Cunningham." Mrs. McGavock's voice carried from the hallway, as did Wade Cunningham's—although with the colonel opening a worn leather-bound notebook and turning the pages with obvious intent, Catriona couldn't make out what was being said. She listened for any sign of Nora or Winder. But either the children were being as quiet as mice, which was highly unlikely, or Mr. Cunningham had managed to give them the slip. Either way, she found herself anxious to check on Nora.

It would help so much if she and Nora were on better footing with each other, something she'd hoped Ryan's return would facilitate. But if he *had* truly met with a tragic fate, how would she and her sister ever reach a peaceable place? Much less make a home, the home she'd promised Mam she'd give Nora. Catriona took a deep breath, loneliness for family and home—a place to call her own—carving out an even deeper well inside her.

The tread of footsteps and snatches of conversation in the hallway faded.

"It took some doing, Miss O'Toole," the colonel continued and then waited for her to look at him. "But I managed to find the files, or at least some of them, from my grandfather's farm in County Antrim. And while I honestly did not expect to find any reference to the charges you laid at my feet the other day, to my profound surprise I did find not only a reference but what I believe may be an answer."

Handling the aging leather notebook with utmost care, he turned to a page marked with a cigar band. Odd pieces of paper had been stuck here and there in the notebook until the binding fairly bulged.

"In recent days, I spent several hours looking through the boxes and crates in the attic I alluded to earlier. I haven't opened some of them since they came into my possession. But I'm pleased to have discovered that my father and grandfather were both most meticulous in their record keeping. With the quantity and detail of entries, it appears they took great care to record even the smallest transactions."

Catriona heard the colonel building a case in his explanation, and she had the distinct feeling it wasn't going to lean in her favor. She also heard the squeak of a floorboard in the hallway and glanced toward the door. Her first thought went to Nora. Her second to Wade Cunningham. She wouldn't put eavesdropping—or much else—past the man. He seemed far too observant for her taste, and she already knew Nora was a little snoop.

"My grandfather and father even recorded receipts for minor farming implements such as a rack or sickle, or even a—"

"Colonel McGavock." Hoping her tone didn't hold too much authority, she was ready to know the truth, for better or worse, and to be done with Carnton and its wealth and privilege. "For both our interests, sir, would you please just be showin' me what you found? Be it in me family's best interest or not."

The colonel's gaze flickered, and for a moment Catriona thought she might have angered him. Then his expression smoothed.

He gave a succinct nod and pointed. "Very well. Note the next-to-last entry at the bottom of this right-hand page."

Her gaze trailed down over the neat, even elegant handwriting, then stopped abruptly when she saw a familiar name. She blinked. It couldn't be. But it was.

CHAPTER 12

Her great-grandfather's name. " 'Tomás O'Toole,' " Catriona read aloud, then continued on to the detail written neatly beside it. " 'Deed for O'Toole land, with exception of homestead, accepted this day in exchange for a loan of' "—her jaw slipped open further—" *two thousand dollars.*' " She swallowed. So much money. Pushing past the silent sense of alarm going off inside her, she read on. And something twisted deep within, hardening in the pit of her stomach. It was all she could do to force out the words. " 'Loan to be repaid within ten years. No interest demanded.' "

Her breath came hard. Her eyes burned, though not due to sorrow. The land *wasn't* stolen? It hadn't been thieved through deception like she'd been told all her life? How could they have done this? How could her family have—

"Wait," she whispered, grasping for even the thinnest thread of possibility. She looked up. "This is only a ledger, Colonel. A record written by *your* grandfather. How can we be knowin' for certain that the man was bein' truthful? Perchance he wrote this in this book of his to be coverin' his tracks for whoever—"

McGavock gently tugged at a piece of paper

that had been stuck into the binding and handed it to her. Catriona took one look at the document, and the bitter taste of metal filled her mouth. The deed to her family's land. And it was authentic too. She knew it not only because she recognized her great-grandfather's illustrative work on the official certificate but because of the embellished O'Toole family crest at the bottom of the page. It was the crest her great-grandfather had taught his son to draw, who had then taught Da, who had taught Ryan—right beside her great-grandfather's signature. And she knew his hand as well as her own, having seen it countless times on old documents in the print shop.

"There's something on the back as well," McGavock urged gently.

Not wanting to—wishing she were miles from this house, from this town, wishing she'd never come here—she turned the document over but couldn't bring herself to read the words aloud this time. *Know all men by this declaration that I, Tomás O'Toole, do hereby grant ownership of the O'Toole ancestral land as described in this deed to James McGavock of County Antrim. This property is put forth as security for a loan of two thousand dollars to be paid back over the course of ten years from the date indicated beside my signature below. This loan is made absent of any charge of interest, and once repaid in full will result in the deed being returned to the signer of this agreement. If the loan fails to be repaid within the stated terms, or upon my death, should that precede repayment of the loan in full, the land described in this deed will forthwith be the legal property of the James McGavock family.*

She stared at the words as they blurred on the page. She swallowed. So it had all been a lie? The famed *McGavock family deceit?* A lie passed down through the years. Coming from Da, she would have expected such a thing. But for the falsehood to have originated with her great-grandfather? And what about Mam? Mam had always nodded her head when the treachery had been spoken of, her frustration and sense of injustice seeming so real.

"Miss O'Toole, please understand that it gives me no pleasure to—"

"No pleasure to what?" Catriona stared up at him, surprised at the anger roiling inside her. As was the colonel, judging by his expression. "To be tellin' me that *your* family is the honorable one? That you stand innocent of the accusation I made the other day? Somehow I have to believe you're takin' at least an ounce of pleasure in it, sir. Because if it was the O'Toole family who had been accused, only to be proven in the right, I'd be relieved. And I, for sure, right or wrong, would be takin' some pleasure in it."

The patience in the man's expression lessened considerably. "What I was going to say, Miss O'Toole, if you'll afford me the opportunity, is that while I'm grateful evidence exists that puts this issue soundly to rest, it gives me no pleasure to reveal it to you. Quite the opposite, in fact. Was I relieved to learn there had been no deceit on the McGavock family's part, as your patriarchs claimed there to be? Of course I was. Because to have discovered that my father or grandfather had treated your family—ancestral neighbors whose land bordered ours in County Antrim—with such blatant disregard and duplicity would have brought shame upon my family name and on my home. A great deal more painful, my opinion of those two men would have been altered to a large degree. And since they have both passed from time into eternity, there would be no way for me to ask why they made the decisions they did. There would be no way for me to reconcile what I always thought to be true with the truth itself. *That* is what pains me the most in this situation . . . on your behalf."

Compassion wasn't what she expected, or wanted, from this man. She wanted the story her family had told her to be true. She'd spent so much time and energy shoring up animosity against John McGavock. And for what? Only to learn that the truth she'd clung to wasn't the truth at all. But John McGavock was not a man free from culpability. She'd asked about him around town. A staunch supporter of the Southern cause, everyone said. "Fine, upstanding, and generous." But how fine, upstanding, and generous could a man be who had bought and sold human beings? And who would likely still be doing just that if the Federal Army hadn't routed the Confederacy so soundly.

Ryan had fought for the South, true. But he'd had no choice. Colonel McGavock and others—Wade Cunningham included—*had.* And they'd made the wrong one.

"I have a great many faults, Miss O'Toole," the colonel said, as though reading her mind. "As my dear wife will attest—"

He glanced beyond her, and Catriona turned to see Mrs. McGavock standing in the doorway, her expression a good deal less magnanimous than it had been when she'd left the room.

"But to rejoice in another's downfall," he continued, "would show a gross lack of moral character. One I sincerely pray I am never guilty of. But in this situation, ma'am, I give you my word, I am not."

Glad that he couldn't read her mind, Catriona wondered how someone could be so blind to their own shortcomings. Still, as clearly as she could read the document in her hand, she saw the sincerity, however tarnished, in the colonel's face. And that, along with the feeling of standing naked and guilty before one's accuser, only served to deepen the sting of betrayal and disappointment. Except she had been the accuser. Not him.

She drew in a fortifying breath. "I'll be takin' me leave of you, then. Once I collect me sister. So if you'd be so kind as to tell me where she is . . ." She'd have had to be blind to miss the look of sympathy the couple gave each other. Or worse, pity. She huffed. Could the man and woman not speak a word without looking at each other first? It was maddening. "Or I'll find me sister meself if that's what you prefer."

Mrs. McGavock's brow rose slightly. "Your sister is with our son, Winder, in the backyard." She gestured toward the rear of the house. "Near the barn."

Catriona tried her best, as Nora had done, not to step on the stains marring the floor as she left the room. But there was no way to avoid them. And to think she was walking over a place where Ryan might have lain . . . An iron fist grabbed her throat and squeezed tight.

She ducked her head to avoid meeting Mrs. McGavock's gaze, then spotted a door in the direction the woman had gestured and took it. Once outside on the back porch gallery, she closed the door behind her and leaned against it. The roil of heartache and grief rose up within her with such ferocity that she clapped a hand over her mouth to contain it. Not here. Not now.

She spotted Nora and Winder beside the barn, crouched near the ground, playing with what looked to be a passel of kittens. She crossed the distance, calling as she went. "Nora! It's time to be goin' now."

Nora didn't bother looking up. "I'm not ready yet. Me and Winder, we're playin' with Bertha and her wee ones. And we went to see a big ol' cow who's got a babe inside her too!"

"I said *now!*"

Both children looked up then. And similar to calling out in one of the caves back home along the shoreline, the sharpness—nay, the ugliness—in her own voice returned to her, and Catriona cringed. But she had to get away from here. *Now.*

"If you're willing, Miss O'Toole," a deep voice said behind her, "I can take you and Nora back to town. I've got a wagon all hitched and ready to go."

Catriona squeezed her eyes tight. *For the love of Saint Peter and Paul . . .* She didn't bother turning. "No thank you, Mr. Cunningham. We can walk."

"But, Cattie, I'm not wantin' to walk! Me boots are hurtin'. I been tellin' you that. They done rubbed me heels raw."

Master Winder nodded. "It's true, ma'am. She's got blood on her stocking feet. I saw it myself. Besides, Mr. Cunningham says I can go along with y'all to town. Says he'll get us some doughnuts at the mercantile for helping him load the crates into the back of the wagon. They're made special every day by a woman at the bakery."

Catriona shook her head. "I'm sorry, Master Winder, but there will be no—"

"Miss O'Toole?"

Catriona turned to see Mrs. McGavock walking toward them, a familiar-looking reticule in hand. Catriona quickly felt her wrist, and though she wasn't one to curse, she thought seriously about it in that moment.

"You left this on the settee. And here's the

215

address to the War Department. I would definitely suggest writing them more than once. They're still being inundated with letters, as I'm certain you understand."

Careful not to meet the woman's eyes, Catriona accepted the reticule and slip of paper, her weak smile demanding more effort than it would take to climb that hundred-year-old sessile oak back home. "Thank you, Mrs. McGavock."

"My pleasure, Miss O'Toole. I sincerely am sorry for your losses, and I wish you and your sister only the best in the days ahead."

Catriona nodded her thanks, picturing a pile of burning coals being heaped onto her head. How often had Mam quoted that specific scripture, wherever it was in the Bible. That if your enemy was hungry, you were to feed him. If he was thirsty, you were to give him drink. And that by doing so, you'd be heaping burning coals onto his head. A humbling thought at the moment, especially considering that Mrs. McGavock had just given her food and drink. Catriona didn't know whether the woman looked upon her as an enemy, but she was certain she did not view her as a friend. What sort of friend came into your home and accused your family of deceit and thievery? Not the sort of friend anyone wished for.

"Mr. Cunningham, Tempy just gave me a list of staples she would like for you to purchase at the mercantile." Mrs. McGavock handed him the paper, her expression turning sheepish. "Your

216

initiation here at Carnton is happening more quickly than we thought."

He tucked the list into his shirt pocket. "Yes, ma'am. But I don't mind. And thank you for allowing Master Winder to come along with us."

Us? Catriona speared the man with a look. She'd already told him no. Yet he acted as though he didn't notice her glaring at him, even though she was all but certain he did.

Mrs. McGavock pointed a finger at her son. "You mind yourself on the way there—*and* back—young man. And help Mr. Cunningham load the supplies."

The boy nodded. "Yes, Mama. I will."

"I'll be helpin' too," Nora parroted, which earned her an approving wink from Mrs. McGavock.

Winder nudged Nora, then gestured toward the wagon. The two of them scampered up into the bed, Virginia in tow.

Only then did Catriona realize that Nora had shed not only her boots but her stockings as well. The girl was running around in her bare feet! Catriona sighed as she scooped the boots and stockings from the ground and placed them in the wagon. What would the mistress of Carnton think of her now? No words came to mind. Except *failure*. And *sapskull*.

Mr. Cunningham extended his hand to her. "May I assist you into the wagon, Miss O'Toole?"

If not for Mrs. McGavock watching them, Catriona would have refused him flat out and toted

Nora all the way back to town on her own steam, which she had plenty of at the moment. She was tempted to do it too. She knew the reason behind Mr. Cunningham's insisting he give her a ride. Carnton's "new overseer" wanted to appear gallant in front of his employer's wife. It was obvious Mrs. McGavock already liked him, too, poor judge of character that proved her to be. But Catriona knew there was no winning this one. If she refused the offer, she'd be lowering Mrs. McGavock's opinion of her even more—*if* that were even possible. That shouldn't matter to her, but for some reason it did. So she begrudgingly accepted his assistance and climbed into the wagon.

He claimed the spot beside her, and the bench suddenly shrank by half. The man had removed the coat he'd been wearing earlier, and the rolled-up sleeves of his shirt revealed tanned, well-muscled forearms. She'd always considered Ryan to be a strapping boy, and he'd become even more so as he'd grown. Yet where Ryan was lean and sinewy, Wade Cunningham's muscles seemed to have muscles of their own. And the man's thighs! Especially next to her own . . .

Eager to distance herself from that thought— and the man—she scooted as far to the right as she could, which proved a futile effort. As soon as he slapped the reins, the mares responded, and the wagon jolted forward. Their bodies couldn't help but touch.

Behind them in the wagon bed, Winder and Nora

chatted away like magpies, but thankfully Wade Cunningham sat silently beside her. In no mood for conversation, it seemed. All the better for her. She gripped the side of the wagon seat, feeling as though she were teetering on the edge of a cliff and that the slightest breath of wind would send her plunging.

How could her family have perpetuated such a lie? And for so long. And why? She was ashamed, aye. And she'd been embarrassed in front of the McGavocks. But it was more than that. Somehow learning this news brought a fresh wave of grief, and she wished Ryan were here so they could talk it through. He would know exactly what to say to help brighten her outlook. She could see his face so clearly in her mind's eye. Her dear, sweet Ryan.

Wade Cunningham guided the wagon onto the main road leading back to town, expertly managing the rig and maneuvering around the deepest ruts in the road. Ryan had been good at driving a wagon, too, and— Nay. Not *had* been. He *was* good at it.

She turned to her right and looked out across the field. This felt like the longest day in her life. Weary from the constant heaviness inside, she fixed her attention on the road, eager to be out of this wagon, done with this day, and living for the moment Nora fell asleep tonight and she could finally give in to the pain.

CHAPTER 13

Wade's grip tightened on the reins. He wanted to look beside him on the bench seat, but he didn't dare. So instead he turned to glance at Winder and Nora, who sat side by side on crates in the back, jabbering away. He could feel the tension in Miss O'Toole's body from where he sat, could see it in her death grip on the wagon seat.

Of all the regiments in the Army of Tennessee, her brother—her *twin* brother—had been in General Cleburne's.

When she'd revealed that fact in the McGavocks' parlor earlier, it felt like someone had slipped a bowie knife between his ribs. He'd had to lean forward in his chair just to gain a breath. And now he couldn't stop his mind from returning to that smoke-hazed battlefield, from trying to recall the blurred face of every man he'd framed in his rifle sights that night. And trying to remember if any of them had borne the distinguishing coloring of the Irish.

But all he'd been aiming at that night was butternut and gray. They were all the enemy. And yet one of them had been Ryan O'Toole. And another, some distance down the line, Wesley Cunningham. He doubted the two young men had ever met, being in different regiments and divisions. But he wondered if they'd met since that night. In the afterlife. Because even though he hoped it wasn't true, in his mind there was little chance that Miss O'Toole's brother hadn't passed through the veil during or following that battle. Wade only prayed he hadn't been the soldier who'd sent him through.

Miss O'Toole, staring out across the fields to the right, drew in a shaky breath, and the knife Wade felt in his chest twisted a quarter turn. She hadn't wanted to accept his offer of a ride into town, and she wouldn't have, he didn't think, if Mrs. McGavock hadn't been there. He didn't know what had possessed him to ask her in the first place. Only that, as he'd listened to her speak in the parlor, she'd seemed so desperate, so weary and beaten down, her hands clenched tight in her lap until her knuckles turned white.

Then when he saw her leaving the house, she'd leaned against the door as though it was all she could do to remain standing. He didn't know her story. Not all of it, anyway. But the part he knew tore at him, and he wanted to do something—anything—to ease the weight on her shoulders. But how to do that when she'd made it clear she wanted little or nothing to do with him?

"Thank you, Miss O'Toole, for allowing me to see you back to town."

She sighed. Or was it a huff? "I appreciate the ride . . . *Mr. Cunningham.*"

Wade raised a brow. That had definitely been a huff. Because the edge to her voice could've cut aged hickory clean through.

Seconds passed, and as the wagon jostled over the rain-rutted road, he sensed something from her. He didn't know what, but curiosity finally got the best of him. He sneaked a look at her. "Are you wanting to say something else, ma'am?"

Her mouth tipped in a semblance of a smile, except one with very little friendliness to it. "Not at all. I'm just sittin' over here baskin' in your chivalry."

He eyed her. "My chivalry?"

"Aye, that's what I said. That's why you offered to drive us back to town, isn't it? So you could show your new employer's wife what a courteous man they've taken into their employ."

Even blind, deaf, and lying half dead in a ditch, he would see that this woman was itching for a fight. But *he* wasn't who she wanted to spar with. Not really. He'd walked a similar road to the one she was walking now, and in his estimation, she needed to aim a whole lot higher than him—all the way to heaven's gates, in fact—to get to the one she was truly angry with. She was lashing out at him only because he happened to be close by. And had flesh.

It was tempting to spar with her. No doubt the woman could hold her own—and then some. But she was hurting and tired, and she had just received devastating news about her brother. So he faced forward, determined not to be drawn in.

"What's wrong, Mr. Cunningham? Am I hittin' a wee bit too close to home for you?"

He gripped the reins. *No. Not doing it.*

"Oh, I see." Her voice turned sugary sweet. "Now that you don't have an audience watchin', you're not nearly so chivalrous as we thought, are you?" She clucked her tongue. "Just like a man. Puttin' on manners and then takin' them off like a set of clothes."

Wade kept his attention on the road, making note of what she'd said—*"Just like a man"*— and finding it revealing. More so than she likely realized. But one thing was clear. No wonder Nora was as spunky as she was. The girl had learned it, at least in part, from her older sister. Even accounting for the difference in their ages, the two seemed fairly well matched in temperament. He could only imagine what sparks flew when their tempers came to a head.

"What are you smilin' at, sir?"

He turned and looked at her. "I'm smiling at you."

Her eyes narrowed, and in that moment he decided that if Catriona O'Toole wanted a fight, he would give it to her. Maybe providing a way for her to blow off some of that steam was how he could best help her. For now, anyway. He sensed she needed a friend. And though under different circumstances he might have hoped for more than friendship with her, anything beyond that was out of the question right now.

"Miss O'Toole, we both know you don't appreciate this ride. You were cornered into it. Still, I'm grateful you agreed to let me take you and your sister back to town."

Her mouth slipped open. "*Och!* So you *were* knowin' I didn't want to come along! You saw the look I gave you yet pretended not to."

"How could I miss it? You about pinned me to the barn back there. But giving you a ride seemed like the right thing to do under the circumstances."

"And I take it you're a man who *always* does the right thing."

The woman had a quick tongue, he'd give her that. "Not always," he answered after a moment. "But I try to."

With a dismissive look, she faced forward again. "When we get to town, deliver us directly to the hotel, please."

"No!" came a cry from behind them. Nora climbed atop the empty crates nested in the wagon bed and pushed up between them. "Cattie, you said we could go to the mercantile!"

"Nay, I never did say that, Nora. Now sit back down before you fall."

Nora whined. "But Wade's goin' to get us a doughnut and—"

Miss O'Toole spun to look back. "That's *Mr.*

225

Cunningham to you, please. And I said to sit down. Now!"

Emitting a low growl, Nora jumped down, then plopped onto the wagon bed. Wade could hear the children whispering back and forth.

"Miss O'Toole," he said softly, "if it's time you're concerned about, what if we were to stop by the mercantile and get the doughnuts first, then I'll take you to the hotel. I can return to conduct my business at the mercantile on the way back."

"Nora is needin' a midday meal, not another sweet. Please be takin' us to the hotel as I asked you. And in the future, you might consider askin' a child's parent or guardian before you go promisin' him or her somethin' that's not within your right to give."

"I meant no harm by it, ma'am. When I took a walk with them earlier, we began talking about our favorite kind of food, and—"

"Do you have children, Mr. Cunningham?"

Wade paused. "No, ma'am. I haven't had that particular pleasure yet."

She peeled a glance at him. "Perhaps when you do, you'll learn that you cannot give children everything they want. They must be taught discipline. Life is difficult, and the sooner they learn that not everythin' will turn out in a way that's pleasin' to 'em, the better off they'll be."

Wade matched her gaze, and she lifted her chin slightly.

"Are we still talking about children, Miss O'Toole?"

Her slender jaw tightened, and she'd just opened her mouth to respond when the stench hit him square in the face, worse than the other times he'd passed by here in recent days. But that was to be expected with the warming weather. Beside him, Miss O'Toole grimaced, revulsion in her expression. Yet beyond that, she offered no response. Behind him, he heard Winder taking charge.

"Cover your nose like this, Nora," the boy said, demonstrating. "And breathe through your mouth. It's that field full of dead bodies over there. My papa says the town is working on getting all that . . ."

Wade glanced behind him, concerned about Nora. Sure enough, the girl was holding her nose like Winder said, and she was staring in the opposite direction from the field. She and Miss O'Toole had passed by here before. There was no way to avoid Lewisburg Pike when visiting Carnton. He slapped the reins, urging the mares to a faster clip.

As they passed the field on the left, he looked out across it and wondered again, as he had before, exactly where Wesley had been buried. All his sister said in her letter last summer was that their brother's body had been exhumed from the west side of the breastworks near where Wesley had fallen in battle, on the opposite end of the Federal

227

entrenchment from where the 104th Ohio had been. A faded wooden marker had still identified his younger brother's grave. Otherwise, with the number of men buried out there, how could they ever have found him?

Wade would have thought knowing where on the line his brother had died would give him a considerable measure of relief. And it had, in one way. But not in so many others.

As they approached town, the field of graves behind them, he took a cautious breath, then exhaled. Miss O'Toole did the same beside him. He checked on Winder and Nora, only to find they were busy whispering again—plotting, no doubt—and also eating some of whatever it was Tempy had given them both in the kitchen, kept in pockets until now. He doubted Nora would want a meal for a while. He dared a look beside him.

Miss O'Toole's features, fetching as always, held clear warning, so he decided not to push the doughnut issue. He'd just have to find some way to make it up to Nora. He guided the wagon onto the main thoroughfare that led to the hotel.

"Whoa there, friend!" a voice called.

Wade looked up ahead to see a man in a suit standing in the middle of the street frantically waving his hat in the air—a mess of squawking chickens racing in all directions, wings flapping. As Wade guided the wagon closer, he realized why and brought the rig to a stop.

"Look at that!" Winder exclaimed, peering over

Wade's shoulder. Nora did likewise. "I bet some-body's in a lot of trouble!"

"Maybe they weren't meanin' to do it!" Nora said quickly, which earned her a doubtful look from her older sister. Nora only scowled.

Wade shook his head to himself. *These ladies . . .*

With a wave, he acknowledged the man jogging toward them, then gestured to the freight wagon turned on its side in the middle of the street, its wheels still spinning. Crates, many of them busted, littered the thoroughfare, their feathered inhabitants liberated. "That freighter was going a little too fast around the corner, I take it."

"A little too fast?" the man replied, his Northern accent thick. "The driver's full of drink, and it's not even two o'clock in the afternoon. He piled those crates far too high on the wagon! Four hundred chickens, and they're everywhere! It's going to take me half a day to round them up. And that's only if I can find them all!"

"For *you* to round them up?" Wade smiled, taking note of the man's fancy suit and bowler. He was an educated man, from the sound of him. But not in animal husbandry, Wade didn't think. Already a crowd of onlookers had gathered to watch the scene, all of them finding humor in the spectacle. But chickens were expensive. And four hundred of them?

The man exhaled and stretched out his hand. "Frasier Martin. I recently purchased a piece of land outside of town. Starting a poultry farm."

Wade shook the man's hand and introduced himself. "A poultry *farm,* you say?"

Martin nodded, his chest puffing. "First of its kind, Mr. Cunningham, to my knowledge. And you'll not find finer chickens anywhere."

Wade couldn't help but laugh. "*If* you can find them."

Martin's chest deflated.

Wade set the brake on the wagon and turned to Miss O'Toole. "I'll still get you to the hotel as promised. It's just going to take a little longer than we thought."

Her gaze moved briefly to Mr. Martin. "That's all right. Nora and I can walk from here."

He wished she would wait, but he knew better than to try to convince her otherwise. Besides, she was already climbing down, not even bothering to wait for his assistance. "Suit yourself," he said under his breath as he hopped down to the ground.

"Where are you from, Mr. Martin?" he asked, already having a fairly good idea.

"Boston." Martin stated it proudly, as though being from the North was a positive thing here in the heart of Dixie. "The wife and I decided we'd had enough of the city and wanted to raise our children on a farm. I sent inquiries out far and wide for affordable land, of which there is none in or around Boston. So one thing led to another, and I sensed the Lord prompting us to move to Franklin, Tennessee. So . . . here we are!"

Not experienced with hearing from the Almighty

so clearly, much less sensing a "prompting" from him, Wade decided he didn't have anything to add to that subject.

Winder jumped down from the wagon bed and joined them. But from somewhere behind them, Wade could hear Miss O'Toole and Nora "whispering" in a heated exchange.

"Mr. Cunningham," Martin began, sparse hope in his eyes, "you look like a man who knows more than a little about farming."

Wade shrugged. "I know a thing or two. And you, Mr. Martin?"

The man's gaze dropped briefly to his fancy hat, now nearly crushed in fidgety hands. "Thus far, my knowledge is mostly from book learning. But I figure if I could become an accountant, surely I can learn how to raise chickens. The husbandry books all say it's not difficult."

Hearing a clear plea in the man's tone, Wade glanced at the squawking mass of chickens headed every which way. "Here's an idea. There's a feed store around the corner. Let's go get some wire and—"

Loud barking followed by heightened squawks and shrieks drew their attention, and they turned to see a hound dog joining the fray. Feathers went flying.

"No!" Martin yelled. "Not my chickens!" The man raced down the street, waving his arms, hurdling over a brood of hens as he went.

Winder laughed so hard he could scarcely catch

his breath. And Wade had to admit the scene was comical. But to see a man losing his investment, his dream, however ill-advised it may be, was not. "You ready to catch some chickens, Winder?"

The boy's face lit. "Yes, sir, I am!" As they hurried down the street, Wade glanced back to see Miss O'Toole with Nora in hand, practically pulling the little girl along. Nora wailed, dragging her tattered doll with her as she went, once again wearing the boots he'd seen her without earlier. And though Wade didn't so much word a formal prayer in his mind, he sensed what sure felt like a prayer rising up from inside him. For Catriona and Nora O'Toole. And for their brother, Ryan, wherever he was.

CHAPTER 14

Chickens everywhere. With a howling Nora firmly in hand, Catriona prodded her way through the flocks of birds, trying to make a path but scarcely finding room to walk. Raucous laughter swelled from onlookers, and Catriona watched Mr. Martin trying to corral some hens with no success. The hound chasing them wasn't helping the man's efforts.

As the dog came closer, she realized it was older and graying around the muzzle. Still a threat, but the mass of frenzied chickens appeared to be a fairly good match for him. She'd never seen so many chickens in her life. In fact, she'd never seen more than a handful together. Ireland was potato country—or had been. Eggs were a luxury. And poultry, even more so. Whoever Mr. Frasier Martin was, he was well-to-do, for sure.

She spotted a man across the street sitting on the ground by the overturned wagon, head in his hands. She recognized that dazed look. The driver full of drink, she assumed. He reminded her of Da after a night at the pub. For all the supposed celebrating that went on in such an establishment, the people who'd been throwing back pints with such merriment never seemed nearly so gleeful the day after.

Nora, now whimpering, squeezed Catriona's hand tight and huddled closer. "I'm not likin' these chickens, Cattie!"

"Just step round them. They won't be hurtin' you."

As exasperating as her younger sister could be at times, in other moments, like this one, Nora's dependence on her made Catriona feel as though perhaps she *could* be what her sister needed her to be. If only Nora would let her.

People continued to filter outside from shops and businesses to watch the birds as they flapped and shrieked each time the old hound dog charged in their direction. Townspeople laughed, but Catriona felt somewhat sorry for the feathered prey. Thus far, the chickens had managed to escape the dog's pursuit, screeching and beating their wings in protest as they ran. Which only seemed to increase the dog's desire to catch them. She'd never realized how fast a chicken could move when properly motivated.

A loud whistle split the air, and she turned to see Wade Cunningham standing catty-corner across the street. He called to the dog and whistled again. This time the hound's head came up.

"Come on, boy. I've got something for you!" Wade bent down and made a kissing sound with his lips, then held out what looked to be a piece of jerky. The dog came running, which of course sent more chickens flying. Mr. Cunningham fed the treat to the hound while deftly slipping a loop of rope around its neck. Winder took hold of the rope, and Mr. Cunningham disappeared into the feed store.

"Cattie!" Nora screamed. "They're eatin' Virginia!"

Catriona looked down to see a clump of hens pecking and scratching at Nora's doll. *"Shoo!"* Catriona waved her hand. "Be gone with the lot of you!" One of the hens, a plucky red female with a distinctive bright red comb, flew at her and caught the back of her hand with its beak. Catriona sucked in a breath. It startled her more than hurt, but the quick peck managed to break the skin and draw blood.

Nora's eyes went wide. "Cattie, you're bleedin'!"

"I'm fine, Nora." Catriona lifted her sister in her arms and balanced her on her hip. "We simply need to get over to the—"

The hens came at them again, pecking mercilessly at the doll's skirt, ripping the fabric. Catriona had never seen anything like it. As though poor Virginia hadn't endured enough already. Catriona kicked at the birds, not wanting to hurt them but feeling far less sympathetic than she had a moment before.

"They're bitin' me legs!" Nora yelled as she tried to climb higher in Catriona's arms.

A rush of protectiveness, hot and fierce, swept through Catriona. "Wrap your legs round me waist, dearest."

Nora obeyed, and Catriona shoved and kicked her way through the squawking melee, working to reach the nearest storefront where she could place Nora safely down inside.

"Miss O'Toole! Over here!"

Catriona looked in the direction of the voice and spotted Braxie standing guard in front of the doors to the mercantile, broom in hand. The girl swatted at a hen headed toward the store, and the chicken changed course. Catriona climbed the steps to the walkway.

"Are you both all right, Miss O'Toole?" Braxie's smile held humor.

Catriona nodded and put Nora down. "Aye, we're fine."

"Nay, we are not!" Nora pointed to the tiny red marks dotting her legs where the chickens had pecked her. "Them blasted chickens are tryin' to kill us!"

Braxie laughed. "I very much doubt they're trying to kill you, Nora. But chickens *can* be right aggressive. Especially when they're scared. Or hungry."

An odd look came over Nora's face.

Catriona eyed her. "You wouldn't be havin' any snacks in those pockets of yours, now would you, wee one?"

All innocence and charm, Nora shook her head. Until her gaze slid down to Virginia. "But she might," she admitted softly.

Catriona took Virginia from her and checked the doll's skirt pockets. Sure enough. "What exactly is this?" Catriona held up the remnants of something resembling a pancake. The rest was crumpled in the pocket.

Nora's mouth pushed to one side. "It might be a corn cake. That Tempy gave me for later."

Braxie began to laugh, then sneaked a look at Catriona and covered her mouth.

Catriona eyed her sister hard. "Do you know what chickens like to eat, Nora?"

The little girl shook her head.

Then slowly, very slowly, Catriona let a smile come. "Corn, you little bog brain!" She tickled her sister in the ribs, and Nora's face lit like a sunrise. "They weren't tryin' to kill you, you daft girl. They wanted your corn cake!"

Nora giggled, then reached for Virginia. Her smile quickly faded. "They got her good, didn't they, Cattie?"

Braxie looked at Catriona as though asking, *Why is she carrying that doll around with her?* Catriona merely shrugged.

"Aye, they did. But we have needle and thread back at the hotel. We can fix her up right well. You'll see."

Nora nodded, features solemn. "This makes her sad, though. Havin' her skirt all torn and dirty."

Catriona was tempted to ask how her sister knew for certain Virginia was sad, seeing as the doll had no face. But clearly Nora cared about her ragged little friend.

"Does that hurt?" Braxie pointed to Catriona's hand.

Catriona examined the dried blood, a welt forming beneath it. "Nay, it's fine. But if I see that little red vixen again, I'll be tempted to give her a good wallop. Either that or stick her in a pot!"

Braxie smiled, then returned her attention to the street. "That poor man."

Catriona followed her gaze and spotted Mr. Martin still chasing his chickens, trying in vain to catch them. Finally he paused in the midst of the mayhem, fancy hat in hand, shoulders sagging. Tired and discouraged herself—and ready to return to the hotel—Catriona also wished she could do something to help him. Honestly, she'd thought Mr. Cunningham had set off to do just that. Yet she saw no sign of him. She sighed. She'd never tried to catch a chicken before, but she guessed there was always a first—

Cheering began a short distance down the street.

Nora raced to the edge of the walkway. "Look, it's Wade!" she yelled. "He's caught himself some chickens!"

Catriona followed. "*Mr. Cunningham* to you, Nora," she said, then peered down the thoroughfare. True enough, he'd caught a chicken—or several chickens judging by the full crates behind him—and was handing off his latest catch to Winder, who popped the bird into a crate. But what was the man holding? It appeared to be a long piece of wire. What that had to do with catching chickens, she wasn't—

In a flash, Mr. Cunningham stuck the piece of wire into a passel of chickens, then swiftly pulled it back and—she couldn't believe her eyes—up came a chicken dangling by its leg, the appendage caught in what apparently was a hook of some sort on the end of the wire. Mr. Cunningham took hold of the bird by its legs, then flipped it upright and handed it to Winder.

"Blimey," Catriona whispered, feeling a little like cheering herself. But she refrained. Her focus went to the crates strewn all over the street. "Braxie, would you keep an eye on Nora for me, please? And on this as well?" She held out her reticule.

"I can keep an eye on meself!" Nora insisted.

Catriona waved away the comment and looked at Braxie again.

"I'd be happy to, Miss O'Toole." Braxie looped the reticule around her wrist.

"Catriona, please."

Braxie nodded.

"And remember, me sister can get into trouble faster than—"

"I'll keep *both* eyes on her. Don't you worry."

Catriona reached over to give Nora's curls a gentle tousle. But Nora evaded her touch, her expression fierce once again. Familiar with that reaction, Catriona waded back down into the sea of flapping feathers and made her way toward Mr. Cunningham, lifting crates as she went, bypassing those too damaged to be of use. She spotted Mr.

Martin working his way in that same direction, doing likewise.

As she came closer, Mr. Cunningham looked her way. Their gazes met, and he gave her a nod, his expression revealing pleasure. "Braving the fracas, Miss O'Toole?"

"If a fracas is a mess of ornery chickens, then aye, I am." Not quite ready to call a truce with the man, she stacked the crates she'd gathered at Winder's feet and gestured. "What can I be doin' to help?"

"I was about to ask that same question." Mr. Martin came alongside them. "*And* ask if you'd teach me whatever it is you're doing. But first, I want to thank you most sincerely for helping me. The books I read clearly did not address this particular set of circumstances." A sheepish look ghosted the man's expression.

Smiling, Wade Cunningham hooked another chicken in one fluid motion and handed it to Winder. "Don't mention it. It's what neighbors do for each other. If you'll hold this, please . . ." He handed Catriona the contraption in his hand and strode to a bench behind him. He grabbed a length of heavy wire, and in no time he'd bent one end to act like a handle and the other like a little shepherd's hook. He handed the wire to Mr. Martin. "Martin, let's see how you do with it. This is the easiest way to catch a chicken. All you do is reach down with your wire, then slip the hook around one of their legs, pull back, and snatch them

240

up. I'm right-handed, so I hold the handle with my right hand, then support the wire with my left as I'm pulling it up. That keeps the wire stable. Then I grab the chicken's legs and flip them upright, all in one smooth motion."

Mr. Martin looked at the thick wire in his hand, then at the chickens clucking and flapping all around him. "I don't want to hurt them."

Cunningham shook his head. "You won't. One smooth motion, like I said. Try it."

Mr. Martin did—and came away with nothing. The second time he managed to hook a chicken, but it wriggled and flapped away.

"Try it again," Cunningham urged. "You'll get the hang of it."

Catriona watched Mr. Martin as he ventured into the chickens and learned from his mistakes. For one, he was taking too long to hook the bird's leg and then pull. The two motions had to be done swiftly, else the chicken got wind that something was up and took off. Second, the man's actions were too timid, which she could understand. Her own heart was racing, and she hadn't even tried to do it yet.

She looked around for her first target, wanting a smaller, sweeter-looking chicken—if there was such a thing. Not a belligerent red vixen intent on pecking her eyes out.

Wade Cunningham turned her way. "All right, Miss O'Toole, are you ready to—"

Wire in hand, Catriona leaned down, slipped

the hook around a little hen's leg, and then pulled for all she was worth. In a flash, she had hold of the chicken by its legs! The bird squawked, and Catriona squealed, careful to keep the chicken at arm's length.

Cunningham's eyes went wide. "Very nicely done!"

She couldn't help but laugh. Holding a chicken was completely foreign to her—and oddly exhilarating. The chicken, however, did not share her jubilation. It clucked and wriggled and tried its best to escape her grasp, but she held on. "What next?"

"Slip the wire out from around its leg, then flip it upright. Be sure to hang on to those legs, though. And tuck the chicken close to your chest so it doesn't flap you in the face."

Heart beating fast, she did as he instructed, and it worked! She handed the chicken off to Winder, who placed it in a crate. She caught four more in no time, then looked to see Mr. Martin doing well too.

Mr. Cunningham counted the crated chickens. Some crates held two birds, others three or four if the chickens were smaller. "Twenty-one. So only . . . three hundred and seventy-nine to go!"

Catriona grinned, then had an idea. "Would you mind takin' me place for a minute?"

His mouth tipped in a wry smile. "Tuckered out already?"

She gave him a look. "Nay, but I need to get

someone I think would enjoy helpin' with this."

His smile mellowed. "I believe you're right."

It took Catriona all of one second to convince Nora to come and help, but minutes more to coax the girl back into the fray. And this, after Nora insisted on leaving Virginia with Braxie at the store.

Catriona held her hand as they waded through the sea of chickens clucking and scratching. "It's much safer, wee one, when you've not stuffed your pockets with corn cakes." Catriona gave her a sideways glance, which Nora ignored except for the tiniest smirk.

Once Nora saw Winder stuffing chickens into crates, the girl's sense of competition kicked in, and for the next two hours, with everyone working together, they managed to find and catch all but twenty-six of the chickens and fit them into the remaining crates.

Mr. Cunningham enlisted the help of three passersby, and along with Mr. Martin, the five men righted the freight wagon. The intoxicated driver was nowhere to be seen. Thankfully, no wheels or axles were broken in the accident, so the group loaded the crates into the wagon bed, distributing the weight more efficiently this time.

When they were done, Mr. Martin shook hands with each of the strangers. "Thank you, friends. Come visit Martin's Poultry Farm, and I'll have two dozen fresh eggs for each of you."

The eldest of the men acted as spokesman and

offered his thanks, but one of the two younger men with him was who drew Catriona's attention. About her own age, she guessed, he instantly looked away and ducked his head when their gazes met. His expression captured an innocence that reminded her of a wee boy.

As the men walked away, Mr. Martin turned to Wade Cunningham. "And to you, sir. I want you and your family to load these dozen chickens onto the back of your wagon."

Catriona exchanged glances with Wade Cunningham, then he opened his mouth to respond.

"Oh, we're not a family," Winder piped up. "I'm a McGavock from Carnton. Those two are sisters all the way from Ireland. And this here is my papa's new overseer."

Mr. Martin looked back and forth between them.

Mr. Cunningham nodded. "I was giving Miss O'Toole and her sister a ride to the hotel. And honestly, there's no need to give us any chickens. At least not for my part. Perhaps Miss O'Toole—"

"I would still be chasing these blasted birds around town if not for you, Mr. Cunningham. If not for all of you. So please, do me this courtesy. And, Miss O'Toole, if you don't have a place to keep chickens, then please come and get eggs for you and your little sister anytime."

Catriona dipped her head. "That's right kind of you, sir. Thank you."

"Well . . ." Wade Cunningham glanced back

down the street toward the wagon they'd taken from Carnton. "Martin, why don't you drive that rig, and I'll drive this—"

Catriona held up a hand. "I'm fully capable of drivin' a wagon. You and Mr. Martin handle this one, and the children and I will come along behind you."

"What about the doughnuts?" Winder asked before Mr. Cunningham could offer argument. "I'm really hungry."

Catriona sighed.

"I'm hungry, too, Cattie," Nora chimed in. "And me throat is dry as dirt."

Right hungry herself, Catriona glanced toward the mercantile. They'd had breakfast that morning, but only cake since. And now a doughnut? That hardly seemed wise. Yet considering the eager faces staring up at her, she smiled. "All right, then."

The children cheered and set off.

"But only one doughnut, Nora," she called after them. "And I'll be payin' for our share." She directed the last comment to Mr. Cunningham, who simply shook his head and walked toward the mercantile with Mr. Martin.

Braxie met them at the counter and handed Catriona her reticule and Nora her doll. While Braxie assisted Nora and Winder with selecting doughnuts from a basket behind the counter, Catriona added crackers, a wedge of cheese, and jerky to their purchases. She'd joined the queue to pay for the items when she felt someone's presence behind her.

"I wish you'd allow me to pay for this," came a deep whisper. "I'd appreciate your allowing me to keep my word to Nora."

Feeling a flush that Catriona chose to attribute to the warmth of the mercantile, she didn't bother turning around but spoke over her shoulder. "We've already discussed this subject, Mr. Cunningham, including makin' promises that never should have been made. So don't be thinkin' I'll be finagled in this manner. Because I wilna." She felt the tickle of a smile but resisted showing it. "Besides, I have me own funds and am perfectly capable of—"

"Call me Wade, please."

Another flush swept through her. Catriona glanced across the store, wondering why someone wasn't busy opening a window. "As I said earlier today, we don't know each other well a'tall, sir. In Ireland, men and women don't begin addressin' one another as—"

"We've just spent the afternoon catching chickens together. And before that"—his voice softened further—"we spent the morning in conversation, much of it of a personal nature. So despite our not knowing each other *well,* I believe we know each other well enough. I hold that international relations between the United States and Ireland will not suffer should we address each other by our Christian names. In fact, a law in this country states that once a man and woman have

246

exchanged more than one hundred words, they must move to a first-name basis."

"You're lyin'. There's no such law."

"Yes, I am. And no, there isn't. But if I *could* write that into the Constitution right now, I would."

With a tiny laugh, Catriona stepped forward in line, more than a little torn. She didn't wish to invite more familiarity with this man than was prudent. After all, she didn't know him. Not really. Yet for reasons she couldn't understand, a smaller but quite vocal part of her did wish to know him. With that in mind, she weighed her knowledge about him. He was the new overseer at Carnton. He was good at catching chickens, and he appeared to be quite clever in regard to thinking outside the usual boundaries. He was overly observant and had fought for the Confederacy, the latter not helping his case in the least. Quite the contrary. And the former not exactly comforting either. He'd also passed muster with Colonel and Mrs. McGavock and had earned the colonel's trust, which was no easy feat, she imagined.

On the other hand, Wade Cunningham's confidence could be completely irritating at times. Close to maddening. Unlike at the moment, however, when that specific character trait came off more as self-deprecating, even charming. Which *also* caused her a fair amount of irritation but for very different reasons.

Hearing Nora's voice, Catriona glanced over to see her and Winder only feet away enjoying their doughnuts. Her sister was smiling. Actually smiling.

"Tell you what," he continued, close enough behind her that she could feel the warmth from his breath on her cheek. "What if we attempt a first-name basis for, say . . . forty-eight hours. And if either of us notices any shift in the earth's axis, or if international relations between our countries suddenly begin to deteriorate, we'll revert to more formal address. Would that be acceptable to you, ma'am?"

Catriona didn't even bother holding back her smile now. Something within her responded to his humor. *To his humor* . . . Her smile took on a sadder feel. *Ryan.* That's what it was within her responding to him. She missed her brother. But Wade Cunningham was decidedly *not* her brother, and she knew the nature of men. Hadn't her upbringing taught her that well enough? No, it would be unwise for her to encourage—

"What I'm trying to say," he added softly, "yet am apparently doing a very poor job, is I'd like to be your friend. That's all I'm suggesting. I think that maybe you could use a friend. I *know* I could."

His tone sounded anything but confident now, and Catriona felt her resistance crumbling, her loneliness responding even before her voice could. She'd missed having a friend.

"Miss O'Toole?"

For a moment, Catriona thought the voice belonged to Wade Cunningham. But when she looked up, she discovered the queue of patrons in front of her gone, and Mr. Pritchard—the ol' tyrant himself—standing there glaring down at her from behind the counter.

She stepped up, only then seeing Braxie standing off to the side, a confused look on her face. Not wanting to get into another row with this man, especially not with Wade Cunningham here to witness it, she reached for cordiality she didn't feel. "Good day to you, Mr. Pritchard."

He continued to stare.

She laid her selections on the counter. "I also need to pay for two doughnuts. The one me sister is eatin' now and another one for me, please."

Braxie reached for the basket of baked goods.

"Leave it, girl!" Mr. Pritchard aimed a fierce look behind him before turning back. "I'd like to see your money first, Miss *O'Toole.*"

Catriona's face burned, especially when Wade Cunningham moved to stand beside her.

"Is there a problem here?" he asked, facing Pritchard square on.

"Nay," Catriona answered, giving the man a look that said she didn't want or need him fighting her battles. "Mr. Pritchard," she continued, "I'd have thought we'd be past this by now. As I demonstrated to you the other day, I have money to be payin' for the items I need."

The mercantile owner gestured. "Money I'm still waiting to see."

She bristled. "Which you *will* be seein' as soon

249

as you're tellin' me how much I owe." She already had the sum figured in her head but wanted the satisfaction of him having to calculate it in front of her.

Pritchard's jaw hardened. He grabbed a pencil and pad, worked the numbers, then looked up. "That will be one dollar and two cents."

Catriona withdrew the money pouch from her reticule, the small purse considerably thinner without the wad of bills she'd deposited at the bank. She opened it and reached for one of the two ten-dollar greenbacks she'd held out that morning, then spotted some change in the bottom of her reticule. She counted it, then laid a crinkled one-dollar bill and two pennies on the counter. "Here you are."

Pritchard picked up the dollar bill and stared at it.

"Is there a problem, Mr. Pritchard?" Catriona pushed, feeling the sting of his prejudice for a second time and promising herself she would never darken the doors of this establishment again.

He didn't answer for a moment, and she glanced beside her at Wade Cunningham, only to find his focus intent on Pritchard, his jaw rigid. Ashamed this was happening in front of him, she hoped he wouldn't cause a scene on her behalf.

"No," Mr. Pritchard finally answered, fingering the bill. "There's no problem." He said it as though he regretted it. "But I still say your kind is robbing me blind."

Wade Cunningham started to say something, but Catriona laid a hand to his arm and squeezed tight. A heavy breath left him.

Pritchard gave a nod to Braxie, who wrapped a doughnut in paper and wordlessly handed it to Catriona.

Catriona nodded. "Thank you, Braxie."

The girl's wary glance toward her uncle spoke volumes.

Catriona collected both Nora and Winder on her way out the door, all while hoping Wade Cunningham would simply chalk it up to one foolish man's ignorance and say nothing more about it. Yet knowing him as she was coming to, she doubted that would be the case.

CHAPTER 15

Wade had seen his share of prejudice, had fought a war against it, but to see it played out against Catriona O'Toole . . . His blood was still boiling. Striding toward the wagon, he gestured to Frasier Martin to give him a moment with Miss O'Toole.

Clearly Pritchard didn't hold the Irish in good opinion, which wasn't a surprise. The agency had already confirmed the man's involvement in the "secret society" bent on terrorizing and assaulting freedmen. If Pritchard would do that, he would certainly think nothing of degrading the Irish. That particular mind-set was prevalent these days, and not only in the South.

Yet he'd noted Pritchard had hesitated after taking the money Catriona gave him. The man had actually paused and studied the bill, meaning he'd likely been checking to see whether it was counterfeit. At a glance, Wade knew it was authentic. But he knew what to look for. What was puzzling was that the man had seemed downright disappointed to discover the money real. In the past, one-dollar bills had been a counterfeiter's favorite to copy. So, no doubt, as a store owner Pritchard had seen his share of those. These days, forgers had moved to counterfeiting ten- and twenty-dollar greenbacks. Greater return for the effort. Wade had seen fifty-dollar denominations as well, but those were rarer, therefore making it easier to catch the person trying to pass fake money as real.

But he knew one thing for sure. He could cross off Pritchard as being part of any counterfeit ring. Anyone who had to look that long and closely at a bill to tell the difference wasn't printing fake money or passing it along. Counterfeiters knew their product well. And so did he.

He caught up with Miss O'Toole and gently took hold of her arm. "Are you all right?"

"Aye, I'm fine." Her expression looked collected enough, but the way she spoke—tight-lipped, unwilling to meet his gaze—told him she wasn't.

Wade glanced at the door to the mercantile, tempted to return and confront the man. But the look she'd given him made it clear she didn't want him to interfere. "I'm sorry for what happened back inside. He had no right to question whether you had money simply because of your nationality."

She gave a quick laugh, her brow rising. "Me *nationality?* You make somethin' so many people seem to hate so much sound so fancy."

"Not everyone hates like that, Miss—" He stopped himself and looked at her, not wanting to backtrack, if indeed he'd made the progress he thought he had. She simply stared up at him, but reading the glint in her eyes, he knew she was following his line of thought. Yet she simply waited. All right, if she wanted him to ask out-right . . . "Would you do me the honor of allowing me to call you Catriona?"

"Nay, I wilna."

He sighed. "But I thought we—"

"Not until you've given me your word that you won't be goin' back inside and speakin' to Pritchard on your own time. I don't need you standin' up for me. I can do that meself."

Wade smiled, liking this woman more all the time. "*That* fact is abundantly clear to me . . . Catriona."

Smiling the slightest bit, she gave him a look of warning. "I'm still waitin' for your word, sir."

Wade shifted his weight. "I promise you I will not confront the mercantile owner about how he just treated you."

She seemed to weigh the statement for any leaks, then nodded triumphantly. "Very well, then."

"But I won't promise not to imagine how good it would feel to walk back inside there and pummel his face."

"Oh aye, I've already done that meself several times. But I believe I'll switch to thinkin' about you doin' it. 'Twould hurt him more."

She smiled, and Wade laughed.

"I was going to say not everyone hates like that, Catriona. Some people believe differently."

Her countenance sobered. "That seems an odd thing for a man such as yeself to be sayin'. And that you'd be gettin' riled at ol' Mr. Pritchard treatin' me that way. After all, did you not fight a war to keep a group of people as slaves?"

An unexpected punch to the gut would have hurt less. Wade glanced away, unaccustomed to being put on the defensive. From the very start, he'd known part of his investigation here in Franklin would involve being seen as an ex-Confederate. What he hadn't counted on was Catriona O'Toole and how much it would bother him to be seen that way through her eyes. Wade looked back to find her studying him. He only hoped the lie he was about to tell sounded more convincing than it had when coming from captured Confederate soldiers he'd interrogated. "Not everyone who fought for the Confederacy supported slavery, Catriona. Some had other reasons."

"Reasons good enough to keep men, women, and children enslaved? If that had been you in their stead, would you have been feelin' the same way?"

Forget the knife in his ribs. The woman went straight for the jugular. He held her gaze. "No, ma'am," he said softly, prouder of her in that moment than he could let on. And more stirred by her than ever. "I would not."

Her eyes narrowed the slightest bit, letting him know she knew she'd won that argument. And rightly so.

Finding it safest to change the subject, he looked beyond her to the wagon. "You're sure you can handle that rig?"

She blew out a breath, her tempting smile

returning. "In me sleep. I used to deliver orders for our family's print shop. Boxes and boxes at a time, and I never lost a one! It's you who's gettin' the greater challenge." She leveled her gaze. *"Wade."*

Watching her walk away, Winder and Nora in tow, he smiled to himself, unable to ignore the shapeliness of her hips and the distinctly feminine way she moved. Upon first glance, one wouldn't look at her and necessarily think *fighter.* Of course, once she opened that pretty little mouth, no one could think otherwise. Still rankled by her holding that opinion of him, he climbed up onto the rig where Martin sat waiting. The man looked from him to Catriona and back, then smiled. But Wade just faced forward, unwilling to take the bait.

On their way out of town, Wade glanced back a few times to make sure Catriona was still behind him and managing all right. True to her word, she could handle a wagon as well as she could a prejudiced shop owner.

Later that evening, after delivering Frasier Martin and the man's poultry to the farm north of town, promising to pick up the gift of a dozen chickens the next day, and taking Winder back to Carnton, he enjoyed dinner with Catriona and Nora at the hotel. They bid one another good night in the hallway outside their rooms, and as he closed his door, he decided he liked having Catriona O'Toole as a friend. Even if his interest in her, however ill-advised on his part, already stretched far beyond friendship.

• • •

"Do you really wish Da was still livin', Cattie?"

Catriona looked beside her at the breakfast table the next morning, wondering where on earth her sister had gotten such an idea. So she asked as much.

"You were sayin' it yeself," Nora responded, her expression convincing. "Yesterday. At Winder's house."

Catriona sifted back through her memory and remembered having said something akin to that, then quickly wishing she hadn't. She sought her sister's gaze. "Aye, you're right, I did say it. But nay, child, I do not wish he were still livin'. I'm not proud of admittin' such a thing, mind you. In truth, it brings me a good measure of shame. But our da was a harsh man, and livin' with him made for harsh days. Especially for our dear mam, God rest her soul."

"God rest her soul," Nora finally whispered when Catriona prodded her with a look. Nora reached over to where Virginia sat in the chair beside her, propped up in all her faceless glory, then pulled the doll into her lap.

A waitress with a pot of coffee appeared and refilled Catriona's cup. "Do you need anything else?" the woman asked.

"Nay, we're doin' fine. Thank you kindly." Catriona tucked her napkin by her plate, the steam rising from the fresh pour.

The waitress gestured to Nora. "Little miss,

would your doll care for another scone?"

Nora's blue eyes sparkled. "Aye, she'd be likin' one for later, I bet."

The woman smiled. "Another blueberry scone coming right up, then."

Catriona nudged her sister.

"Thank you kindly, ma'am," Nora added as the waitress moved to the next table.

Catriona thought again about the bill she'd received yesterday when they returned shortly before dinner. The hotel was requesting she pay for the entire next week in advance, and she'd lain awake last night, exhausted, waiting for sleep to come, mulling it over. Every time she'd closed her eyes, haunting images roused by the McGavocks' descriptions of the battle filled her head, and to think of her dear Ryan enduring that horror tied her stomach—and hope—in knots.

But somewhere during the night, what she had to do came to her. Especially in light of what she knew about the battle now. Sleep evading her, she'd risen and penned a letter to the War Department. Five letters, in fact. Identical in wording. She planned on mailing a letter every two to three days and would continue writing until she received a response. She'd also decided she would have to wait until the exhumations were completed before she could even think of leaving Franklin. Because, even though she loathed this possibility and hoped it proved false, the answer to where Ryan was might well be buried in that horrible field.

She'd also written a letter to Miss Maeve back home, telling the elderly widow where she and Nora were on the off chance that a letter from Ryan had arrived. Or that it still might. After much consideration, she'd used the bank's address for her personal return address since that was the most permanent location she had. She and Nora couldn't stay in this hotel indefinitely. The accommodations and food were splendid, and they'd been made to feel welcome. But it was too costly.

Aye, on one hand, she had more than enough funds safely deposited with the bank. But on the other, that money was for her and Nora *and Ryan* and their start at a new life. So today she would begin looking for less expensive accommodations. A boardinghouse, perhaps. Or even a single room for rent. Nothing fancy. Just something safe and clean. Or she'd settle for safe and could clean it herself.

A deep voice from behind drew her attention, and Catriona turned, half expecting to see Wade. But it wasn't him. He'd told her last night he planned to check out of the hotel early that morning and run errands in town—including circling back by Martin's Poultry Farm for the dozen chickens the man had insisted on giving him—before heading out to Carnton. Since she and Nora had slept in later than planned, she figured he'd left a good while ago.

"I'd like to be your friend. That's all I'm suggesting between us."

She'd turned those words of his over and over and found herself wanting to believe them. She could use a friend. His tone and manner toward her yesterday had her mostly convinced of his claim, although the way she sometimes caught him looking at her made her wonder otherwise—like after she'd confronted him about fighting on the side of the Confederacy.

He hadn't appeared so much angry with her at the combative question as impressed. Perhaps Southern men weren't accustomed to a woman speaking her mind so plainly. If that were the case, heaven help him, because she'd been holding back. But when he'd said Mr. Pritchard had been wrong for treating her in such a manner, it didn't make sense. How could a man come to the defense of the Irish while fighting a war to keep Negroes enslaved?

" 'Twas the bottle what made Da mean, weren't it, Cattie?"

Catriona blinked, then looked at Nora. Even at so young an age, her sister had seen it. Mam had done her best to shield Nora from the truth, always covering for Da's drunkenness with excuses. *"Da's a wee bit sick this morning with the collywobbles. It's makin' him unsteady. So best let's be like mice and tiptoe round him."* Catriona had gone along with it only because Mam asked her to. She wasn't at all convinced a parent could fully shield a child from life's cruelties. Life always had a way of winning out, it seemed.

"Aye," Catriona answered softly, choosing her words with care. "It was his drinkin', dearest. But it went further than that, I think. People deal with their hurtin' in different ways. And some people can't seem to deal with it at all, so they do their best to *not* think about it."

Nora's brow furrowed. "Drinkin' makes you forget you're hurtin', then?"

Catriona detected curiosity in the simple question and rushed to dispel any misconception. "Nay, turnin' to the bottle only covers up what's worryin' you for a time. And over time, drinkin' makes it even worse." She read confusion in Nora's eyes and pondered how to explain what she meant. She gestured to the doll in Nora's lap. "Take wee Virginia's skirt, for instance. When those chickens scratched and clawed it yesterday—"

"Those *dang* chickens," Nora supplied, brow scrunching tight.

Catriona raised a forefinger. "You know as well as me that our dear mam would be castin' you a witherin' look for usin' that word."

"Winder uses it!"

"Winder's a boy. And we're both knowin' that boys aren't nearly as keen in the mind as girls." Catriona slowly smiled, wondering if her sister remembered that Ryan had often said something similar when boys Nora's age teased her until she cried.

Nora's faint, sad smile said she did.

"So don't get all your learnin' from Master

Winder. Use your noggin and remember what you already know."

Nora nodded, not looking fully convinced.

"Now back to wee Virginia's skirt. We could shove your doll into a drawer and let her stay there till summer turns to fall and fall to winter."

Nora's frown deepened, and she clutched Virginia closer.

"But would that do anythin' to fix what happened to her yesterday?"

Nora gave a tiny shake of her head.

"Nay, 'twould not. Simply hidin' something away where you can't see it, where you're not havin' to face it, that's not fixin' anything." Catriona leaned closer. "Remember when we used to take our clothes from the trunk every week and shake them out, lookin' for moths so those little buggers wouldn't eat up everything?"

"Aye," Nora said softly.

The waitress stopped at their table and sneaked a small napkin-wrapped bundle beside Nora's plate. Catriona thanked her with a smile, then turned back to Nora.

"That's what I'm talkin' about, wee one. Facin' things straight on. Gettin' them out in the open and doin' all you can to make things right. But facin' life like that 'twas never Da's way. At least not by the time I was old enough to know what was what. And certainly not when you were born." She gently tugged a curl at Nora's temple, pleased when her sister didn't pull away.

263

Catriona gestured to Nora's nearly cleaned plate. Even now, it was difficult for her to see even the tiniest bit of uneaten food left behind to be tossed. "Are you finished, dearest?"

Nora nodded and downed the last of her milk.

"We'll run back up to the room to use the chamber pot," Catriona said quietly, mindful of other diners nearby. "Then we'll take a walk about town. It's a beautiful day, and I need to post some letters. Who knows, maybe we'll find ourselves walkin' by a fabric shop with some time to look for a pretty scrap of floral to sew Virginia another skirt."

Nora's eyes lit. "She'll be smilin' for sure when she's wearin' that!"

Doubtful on the smile, Catriona thought, looking at the pitiful little doll. She found herself contemplating how she could make her another face, but that was hardly a priority at the moment. She pushed back from the table, and Nora grabbed the wrapped scone and shoved it into her pocket, then hopped down from her chair.

Catriona had decided not to tell her they would be looking for a new place to live. Change seemed to send her sister into a tizzy these days. Best to share that news only once she knew where they were going.

Nora raced up the stairs and beat her to the room, a spring in her step. Her sister's spending time with Winder yesterday had been a good thing. Not that the two children would be friends. Perhaps a hundred years ago in County Antrim, but not here. Yet watching the two of them crate the chickens, then make faces at the birds through the slats was like glimpsing who Nora was before Ryan left for America. Before Mam and their sisters died. Even for herself yesterday, there'd been moments when the weight of grief and worry resting on her chest like an anchor had lifted long enough that she could actually feel her soul begin to breathe again.

At first she'd wondered whether it was the company she'd kept, which likely played a part in it, she couldn't deny. But the greatest boon was that she'd had a purpose, albeit a minor one, in Mr. Martin's fiasco, and helping someone else had taken her mind off her own troubles for a while. And Saint Peter be blessed, but it had felt good not to be thinking about death for more than five minutes straight.

They finished quickly in the room, and she locked the hotel door behind them.

"Don't be runnin' down the stairs," she called.

Nora slowed her pace enough that Catriona could keep an eye on her as she clomped down the stairs, but by the time Catriona reached the lobby, her sister was waiting near the front door. An older gentleman stood conversing with her, and while Catriona found his profile familiar, she failed to place where they'd met. Until he looked her way. It was the manager from the bank.

"Mr. Grissom," she offered, crossing the lobby. "How good to be seein' you again."

He dipped his head. "Good day, Miss O'Toole. And you and your sister as well." He glanced about. "I was hoping I could have a word with you, ma'am."

"Nora and I were just headed out, but we can spare a few minutes, if you need." She started toward the dining room.

"Miss O'Toole," he said softly.

She turned.

"The hotel manager has kindly offered us the use of his office. Just here." Mr. Grissom indicated a door off to the left. "That will afford us more privacy."

Catriona hesitated. Not that she distrusted the man. At least not any more than she distrusted anyone else she didn't know, but . . . "Is something wrong, Mr. Grissom?"

He opened the door to the manager's office, and Catriona spotted the hotel manager himself seated inside. Her gaze met his, and the lack of surprise in his expression clearly communicated he was waiting for them.

Mr. Grissom smiled. "Please, Miss O'Toole. This way, if you would."

"Cattie, it's such a pretty day!" Nora called in a singsong voice, still standing by the front door. "We need to be goin'! We need to be lookin' for a scrap of floral for wee Virginia, like you said."

A bad feeling coming over her, Catriona nodded. "Aye, and we will, dearest. But first I need to be havin' a word with Mr. Grissom." She glanced toward the empty concierge desk, then to the dining room, looking for the woman who'd served them breakfast this morning. But she didn't see her anywhere, and she didn't recognize anyone else. That meant Nora would have to come with her.

Catriona held out a hand to her sister.

Nora shook her head, her smile disappearing. "You said we were goin' now."

"Aye, and we will. As soon as we're done here." Already chiding herself for it, Catriona saw no other choice. "If you'll sit quietly for me inside the office, we'll go by the bakery and get something sweet!"

Virginia in her arms, Nora beelined into the office and claimed one of the chairs opposite the manager's desk. Catriona took the seat next to her, and only then did she see a third man standing off to the side. She sat up straighter, determined to look more confident than she felt. But when the door latched firmly behind her and Mr. Grissom put away his smile, her confidence threatened to buckle at the knees.

CHAPTER 16

"Miss O'Toole," Mr. Grissom began, "we're meeting with you because of an issue with your deposit—"

"Wait!" Catriona held up a hand, feeling off balance—and outnumbered. "First, who is he?" She looked at the man standing quietly to the side, intuition telling her he played an important role in this gathering despite his lack of presence. In fact, without looking at him again, she wasn't certain she could have described him on first glance alone. Of average height and build, his features neither handsome nor unattractive, the man possessed little about him that stuck in one's memory. Except for one thing. She had the uncanny sense that nothing, not the slightest detail, escaped his attention.

Mr. Grissom hesitated. He shot the man a look, his expression hesitant almost to the point of appearing somewhat frightened. "This . . . *gentleman* is here because of the issue I'm attempting to"—he cleared his throat—"explain to you in a way that—"

"My name is Frank Bonner, Miss O'Toole." The man took a step forward. "I'm a government operative with the United States Treasury Department, and you, ma'am, are the sole reason I am present."

His eyes were as steady and penetrating as those of an eagle, and Catriona felt her defenses rise fourfold.

He strode to the desk where the hotel manager was seated. "Leave us, please."

The manager looked up, surprise in his expression.

"Now, Mr. Harper," Bonner said calmly, and immediately the manager vacated his chair and exited the office, closing the door behind him. Mr. Grissom, standing off to the side, shifted his weight, his expression silently inquiring whether he, too, should take his leave. A subtle shake of Mr. Bonner's head settled the issue, and Grissom all but faded into the wall.

Mr. Bonner seated himself behind the desk, then removed a small journal and pen from his inner coat pocket and set them in front of him, his gaze fixing on Catriona. "You made a deposit with Mr. Grissom's bank yesterday, Miss O'Toole. It was an inordinately large sum of money. Especially for someone who has so recently immigrated to this country, and from Ireland, no less. No offense to County Antrim, but that area isn't known for its *wealthy* citizens."

Catriona swallowed. His knowing she was from Ireland wasn't surprising. Her accent—not to mention her copper hair—gave that away. But knowing she was from County Antrim? Who *was* this man? And what business did he have inquiring about her money? He seemed to be waiting for a

270

response, but he hadn't asked a question, and a clarion voice inside her told her the less she said, the better.

Seconds ticked slowly past. His focus was unrelenting, and though tiny beads of sweat trickled down beneath her bodice, Catriona clung to the counsel of that inaudible voice.

A corner of his mouth lifted, but the gesture in no way resembled a smile. "What brings you to this country, Miss O'Toole?"

In a blink, she sorted the various responses she could give him. The one on the tip of her tongue— *To find me brother*—came with the greatest caution. Right or wrong, instinct told her to leave Ryan out of this. "Life in Ireland is hard, sir. As I'm sure you're knowin'. And I've come with me sister to start afresh, as so many others have done before us."

His eyes narrowed. Then his gaze shifted to Nora, and Catriona looked beside her, hoping her sister wouldn't choose that moment to chime in. Nora seemed oblivious, counting the tiny diamond shapes in the fabric covering the chairs.

"So you plan to stay in America, then?" Bonner asked.

"Aye, we do."

He picked up his pen and scribbled something in the journal. It took Catriona every ounce of control not to try to read what he'd written.

"You're pleased with what you've seen of our country thus far?"

"Aye," she said again, hearing the trepidation in her own voice. "We haven't been here long, but—"

"Do you know anyone here, Miss O'Toole?"

She opened her mouth to respond, then hesitated. "Are you meanin' here in Franklin, sir? Or do you mean in America as a—"

"Let's start with Franklin."

She shook her head. "Nay, sir. I'm not knowin' any—"

"You haven't visited anyone's home since you've been here? No one at all?"

She looked at him, suddenly feeling like a fly with one wing caught in a web, the spider perched off to the side, waiting, watching as its prey struggled hopelessly to break free. "Beggin' your pardon, Mr. Bonner, but I'm not understandin' why you're askin' me these questions. Perchance, if you'd be tellin' me what you're wantin' to know, then—"

"I want to know where you got the money."

He leaned forward, the hush of his voice and the intensity in his expression sending a shiver through her. Catriona looked from him to Mr. Grissom and back again.

"You're meanin' the money I deposited at the bank?" As soon as she said it, she realized she'd made a misstep. What other money could they be talking about? Mr. Bonner's eyes narrowed again, cautioning her to choose her next words carefully.

She clutched her reticule in her lap, imagining that at any moment the two ten-dollar greenbacks in her money pouch would begin burning a hole right through the fabric. Maybe if she gave the man a scrap of truth, that would be enough, and Ryan's name would never have to be mentioned. "I brought the money with me from Ireland, sir. It came from there. From me family." She swallowed hard, as though the knot working its way up her throat was the rest of the truth begging to be told.

Mr. Bonner's mouth slowly curved. He sat back in his chair. "You arrived in the United States nine days ago, Miss O'Toole. In New York City. You spent a ten-dollar bill purchasing tickets for the trains you and your sister took to Nashville and then to Franklin."

Catriona's jaw went slack.

"Next, you presented a fifty-dollar greenback at a mercantile here in town. And based on the mercantile owner's sworn statement, you received nearly twenty dollars in change. Even though that was a hefty amount to spend in one transaction, ma'am, I must say that for having had such a sum of money in your possession, you were spending most frugally. All that to say, yes, we already assumed you brought the money with you from Ireland."

"I . . ." Catriona shook her head, resisting the irrational urge to grab Nora and run. "I'm not understandin' how you're knowin' all this, sir. Or why you're—"

"The money you deposited with the bank is counterfeit, Miss O'Toole. And not just any

273

counterfeit, but a *very* good one. The best fake I've ever seen, and I've seen them all. Whoever forged those bills is a real artist. What I want to know from you right now is where you got that money."

Catriona stared. Time slowed to a crawl even as her thoughts fired at rapid speed. Torn snatches and bits of memories collided, fighting to fit together yet failing to do so. "Counterfeit?" she finally managed. "I don't understand your meanin', sir. 'Twas real money. I gave it to Mr. Grissom. He saw it as well as I did." She looked at the bank manager. "Tell him, sir. Tell him it was *real!*"

Mr. Grissom shook his head. "It indeed looked real, ma'am. Even to me, at first. But upon closer—"

"All that is secondary to my question for you, Miss O'Toole." Bonner's tone hardened. "*Where* did you get the money?"

Her heartbeat thrumming in her ears, Catriona sensed the air in the office growing thinner, and she wished Mr. Grissom would open the door. But he simply stared at her, same as Mr. Bonner. She glanced at Nora to find her sister finger-combing the doll's hair. But Nora was combing the same strands over and over and over again. Were little ears listening? And if they were, could Nora understand the accusation being made?

Catriona took a needed breath, struggling to wrestle her thoughts in line and rejecting outright the one thought forcing its way through the door, grappling to take hold inside her even as she ripped it up by the roots. *"Whoever forged those bills is a real artist."* The phrase pounded away in her mind. But nay, it couldn't be. Ryan would never do such a thing. If that money *was* counterfeit, Ryan had been deceived. Her brother was incapable of committing such a wrong.

"Do you know the penalty for forging United States currency, Miss O'Toole?" Bonner said quietly.

Hearing the unveiled threat in the question, Catriona determined to protect her brother from the barest hint of accusation. After all, the Irish weren't looked upon kindly in this country. Some, maybe even this man, would find Ryan guilty simply by way of his last name. She forced herself to meet his gaze, her desire to believe in her brother's innocence outweighing the intimidation in Bonner's eyes. "So you're thinkin' I'm a counterfeiter, sir?"

He stared, unblinking, and it felt as though he could see straight through her, all the way back to Ireland. "No, I don't. But you haven't answered my question yet, which tells me you feel as though you have something to hide. And the longer you insist on not answering that question, the more I'm convinced you do."

Catriona blinked, a prick of emotion burning her eyes. Who was this man? And how did he know everything about her? He said he was a government *operative*. What did that mean? And what kind of country had she come to that certain people could follow her whereabouts so closely? As the walls closed in around her, her thoughts narrowed, and recent events suddenly gained clearer focus. No wonder Mr. Pritchard acted the way he had yesterday.

A thought struck her like blinding sunlight through the trees, and she squeezed her eyes tight. If the money really was counterfeit, if what this Mr. Bonner said was true, then *all* the purchases she'd made here in town, in Nashville, in New York, even since before leaving Ireland, *everything* . . . none of it had been paid for honestly. She put a hand to her abdomen. She'd cheated all those vendors. Unknowingly, aye. But she'd cheated them just the same. How would she repay those debts? Worse yet, what would she do for the present? How would she care for Nora? She swallowed again, this time tasting bile at the back of her throat.

Bonner sighed. "I sense the weight of whatever it is you're hiding is coming to bear on you. So please, for all our sakes, Miss O'Toole . . . *where* did you get the money?"

"Cattie, we need to be goin'." Nora hopped down from her chair.

"Not yet, Nora," Catriona whispered. "In a moment."

Nora's chin quivered. "But you *s-said* we'd be gettin' some f-floral for Virginia's skirt!" she shot back. But her voice gave her away, as did the way she looked at the two men, then to Catriona again, her eyes hot with anger. And fear.

Catriona's lungs emptied of air. How much of this conversation her sister comprehended, she didn't know. But Nora understood enough to be afraid, and Catriona felt something fracture inside her. *"Go to America, find Ryan, and make a good home . . . the three of you."* Mam's voice was as clear inside her mind as the *tick-tick-tick* of the clock slicing off the time on the desk in front of her. Catriona began to tremble.

Despite trying to do everything right, she'd failed Nora. She'd failed her mother. And now she'd failed Ryan. Or was about to. She bowed her head, wondering just when the Almighty had started despising her so. If she knew what she'd done, perhaps she would know how to appease his anger. How to get back on his good side.

Struggling to find her voice, she turned. "Mr. Bonner, w-would you permit me to see to me sister?" She wiped away the tear sliding down her cheek, not daring to wipe away those on Nora's. "Then I'll tell you everything I know about the money."

"A wise choice." He rose from his seat.

Catriona guided Nora from the office but paused at the door and turned. "Mr. Bonner?"

He looked up.

"What *is* the penalty for forging money, sir?"

"Prison. A sentence of twenty years . . . to life."

CHAPTER 17

"There's no need to be nervous, pretty girl," Wade whispered. He lowered his head a little as he approached the quarter horse, never breaking eye contact. "We've already got the saddle on. Next comes the rider. We'll take it slow and smooth."

The mare took a cautious step back, the muscles rippling in her hindquarters. True to the breeder's word, she was harness broke but still shied at taking on a rider. It hadn't taken Wade long to get her saddled in the stall. She'd settled right down—until he brought her out into the round. She was a smart little thing. Stubborn too. She took one look at the corral and insisted on maintaining her distance from him as though she knew his intentions.

"Easy there, Sassy," he said softly.

Her ears pricked as if she already recognized her name. Cassandra's Legacy was fine for registered paperwork but far too fancy for every day. He smiled. The first time he caught a glimpse of her personality he knew what he'd name her if she were his. And while she wasn't his outright, she *was* his as long as he occupied the position of overseer at Carnton—short-term though that would be—and he planned on winning over this feisty little copper mare.

Wade sidled up beside her and took hold of the reins. "That's it, girl. You're doing fine," he whispered, reaching for the saddle horn.

The clang of metal on metal broke the calm, and Sassy spooked and trotted to the opposite side of the corral. Wade heaved a sigh and looked behind him at Winder seated atop the corral fence. The boy's ladle and pail of fresh milk lay spilled in the dirt.

Winder pulled a face, a frothy mustache along his upper lip. "Sorry, Mr. Cunningham," he said in a loud whisper.

Wade gave him a look that told him once was forgivable, twice wouldn't be. Winder had asked if he could watch him ride the quarter horse for the first time, and Wade agreed, provided the boy wasn't a distraction. Wade ran a hand through his hair, the sun beating down overhead. Maybe he should have been clearer on his definition of *distraction*. But Winder *was* the colonel's son.

The boy wiped his mouth with the back of his sleeve and nodded succinctly as if reaffirming their agreement. Wade tugged his grandfather's pocket watch from the pocket of his shirt and flipped open the lid. Nearly noon already.

He'd checked out of the hotel early this morning, then quickly put his errands behind him before meeting with the colonel in the farm office for a good two hours. The colonel gave him quite a list of responsibilities, mainly managing the various aspects of the estate. But to Wade's pleasure, in the process of discussing those responsibilities, he'd gained valuable information about several of the prominent businessmen in town simply by listening and sprinkling in a leading question here and there. Gossip wasn't just for old ladies and quilting groups.

He'd learned who besides Whitley Jacobs had recently built a new house or barn, who'd acquired land, and even whose wife had purchased new furniture for the entire home—all from reviewing the various accounts of people who did business with Carnton. And everyone in town did business with Carnton, it seemed. Not that building a new house or barn or buying new furniture indicated someone was guilty of counterfeiting. But it did indicate they'd come into some money. It was Wade's job to make sure that money trail was clean.

For today, however, he had two primary tasks. First, make certain the repairs on the sawmill were complete and confirm that orders were being delivered to buyers as expected. Especially a large order due in less than a week, which represented a sizable chunk of income. He looked forward to meeting with Isham today, too, if they could manage the privacy. He had yet to speak with his former fellow captain since their first encounter, and he was eager to catch up.

His second task was to make a visit to none other

than McGavock's accountant—Woodrow Cockrill, one of the leading suspects in the counterfeiting scheme. McGavock said he'd get the "important paperwork" for his accountant completed this afternoon so Wade could hand deliver it to him at his home tonight. Wade couldn't have set up the meeting better himself.

He closed the lid of his grandfather's watch and ran the pad of his thumb over the initials engraved on the top. *W. R. C.* Wade Robert Cunningham. His grandpappy's namesake, Wade was deeply grateful for the life and work of the man who'd left this tangible reminder to him. Wade hadn't been there to bury his own father beside Grandpappy in December of '64. He'd been away fighting. But now Grandpappy, Papa, and Wesley—three generations of Cunningham men, the last gone far too soon—lay buried beneath the canopy of that ancient oak up on the ridge, along with his mother and grandmother. A pang of homesickness crowded the moment, and that ridge and the family homestead, so familiar to him, felt another world away, as did any permanent sense of belonging.

Having no desire to tug at that particular thread of thought, Wade tucked the watch back into his pocket and directed his gaze across the corral at Sassy. She was watching him, which he took as a good sign. He strode toward her once again.

"Okay, pretty girl . . ." He pulled a chunk of apple from his pocket and took a bite, crunching where she could hear it. "Mmm. This is good." He held out a piece. "I'll share some with you, and then we can get this done, Sassy."

She dipped her head and snorted but didn't back away.

He came alongside her. "That's it, just you and me, taking it real slow . . ."

Wade saw movement from his peripheral vision and looked over to see Winder with his hand raised high as though he were in a schoolroom. Wade leveled a stare, and a flush of guilt swept the boy's face.

"What?" Winder whispered. "I didn't say anything, Mr. Cunningham. And I didn't make any noise this time. I just raised my hand."

Briefly looking down, Wade thought of Catriona's occasional frustration with Nora and had to smile. "What is it now?"

"Well, sir, I'm just wondering why you don't just take a whip to her. Or a stick. That's what the last overseer did if a horse wouldn't come round. He said you had to show them who the master is."

Wade took a deep breath. "Come here, Winder."

He hopped down and ran over.

"Stand right here. Just to the side." Gripping the reins in one hand, Wade positioned the boy a couple of feet in front of the mare and slightly to the left. Uncertain about how much time Winder had spent with horses or how much he'd been taught about them, he decided to seize the moment. "If you stand straight in front of a horse, it can't see you because of how its eyes are positioned on

283

the sides of its head. This pretty little mare's name is Sassy, and I want you to look straight at her and tell me what you see."

Winder squinted, then leaned forward a little before looking at Wade, then back at Sassy again. "I see big black horse eyes."

Wade smiled. "Look again and talk to her this time."

"Talk to her?" The boy frowned. "What should I say?"

"Tell her she's a good girl. Tell her she's strong and fast. Tell her what you see when you look at her."

Winder appeared to weigh the idea for a second or two, then nodded as though accepting a challenge. "I think she's a good—"

"Don't tell me. You're talking to her, remember? And keep your tone gentle."

Winder thought for a moment, then nodded. "You're a *good* girl." He spoke softly, slowly. "You're strong. And you're fast. And your eyes are *really* big. But they're pretty! Kind of like glass. Or a mirror. And they're black. Like the coffee Tempy makes. And your ears are real pointy, too, but—"

"Do you see any difference in the way she's looking at you, Winder?"

Winder stared, his eyes narrowed. Then he smiled, and Sassy snorted.

Winder laughed. "She sees me! I mean, she's looking back at me."

Wade rubbed Sassy's forehead. "That's because horses can form an attachment to people, just like dogs do, *if* we're patient enough to let them. You have to earn a horse's trust. Yes, you need to show them who the boss is, or they won't listen to you. Won't do what you need them to do." He paused. "But do you think taking a stick or a whip to a horse teaches it to trust you?"

Winder didn't respond, his expression conflicted, and Wade decided to take the lesson a step further.

"Do you think someone taking a stick or a whip to you would teach you to trust them?"

Winder frowned and shook his head. "No, sir!"

"Of course it wouldn't. It's wrong to do that to a horse, or a cow, or any other animal. And it's wrong to do that to another person. No matter who that person is. Because the Almighty made all of us, no matter our differences on the outside."

Winder looked up at him, his expression thoughtful, then his brow quirked. "If that's true, how come we slaughter cows and pigs and eat them?"

Wade grinned. Smart kid. He thought fast. "Well, some animals are raised specifically for the purpose of being food. Like cows and pigs. And yes, when the time comes, they're slaughtered and eaten. But that still doesn't mean we shouldn't treat them humanely while they're in our care. Animals are a gift. From the Almighty. Some we eat and some we don't. But we should be appropriately respectful of them all. And grateful too. But people are not animals. People—*all* people—are image-bearers of the living God. Does that make things a little clearer?"

Winder nodded.

"And in some places in the world," Wade continued, leaning closer, "horses are raised to be eaten too. Just like we eat cows or pigs or chickens."

The boy scrunched up his nose, and Wade laughed.

"Bottom line, Winder, anyone who has to take a whip or a stick to a horse to get it to do his bidding isn't its master. That person is simply cruel." Wade lightly gripped the boy's shoulder, and Winder nodded again.

But a trace of question seemed to linger in his eyes. "You think I could touch her now, sir?"

"Sure you can. Rub her on the neck just here. But reach out slowly and stay to the side where she can see what you're doing. Surprising a horse is *never* a good thing."

"I'm going to rub you now, girl," Winder announced, then carefully ran his hand down her neck. After a few strokes, he peered up. "I'm a little scared of horses, Mr. Cunningham. Especially Papa's thoroughbreds."

"It's good to have a healthy respect for horses, son. Thoroughbreds, especially. Blood horses can be unpredictable. But you and Sassy here, you'll be good friends in no time. Now, if you'll hop back up on that fence, I'm going to finish what I came out here to do."

Winder ran back to the fence and climbed to the top rail.

Wade took the piece of apple still in his palm and held it out. "You ready, girl?" he whispered.

Sassy took the apple from him, and in one smooth motion, Wade swung up into the saddle. Sassy whinnied and tossed her head, and Wade pressed his heels down in the stirrups in case she tried to buck. She trotted a few feet and blew out a breath, her muscles quivering, and he ran a hand along her withers. She pawed the dirt, and he sensed she wanted to run.

"Winder, would you get that gate for me? And be sure to close it back."

"Yes, sir!" Winder scampered down and swung the gate wide open.

Sassy trotted into the field, but Wade kept her reined in, reminding her who was in control. He gradually eased her into a canter, then a gallop, and the mare flew across the field, her gait smooth and even. It felt good to be riding again, felt good to experience the singular sense of freedom that came from riding. Wishing he had more time, he knew better, and after a few minutes he eased the mare back to a trot and headed in the direction of the corral behind the barn. Still a ways away, he spotted someone waving to him. It was the colonel.

Wade changed course and reined in by the back porch.

"Cunningham." McGavock met him at the steps. "I'd like for you to come inside and meet the exhumation team for the project. We just shook on the deal."

"Lead the way, Colonel." Wade dismounted, looped the reins around a low-limbed poplar, and trailed McGavock's path.

The colonel held the back door open behind him. "Between you, me, and the committee, this team's bid came in at less cost than any of the other applicants. In my mind, it's a price as low as can be done. *Five dollars* for each set of remains. And they'll do the work in advance of payment."

Wade raised a brow. "That's a mighty fair bid *and* deal, in my mind . . . considering."

McGavock nodded. "I agree. But with the hundreds of bodies buried out there, the burial committee needs to step up our efforts in fund-raising."

Wade closed the back door behind them. Five dollars wasn't an insignificant amount of money. But exhuming those bodies, especially over a year after they'd been hastily buried in shallow graves—no coffins, no other care taken—was an unenviable task. It made the twenty-five dollars a month McGavock had agreed to pay him as overseer seem like easy money, especially since it included room and board. He'd briefly visited the overseer's cottage that morning, and it was nice aplenty. But he had yet to summon the courage to enter the kitchen—Tempy's domain. However, hunger was a powerful motivator, and he knew that showdown was coming. He also knew who was likely to win it.

McGavock paused inside the entrance hall, his voice hushed. "As I said this morning, I'd like you to work closely with this team as the project progresses. The task itself will be monumental. I'd appreciate your oversight and availability to them should they have questions or should issues arise along the way."

Wade nodded. "Glad to do it, sir." He followed the colonel down the front hallway and into the office just across from the fancy parlor they'd been in only yesterday morning, along with Catriona and Mrs. McGavock.

Wade wondered how she and Nora were faring after the chicken caper. They'd both seemed tired last night during dinner. Catriona, especially. She'd seemed preoccupied, too, and worried, which was understandable given her circumstances with her brother. He'd tried to get her to open up some to him during the meal, but the lady wasn't onc to share items of a more personal nature.

"Gentlemen," the colonel began, gesturing to the three men standing in the office, "allow me to make introductions."

Wade took one look at them and returned the smile lighting George Cuppett's face. Before the colonel could get out the names, the eldest Cuppett brother reached for Wade's hand.

"Mr. Cunningham," George said. "Good to see you again."

"Mr. Cuppett." With a glance, Wade acknowledged his two brothers with him, remembering how one of them seemed to take an instant liking to Catriona yesterday, judging by the blush that had crept over his face. And who could blame him? "It's good to see you all again. And so soon. Thank you once more for your assistance yesterday afternoon." Reading bafflement on the colonel's face, Wade hurried to explain. "Remember, sir, when I told you that three men helped us flip that freight wagon upright? That was these strapping fellows right here."

Lively conversation ensued as they took their seats.

Wade mostly listened, which was always his preference. It seemed a search for work had brought George Cuppett and his brothers to Franklin. The men were Texas boys, which Wade would've guessed judging by their accents. The topic quickly turned to the cemetery, and George—a former Confederate who had served in the 8th Texas Cavalry, known in Federal ranks as Terry's Texas Rangers—said he would be heading up the project.

"My brothers here," George continued, "Marcellus and Polk, will assist me, as well as two others. Robert Sloan is to join us any day now. And Charley Baugh, a young man who's got a good hand at carpentry, will be making the wooden boxes to hold the remains."

George presented a detailed plan for the process,

demonstrating he'd already given the endeavor much thought, and Wade could tell McGavock was pleased.

A few moments later, the colonel stood, shaking George's hand and his brothers' as well. "You all are an answer to many prayers. I hope you realize that."

"Thank you, Colonel," George and Polk said in unison. Marcellus simply nodded.

Wade shook hands with the brothers as they exited the farm office, then followed the colonel with them to the front door.

George paused on the front portico. "Colonel, we'll start gathering supplies immediately and staking out the boundaries as discussed. We plan to begin the process of moving the bodies within the week."

"Very good. I'll inform the committee of everything we've discussed here today. This is a task too long in coming. It's high time we give those soldiers their due."

A somber mood fell over them as Wade walked with the brothers to the hitching post where they'd tied their mounts. George glanced in the direction of the battlefield. "From what I've heard, they fought those Yankees with everything in them. They kept pushing toward that Federal line, even outnumbered and outgunned. We heard that some of our boys surrendered themselves to the Federals only to have the Federals shoot them down in cold blood." He looked back at Wade. "Can you believe that, sir? Where's the honor in that?"

Wade searched his expression, looking for the least indication that George Cuppett was fishing for something, that the man knew who he was talking to. But Wade saw nothing but gut-level honesty in the man's face. "If that happened, Mr. Cuppett, I agree. That truly is reprehensible."

His business at the house finished, Wade rode Sassy to the sawmill. On the way, he looked toward town and thought maybe, since he and Catriona O'Toole were on friendly terms now, he'd stop at the hotel to say hello after his meeting with Cockrill. Maybe she and Nora would have dinner with him if they hadn't eaten already. Then again, Catriona might not welcome a visit from him this soon. Or at all. Maybe he should just wait until their paths crossed again by happenstance. But considering the odds of that happening, the idea didn't hold much appeal. Then reality delivered a swift kick.

Despite his surroundings and current position at Carnton, he was an operative for the Secret Service. His life had no place for anyone or anything other than the job. He knew that—even though in some moments, like now, it seemed there should be more to life.

His decision made, he spurred Sassy on, firmly putting Catriona out of his thoughts while hoping against all reason that George Cuppett and his team would find no trace of her brother's remains in that field.

CHAPTER 18

"You're quite certain, Miss O'Toole, that you've never heard of Peter McCartney?"

Frazzled from the past hour of Mr. Bonner's endless interrogation, Catriona looked across the hotel manager's desk at him, her frayed nerves brittle with fear and uncertainty. She'd thought it might somehow be easier to answer these questions when Mr. Grissom had taken his leave. But Mr. Bonner had a way of crawling under a person's skin and staying there. And he kept asking her the same questions over and over, only in different ways.

"Sir, with all due respect, I've already responded to that inquiry, and me answer is still the same. Nay. I've never heard the name Peter McCartney. I don't know who the man is." A thought occurred. "Did he come over from Ireland on the same ship as me and me sister, by chance? Is that how you're thinkin' I may be knowin' him?"

Saying nothing, Mr. Bonner returned his attention to the notes he'd been taking, tapping his pen in a steady, perfectly maddening cadence.

She massaged her left temple, trying in vain to keep the constant barrage of what-ifs at bay. What if this man ended up finding her guilty in some way? What if Mr. Bonner demanded she repay all those debts? What if she went to prison? What if Nora were left alone? What would happen to her sister then? What if—

Nay, she told herself. *Stop it. "Imaginin' the worst never brings about the best."* Recalling Mam's frequent counsel quieted the bombardment—for now—and she wiped her moist palms on her skirt. She'd done nothing wrong. She hadn't known the money wasn't real. And neither had Ryan, she was certain.

"What about Thomas Ballard?" Mr. Bonner continued. "Or Henry C. Cole? Have you ever heard of those men?"

"Nay, sir. I have not."

"So you have never worked with these men? Any of them? Not in any capacity?"

She stared. "Mr. Bonner, if I'd worked with them, I guess I'd be knowin' them, now wouldn't I? And I'd have answered that question differently."

His right brow rose slightly, and she bit her tongue. She knew better than to give in to frustration, not with a man who had ways of knowing so much about her. When she came and when she went, where she traveled, where she spent her money. *Her money.* But it wasn't her money anymore, was it? And with no funds at all, even if they let her go, how on earth would she care for Nora? For herself?

She glanced behind her through the open door and into the dining room where her sister sat at a table drawing with pen and paper. The waitress who'd served them before kindly agreed to keep watch over Nora for a bit. But knowing her sister, Catriona insisted the door to the office remain open so she could do the same.

"This note you claim is from your brother, Miss O'Toole . . ."

Catriona turned to see him hovering over Ryan's note that lay beside the two counterfeit ten-dollar bills she'd offered up earlier. He'd insisted she fetch the note from her room, but she intended to get it back.

"You say he included this with the money. You're certain this is his handwriting?"

"Aye. The note *did* come from me brother, as I've said. I'd know his script anywhere, all cobbled together though 'tis."

"And was anything else in the package he mailed to you? Other than this note and the money? Something you've perhaps forgotten to mention?"

Hearing yet another insinuation in his tone, she clenched her jaw. "Me brother mailed the package to *our family*," she gently corrected. "Not only to me. He sent the money to all of us. And nay, sir. I've not forgotten anything. I'm tellin' you everything I know."

He held her gaze. "You said you received the money in approximately June of last year, and that your brother sent it so you and your family could come to America. Yet you didn't act on that plan—on your brother's most earnest wish, as you

295

stated—until recently." He glanced again at Ryan's note. " 'Come as soon as you can,' " he quoted. " 'So me heart can feel whole again.' "

Hearing him read those precious words in his grating American accent, the last words she'd received from Ryan, tarnished the sweetness they had in her memory.

"Why did you not come as he requested?"

Catriona took a breath. "I've already been tellin' you why, sir."

He placed the pen on the desk. "I'd like for you to tell me again."

Her eyes watered, and the fear in the pit of her stomach curdled like day-old porridge. "Me da was the first to take sick. Then me two sisters, followed by Mam, who suffered for several long—"

A heavy thud outside the office drew her attention, and she looked back.

"Wait . . ." She rose. "That's our trunk!" She hurried into the lobby and saw the hotel manager with the concierge. "Why are you bringin' our trunk to—"

The manager turned to face her. "We have taken the liberty of removing your items from the room."

"But those are our personal belongin's that—"

"Are on *our* property, Miss O'Toole. Do you possess the means to pay your hotel bill, ma'am? You have five days outstanding already, not to mention the meals you've charged to your room."

Catriona swallowed, reading accusation in his eyes. He thought she was guilty as well. The creak of a floorboard behind her demanded attention, and she turned to see a well-dressed man and woman standing in the entryway of the hotel, both staring at her.

"Well?" the manager asked. "Do you have the means to pay or not?"

She met his gaze as steadily as her wounded pride would allow. "Nay, sir. I do not."

"Then neither do we have accommodations for you." He held out his hand. "The key to your room, please."

She withdrew the key from her skirt pocket and gave it to him, then quickly checked the left sleeve of her shirtwaist to make sure she'd remembered to get the dagger from the bedside table. She had.

The manager nodded a silent greeting over her head to the couple by the door, then looked back. "When your meeting with Mr. Bonner is completed, we invite you to promptly leave the premises."

By sheer willpower, Catriona kept her head erect. "Aye, sir. I'll do as you ask. And I truly am sorry for—"

He walked away, and the couple quickly skirted past and followed in his steps.

Catriona glanced toward the dining room to see a handful of patrons looking her way as well, and she wondered if they, too, had overheard the exchange. But Nora, to her relief, remained bent over her paper, intent on her drawings.

"Miss O'Toole?"

Reaching for strength and finding none, Catriona stepped back into the office. Mr. Bonner stood beside the desk.

"One last question. Upon making your deposit with the bank, did you or did you not ask Mr. Grissom"—he read from his notes—" 'Will I be getting this same money back when I take it out of the bank again?' "

Catriona's throat closed tight, quickly reading between the lines and understanding his accusation. So Mr. Grissom did consider her guilty as well. Was there no winning with any of them? "Aye," she finally said. "I asked him that. But only because—"

"That will be all, Miss O'Toole."

He gathered his notes and moved to step around her, but she held her ground.

"You asked me a question, sir, and I aim to be answerin' it."

He stopped beside her, a flash of warning in his expression.

"I asked Mr. Grissom that question because that money was the last thing me brother sent to us. 'Twas the last thing of his I had, that he'd held in his own hands. And givin' it over to Mr. Grissom felt like givin' part of Ryan away."

He stared, emotionless. "And you still maintain you don't know where your brother is. Whether he's 'alive somewhere or buried out in that field.' "

Hearing him parrot her own words, Catriona

298

could scarcely look at him. "I still maintain that, sir, because it's the truth."

He gave a slow nod, the act conveying distrust. "Last spring we confiscated numerous bills matching the same quality and having the identical signature plate as the counterfeit bills you had in your possession. We tracked them to Nashville, and then suddenly everything went quiet. It's as if, just like that"—he snapped his fingers—"the bills and the counterfeiters disappeared. All of it . . . gone. Until you arrived into the country nine days ago." He slipped his pen into his pocket. "I trust you'll be staying in Franklin."

A puff of air threaded her lips. "Where else would I be goin', Mr. Bonner? Now that I've been booted from the hotel, I've got nowhere to go. And nothin' left."

"Indeed," he said, brushing past her.

CHAPTER 19

The trunk was heavier than Catriona remembered, and no sooner had she and Nora walked a block from the hotel than she needed to stop and rest. "Nora, let's sit a moment. Let me catch me breath." Hot and winded, Catriona lowered the trunk to the ground, the muscles in her back paying dearly for the strain. She sank onto a bench.

Nora perched beside her, Virginia in her arms. "Cattie, I don't like your idea of campin' somewhere tonight. I like me bed at the hotel. I want to go back. And I'm hungry. I'm wantin' me lunch. They were servin' roast, and that's what I want to be havin'. Roast beef for lunch. They were havin' pie too. I saw 'em bringin' it out, and . . ."

Catriona rested her head in her hands, her sister's voice a blur. Twenty-two cents. That was all the money she had left. That, and a half-full box of crackers. Nora had eaten everything else. The cheese, the jerky, all the staple items. Everything. The girl was like a pot with no bottom. Catriona sat up straighter and smoothed the sides of her hair. She'd put it up that morning, taking extra care, but numerous strands had worked their way free, little it mattered now.

Before they'd left the hotel, she'd checked the

trunk to make sure the manager and concierge hadn't missed anything. All pieces of clothing, what few there were, as well as their personal items were accounted for from what she could tell. She'd asked if she could go back to the room to make certain nothing was left behind, but the concierge said that wasn't permitted since she was no longer a patron of the hotel.

Catriona looked at the people walking by them. Going to their homes, to their places of work, walking with people they knew. *Neighbors*. Few of them looked her way, and when they did, it was with a dismissive air. Because she wasn't one of them. She hadn't had the good fortune of being born on what some might consider the right side of the ocean. That, and her family hadn't immigrated to America years ago, long enough for time to erode the accent from their voices and the time-honored traditions of the homeland from their lives.

She picked up a sliver of a broken branch and fingered the recently budded leaves. They'd held such promise, yet now were shriveled to nothing. Why had she come to America? She wished she could go back and rethink the decision to leave her beloved Emerald Isle. At least they had a house there, if not a home. They had an ample plot of garden, a roof over their heads, and vegetables aplenty. They'd known people there too. They'd had friends. People who would have come to their aid at a time like this. She and Nora wouldn't have been alone, destitute. Life hadn't been as bad there as she'd thought.

Abruptly, her thoughts went stock-still, and in the sudden silence, she recognized the thoughts for what they were. *Lies*. All of them.

Aye, they'd had a cottage, but it was falling down around them, the thatch roof a leaky sieve and the main support wall leaning to one side like a crippled beggar on borrowed time. Years of repeated planting had leached all the goodness from the soil, and only stunted cabbages and blight-riddled onions would grow. Of course, right now, a pot of hot cabbage and onion soup, even blighted, didn't sound half bad. The people they'd known . . . Those people were mostly gone now. Passed on or close to it. They couldn't have provided aid because they couldn't even feed themselves.

Nay, coming to America hadn't been a mistake. Ryan had sent for them, after all. Yet this land wasn't proving to be the "land of opportunity" she'd heard touted. And whether they starved in Ireland or starved in America, they would still be starving. She'd gone without food before. She knew what that was like. Nora, however, did not. Oh aye, her sister knew what it was like to be in want of a meal. But the child had no idea what hunger was. *Real* hunger. When your body felt like it was shutting down to die, and your stomach, stuck to the back of your ribs, ached, pining for anything more than water. But they weren't nearly to that point yet, and Catriona determined they wouldn't be. Not while she still drew breath.

So far they'd missed only lunch. And no matter how Nora carried on about roast beef and being hungry, the girl was fine—and would be. Catriona had learned years ago where to ferret out wee bits and scraps of food. And some lessons, once learned, were never forgotten.

She stood and picked up the trunk, resolved to keep the truth of their circumstances from Nora as long as she could, which would prove difficult with her sister's curious nature. "Let's be on our way, wee one."

"Cattie, were you not listenin' to me at all?"

"Aye, I was listenin'. But we need to keep movin' if we're goin' to find a good place to hunker down for the night. We don't want others to take all the best places."

"Let 'em take 'em! I want to go back to the hotel. That's what I've been sayin' to you."

Catriona gestured with a tilt of her head and continued walking, certain she heard the words *daft* and *sister* uttered in some combination behind her. But given their circumstances, she ignored them. Nora was following for now, albeit begrudgingly.

When they reached the post office a few minutes later, Catriona set the trunk down off to the side and gave the knots in her shoulders a quick rub. She reached into her reticule and withdrew one of the five letters she'd written to the War Department, as well as the one she'd penned to Miss

Maeve. She took Nora by the hand, and they went inside and purchased two stamps. That left her with only sixteen cents now, but these letters were important. They could provide answers.

Catriona explained what the letter to the War Department was for, then let Nora slip it into the box on the counter. Followed by the one to Miss Maeve.

"That first letter will tell us where our Ryan is?" Nora asked, her gaze holding reservation.

"I'm not knowin' that for certain. But if anyone *can* tell us, I'm believin' it's the people I wrote that letter to."

They continued on their way, the handles of the trunk biting into Catriona's palms. So much so, she finally had to stop again.

"Why are we stoppin', Cattie? I thought we were goin' to find 'a good place to hunker down for the night.'" Nora looked at her askance, her tone sharp with sting for one so young.

Catriona narrowed her eyes. "We are. I just have to rest for a minute. This bugger is heavy." She gestured to the trunk.

"Why are you bringin' that anyway? We won't be needin' all our things for just a night."

Catriona briefly looked away. "We might. And I believe in bein' prepared."

Nora rolled her eyes.

Catriona peered across the street, and for an instant, she questioned what she was about to do. But of all the people she'd met in this town, there was one person she couldn't abide thinking the worst of her. Actually, two. But Wade Cunningham would have no way of knowing what had happened to her if she didn't tell him. And she had absolutely no plan to do that. But Braxie . . .

Catriona could well imagine what lies the girl was being fed by Mr. Pritchard. Although, looking at the situation honestly, Catriona knew the man had every right to think the worst of her now. So waltzing through the front doors of his mercantile wasn't an option. Not when he'd already threatened to call the authorities on her once and might well again, for all she knew. Mr. Bonner at the hotel could have done that as well, she figured. Yet for whatever reason, he'd chosen not to. Grateful that had been the case, she still had trouble making sense of it all. But of one thing she was certain . . .

She hefted the trunk and headed across the street toward the alleyway.

"Why are we goin' *this* way?" Nora peered up, sweat beading on her upper lip. "Why aren't we goin' inside? We could get somethin' sweet, Cattie. And a drink too. Each of us!" Her voice rose an octave.

"We're not comin' for somethin' sweet today, Nora."

"But I'm hungry!"

"I know you are, dearest. And I've got some crackers for you right here."

"Crackers! For lunch? But I'm wantin' roast. I been tellin' you that."

With a grunt, Catriona lowered the trunk to the ground, her palms throbbing. Deep red creases ran lengthwise from side to side. The skin wasn't punctured, so there was no bleeding. Yet. But blisters were already forming. Moving gingerly, she lifted the lid. "There'll be no roast today, wee one. Because today we're campin'! And that means crackers." She handed the box to her sister.

Nora sighed, opened it, and shoved a cracker into her mouth. "I hate crackers," she said between bites, crumbs pluming from her lips.

Catriona pushed the trunk back a couple of feet so it sat nestled between two stacks of empty crates, hidden from view. She'd chosen a shaded place near the back door of the mercantile so she could see who came and went but not so near that she and Nora would be easily spotted.

She situated two crates on the ground and sat, pressing her back against the wall of the building, the brick still warm from the morning sun. It might have felt good on her sore muscles if she hadn't already been overheated. She unbuttoned the top two buttons of her shirtwaist and fanned the fabric in and out, trying to get cool. She patted the crate beside her, encouraging Nora to sit.

"I'm thirsty," Nora mumbled, sitting, her mouth full.

"We'll get a drink from the creek in a few minutes. But first, I need to speak to Braxie."

"What about?"

Catriona looked down beside her, having no

intention of telling Nora why they were here. "Well, aren't you bein' a nosy little bird!"

Nora shrugged and pulled another cracker from the box, then paused. "I know! You're goin' to ask her to go campin' with us!" Her mouth formed a perfect little O.

Thinking fast, Catriona made a face as though she could scarcely believe Nora had guessed her surprise. "And a *smart* nosy little bird you are too!"

Her sister sat up straighter, pride brightening her eyes.

"But I'm thinkin' Braxie will likely have to work," Catriona continued. "And her mam and da will probably be needin' her help at home tonight. So I'm doubtin' she can come."

"But at least we can be askin' her!"

Catriona gave a noncommittal shrug. Braxie *camping* with them was not part of her plan. But if she handled things right, that wouldn't be an issue.

Even though she'd chosen a shady spot, the cloudless sky overhead gave the sun free rein, and she soon had visions of doing more than just drinking from that creek. She leaned her head back and drifted a bit, the lack of sleep last night catching up with her. Sweat trickled down her neckline and into her bodice. Thirsty, she licked her lips, eager to—

The back door to the mercantile opened, and Catriona sat up. Nora did too. They peered around the stack of crates. Seeing Mr. Pritchard, Catriona pressed a forefinger to her lips, and Nora nodded, thunder forming in her blue eyes as she glared at the man.

A stack of boxes in hand, Mr. Pritchard called over his shoulder, "Braxie! I told you to take out the trash!"

"I did, Uncle Laban," came the girl's voice. "But I'll do it again."

Pritchard muttered something under his breath, laid the boxes aside, and stomped back in, slamming the door behind him.

Catriona stood. "Wait here, wee one, just in case the ol' tyrant comes back out."

Munching on another cracker, Nora nodded.

Catriona stayed half hidden until Braxie was outside and had closed the door, then she hurried over. "Braxie," she whispered, not wanting to give the girl a fright.

Boxes of trash in hand, Braxie turned and saw her, and Catriona detected a measure of light fade from her friend's eyes. That told her she'd done the right thing in coming here.

"Hello, friend," Catriona offered first.

"Hey, Catriona." Braxie's gaze went anywhere but to her.

Catriona stepped closer. "I had to come and see you, Braxie. I know we don't have long, and I'm not wantin' to get you into trouble. But I had to come and explain." She bent down a little, hoping to gain the girl's attention.

Braxie gradually looked up. "My uncle already told me."

"But that's just it. What he's tellin' you isn't the whole truth. Leastwise, I'm fairly certain it's not." Keeping her voice quiet, Catriona checked to make sure Nora was still seated on the crate and out of earshot. "Aye, the money I spent at your uncle's store was counterfeit, or so I'm bein' told. But I didn't know the money wasn't real, or I never would have used it. I want you to be knowin' that."

Wordless, Braxie searched her expression, and Catriona sensed the girl struggling with whether to believe her.

Catriona rushed to get the words out. "I know I owe your uncle a bucket full of money. And I don't know how I'll be payin' it back, but I will. Every penny. I give you me word on that."

Braxie nodded, the gesture lacking conviction.

"I don't blame you for feelin' badly toward me, Braxie. Even for not believin' me. You don't know me well, not really. We only just met. But your friendship means a great deal to me. You were the first friend I made here in Franklin. And I simply couldn't be bearin' you thinkin' that I did this straight to your face. That I would cheat a friend in such a way. Because I never would. You, especially."

Braxie's eyes glistened, yet she said nothing.

"Well . . ." Catriona managed a weak smile and glanced back to see Nora still seated on the crate—but barely. The girl looked as though she were ready to bolt at any minute. "Thank you for lettin' me say me piece."

"You say you didn't know the money was fake." Braxie's voice came softly. "So . . . where did you get the money, Catriona?"

A sinking feeling pulled Catriona's heart to its knees, taking her breath along with it. "If gossip here is what it was back in County Antrim, I'm guessin' you'll be hearin' this soon enough. 'Twas me twin brother who sent us that money. To me family, back when we were still in Ireland. That's how Nora and I came to be here. But I'm certain that Ryan wasn't knowin' it was counterfeit. He would *never* do such a thing. I know him, and he doesn't have such deceitfulness in him."

"Ryan's the brother you said fought in the Army of Tennessee?"

"Aye."

Braxie frowned. "And where is he now?"

Catriona shrugged. "I don't know. That's what we're doin' here. Nora and me. We're lookin' for him. The last time we got word from him was when he sent us the money and told us to come over. Franklin is the last place he mentioned bein'." She hesitated, almost dreading Braxie's reaction. "Me brother fought with General Cleburne's division."

A pained look moved into the girl's eyes. One Catriona felt deep inside herself. Then Braxie's gaze shifted beyond her, and Catriona heard the patter of footsteps coming fast.

"Did Braxie say aye to campin' with us?" Nora called.

Catriona quickly grabbed Braxie's hand and gave it a squeeze, her own palm aching. "Braxie, *please*," she whispered. "Me sister isn't knowin' any of this. About the money bein' fake. And I'm not wantin' her to. She'll just go worryin' herself to bits over it."

Nora ran up beside them, Virginia in tow. "So are you comin' campin' with us tonight, Braxie?"

Catriona waited, hopeful. Then her hope began to drift. She released Braxie's hand, but to her surprise, Braxie held on. The girl searched Catriona's eyes, and a smile began to bloom. She gave Catriona's hand a gentle tug.

"Thank you," Catriona whispered. "So very much."

Braxie nodded. "I knew deep down it couldn't be true."

"What couldn't be true?" Nora asked, looking between them.

"That the two of you would go camping without me!" Braxie said, not missing a beat. "But," she added, glancing back toward the door, "it's Thursday, which means I have to work late tonight cleaning the store, then I have chores in the kitchen."

Nora's face fell.

Catriona brushed an unruly red curl back from Nora's forehead. " 'Twould have been far more fun with Braxie joinin' us, but we'll still have a good time, wee one."

Nora sighed, then looked up, expectant. "Maybe you could ask your mam and da if you could be comin' with us after your chores are done?"

Braxie's smile diminished. "I wish I could come, Nora. But I can't this time. And I don't have a mam and da. They died during the war. I live with my uncle and his wife." She glanced up. "Above the mercantile."

Catriona followed her gaze, the world she'd imagined Braxie living in changing in a blink. "I'm so sorry to hear that about your parents," Catriona said gently. "I didn't know."

Braxie shook her head. "Of course you didn't. Papa died in battle. At Shiloh. Mama shortly after. Doc said her heart just gave out from grief. So I came to live with my mother's older brother and his wife. They never had any children of their own, so . . ."

Sadness weighed the girl's tone, and Catriona hoped Nora wouldn't pry further.

"So you're an orphan, then," Nora continued. "Like me and Cattie."

Braxie nodded. "I am. But I'm grateful to have a home."

Catriona smiled, seeing evidence of gratitude in the girl's expression but hearing the hollowness in her voice.

Braxie turned back to the door. "I'd better go before he comes back out. Once riled, Uncle Laban's temper stays hot. I hope you two have a fun time camping."

Nora pouted. "I'm not wantin' to go. But Cattie's makin' us."

Catriona put an arm around Nora's shoulder. "We need to be goin' now."

"Are we takin' the trunk with us, Cattie? Or are we hidin' it here?"

Braxie paused and looked past them. She walked a few steps, apparently spied the trunk, then looked back at Catriona, who gave an almost imperceptible shake of her head.

"We'll keep in touch, Braxie." Catriona gave the girl a quick hug. "And we'll be fine. You take care of yeself, too, and—"

"Braxie! How long does it take to empty the trash, girl?"

Catriona picked up Nora and ran, barely reaching the safety of their little alcove in the crates before Mr. Pritchard threw open the door.

"What have you been doing out here, girl?"

"I was just dumping the bins and—"

"Get back inside and get to work. If I didn't stay on you every minute, you'd . . ."

The door slammed shut, and Catriona let out her breath, contemplating again if it was possible for a parent to ever truly shield their child from the cruelties of this world—yet already knowing the answer.

CHAPTER 20

Wade dismounted, then gave Sassy a rub on the neck before looping the mare's reins to a post beneath a broad-limbed poplar. Even at a distance, he recognized the familiar, rhythmic roar of the water-powered saw, which told him the mill was up and running. That boded well for the recent repairs. Hopefully, they would hold.

He was arriving at the mill a little later than planned. He'd run into some of the sharecroppers on his way and had taken the opportunity to visit with them, to introduce himself and get a handle on the progress each of them had made. To a man, they treated him much as he expected. With kindness and respect but with a watchful eye. And he didn't blame them one bit. Not after the life they'd lived.

He had no idea what kind of contracts McGavock had drawn up with them, but he planned on reviewing them at first opportunity. The position of overseer was only a cover, a way to gain information while avoiding suspicion, but he figured he might as well do as much good as he could while he had the chance. And if he found even a scrap of disparity in the employment contracts McGavock had drawn up with the sharecroppers, he wouldn't hesitate to report McGavock to the Freedmen's Bureau. They'd make certain the former plantation owner was in compliance with the Freedmen's Bureau Bills.

The creek was running high after the recent rains, and the water level in the pond was ample. Since water meant power, the sawmill could run at top capacity. He inspected the mill gate in the dam where water flowed from the pond through the headrace and into the tank on the lower mill level. All looked in good working order, as did the turbine and main control gate. If the turbine failed, it would mean he'd be taking a dive. He didn't mind swimming, and deep water wasn't an issue. It was diving under a sawmill he wasn't particularly fond of.

Working in a sawmill before had taught him to have a healthy respect for those turbines. Once the control gate was opened and the force of the water unleashed, that turbine began spinning like a top and could take off a man's arm—or worse. It would suit him fine to never have to make that dive again.

He opened the door to the mill and stepped inside, giving his eyes a minute to adjust. The sash blade pumped up and down, up and down, and a man he assumed was the other sawyer, in addition to Isham, stood with his back to him, inspecting every swish of the blade.

"Howdy," Wade called out over the roar.

The man turned and made his way toward him.

Wade extended his hand and gave his name. "I'm the new overseer."

The man's grip tightened. "Yes, sir. I's heard you was makin' the rounds. The name's Samuel. I'm one of the colonel's sawyers."

Wade gave a nod. "Sounds like things are running well today."

"Had a little bindin' earlier, but she's runnin' smooth as molasses now. I guess you're knowin' your way around a mill, sir?"

Wade gave a tilt of his head. "Not as thoroughly as you do, but I've had experience with the sash blade. What are we producing here? About two thousand feet per day?"

Samuel's face lit. "You got that right on the mark, sir. On a real good day, if the blade holds steady, we can do a little more."

Wade asked him a few more questions. Samuel updated him on the progress of current orders for lumber, then gave him a quick tour. As they walked and talked, Wade looked around for Isham but saw no sign of him. The mill reminded him of the one he'd grown up working in, and while he had some good memories of those times, he was grateful to be doing what he was doing now, not milling. Sawyering was difficult and dangerous work. He noticed Samuel was absent two fingers on his right hand. Not uncommon for a sawyer.

It still bothered him that Isham was working in this capacity. Back during the war, they'd both held high aspirations for how life would change for

Negroes once the North won. How opportunities would open. Wade didn't like to think of himself as an idealist. He was more practically minded. But things simply weren't changing as quickly as he'd thought they would. Even for someone like Isham.

Wade thanked Samuel for the tour and headed for the door, then turned back. "Is the other sawyer around? Pender, I think his name is?"

"Yes, sir. Isham was here. But a boy come down from the cattle barn askin' for him. Said they's needin' help with a birthin'."

"A birthing?"

"Yes, sir. Ol' Thomas usually sees to birthin's, but he's down in his back. So Isham went to help. I think it's one of them special cows belongin' to the colonel."

Hearing that, Wade wasted no time in taking his leave. He mounted Sassy and set out in the direction of the cattle barn. He gave the mare her lead, and she flew across the fields.

Late yesterday afternoon he'd checked with ol' Thomas on the Ayrshire heifer set to give birth. While the mother-to-be had showed signs of nearing labor, her time hadn't yet come. McGavock took great pride in the fact that he'd imported the Ayrshires from Scotland, and he'd spent a small fortune on those cows too. But Wade didn't care a lick about that. In his opinion, whatever McGavock might lose, the man had it coming after all he'd stolen from so many lives through his perpetuation of slavery. No, Wade's main concern was Winder.

Penelope was the boy's "special cow," and Wade knew if anything happened to her or her calf, Winder would be crushed. So would Nora. Apparently the boy had promised to name the calf after her.

Looking ahead, Wade remembered the shallow stream that cut across the field, and he debated whether to rein in. He had no idea how Sassy would react. Earlier, she'd trotted right across it. But she was galloping at full speed now. Yet the clock was not on his side—and there was always a first time.

The creek came into view, and he spurred her on, certain he felt a quiver of excitement pass through the horse's withers just seconds before she launched into the air. She cleared the creek with feet to spare. This filly was born to fly!

"Good girl!" he shouted.

Sassy snorted as she rounded the final turn leading from the field toward the barn, cutting the corner like she'd been doing this all her life. Wade reined in and dismounted, out of breath and feeling like the mare had just given him a gift. She had. He rubbed her behind the ears and tossed the reins to one of the young saddle hands. "Treat this pretty girl to the finest bucket of oats you've got. And be sure to water her well."

The boy nodded. "I will, Mister Cunningham! I brush her down real good for you too!"

Before Wade even entered the barn, he heard Penelope bellowing. He followed the sound to the last stall on the right and found the massive twelve-hundred-pound heifer lying on her side, legs thrashing, her distended belly appearing even larger than when he'd seen her the day before. Isham and another man knelt behind her, their backs to the stall door.

Wade recognized the second man as one of the sharecroppers he'd met that morning. Both men stroked the heifer's neck and withers, trying to calm her. "How's she doing?" Wade asked.

Isham looked back, and recognition flashed across his face before he masked it. "She's having trouble. Looks like the calf is stuck in the birth canal. We've already sent for the veterinarian, sir."

Wade understood the reason for Isham's formal tone and went along with it.

"But I'm thinkin' we can't just sit here waitin' for that doctor." The man beside Isham rose, worry lining his face. He was tall and muscular and wore a slouch hat, which he promptly removed. He looked directly at Wade. "We met this mornin', Mister Cunningham. My name's—"

"Miles McConnico," Wade supplied, reaching out his hand and noticing how McConnico stared at it like it was a snake ready to strike, same as he'd done that morning. Wade had hoped to put the man at ease by using his name, but McConnico only nodded and regarded him with uncertainty— and even distrust.

"Yes, sir, that's right." McConnico's grip was firm, his gaze unflinching. "I been comin' alongside ol' Thomas for a while now. Colonel McGavock asked me to help with these Ayrshires. To be learnin' more about 'em, with Thomas gettin' on in years and all. But I don't know all that ol' Thomas knows. And this birth"—he shook his head—"this one ain't goin' like any I ever seen."

The heifer let out a high-pitched bawl, then reared her head and tried to stand. It took all three of them to keep her down. Gaining her footing at this stage of birth could mean disaster.

Wade ran a hand along the animal's withers. "How long has it been since her water sack broke?"

"Almost two hours." McConnico twisted the hat in his grip. "Ol' Thomas says if the calf ain't out by then, it's all but done for. This heifer, she's havin' the birthin' pains. You can see 'em ripplin' over her belly. But the calf, it just ain't comin'. I asked ol' Thomas, but he say he don't know what to do. And no matter that the colonel's wantin' me to learn, I for sure ain't got the know-how for doctorin' this."

Wade clearly heard what the man wasn't saying. In Thomas's absence, McConnico was in charge. And the man feared that if this calf died, McGavock would hold him accountable. Chances were good he was right. In Wade's experience, wealthy men always looked for someone else to blame.

Mindful of the Ayrshire's hooves, Wade moved around to her hindquarters.

"You know something about birthing cows, Mister Cunningham?" Isham asked.

Knowing Isham already knew the answer to that question, Wade figured his friend was asking for McConnico's benefit. "My father knew everything about cattle there was to know." Wade rolled up his sleeves to make a quick examination. "And though now I'm wishing I'd paid a little more attention, I did manage to pick up some knowledge." He concentrated, doing his best to determine the problem without causing the heifer any more pain. After a moment, he paused, his worst fear—and McConnico's prediction—looming large. Wade grabbed a towel and wiped his hands. "Well, the good news first. The calf is still moving, so it's alive. The bad news, it's posterior-facing. Coming out backward," he added, reading uncertainty in McConnico's expression.

The man looked away, shaking his head.

"So what we need to do," Wade continued, "is give the calf a chance to turn itself."

"And if it don't?" Dread weighed McConnico's voice.

Wade met his stare. "Then chances are good we'll lose both."

McConnico said something beneath his breath, then looked at Isham, who looked up at Wade.

"Tell us what to do, sir, and we'll do it."

Isham had said much the same thing to him the day Wade took command of the colored troops. To a man, the soldiers in that regiment proved to be among the bravest and most dedicated he'd fought with. Isham most of all.

Wade grabbed a coiled rope from a peg and fashioned it into a harness. "There's nothing *we* can do to turn this calf. But if we can manage to get this hefty mama on her feet, the calf *might* turn itself."

McConnico stared hard at him. "What kind o' foolery you tryin' to get me to do, sir? Get me thrown off o' my land, or worse?"

"Miles!" Isham stepped forward. "I can tell you that—"

McConnico held up a hand, his focus glued on Wade. "Everybody know that havin' a heifer come to standin' while she got a calf comin' down ain't to be done, Mister Cunningham. Sir, I can't lose all I put into my time here at Carnton. Into this land I'm sharecroppin'. I's barely makin' it now. My wife's with child, and we got three others besides. So what I *need* is a way for this new mama *and* calf to live. But what you wantin' us to do is gonna surefire kill 'em both."

Wade took a step toward him, seeing a lifetime of bone-deep scars from treachery and deceit etched in the man's features. "I'm not trying to fool you, friend. And you're right. Usually, that's the case. But I'm telling you, unless we get her to standing, and *fast,* they're *both* going to die." Wade held out the harness.

The heifer let out a primal cry that Wade felt all the way inside him. McConnico must have, too, because the man grabbed the harness and quickly fit it over the heifer's head.

Wade moved to stand with Isham near the

mother's backside. "McConnico, when I give the signal, pull for all you're worth and we'll try to push her up from this end. But watch yourself. If she comes to her feet, she's going to bolt forward, so be ready to move."

McConnico nodded.

Isham shot a look at Wade. "And if she gets halfway up and comes back down?"

Wade gave a flat laugh. "Then we'd better not be where we are now."

They all got into position.

"On your mark." Wade took a deep breath. "Get set. *Go!*"

Wade pushed with everything he had, watchful of the animal's massive hooves but even more so of McConnico's footing. Isham could handle himself. That was never a question. However, Wade couldn't gauge the other man's reflexes.

The heifer didn't budge. She continued to thrash, however, and Wade narrowly missed getting kicked.

"Okay, stop," he said, panting. "Let's rest for a minute, then try again."

They did, and on the third attempt, Penelope bolted upright—straight toward McConnico. With surprisingly quick reflexes, the man sidestepped to safety, and after the initial shock wore off, he smiled. "We got her up, sir!"

Wade nodded, relieved. "Remove the harness, if you can."

He did, and they gave the heifer some room— and waited.

After a few minutes, Penelope let out a low bellow and staggered to one side. The faint outline of life within her could be seen shifting and moving, and Wade prayed the calf would turn the right way. With a keening cry, the heifer's hind legs suddenly gave way, and her massive bulk sank into the straw. She rolled onto her side. The calf was starting to crown—but it wasn't the calf's nose and front hooves presenting.

"Oh dear Jesus," McConnico whispered.

"McConnico, throw me that rope!" Wade caught it midair, then dropped to his knees and grabbed hold of the calf's hooves. He looped the rope over and pulled the slipknot tight, wishing that Winder and Nora hadn't chosen this specific heifer to be so partial to.

Wade exhaled, waiting for the telling ripple of muscle in the heifer's belly. Then, gritting his teeth, he pulled. She let out a cry. The calf's legs were slippery from birth fluid, and the rope lost hold. Wade hurriedly looped the rope around the hooves again, then waited for the next contraction and pulled. But little progress was made, and Penelope shuddered and moaned.

"Come on, girl," Wade whispered, but he could feel the strength ebbing from his back and shoulders.

"Let me do it, sir."

Wade looked up to see McConnico's outstretched hands. He handed off the rope and moved to the side as McConnico took his place.

Wade's breath came heavy. "Wait for the next contraction." Seconds passed. "Now!"

McConnico pulled, teeth gritted, the tendons in his neck going taut, and in a wash of birth fluid, the calf finally slipped free of its mother's body. McConnico let go of the rope and scooted back. Then for a moment, the three of them just stared at the wonderment of life. The newborn calf was perfect and already struggling to stand.

Penelope lifted her head as if eager to see her daughter, and Wade gave the new mother a quick going-over before untethering the rope from the newborn's legs. The feisty little red-and-white-spotted calf tried to kick him in response. Wade laughed, knowing Winder had chosen the right name.

Penelope gained her footing and turned to nudge her baby. Nora O'Toole's little namesake shook her head, her still-slick body wet and shiny as Mama began to lick.

Wade stepped from the stall, Isham and McConnico following. They washed their hands and arms in a water barrel, then dried them with rags before turning back to watch the scene. Wade said a silent prayer of thanks to his papa for all he'd taught him. And to his Father, too, for bringing him back to a place he'd sworn never to return to.

"Mister Cunningham?"

Wade turned to see Miles McConnico's out-stretched hand and accepted without hesitation.

"I was wrong about you, sir. And I want

to thank you for doin' what you did in there."

Wade met his gaze. "Actually, *you* pulled that calf free. And that's exactly what I'll be telling the colonel—and anyone else who asks."

McConnico's grip tightened as his grin went wide.

Wade gestured. "Now go on and spread the good news. And be sure to tell the main house, if you would. They'll be eager to get word."

No sooner had McConnico left them than Isham began to laugh.

Wade looked at him. "What?"

"It's good to see you again, old friend."

Isham grabbed him in a bear hug, and Wade pounded him on the back.

"It's good to see you too." Wade took a step back. "But when I turned around and saw you standing there yesterday . . ."

Isham shook his head. "You're the *last* person I ever expected to see here at Carnton."

"I could say the same about you."

A telling look came over his friend's face. A look Wade knew only too well.

Wade narrowed his eyes. "So what are you *really* doing here, Isham?"

Isham looked away. "Things haven't turned out like I thought they would. Like we dreamed they would back during the war. So I'm a sawyer here at Carnton. And I'm a good one too." Isham returned his gaze and held up his hands. "See? Still have all ten fingers."

327

Wade mirrored his smile but sensed something *off* in the man.

"McGavock pays us pretty well," Isham continued. "And I've got a house on the property. An old slave house, but I'm fixing it up."

Wade gripped his shoulder, shaking his head. Isham only nodded.

"So what about you?" Isham frowned. "You swore you'd never come back to Franklin. Not after all we went through. Not after—"

"I know I said that, but . . ." Wade shrugged. "Like you, life just hasn't turned out like I thought it would."

Isham said nothing, just nodded again. "Does McGavock know you fought for the other side?"

Wade laughed. "What do you think?"

"Yeah, he doesn't know about me either."

They talked until they heard a commotion of people coming, then they resumed the pretense. But as Colonel McGavock and his family, along with freed men and women and other workers, flocked to see the newborn calf, he watched Isham, unable to shake the troubling feeling within him. Because for the first time since Wade had met the man, Isham Pender had lied to him.

"Now see? This isn't so bad, is it?" Lying on her back, Catriona stared up through the branches into the night sky, the breeze whispering through the canopy of walnut trees.

Nora shifted beside her. "The ground is bumpy."

"Here, stand up. Let's get your cloak better situated beneath you."

Nora rose, and Catriona took up the garment. She felt along the ground for bigger rocks she might've missed the first time and found a couple. She tossed them aside, then spread out the cloak again, folding up the hood of the cape like a little pillow.

"Here, try that."

Nora lay down.

"Any better, dearest?"

"A wee bit . . . maybe."

Hearing the disappointment in her sister's voice, Catriona resisted the inclination to feel like a complete wastrel. Which was difficult, seeing as how only an hour earlier she'd been rummaging through trash bins in alleyways behind local eateries, scrounging for food. She'd waited until after the dinner hour, once kitchen workers had tossed scraps and were busy washing dishes. The real challenge had come in keeping Nora occupied. But the pen and paper the waitress at the hotel had sent with them proved a wonder. It had taken some noggin work, as Ryan would have said, but Catriona finally concocted a game.

She'd been responsible for educating all three of her sisters, yet she hadn't so much as cracked a primer with Nora since before leaving Ireland. So that afternoon she'd filled a page, front and back, with arithmetic problems for Nora to work. But she'd divided them into blocks with the catch that Nora had only three minutes at a time to work a single block, long enough for Catriona to whip around the corner and scour a bin. She'd managed to find food enough to keep hunger at bay for the night. Bread, mostly. But also half an apple and two partially eaten pieces of ham. Food people would have fought, if not killed, each other over during the famine back home.

Deliberately setting those thoughts aside, she breathed in, filling her lungs, and caught the scent of something sweet in bloom. Mercifully, the sun had set an hour earlier, and the heat of the day was dissipating to a mild—

Hearing the crack of a twig behind them, Catriona rose on one elbow and looked at the ghostly line of trees a few feet away.

"What're you doin', Cattie?" Nora said sleepily.

"Nothin'. Just lookin'."

Catriona studied the edge of the woods but didn't see anything unusual. Still, she reached beneath her cloak and made sure the dagger was there. She didn't like the dark. She wasn't afraid of it, really. She simply didn't like not being able to see what was just beyond her.

Looking through the trees, she could just make out the Franklin Presbyterian Church, its steeple rising high into the night sky. She'd knocked on the front doors of the church earlier. When no one answered, she'd tried the handle. Locked. What church locked its doors? She'd then tried every other door she could find. No one was there to

330

help. Which wasn't surprising, considering whose house it was and that the two of them weren't on speaking terms. She'd been tempted to try the windows too. But on the off chance the Almighty happened to be watching her at the moment, she resisted. Not that she thought she would fall out of favor with him if she had. She would have to be *in* favor with him first for that to happen. And heaven knew she was not.

She looked heavenward, and her eyes filled unexpectedly. She shook her head, not welcoming the gentle tug of yearning deep inside her, like something long forgotten calling out to her, wanting to be reclaimed.

Nora turned onto her back and gave a deep sigh.

Grateful for the distraction, Catriona cleared her throat, making sure her voice would hold. "Can you not get comfortable, wee one?"

"Not very. I'm still hungry."

"Would you like another piece of bread?" Catriona reached into the trunk and pulled out the last roll, the lid to the trunk creaking something awful. She'd been saving it for their breakfast, but if it would help Nora sleep . . .

"Nay, I don't want it."

"So you're full now, then?" Hopeful, Catriona waited.

"Nay, I'm just dreamin' of havin' me some roast."

Suppressing a sigh of her own, Catriona lay back down. She would've felt worse if not for the touch of drama in her sister's tone. "Are you needin' another drink before we go to sleep?"

Nora said nothing, but Catriona could see the smudgy outline of her profile and the subtle shake of her head. Catriona took a long drink of water, then set the chipped coffee cup back on the ground near the trunk. She'd found the cup in her foraging and had washed it thoroughly in the creek. Amazing how a broken thing cast off by one person's hand as useless became such a treasure in another's.

She felt so small peering up at the vast darkness above. The stars were sprinkled like tiny candles across an endless expanse, their smoldering wicks flickering through windows another world away. Mam had made certain to read the Bible to her children, and though Catriona couldn't remember where it was written, she recalled that somewhere it claimed there would be no night in heaven. No darkness. Which was good for heaven, wherever that was, but what about the grave? She grimaced imagining that field not far away, so many bodies buried in the cold, dark ground. But even more, that Ryan might be among them. *Brother, where are you, dear one?*

With that thought on her mind, she turned onto her side toward Nora, already hearing the little girl's soft intake of breath. Catriona tugged the edges of her sister's cloak around her wee body. Not that she expected the night to be cold but more from habit of tucking her sister in for seven years

332

now and counting. Catriona pulled her own cloak over her body and cradled her arm beneath her head.

This morning she had been a wealthy woman, of sorts. And tonight she had nothing. Only sixteen cents to her name after mailing the letters. *"The best fake I've ever seen. Whoever forged those bills is a real artist."* Catriona turned onto her back, Mr. Bonner's voice the last thing she wanted in her head before she went to sleep.

No matter what he said, she would never believe that Ryan had done such a thing. Da? Aye, given the chance, he would've done it and for far less money. But Ryan? *Never.* A thought occurred, and she frowned. Ryan's note. Bonner had never given it back to her, and she'd been so befuddled in the moment she'd forgotten. She sighed. Yet something else dear stolen away.

From somewhere in the tree branches above her, the gentle *coo-coo* of mourning doves drifted down, and she took strange comfort in the sadness inherent in their call. As she drifted toward sleep, the image of all those chickens from yesterday came to mind, and she smiled sleepily, picturing the chaos of all those flapping—

The chickens! She blinked and came fully awake.

Frasier Martin had offered her chickens. Eggs, too, most certainly. But chickens! Chickens were worth money. Quite a bit of money. She could scarcely lie still. Wade had said he was going to pick up the chickens from the Martins' farm this

333

morning. She was certain he'd taken them back to Carnton. Where else would he take them? And even if he'd put the chickens from Mr. Martin in with the McGavocks', surely Wade would still let her have her share. After all, she'd caught dozens of chickens with that little contraption of his, and she had done as well as he had. Well, almost as well. And she knew Frasier Martin had placed a particular hen in the dozen he offered them.

Wondering if she'd ever be able to get to sleep now, she ran her hands through her hair, having dispensed with the pins hours ago. She could scarcely wait for the sun to come up. She would stash their trunk in the walnut grove, and then they would walk to Carnton and get their chickens. It wasn't near the fortune she'd lost, but it was something. Eggs were expensive, and surely chickens couldn't be that difficult to keep. Of course, she had no chicken coop or house behind which to keep it. So perhaps it would be best to sell the chickens outright.

Somewhere between wondering how much a chicken was worth and how many eggs a hen could lay per day, sleep claimed her. Until the creak of the trunk being opened brought her awake. She blinked.

It was still dark, and her mind was groggy from sleep. But when she saw Nora's sleeping form still cuddled beneath the cloak beside her, her head instantly cleared.

She turned and spotted a shadow hulking over

the trunk, and her heart went from near standing still in her chest to all but thrashing out of it. She reached into her sleeve for the dagger—and panicked. Then remembered and pulled it from beneath her cloak.

She stood, sliding the blade from its leather scabbard. "W-what do you think you're doin' there!" she whispered, hoping not to wake Nora.

The figure spun to face her, and Catriona caught a whiff of whiskey and days-old sweat. The man was tall and thick around the middle, and he appeared none too steady on his feet. But she knew better than to trust that. Some revelers, once riled, remained surprisingly agile despite the number of pints in them. Others saw their suggestibility increase with every drink. She hoped this man was the latter.

"I'm taking this," he said matter-of-factly, slamming the lid down on the trunk and bending to pick it up.

"Nay, you are not!" Catriona inched forward, blade in hand. "You're goin' to leave it right there and go on back to the pub!"

He lifted the trunk as though it weighed nothing and laughed, the sound gurgling in his throat. "Ain't no use goin' back. Ain't got no more money." He looked in her direction. "But I'm bettin' *you* do."

"I *don't* have any money! That's only clothes, so put it down! Unless you're needin' a dress to be wearin'," she taunted.

But he didn't put it down. A rush of anger heated her body. Maybe it was all she'd lost that day or the thought of losing the few personal items left to them—the bundle of Ryan's letters he'd sent during the war, Mam's Bible filled with her handwriting, a worn image of her maternal grandparents—but a fierceness rose up in her, and she called to memory everything Ryan had taught her.

She gripped the blade with her left hand and took a step forward, the smell of soured mash turning her stomach. "I said put the trunk down. Do it now, or I'm goin' to stick you good!" She held up the dagger, the tip gleaming in the moonlight.

He smiled and tilted his head as though he were taking a closer look at her, his fat cheeks pudging out on the sides. "Instead of you stickin' me, maybe I oughta—"

Quickly catching his intent, her stomach turned. "I'm warnin' you for the last time. Drop the trunk and—"

"Cattie, what's wrong?"

Wincing, Catriona looked to see Nora seated on her cloak. "You stay right there, wee one! You hear me?"

The man dropped the trunk, and Catriona spun.

He took a step toward her. "Maybe afterwards, I'll get friendly with her too."

He lunged for the dagger, and Catriona braced herself even as, with a flick of her wrist, she flipped the blade from her left hand to her right, then shuddered as it sank into folds of soft flesh.

She stepped back, bringing the blade with her, her body shaking.

The man groaned and muttered a curse. "You cut me, you vile little . . ."

He came at her again, and she moved swiftly, catching him on the forearm this time. He stumbled to his knees and spat out a string of profanities she hadn't heard since before Da's final days. She had quickness on her side, but she was no match for the man's strength, even drunk as he was.

He staggered back to his feet, his breath coming hard. With a low growl, he bent down, then picked up the trunk and heaved it at Nora.

Catriona screamed her sister's name, and Nora, watching, huddled on her cloak, managed to duck at the last moment.

Seething, the man doubled over. "I'm gonna take that blade and cut you both to . . ."

Catriona slipped the dagger back into the scabbard, then grabbed Nora in her arms and ran.

They reached the edge of the tree line, and Catriona kept running. "Keep your head down," she warned, and Nora tucked her face into the curve of her neck. Branches slapped at them, and Catriona stumbled more than once but caught her balance and kept running. When she reached the other side of the walnut grove, she paused, hearing only the rush of her pulse in her ears.

"Cattie!" Nora cried.

"Shhhh . . ." Catriona stroked her curls, straining to hear. "Be quiet!"

Nora trembled in her arms. Then Catriona heard thrashing through the trees behind them. She took off for the church, struggling to remember the outside of the building and where the best hiding places would be. Not knowing if the man could see them, she ran to the back of the church, then circled again to the front, the breath in her lungs churning. A wash of moonlight helped light the way, but she knew it was doing the same for him.

Catriona stopped, breathless, and Nora peered up. But Catriona forced her head back down.

"Hold on tight to me," she whispered, then felt Nora's arms and legs clamp around her neck and waist. Catriona pushed through a thick stand of shrubs and low-growing trees, the branches tearing at their clothing. Once through the wall of foliage, she huddled down against the foundation of the church, laid the scabbard on the ground close beside her, then cradled Nora in her lap, rocking her sister back and forth as she'd done when Nora was just a bairn.

"We're all right," she whispered. "He can't find us."

Nora shook her head, crying. "I'm wantin' to go back to the hotel, Cattie. *Please . . .*"

"Shhhh . . ." Catriona's throat tightened. "We'll be all right, dearest. We'll be all right."

Heart thudding, she waited, listening, already grieving the loss of the treasured items in the trunk. Perhaps the man would simply scrounge for money, find none, and leave the trunk be. A branch snapped only feet away, and feeling Nora take a breath, Catriona gently slipped her hand over her sister's mouth and waited.

How long they sat there, she didn't know. Had the man given up? Had he gone on? Wanting to believe that, she felt her pulse beginning to slow, even as the anger inside her simmered. She pressed a kiss to Nora's head and tried not to think about what could have happened to them. To her sister.

Within minutes, Nora was asleep again, and Catriona's arms went numb from supporting the weight of her body. Not knowing the time, she searched the swathe of sky within her view for any sign of dawn, but she saw only pitch black. Hearing no sign of the man's pursuit, she debated leaving the secrecy of their nook but finally decided to stay until first light. Yet sleep was miles away.

Weary, she leaned her head back against the rock and spotted, directly above them, the steeple of the church spiraling high into the night. From this vantage point, it appeared as though the spire reached all the way to heaven's gates. She exhaled. Of all the places she could have chosen to hide. "I'm guessin' you're findin' humor in this, aren't you?" she whispered, shaking her head.

Mam always said she should tell God whatever was in her heart. But what was in her heart right now wasn't like any prayer she'd heard in any church in all her life. Her eyes burned. She tightened her jaw. What she wanted to say to him would not be welcome, nor would it be honoring, and she knew better than to pick a fight she could never win.

Yet the longer she stared at that lofty spiral, the more the words burned inside her. Was he daring her to say it? Did the Almighty do that? "All right, then," she whispered, searching the darkness above. "I don't know if you're listenin', but if you are . . ." She hesitated, her voice breaking, the words more difficult—and more painful—to say aloud than she'd expected. "I-I know I'm a disappointment to you. You've made that clear. 'Cause your anger's always burnin' against me. I'm tryin' to do right, yet bad things keep happenin'. And while I can learn to live with that"—she shook her head—"I'm wantin' better for me sister. I promised Mam I would give that to her. So please, Lord"—tears came despite her squeezing her eyes tight—"be merciful to Nora, I'm beggin' you, even if not to me. Make a way for her in this life. I'll do whatever I need to for her. Only please don't make her pay for your displeasure with me. Let me be bearin' the brunt of that alone."

She searched for any more words inside her and found none. So she bowed her head, a little late, she knew, and said a quiet "Amen." Then she waited—for what, she didn't know.

But nothing happened. Not the least stirring of wind. Not the slightest prickle on her skin or sense of acknowledgment. Nothing. So much for God's help being nearer than the door. It was as if she'd been sitting there talking only to herself. And who knew, maybe she had been. But at least she'd said her piece, whether or not he'd ever answer her.

Gradually, her eyes grew heavy, and she closed them, determined to get some rest. But equally determined to get to Carnton first thing come sunup and get what was due her. Including one little red-feathered vixen.

CHAPTER 21

Wade awakened with the sunrise—and with roosters crowing just outside his window. Why anyone would build chicken coops so close to a cottage, he didn't know. But he'd like to have a word with that person.

Yawning, he rose and stretched, then sat on the edge of the bed for a minute, the muscles in his shoulders and back sore from delivering the calf yesterday. The brief meeting with the accountant last evening played over in his mind, same as it had as he'd drifted toward sleep. He couldn't pinpoint exactly why, but something about Woodrow Cockrill told him the man was hiding something. Then again, he'd never liked accountants much. Always thought they were charging for services that weren't necessary.

His father had always kept the farm records himself until Wade came of age and took over the task. Of course, their family farm hadn't been an estate the size of Carnton. Still . . . he wouldn't trust Woodrow Cockrill with five dollars, much less a fortune the size of McGavock's. To make matters worse, he hadn't picked up on anything that would indicate that Cockrill was involved in counterfeiting.

But even more frustrating, following that meeting, he'd stopped by the hotel to see Catriona and Nora, only to be informed that Miss O'Toole and her sister were no longer patrons of that establishment. Catriona hadn't mentioned one word to him about leaving. Either the hotel or town. And though it wasn't his business, and shouldn't be for so many reasons, that didn't stop him from being curious.

Yet thrumming beneath all that was the fact that Isham, a man he'd once counted as a dear friend, had lied to him. Isham Pender was no more just a sawyer here than he was an overseer. So what was his old friend really doing at Carnton? He didn't know, but he was determined to find out.

He rummaged through his satchel, not having bothered to finish unpacking yet, and pulled out a clean pair of drawers and socks, a towel, and a bar of soap, and laid them on the bed. With the last item came a familiar photograph, the edges bent and worn. Wade read the name on it—Harvey—and had to smile. Harvey, the 104th Ohio's mascot, and what a good one he'd been. The spirited little dog had made it with them through the war and all the way to the Battle of Nashville, then had vanished. As far as he knew, no one had seen him since. Wade hoped the smart little pup had made it through. That perhaps some local had picked him up and given him a good home.

Tucking the photograph back in his satchel, he spotted the rolled-up poster, crunched and wrinkled, half-hidden beneath his clothes, and pulled it out. He didn't bother unrolling it. Didn't need to. He already knew the illustration by heart, and so had every member of his colored regiment. He'd made sure of that. Back during the war, he'd hung the poster by Thomas Nast in a prominent place so there would be no doubt where his loyalties lay or his reasons for fighting in the war. Someday, God willing, the image in the center of that poster would become the reality in this country. Wade only hoped he lived long enough to see it.

He placed the poster on the bottom shelf of his bedside table, toward the back, then pulled on a pair of trousers and his boots. He tucked the revolver from the bedside table inside his waistband, gathered the pile of clothing and items from the bed, and left the bedroom.

His plate from dinner last night still sat on the table where he'd left it, right next to the portfolio containing the detailed weekly report he'd stayed up late writing for Chief Wood. The report included all his findings and interactions in recent days, plus some confidential information on several of the suspects. He placed the portfolio in the empty iron skillet atop the stove and popped on the lid, then slid it into the cold oven. Amazing some of the places people never thought to look.

Glancing back at his plate on the table, he eyed the last half of a muffin—one of the tastiest he'd ever eaten—and popped it into his mouth. The

345

portions of meat loaf and vegetables had been generous, and he'd wolfed down the meal. If that was a sampling of Tempy's cooking, it was a good thing the duties of overseer of Carnton were physically demanding. Chief Wood was always harping on his operatives to keep fit. It was part of the job, the chief said.

Upon returning to Carnton last evening, Wade had been about to brave Tempy's kitchen for the first time when Mrs. McGavock met him on the back porch. *"When you didn't come to the kitchen for dinner, Tempy delivered your plate to the cottage. She's a woman who appreciates keeping to her schedule."* Mrs. McGavock's expression held a hint of mirth, but Wade knew the real reason Tempy had delivered that plate. She didn't want him in her kitchen.

But that time was coming. He enjoyed a little challenge, and Tempy had a wealth of knowledge about Carnton and this community. Knowledge he needed.

The creek was an easy walk down a trail behind the cottage. Squirrels chittering and racing through the branches overhead drew his attention, as did the sunrise over the hills. Soft brushstrokes of pink and purple cast the eastern horizon in a wash of color, and he could all but hear his mother's voice. *"Drink in beauty wherever you can find it, son. And be grateful. Beauty is a treasure and a foretaste of heaven."*

He missed his mother so much. Missed her

346

laughter, the way she'd smiled up at him when he walked into the kitchen. He still regretted not being there with her when she passed. The war had taken so many things from him—and not just him alone. War stole with both hands and from both sides. He only hoped the deep rifts in this country could soon be healed and that the chasms present for so many years would finally be bridged.

He scouted the creek bank and picked a secluded spot where the water ran deep, then shed his boots, trousers, and drawers, grabbed the soap, and waded in. He sucked in a breath, the chill of the water bracing. After a minute or two, once he'd acclimated, he sank down. He submerged his head a couple of times, then rubbed the bar of soap into a lather and worked it through his hair.

He didn't think Catriona would just up and leave town without saying anything. Not when she was still looking for her brother. Maybe she'd found a better place for her and her sister to stay. Something less expensive, perhaps. He had no idea what her financial situation was. She'd never made a show of having money, but obviously she must have some if she'd just arrived from Ireland and was staying at the hotel and taking her meals there. He rinsed the soap from his hair, reminded yet again that he needed that haircut and shave.

He finished bathing, then toweled off and pulled on his drawers and trousers, then socks and boots. Damp towel over his shoulder, he grabbed the rest of his clothes and his gun and strode back toward the cottage, mentally reviewing all he needed to get done in the next few days. Yesterday McGavock told him he'd scheduled another meeting with the burial committee, which meant the town leaders would be gathering at Carnton again soon. He didn't know how he would manage it, but he planned to be part of that gathering. The more time he spent in the company of those men, the greater likelihood he'd see or hear something important. Something incriminating to one or more of them.

Nearly halfway back to the cottage, he paused and cocked his head, certain he heard the tread of steps somewhere in the brush around him. He waited, listening, his hand instinctively closing around the revolver nestled in the bundle of clothes. But whatever—or whoever—was out there had gone quiet.

McGavock had warned him that they'd had some trouble lately with cougars in the area. About a month ago, one of the cats had taken down a newborn calf. But cougars were usually shy, secretive animals, preferring to hunt at night, so maybe it was a coyote or a fox. Those were plentiful.

Yet never far from his mind was the note slid beneath his door at the hotel. *Anson Bern.* Whoever had written it knew he worked for the Secret Service, but they hadn't contacted him again, nor had they revealed his identity. But they likely would as soon as it proved to their advantage.

Hearing nothing else, he continued on, watchful.

As he passed the chicken coops, he spotted a couple of the chickens Frasier Martin had given him. He knew they were Martin's because the man had insisted on marking the dozen russet-colored chickens by brushing the tips of a few of their feathers with brown paint. When Wade questioned why, Martin explained that since Wade would no doubt be adding the chickens to those already at Carnton, he wanted *his* chickens to be distinguishable so that the quality of Martin's Poultry Farm would stand out. Wade laughed to himself, looking at those paint-tipped feathers and wondering if Frasier Martin had ever heard of molting.

Back at the cottage, he took the two steps up to the porch in one stride, grateful for the independence this situation at Carnton gave him. He could pretty much come and go as he pleased, day or night, as long as he got his work done, and the overseer's lodgings were more than ample.

The cottage, located a hefty stone's throw from the barn, consisted of just the two rooms—the kitchen with a table and chairs and a small sitting area, then the bedroom beyond. The furnishings were simple, and they suited him. He'd always put more stock in function than in fancy.

He dumped his clothes on the floor of the bedroom and tossed his gun on the bed. He pulled his last clean shirt from the satchel and attempted to shake out some of the wrinkles. He needed to do laundry—or have it done somewhere in town. He smiled, imagining Tempy's reaction if he asked her to do it. Might be worth it just to see the woman's expression. He bet she'd have a pot of coffee boiling on the stove by now, and he hoped—

Spotting an envelope lying on the bedside table, he stilled. An envelope that hadn't been there when he'd left for the creek. He was certain because that's where he'd kept his gun. Feeling an uncanny sense of déjà vu, he slid his finger beneath the seal, remembering the note he'd found while at the hotel.

He pulled out the single sheet of paper, and as he read the instructions, a sense of satisfaction moved through him. Chief Wood had said the courier would be in touch when they had news. And apparently they did. His next move would be to locate the specific place described in the note where—

A ruckus broke loose just outside his bedroom window. A hysteria of squawking and cackling. Tossing his shirt on the bed, Wade pulled back the curtain. Hens and roosters running everywhere! Feathers flying! It had to be a coyote or a fox, for sure.

He stuffed the note in his pants pocket, then grabbed his gun and raced outside, knowing there'd soon be one less chicken predator to worry about. And maybe one less rooster, if the fox got lucky.

CHAPTER 22

Catriona grimaced and rubbed her shin. That blasted pail! How had she not seen it? She'd tripped over it on her way into the chicken run, and now the chickens were making enough noise to wake everything for miles around. She huffed, wishing she could kick the pail again just for spite.

She looked around to see if anyone was coming, but she saw no one. Could she be that lucky? The chicken coops *were* a fair piece from the McGavocks' house and situated behind the barn. Perhaps the family was still sleeping and hadn't heard.

If she'd known where Wade was staying on the property, she would have gone to him straightaway. She was only trying to find out if the chickens from Frasier Martin were here, and if she found that one—

"Look out, Cattie!" Nora called. "There she is! There's Brunhilde!"

Catriona turned to see the ornery little vixen that had pecked her hand the other day. The plucky red hen was strutting straight for her. She and Nora had named the chicken on their walk to Carnton that morning, partly an attempt to give her sister something else to focus on while they passed the field of graves. And partly revenge. Nora had declared Brunhilde to be the least attractive name she could think of.

"Cattie, be careful! She'll peck your eyes out!"

Catriona shushed her. "She can't reach me eyes, Nora. Besides, she doesn't peck that hard."

The deep red of the hen's feathers, not to mention that bright red comb, was unique enough to stand out, and it assured her that those twelve chickens were likely still here. And if Wade agreed to give her six—and she didn't plan on leaving with any less—she wanted Brunhilde to be among them.

"I'm hungry, Cattie. Get us some eggs so we can fry 'em up!"

"Nay, dearest, I can't. Those eggs are not belongin' to us. And besides, we've got nothin' to cook them in." But eggs did sound delicious. Anything sounded good. And though she'd never wrung a chicken's neck, she'd be willing to have a go at it right this minute if it meant the two of them could eat. She knew which bird she'd start with too.

As soon as they finished here, they'd head back to town, and she would do her best to find food. Even if it meant spending a few precious pennies on a loaf of bread to tide them over until she could sell her share of the—

"Cattie! Someone's comin'!"

Knowing it was useless to try to hide, Catriona turned in the direction Nora was pointing, only to see Wade coming around the corner running full steam. When he saw her, he slowed, and Catriona knew the surprise she felt must be written on her face for all the world to see, including him. But *blimey,* friend or no, the man was a sight to behold. Bare-chested, hair mussed and damp, unshaven, and with a revolver in his grip, he looked more like one of those Colorado mountain men she'd read about in a dime novel on the train from New York than the overseer of a fine estate. She felt a heat rising within her, similar to a flush in her face but more potent—and not at all keeping to her cheeks this time but traveling to other parts of her body she didn't know could blush.

He slowed his steps, consternation darkening his rugged features. She attempted to run a hand through her hair, knowing she looked a fright after last night's ordeal. But the mess of matted curls prevented it.

Wade strode toward her, tucking the gun into the front waistband of his trousers. Her gaze followed his movements—until she realized it was probably best that it not.

"What in the *world* do you think you're doing, Catriona?"

She held up a hand. "I know findin' me in here is a wee bit of a surprise."

"A wee bit?" His brows rose.

"But I've come for me chickens. The ones Mr. Martin said I could be havin'."

His eyes widened. "It's barely six o'clock in the

353

morning! What are you doing here so early? And where's Nora?"

"Here I am!" Nora perked up and ran straight for him.

Wade caught her up in one arm, and to Catriona's surprise, Nora hugged his neck. The same way the girl would have hugged Ryan. *Like she used to hug me.* Seeing her sister react to Wade like that stirred sour jealousy in the pit of her stomach. Which, when combined with her hunger, did not make for a good feeling.

Wade set Nora down and gave her curls a tousle, then looked back. "You're welcome to all twelve chickens. But what do you aim to do with them? I *would* say I don't believe the Williford Hotel will allow additional guests in your room. But I stopped by there last night to ask you two ladies to have dinner with me, only to be told you're no longer staying there."

Catriona quickly looked at Nora, whose expression clouded. Clearly, the girl was trying to make sense of Wade's comment.

Catriona had not yet told her they weren't returning to the hotel, and she'd also done her best to convince Nora that the less said to others about last night's camping incident, especially the visitor they'd had, the better. Nora had reluctantly agreed. And though Catriona wasn't overly proud of it, she'd also conveyed to her sister—as part of the attempt to keep her quiet—that they'd camped on someone's land *without* permission and that

354

Catriona didn't want the two of them to get into trouble. So the fewer people who knew about it, the safer they'd be.

It was mostly true, Catriona reasoned. She hadn't sought anyone's permission, and trouble was exactly what they'd gotten.

"While that's true, Mr. Cunningham"—Catriona jumped in, addressing him formally for Nora's sake—"that we're not stayin' at the hotel currently, it doesn't mean we might not be choosin' to stay there again. Sometime in the days ahead."

Nora's eyes narrowed. "I'm not campin' again, Cattie. It was no fun at all! It gave me a fright to me bones, and I *won't* be doin' it twice!"

"Nora." Catriona pointed a warning. "You wilna—"

"Wait." Wade exhaled. "You two were *camping* last night? As in sleeping outside?"

Catriona shot Nora another warning glance for her mouthiness but also to remind her of their agreement. Nora's chin rose ever so slightly, telling Catriona their agreement was in serious peril.

"Aye, we did," Catriona said quickly, exiting the chicken run and making her way around to join them. Perhaps proximity to the conversation would help her feel more in control. But she quickly realized it only made her more aware of Wade's muscular physique. And his lack of a shirt. " 'Twas a lovely night for campin'," she continued, forcing her gaze upward. "Mild, and no rain. Isn't that right, Nora?" She placed a light hand on her

355

sister's shoulder, mindful of the tender blister on her palm.

Nora looked up, and her pretty pink lips slowly crooked to one side, which meant Nora not only knew she had her over a barrel but was pondering even then what she wanted in exchange for keeping quiet. The scheming little ragamuffin . . .

Meanwhile, Wade stood watching them both, and Catriona felt as though he was absorbing every detail. Considering how she looked at present, she did not welcome a close perusal from him. In truth, she didn't welcome anything from him at all, because what scared her even more than being on her own was being forced to trust someone. Nay, not just someone. To trust a man. To trust *him*.

Yet her confidence in the plan she'd formed suddenly made her think of that old coracle she and Ryan had found washed ashore one summer. They'd pushed the wee boat out to sea, not knowing the bottom was nearly worn clean through. It had taken only minutes for it to take on water and sink, and she feared the same fate awaited her now.

Aye, Wade had said she could have the chickens. But where was she to sell them? How was she to get them there? And after the money from the chickens ran out, what then? She could not, and would not, put Nora in danger like she had last night. *Och,* just thinking about that man made her ill. His stench, the way he'd looked at her and Nora . . . A pang of desperation mixed with the hunger and jealousy already swirling inside her, and she thought she was going to be sick. Only, her stomach had nothing to give up. *And* she had no other plan.

"Where are you staying tonight?" Wade asked softly, skepticism lining his tone.

"I've not decided yet," Catriona answered honestly, standing a little straighter, aware of Nora watching them. "But I will. What I'd like to know for now, though, is where I might find a place to be sellin' these chickens."

The kindness in his eyes reached inside her, doing things it had no right to do, and she found herself wanting to run and never stop.

"So you're going to sell them? All of them?"

"Aye. As you all but just said, I've no place to be keepin' them. So sellin' 'em makes the best sense, don't you think?"

He didn't answer.

"Cattie, where *are* we stayin' tonight?"

"Later, Nora. Not now."

"And what about breakfast? I'm *hungry!* That wee roll wasn't enough. And it was *hard!*"

Weary of her sister's belligerence, Catriona placed a hand on Nora's shoulder. "We'll talk about this more in a minute. For now, I want us to go fetch our chickens and—"

"You're not listenin' to me, Cattie!" Nora stomped. "You never listen! You're always tellin' me what to do and talkin' about me like I'm not here. Well, I'm not doin' it no more!"

"*Nora!*" Catriona grabbed her sister's arm,

357

but Nora wrenched away. Catriona winced, the blister on her hand suddenly burning like fire. She squeezed her hand tight, her palm slick with moisture. But she dared not peek at it. Not with Wade looking on.

"Nora," Wade said softly. "Do you remember where the kitchen is in the main house? Where you and Winder had some of Tempy's cookies the other day?"

In a blink, Nora's expression transformed from angry to hopeful. "Aye! I do!"

He smiled down. "Run on up there, if you would, and ask Tempy if she'll fix us all some breakfast."

Catriona shook her head. "Nay, we're not wantin' any—"

"And tell Tempy," Wade continued, matching Catriona's gaze, "that your sister and I will be up directly."

Catriona stepped forward. "Nora, you are *not* to go. You will obey me and—"

Nora took off running. She rounded the corner of the barn and headed in the direction of the house, and she never looked back.

Catriona squeezed her fists tight, the pain in her palm nothing compared to the anger coursing through her. She whirled around. "You had *no right* to be doin' that! *I* am her sister. *I* will be decidin' what—"

"Catriona, what's happened?" The earlier kindness in his blue-gray eyes now filled his voice.

But she wanted none of it. "Nothin' has happened! We're *fine!*"

As soon as the words left her mouth, she heard Nora's voice from that day at the bank—*"You're lyin', Cattie. Just like Da used to do! You're just like him!"*—and the truth cut her to the quick. Feeling as if she'd been gut punched, she pressed a hand to her midsection, finding it difficult to breathe.

"Catriona, are you all right?"

Wade gently took her by the arm, but she pushed him away. She *was* lying. To Nora, most certainly. But even more to herself. And to Wade. She and Nora weren't fine. Gradually, the ache in her midsection eased, and she lifted her gaze to find Wade staring down at the faint reddish outline of a handprint on his chest.

Frowning, she slowly turned her palm up.

"*Catriona* . . . What happened to your hand?"

She shook her head again, then with effort perfected by practice, she stuffed all the pain and disappointment back down inside. Or tried to. This time it refused to go, and she panicked, not knowing what to do with it all. *Oh Ryan* . . . She missed him so much. If here, he would've hugged her tight and told her all would be well. Then he would have made it so. Because that's what he always did. He always made a way. For her. For their family. With little thought of himself. But Ryan wasn't here. And she had no one to turn to.

Her head down, she looked at Wade's worn

359

leather boots and wrinkled trousers, then at his hands, steady and strong, hanging by his sides. He'd said he wanted to be her friend. But did he really? Could she trust him? She briefly closed her eyes. Did she have a choice? She needed help, and she knew it. Reaching for courage and scraping the bottom, she slowly lifted her face.

Without a word, he turned and walked away.

Heart in her throat, she watched him go, knowing then that her first inclination had been the right one. Would she never learn? Trust came at a steep price. If Wade would give up on her so easily—

He stopped at a water barrel. Then dipping a bucket deep, he withdrew it and strode back.

She stared.

"Sit down." He pointed to a tree stump.

Numb, she did as he asked. He knelt beside her.

"Give me your hand," he said gently.

She held it out, and he cradled her right hand in his left. He filled the ladle with water and slowly poured it over the open blister. Teeth clenched, Catriona sucked in a breath.

"How did you do this?" he asked. "And don't tell me it doesn't matter. It does. To me." His gaze searched hers.

The words *It doesn't matter* had indeed been on the tip of her tongue. Tears formed, and she bit her lower lip until she was certain she would taste blood. "I was carryin' our trunk," she finally managed, watching his actions, surprised such tenderness could come from such hands.

He glanced around. "Where's the trunk now?"

She briefly bowed her head, knowing to trust her instincts on this one. "I left it back in town. Well hidden in a walnut grove by a church." Come sunup, she'd found the trunk smashed in on one side and the lid hanging open. But she'd been so grateful it was still there. The man had rummaged through everything and taken what he wanted. But none of the treasured, irreplaceable items, thankfully—though he had taken the time to leave his "mark" on their clothes. But the garments would wash well enough, and she had scrubbed clothes clean of worse.

"Let me have your other hand."

She hesitated, wondering how he knew, then saw a smile slip in behind his eyes.

"A trunk has two handles." He shrugged. "So I'm only assuming."

He washed her other hand, the blisters on that palm broken as well, the flesh the same watery mess. As he tended her sores, she let herself look at him. *Really* look at him. He was handsome, just like Da had been. Dark-haired, broad-shouldered, well-muscled. Wade had that same easy charm about him too. She'd seen Da charm others to get what he wanted countless times. Only, never in all her life had she seen him treat Mam, or her, or her siblings with one ounce of the kindness Wade was showing her now.

He rose. "Tempy will have some salve, I'm sure. And bandages. Shall we? Once I go grab a shirt, of course. I don't think Tempy will allow me into her kitchen otherwise."

Despite his actions in the moment, Catriona found herself weighing what little she knew about Wade Cunningham against all she didn't. And though part of her wanted to believe he was a man who could be trusted, the internal scales within her still dipped heavily toward caution.

On their way toward the house, they made a quick detour to a pretty little cottage nestled in a stand of pine trees—the overseer's cottage, he called it—where Wade ducked inside for a moment, then returned sporting a shirt almost as wrinkled as his trousers. Together, they walked in the direction of the McGavocks' house.

The chickens had quieted, and the trill of birdsong filled the morning. From a distant field, the low of cattle drifted toward them, and a sweetness layered the air that could only be described as the promise of spring. It tugged at the homesickness inside her.

A good distance off to their right stood a cluster of tombstones. The McGavock family cemetery, she assumed. Towering over the graves hulked an ancient oak whose branches reached from one side of the picket fence encircling the cemetery to the other. The tree resembled a sentinel taking rest after a long night's watch, and she wished again that she could have given Mam, Bridget, and Alma a finer resting place than a pauper's field. A resting place like this. Thinking of their precious bodies being so far outside her care still left her with an empty feeling.

She sneaked a look at Wade beside her. Sensing he was waiting for her to answer his earlier question about what happened—and that he wouldn't wait much longer—she was tempted to let the whole truth just spill out. To tell him everything. But prudence tugged at the hem of that choice, reminding her of past occasions when she'd trusted only to regret it.

"I'm out of money," she said simply, keeping to the truth. "I thought I had more than I did. But in the end . . ." She lifted a shoulder, then let it fall, hoping that would spare her from having to say more.

His silence challenged that hope, and when they reached the outside door to the kitchen, he paused.

"So you have nothing left, then?"

"Sixteen cents." She gave a humorless laugh. "And a dozen chickens, if you don't go changin' your mind about givin' me your share."

He smiled, his gaze holding hers fast. She told herself to look away, knowing full well that the eyes revealed a depth of truth about a person. *"Windows to the soul,"* Mam called them. And his eyes, with that bluish-gray color, were kind—and astute and discerning. Catriona looked away first.

Her palms ached, and she glanced down at them, worrying over how long it would take for them to heal. Time was not on her side. She needed a job. A way to earn a wage. But who would care for Nora while she worked? Aware of his continued stare, she looked up. "I do have a plan, though," she said quickly. "I'll head back into town and—"

"Why don't we just have breakfast for now, Catriona." He reached for the door. "Then we'll talk about your plan."

CHAPTER 23

"I 'bout got your poultice ready, *Miss* O'Toole." Tempy stood across the kitchen stirring a pot on the stove, but Wade didn't miss the look she threw him over her shoulder.

He caught the slight inflection in her voice too. But Catriona, seated at the table in the corner with Nora—both of them intent on a breakfast of eggs and bacon—didn't appear to.

Tempy was letting him know she hadn't forgotten about catching him eavesdropping in the entrance hall that first day. And as if that incident hadn't adequately sabotaged her opinion of him, she'd also caught him in a lie of sorts when he'd said he hoped to walk Miss O'Toole back to town. And this, after he'd already mistakenly referred to Catriona as *Mrs.* Granted, not one of his finer moments as an operative for the United States Secret Service.

Tempy removed the pot from the stove. "Let's just let this cool for a bit, then we'll get those hands o' yours fixed up, ma'am."

Catriona offered a grateful smile. "I'm most grateful to you, Tempy. And for this breakfast too. It's tastin' so good."

Beaming, Tempy smoothed her tiny hands down

the front of her apron, humble pride in the gesture. Wade knew the two women had seen each other previously, but they hadn't been formally introduced. He'd seen to that right off. Tempy had taken an instant liking to Catriona, which wasn't surprising to him. Tempy hadn't peppered her with questions either but seemed to know intuitively that her situation was dire.

"I'm out of money," Catriona had told him a while earlier. *"I thought I had more than I did."*

Wade wanted to take her comment at face value, but he couldn't. Something didn't fit. Not that people couldn't miscount—and even mismanage— their money. But to go from staying in a hotel one night to sleeping outside the next? A piece of the puzzle was missing.

Catriona O'Toole impressed him as being entirely more organized and conscientious than that, and he knew Nora's welfare was of the highest priority to her. And that little shoulder shrug she'd given him. He'd seen that often enough from people eager to change the subject. Or evade the truth. But one thing he knew for sure. He needed to apologize to her for interfering with Nora earlier. In that moment, however, sending the child away had been the only option he could think of so he could talk to Catriona privately. To try to get through to her.

She'd looked so lost and broken yet so determined to keep that wall up between them. Gradually, she had let him in, at least a little. And he was glad she had. Because they were friends. *Friends*. That word caused a little hiccup in his thoughts, but he ignored it, much as he needed to ignore his growing attraction to her and move on. Which he determined, again, to do.

Already finished with breakfast, he savored a long sip of coffee, purposefully redirecting his thoughts to the note in his pocket. He was eager to retrieve whatever had been left for him at the coordinates listed therein. He hoped something substantial had turned up. Information on someone in town, perhaps.

Aware of Tempy's attention drifting over to him, he caught the woman's gaze and raised his mug in mock salute. "My compliments to you, Tempy. Best coffee I've had in ages. Thank you, ma'am."

She gave him a knowing look. "Mmm-hmm. You's *so* welcome, Mister Cunningham."

Wade smiled. One uphill step at a time.

"May I be havin' more bacon, Tempy?" Nora asked.

"*Nora.*" Catriona shook her head. "You've had enough of that bacon. No more."

"But, Cattie, I'm—"

"Nay, wee one! Don't you be sayin' those words to me again. You cannot be hungry after all you've been stuffin' into that belly."

One side of Nora's mouth tipped.

"Miss O'Toole"—Tempy held up a spatula—"I got plenty more if your little sister wants some, ma'am. Master Winder, he eats just like that.

Stuffs hisself like a prized hog at a county fair. But I guess these children, they need to 'cause they gonna be runnin' it off when they play today."

Catriona rose and carried her empty plate to the wash bucket. "Oh, we're not stayin'. I'm just gettin' me chickens a man in town gave us, then Nora and I will be on our way."

Wade perked up.

"But I want to *stay!*" Nora whined. "I want to play with Winder. He's me friend!"

With a severe look, Catriona silenced her sister, but Wade could still hear the two ladies' fiery exchange without either of them uttering a word.

He tried for a casual tone. "I thought we agreed to discuss your plans after breakfast, Miss O'Toole."

Catriona looked over. "Aye, and we still can. But I've had time to think about what it is I'm wantin' to do."

Wade nodded, knowing better than to disagree with her outright. Especially seeing that determined expression. Gone were the humility and brokenness from moments earlier. Back in place, stubbornness and hardened resolve. Which meant the idea he planned to present to her would likely be met with opposition, and that was putting it mildly. He needed to broach it carefully.

He carried his mug to the wash bucket and sidled up beside her. "What if—"

"Miss O'Toole, I's ready for you over here, ma'am!" Tempy announced, her voice seeming overly loud in the quiet.

Wade turned to see the woman holding up the pot from the stove. Maybe it was his imagination, but he thought he detected a spark of protectiveness in her tone.

"Let's get them blisters of yours seen to. The sooner, the better."

Deciding it *was* his imagination, Wade resigned himself to waiting—and to another mug of coffee.

Catriona joined Tempy at the table, and with the tenderness of a mother and the expert touch of a nurse, the older woman applied the poultice to her palms.

Nora joined them, wrinkling her nose. "That's smellin' awful."

Tempy laughed. "It ain't got the best smell, you's right. But it sure will help with the healin'."

A gentle breeze rustled the blue-and-white-checked curtains in the open windows looking out toward the barn, and a large pot of something savory Tempy was cooking simmered on the stove. Wade leaned up against the cupboard, enjoying his coffee, and watched from across the room.

Catriona sighed. "The pain is already startin' to ease some. Thank you."

With an endearing look, Tempy wrapped Catriona's palms in clean strips of cloth. "My mama done taught me how to make this poultice when I's just a girl. Come in handy through the years too. Little bit of mustard and some herbs. Stir that with a measure of milk and an egg or two, then throw in some chunks of day-ol' bread for the bindin'."

Catriona's features softened. "Our own dear mam, Nora's and mine, God rest her, had her own recipe for poulticin' wounds. As I'm rememberin', it had a smell to it much like this one does."

Tempy snipped the tails of the bandages, ripped them down the middle, then gently tied them off. "She been gone long, Miss O'Toole? Your *mam,* you called her?"

"Nay," Catriona whispered. "We buried her in December."

Wade paused, coffee mug to his lips. That was scarcely three months ago. So recent. Catriona kept her eyes down, and Nora turned away as though not wanting to see her sister's sadness. Watching them, he felt the weight of their loss in his own chest.

So not only was their brother missing—or most likely dead, if indeed Ryan had been with Cleburne's men the night of the battle—but they'd also had to say good-bye to their mother. Both separations he knew only too well. They hadn't mentioned their father, so he figured it was safe to assume he had already passed too.

Tempy patted Catriona's arm. "The hurt's still feelin' fresh for you, I know. Feels fresh to you both." She touched Nora's cheek, and the girl's eyes filled with tears. "But it gets better. The pain don't ever go 'way, really. Leastwise, not the whole of it. But over time, your heart soaks it up. Then the good Lord comes along and slathers a salve right over what's left of the hurt." The lightness of hope filled her voice. "Same as he'll do for the pain you feelin' over missin' your mam. Only, *his* salve is sweeter smellin' than mine—and heals a whole lot better too!"

Catriona gradually lifted her gaze, a trace of tears in her eyes—and what Wade interpreted to be disbelief as though she doubted Tempy's counsel would hold true for her. He read the same in Nora's expression, along with confusion.

The little girl shook her head. "But what about Bridget and Alma? Will God be slatherin' our missin' them too?"

Tempy looked at Nora, then Catriona, her brow furrowing.

"Bridget and Alma were our sisters," Catriona offered quietly. "They were twelve and ten when they died . . . weeks before Mam."

For the longest time, Tempy stared, then slowly exhaled, shaking her head. "I ain't one to question the Lord's goodness. But sometimes it sure feels like he can give a body too much to bear, don't it?"

Catriona and Nora offered no response, but Wade found his own thoughts reflecting Tempy's. Their entire family gone. In a handful of months, it sounded like. Then to leave their home and come to a land so far away. In search of a brother they couldn't find and likely never would. A heavy burden indeed.

For a long moment, Tempy simply held their hands, the three of them sharing a silent, intimate kinship of grief. Wade watched from across the kitchen, feeling like an outsider, completely excluded from the conversation, all but forgotten—and privileged beyond words.

"Where is your mam, Tempy?" Nora finally asked, such innocence in the question.

The older woman smiled. "Oh, I said good-bye to my mam years ago, darlin'. She long gone to be with Jesus now. My husband too. He was a big ol' mountain of a man." Her mouth tipped further. "You woulda liked him, and he woulda made you laugh! He had a way of grinnin' that got your own mouth just to twitchin'. We ain't never had children, Isum and me. So I's the only one left. 'Cept for a brother and sister I had once. They was younger than me. But I ain't seen 'em since I's a child."

"Where are they now?" Catriona asked.

Wade winced, knowing Catriona hadn't thought the question through. Then again, she might not be as familiar with the former practice of slavery in this country as he'd assumed.

Tempy squinted as though trying to see something far away. "Oh, they was sold separate from Mama and me, 'fore we was brought here to Carnton from over in Montgomery in Alabama. And that was nigh onto . . . sixty-seven years ago now, I reckon. I cried over Rufus and Jinsey for months, Mama told me. Still miss 'em too." She lowered her eyes. "No matter that I can't even remember what they looked like."

A shadow crossed Catriona's expression as truth apparently took deeper hold. She reached over and covered Tempy's hand, and something Wade felt deep down inside him passed between the two women.

As Tempy instructed Catriona on when to change the bandages, Wade busied himself at the wash bucket, rinsing his mug, more determined than ever to help Catriona and Nora in any way he could.

He watched for the right moment to pull Catriona aside. It finally came when Nora and Tempy began talking about baking some cookies. He gestured to Catriona and moved closer, then leaned in.

"I have an idea," he whispered. "If you're finished in here, why don't we talk outside for a minute?" He pointed toward the back door.

She gave a slight nod, but her expression seemed hesitant.

"Anything else you be needin' over there, Miss O'Toole?" Tempy asked, her tone undeniably attentive.

"Nay, I'm fine. Thank you again for the breakfast"—Catriona held up her hands and smiled—"and for this." She looked at her sister. "Nora, let's be goin' now."

Wade gave Catriona a look. "I was hoping we might speak outside *alone*."

She eyed him. "And I'm just supposed to be leavin' me sister behind?" she whispered. "Nora's not Tempy's responsibility. She's mine."

With that, she skirted around him, and Wade realized then what she'd done. He couldn't fault

373

her for it. She was keeping Nora close at hand in the hope of avoiding a frank discussion with him. Whereas, earlier, he'd sent Nora on an errand in the hope of having one.

Touché, Miss O'Toole.

Wade opened the back door and indicated for Catriona and Nora to precede him outside.

"I'm goin' to go find Winder!" Nora yelled as she took off for the barn.

"Nay, you are *not!*"

Catriona's firm tone stopped Nora short.

"You're stayin' right here with me, child."

Nora sighed. "But why? You're not needin' me, Cattie."

Wade hung back a little, observing the exchange. The barbed back-and-forth between them was becoming familiar.

"In fact, I am needin' you. I'm needin' your help in gettin' the chickens together."

"Och!" Nora made a face. "I'm hatin' them chickens!"

"Hatin' them or not, they're ours. And we're takin' them to town to sell."

Nora's expression perked up. "Then we're comin' back here?"

"Nay. We'll find another place to stay for the night. Perhaps a—"

"I'm not campin' no more, Cattie! I'm not havin' some stinkin' oaf of a man bellowin' about, throwin' our trunk and almost wallopin' me in the—"

"I said nothin' about more campin'!" Catriona countered quickly, raising her voice.

But Wade found the sideways glance she slid him almost as revealing as Nora's statements. "A stinking oaf of a man who threw the trunk?" He looked from one to the other, his imagination running rampant.

"Aye," Nora said. "He was a big man too. With a whale of a belly, and he—"

"Nora!" Catriona bit out. "Are you forgettin' what you said to me earlier?"

"Nay, I'm not forgettin'. But the oaf threw the trunk straight for me. Meanin' to bash me head in! Then he chased us." The girl's attention swung back to Wade. "We had to hide in the—"

"That is enough, Nora!" Catriona stepped forward. "I know full well what you're tryin' to do. And it won't work."

Nora's eyes went hot. "Well, we shouldn't be stayin' where I could get walloped in the head! You promised Mam you'd take care of me. And if she could be seein' us, I don't think she'd be approvin' of your *campin'*! Or of us not havin' anythin' to eat. That's *not* takin' care of me!"

Catriona opened her mouth as if to respond, then clamped her lips closed tight. A stricken look came over her face, Nora's comments apparently finding their mark.

Nora's expression, on the other hand, was defiant. The girl looked ready to do battle. Yet as the sisters stared at each other, the tender thread of family binding them together pulled tighter and tighter until Catriona's breath quickened and Wade sensed the balance shifting.

"I'm far from perfect, wee one," Catriona whispered, her voice fragile. Her gaze was centered on Nora, yet Wade sensed she intended the comment for him as well. "I'm knowin' that full well. I also know that campin' last night 'twas not for the best. I won't be takin' that kind of risk again. And while I'm not knowin' whether Mam can see us, I *am* doin' me best, Nora. I g-give you me word."

Wade felt his heart react to the stumble in her voice and then again when Nora's expression faltered. Frowning, the girl looked downward and away in a silent acknowledgment of guilt, and regret drained a measure of defiance from her diminutive features.

Seeing an opportunity and wanting to help, he took a step forward. "If I may, I'd like to offer a suggestion in the hope of improving your situation."

Catriona looked at him, her eyes glassy yet the determination in them undeniable. "Mr. Cunningham, while I appreciate your—"

Nora sucked in a breath and pointed. "Look!"

Wade turned to see the mother cat sauntering from the barn, her litter of kittens frolicking behind her.

"*Please,* Cattie, can I go see Bertha and her wee kits?"

Catriona hesitated, and Wade clearly saw the

conflict within her. If she kept Nora here, the girl would hear the suggestion he had, and no doubt Catriona dreaded Nora favoring any idea she did not. That meant another battle would ensue. But if she let Nora go, she'd be faced with a discussion she didn't wish to have.

So he simply watched and waited, fairly certain the odds were in his favor.

CHAPTER 24

"Aye, Nora, you may go," Catriona finally managed to say, keenly aware of Wade's close attention. The girl made a beeline for the cat and her kittens, and Catriona turned to confront Wade, her pride battered but her ire sufficiently stoked. Did the man think she lacked the sense to see what he was trying to do?

"Wade, I—"

"What I want to suggest," he began again, speaking over her, "is that you allow me to let the two of you stay in the—"

"*Wade,*" she tried again, more forcefully this time. She met his surprised gaze straight on, her tone unexpectedly firm compared to the brokenness she felt. "First, while I sincerely appreciate the kindness you've shown to me and Nora since we met, I cannot—and *will not*—abide you intentionally tryin' to pit me sister against me."

He briefly looked away. "Catriona, I was actually going to—"

"I'm not finished," she said, needing to get through this, collect Nora, and be on their way.

He stared, looking none too pleased—which, oddly, fueled her gumption.

"I'm havin' a big enough challenge with Nora

as 'tis, which I'm sure you're seein' only too well for yeself. So I don't need anyone else conspirin' against me." She briefly glanced behind her to make sure her sister was still with the cats. She was, although the girl was slowly following the entourage around the corner of the barn. Catriona started to call out to her, but she didn't want to risk another "You're always tellin' me what to do" tantrum. But oh, she *had* to get control of her. And swiftly.

A reprisal of desperation rose inside her, and the same questions flogging her confidence earlier renewed their defeatist chant. After the money from the chickens was gone, what then? How would she earn a wage? Who would care for Nora while she worked? Where would they live?

She still didn't have any answers, but the breakfast Tempy served them had renewed not only her physical strength but her determination. Not to mention how the woman had doctored her hands. The blisters still stung but not nearly as much. The pain was negligible, and Catriona felt her self-assurance returning. She could do this. She *would* do this. She looked back at Wade.

"So while I appreciate the offer you were goin' to make, to pay for our stay at the hotel, I'm not at all comfortable with that arrangement. As I said before, I'll be gettin' me chickens and will sell them in town, then I'll find a suitable place for us to stay. Next, I need to be findin' a way to earn a wage."

He opened his mouth.

"*And* before you go askin' again"—she held up a bandaged hand, then quickly lowered it, the sight of the damaged appendage not inspiring confidence—"I don't wish to talk further about what happened with the campin'. It's done and over with." She nodded as though that gesture alone would prevent him from pursuing the topic. "Now, if you'd be so kind, let's get me chickens." She glanced toward an empty wagon, one of three parked off to the side of the barn. "And perhaps I can borrow a conveyance. I'll promptly be returnin' it before the day's out, of course."

He said nothing. Only stared.

She waited as frustration darkened his handsome features.

"Are you quite finished, Catriona?"

"Aye," she responded, suddenly feeling significantly smaller beneath his unwavering appraisal. She squared her shoulders, his own looking formidable in comparison.

"Good." He sighed. "First, I was *attempting* to apologize to you a moment ago for my interfering with Nora earlier. It was wrong of me. I shouldn't have done that, and I'm sorry. I hope you'll forgive me."

Catriona blinked. The man was admitting he was in the wrong? And asking for her pardon? That was the last thing she'd expected—and more than a smidgen of doubt clouded the moment. But his gentle tone mirrored the sincerity in his expression. "Wade, I didn't realize—"

"I'm not finished yet," he continued, the barest hint of a smile tipping one side of his mouth.

Catriona promptly closed hers.

"Second, I was *not* going to offer to pay for you to stay in the hotel in town. What I was—and still am—offering is for you and Nora to stay in the overseer's cottage. Just temporarily, until you can find appropriate accommodations." He nodded in the direction of the quaint little dwelling they'd visited earlier. "I'd need to secure the McGavocks' permission, of course. But given the circumstances, I don't think they'll object."

She shook her head. "Wade, I don't—"

"And before you say no outright—" He held up a forefinger as though to shush her.

For a moment, she thought he was going to touch her lips. But he didn't. So why did a warm tingle still work a slow-spinning spiral down inside her?

"I think you should come and see the cottage for yourself," he continued. "It's quite comfortable, and it won't cost you anything. Not even sixteen cents."

He smiled, and for the first time she noticed the faint laugh lines framing the corners of his eyes and mouth, which only served to make him even more appealing. She wondered again if her first impressions of the man had been wholly off the mark. Yet she didn't think so. Even now she sensed that silent voice of warning deep inside her. Only,

382

the warning itself felt different somehow—and even more urgent.

There was no way she could accept his offer, not when doing so would make her beholden not only to him but to the McGavocks as well. That was part of her family history she would *not* be repeating. "Wade, while I appreciate your willingness to—"

"Just come and see it," he insisted, then offered his arm.

She looked down at it, then up at him, a little taken aback yet again by his gentlemanly insistence but also surprised at how tempting it was to slip her hand through. How wonderful it would feel to be taken care of. How long had it been since she'd known that luxury? Yet the silent warning within her escalated with each passing second.

The kitchen door burst open.

"Miss O'Toole!"

Tempy bustled toward them, her white apron wafting. The tiny slip of a woman covered ground faster than Catriona would have imagined a woman her age could, and her expression bordered on fierce.

"I'm needin' you in the kitchen, ma'am!" Tempy called, out of breath. "I can't wait for later neither!"

Upon reaching them, Tempy all but inserted herself between Catriona and Wade, giving him a wilting stare. Wade responded with a slightly raised eyebrow, and Catriona looked from one to the other, confused. She'd been under the impression that Tempy was smitten with Wade Cunningham, but apparently she'd been mistaken. She wasn't wearing the look of a woman smitten. More like a woman wanting to *smite!*

Tempy gestured toward the house. "You come on with me, Miss O'Toole. I . . . I got somethin' to show you in the kitchen right quick."

Catriona sensed the older woman was simply making that up. But for all the world, she didn't know why. Unless it had something to do with Tempy's aversion to Wade. "All right. I'll be comin' with you—"

A scream split the air.

Catriona turned in the direction of the barn, knowing that voice. Her heart leapt to her throat. "Nora!" she yelled and then took off running. Heavy footfalls behind her told her Wade was following.

No sooner did she round the corner of the barn than she saw a Negro man striding toward her, carrying Nora in his arms.

"It's hurtin' me!" Nora cried, cradling her right arm to her chest, her face pale and tear-streaked.

Catriona hurried to meet them. "What happened?" She reached out to take her sister.

"No, Cattie! Don't touch it!" Nora screamed and clenched her jaw. Her breath came in gasps.

Then Catriona saw it—a slight protrusion beneath the skin of Nora's forearm—and her knees went weak. "Oh, dearest . . ."

"I called you, Cattie, but you didn't come!" Nora

cried. "I slipped and I tried to hold on! And you never came!" She looked down at her own right arm, and her eyes widened. She opened her mouth as if to scream again, and Catriona braced herself.

"*Nora,* look at me," Wade commanded, compassion softening his voice.

Nora blinked. Her teary gaze shifted, her chin quivering.

"You've broken the bone in your arm," he continued, "and I know it hurts, honey. But you're going to be all right, I promise."

He exchanged a look with the man holding Nora, and Catriona got the distinct feeling they already knew each other.

"Pender here is going to carry you inside the house. Your sister will go with you, and I'll go fetch a doctor."

"Nay," Nora whined, her features growing even paler. "I'm not likin' doctors! They say they'll fix things but never do!"

He smoothed a hand over her red curls. "It's going to be all right," he whispered.

Nora drew in a ragged breath, and even as Catriona detected the bloom of trust in her sister's eyes, she felt the subtle stir of jealousy in her own chest.

She pressed closer. "I'm goin' to take care of you, wee one, so don't you go worryin' any about it." Ignoring the uncertainty slipping into Nora's expression, Catriona looked up at Pender. "Did you see what happened?"

He shook his head. "I didn't, ma'am. But I found her at the base of the loft ladder in the barn. My guess is she was trying to climb up to the hayloft. I happened to be passing by when I heard the screaming."

The guilty scowl crossing Nora's face told Catriona that was likely the truth of it, her sister going where she had no business going.

Tempy joined them. "Oh, gracious sakes alive," she whispered, huddling close. She motioned to Pender. "Get this sweet child to the kitchen, Isham. Meanwhile . . ." She looked at Wade. "Sir, you go fetch ol' Caesar and ask him to come and set the bone."

"Old Caesar?" Wade frowned. "I was headed into town to get a doctor."

Tempy shook her head. "Ain't no need for that. Ol' Caesar can set a bone better than any doctor I ever seen. And this one don't look too bad. You can find him over yonder at the smithy."

"He's a blacksmith?" Catriona and Wade questioned in unison, and Catriona resisted the urge to sneak a look at him.

Tempy leveled a gaze at them both. "That's right. And he's the best bonesetter I seen in all my livelong days. He got a gift for it. And he don't cost you a lot of coin like a doctor either, ma'am, if that matters. He treats a person fair, and he sets the bone so gentle-like, the healin' comes swifter too."

Catriona hesitated. A *blacksmith* setting a bone?

386

That didn't sound promising. Yet she trusted Tempy. Look at what the woman had done with the wounds on her hands. Catriona glanced at Wade in an attempt to read what he thought, but she found him looking at Isham Pender. She saw an almost imperceptible nod pass between the two men, and she quickly looked away, not wanting either of them to know she'd seen it. But there was no question in her mind now. The two men indeed knew each other—and well.

Nora's breath quickened. "It's hurtin' somethin' awful, Cattie."

Catriona included Tempy and Wade in her glance. "Please, let's be askin' ol' Caesar to come and help us."

Wade took off in what she assumed was the direction of the smithy, and Tempy led the way back to the house. Catriona fell into step beside Pender and gently laid a bandaged hand on her sister's leg, half expecting Nora to object. But her sister's eyes were closed tightly, and she whimpered as though every step brought a spike of pain.

The man carefully adjusted Nora in his arms. "You won't regret your decision, ma'am," he said softly. "If I had a bone needing to be set, I wouldn't want anyone but Caesar doing it."

"That's mighty good to be knowin'."

Tempy held open the door to the kitchen. "Come on inside, Isham. Let's take her up to my bedroom. She'll be more comfortable on the bed."

Catriona followed them up a narrow flight of stairs that led from the kitchen to a hallway on the second floor. The hallway opened to three rooms. Bedrooms, she assumed, the first belonging to Tempy. The furnishings were sparse and simple, but the room was neatly kept. A Bible lay in a prominent position on the bedside table, and as she drew closer, she saw tiny slips of paper sticking out from the top of the pages.

Pender gently deposited Nora on the bed, and Catriona knelt beside her. Mindful of the bandages wrapped around her palms, she felt the girl's forehead with her fingertips. Nora's skin was clammy to the touch.

Still cradling her arm to her chest, Nora hiccupped a breath and opened her eyes. Tears slid down her temples. "Am I dyin', Cattie?"

Catriona smiled down. "Nay, dearest, you're not dyin'. The bone in your arm needs a little mendin', that's all. And Mr. Cunningham is fetchin' someone right now who's goin' to come and do just that."

Tempy covered Nora's legs with a light blanket. "I'm gonna make the child some tea with herbs and such that'll help with the hurtin'."

"Thank you, Tempy," Catriona whispered, then noticed how featherlight the woman's steps sounded as she descended the wooden staircase. Catriona stood. "Thank you as well, Pender."

The man smiled, and the gesture did wonders to soften what was otherwise a most serious countenance. "I'm glad to be of help, ma'am. As you heard, the name's Isham Pender. I work over at the sawmill."

He kept his voice soft, and she did likewise, watchful of Nora. Of average height, he was broad-chested, strong-looking, and had a quiet but commanding presence. He reminded her of someone, but she couldn't think who. Then it occurred to her. He reminded her of Wade. He carried himself with the same confidence and conveyed the same self-assured demeanor. Which made her earlier assumption about the two men even more intriguing. They'd conducted themselves as near-strangers, yet the look she saw pass between them said otherwise.

"I'm Catriona O'Toole. And this is me sister, Nora."

He nodded. "Good to meet you, ma'am. I take it you're a friend of the McGavocks'."

She let out a breath. "Nay, not at all. You might be sayin' I'm more a friend of Mr. Cunningham's."

Surprise showed in his eyes. "Have you known each other long?"

She shook her head. "We met only recently. But he's been of some help to both Nora and me." She paused. "What about the two of you? Have you been acquainted for some time?"

"Oh, I was just recently introduced to our new overseer. The colonel just hired him."

Catriona nodded but said nothing, weighing his response.

"Have you been in Franklin for a while, ma'am?"

"Nay. Only a few days now."

"Well, it's a good place to set down roots."

"Oh, I doubt we'll be doin' any of that."

"Why not? It's a nice enough town."

"Aye, 'tis. But we're findin' our circumstances have changed, and—" Realizing the conversation was taking a turn she didn't wish it to take with someone she didn't know, she hurried to change the subject. "We'll simply have to see what comes next and then decide. Have *you* been at Carnton long?"

"Only about four months."

"And what brought you here?"

"The work," he said simply. "I needed a job, and the colonel had an opening in the mill."

While the man's Southern accent was pronounced, his pattern of speech differed from Tempy's and the other freed men and women she'd met. *Freed men and women.* That's what she'd heard other people call the former slaves. Isham Pender's speech was more formal sounding. Like Wade's.

Then a thought occurred to her. Maybe he hadn't been enslaved. Had all colored people been slaves before the North won the war and set them free? She didn't know. Either way, she was grateful that those who were had been granted their freedom. Surely Ryan had wrestled with fighting a war on the side that favored enslavement. Not that conscription had given him a choice in the matter.

But she could imagine how that would have bothered her brother.

Had it ever bothered Wade? She hoped it had. Yet he'd given no indication of such when she'd confronted him about it. And he had most definitely had a choice.

Boot steps sounded in the kitchen below, followed by heavy treads on the staircase. Wade entered the bedroom first, then Tempy behind him, cup and saucer in hand. They were followed by a man who looked every bit a blacksmith but nothing at all like any bonesetter she'd ever seen.

CHAPTER 25

Catriona fought the urge to tell them all she'd changed her mind. That she didn't want this massive mountain of a man with hands as huge as meat cleavers laying hold of her sister's wee, injured arm. What if, even by accident, he did more harm than good? She'd seen the results of bones badly mended after poor setting, and she couldn't stand the thought of that kind of deformity following Nora throughout her life.

Tempy came alongside her. "Miss O'Toole, this here's ol' Caesar. He been at Carnton 'bout long as I have, and he's as good a man as ever was."

Sweat beaded the man's brow, and an unruly salt-and-pepper beard all but masked the smile ghosting his mouth. "Now, Miss Tempy . . . You oughtn't lie like that, ma'am. And you bein' a God-fearin' woman and all." His deep voice resonated in the quiet of the bedroom.

With a kind look, he acknowledged Catriona, then his gaze slipped past her to Nora.

He walked as far as the foot of the bed, where Catriona intercepted him, her heart beating like a snared bird's. She swallowed and tried to speak, but the words wouldn't come. His eyes were the color of sunlight shining through honey, and she could almost feel the warmth on her face.

"I ain't gonna hurt your sister none, ma'am. Miss Tempy done told me what happened, and I believe I can fix it. If'n you want me to."

From the corner of her eye, Catriona saw Wade give a slow nod, and somehow she knew he meant it for her. Still, she couldn't quell the trepidation inside her. Should she insist on fetching a real doctor from town? A physician who had the education and skills to perform a proper procedure? Or did she say aye to this man who had no credentials but clearly held the trust of the people in this room?

Acting on borrowed faith, she stepped to one side. "Aye, Caesar. I do."

The blacksmith walked to the bed and leaned over. Nora's gaze on him was wide and watchful.

"Bless you, child," he whispered, then tenderly touched her forehead and closed his eyes. Catriona watched, not knowing what he was doing but aware of his lips moving.

"Now, Miss Nora," he began after a moment, taking hold of Nora's sound arm, "I'm gonna get a readin' on your good arm first. See how the good Lord knit you together in your mama's womb. This part won't hurt none. Not even a little."

He encircled the top of her left arm in his enormous grip, his dark skin a sharp contrast to her pale complexion. Then he closed his eyes and slowly moved his hand down her arm bit by bit, stopping at some points, his brow furrowing in concentration.

"You a strong little thing, ain't you?" he said, opening his eyes long enough to see Nora's meager nod in agreement.

When he reached her wrist, he straightened a little and turned his attention to her right arm. But Nora whimpered and pressed farther back into the bed.

"It's all right, little miss," he said gently. "I ain't gonna do nothin' without tellin' you 'bout it first. You got my word on that. Ol' Caesar don't like surprises no more'n you do."

He glanced back at Tempy, who still held the cup and saucer in her hand.

Tempy gently eased onto the side of the bed. "I made you some tea, sweet one. It's gonna make your belly feel real warm. How 'bout you just pretend it's some of Tempy's hot cocoa and take some good long sips."

Nora's expression clouded. "What's . . . hot chocolate?"

Tempy's mouth dropped open. "You ain't never had hot chocolate, child?"

Nora shook her head, her expression leaning toward distraught.

Tempy laughed softly. "Well, we'll have to fix that right up soon as you're able."

Nora smiled a tiny bit, but the fear in her eyes overpowered it.

Tempy held up the teacup. "This is gonna make

you a mite sleepy, too, like you's driftin' on a fluffy cloud on a summer day. Just floatin' along with all them butterflies and birds flittin' round. You think you can drink a few swallows for me?"

Nora nodded and started to rise up when her face pinched in pain.

"No, darlin'." Tempy patted her little chest. "You just lay right there. Let Tempy bring the tea to you." The woman pulled a soup spoon from her apron pocket and proceeded to dip it, then hold it to Nora's lips. Dip and drink. Dip and drink. A handful of moments later, the cup was empty, and Nora's eyes grew heavy.

Catriona watched the scene, and for an instant she was pulled from the moment. She looked around the room. How had she and Nora arrived here? Not in Franklin. She knew the reason behind that journey only too well. And the one to Carnton too. Nay, how had they arrived among these people who, only days earlier, had been complete strangers? If something like this had happened to Nora elsewhere—say in town, perhaps, or while they'd been traveling somewhere along the way—what would she have done? How would she have cared for her sister? Tears pricked her eyes.

"Miss O'Toole?"

She blinked and looked at Caesar. The question in his expression led her to think he'd said her name once before. "Aye, sir?" She noticed Wade standing close to the bedside.

396

Kindness lit Caesar's face. "I'm gonna need your help, ma'am. If you'll get on the other side of the bed there . . . Ease onto it so as not to give her a jolt. And, Mister Cunningham, if you'll move that table away from the bed and get where you can hold Miss Nora's shoulders when the times comes . . . Then I'll tell you both what to do as we go along."

Catriona did as he asked, aware of Nora's eyes opening and closing. She was struggling to remain conscious, and Catriona didn't blame her one bit.

"All right, little miss . . ." Caesar leaned close, the smell of hard work clinging to his clothes. "Can you still hear me?"

Nora exhaled. "Aye. But why are you swayin' like some bloomin' tree?"

Caesar smiled in response, but his attention was focused on her arm and the bone protruding beneath the skin. He studied the wound, the area around the break already beginning to bruise. "I want you to take some deep breaths for me, little miss. Will you do that?"

Nora complied, and each time she exhaled, her eyes stayed closed a bit longer, her hold on consciousness gradually slipping away. Part of Caesar's objective, no doubt.

"While you keep breathin' deep," he continued, "I'm gonna slip your bone back into place, so it can mend up just as good and strong as it was before. That way you can run and climb with the best of 'em. Does that sound good to you, child?"

Nora didn't respond, her breathing quiet and even, her chest moving rhythmically up and down.

Catriona brushed a curl back from her sister's forehead, regret sinking its teeth deep. She should have called Nora back from following after those kittens. If she'd done that, this never would have happened. What kind of parent was she? Not a good one, that was for certain.

"Little miss?" Caesar said firmly. "Can you hear me?"

Nora didn't move.

The blacksmith looked over. "Miss O'Toole"— he glanced at Wade—"and sir, we'll be workin' real quick. We only got a few minutes 'fore she wakes up again. And we *all* want her asleep while we do this."

Wade nodded, and Catriona did likewise, her stomach a little queasy.

"It's a clean break," Caesar continued. "I ain't seen or felt any shards of bone, which is a good thing. The most important part for you two is that you keep her still while I set the break. The pain's gonna wake her up soon enough, and when that happens, we can't have her jerkin' and movin' about. 'Specially if I'm not done yet. So hold her shoulders secure."

Catriona nodded again. "I understand."

"Will do," Wade said quietly.

Caesar cupped his enormous hands around the top of Nora's right arm, first one, then the other just below it, and with painstaking slowness, he inched his way downward, his face bathed in sweat. "When I get to where the bone is broke, you gonna hear somethin' that sounds a little like crunchin', ma'am. But don't you mind it none. It's just the bone goin' back into place like it should. Your little sister ain't gonna feel a thing. Miss Tempy done seen to that."

Catriona nodded, her stomach moving from queasy to a full-on roil. She breathed in through her nose and out through her mouth, keeping her gaze on Nora's beautiful face. On her eyes and the gentle upsweep of her pretty lashes, on her button nose and her rosy cheekbones—

Then she heard it. A sound like boots on crushed gravel. A chill swept through her. She couldn't keep the tears from coming. *Oh Lord, please let this man be makin' me wee sister whole again. Don't let her go through life with an arm all mangled and twisted. Help me be what she's needin' me to be. Because right now, as we both know, I'm sorely failin' at it.*

She recognized the words for what they were. A desperate prayer for help, and the first she'd uttered in some time. The words felt traitorous somehow, in opposition to the silent wall she'd constructed and reinforced in recent months. Years even. Would the Almighty answer a plea from someone who wasn't even certain he was watching anymore? Or that he even cared enough to listen, much less respond?

"Are you all right, Catriona?" Wade whispered.

Without looking at him, she nodded, uncertain whether she was.

Nora's eyes fluttered, and Catriona's pulse ticked up a notch. "Hurry, *please,*" she whispered. "She's comin' awake."

"We're almost there." Caesar's deep voice was strained as he tenderly probed Nora's arm again. "I just wanna make sure the bone's back in place good and sound 'fore we go wrappin' it up snug. Miss Tempy, I'm gonna need those—"

Tempy appeared by the bed, long strips of bandages in hand.

"We gonna do this together," Caesar said, glancing at each of them. "And we gonna do it quick but good. Don't want that bone movin' any."

Working together, the four of them carefully wrapped Nora's right arm, then fitted her with a sling, lifting her lithe frame from the bed just enough to slip the fabric beneath her, then cinch it snug to keep the arm immobile.

When they finished, Caesar finally straightened, his expression pained. He rubbed his lower back and wiped the sweat from his face. Only then did Catriona realize how uncomfortable bending over the bed for that long must have been for him.

"You need to keep her in tow for a few days, ma'am," he said.

"So only bedrest, then?"

"Oh no, ma'am. She can get up and move around, if she feels like it. But she gotta be careful. And no movin' that arm, for sure. Rest is what her little body wants right now. Rest and plenty of good food, so that the bone can start mendin' proper-like."

Catriona listened to his instructions, taking them to heart. But they only served to feed the uneasiness simmering just below the surface. She glanced at Wade and found him studying her. Was he thinking what she was thinking? That she had no choice now but to accept his offer of staying in the overseer's cottage? So much for not being beholden to the man.

Once Caesar finished, Catriona briefly took his hands in hers. "I'm appreciatin' what you've done for me sister, sir, and I'll be workin' to pay you whatever you—"

He shook his head. "Don't you worry none 'bout payin' me, ma'am. You just take care of this sweet little one. I got a feelin' the Lord's got big plans for her life." A slow smile turned his mouth. "And that she's gonna give him a whole lotta what-for along the way."

Tears rising, Catriona smiled despite her doubts. "I have a feelin' you might be right on that count, sir. Because she gives me that and *more* every hour of every day." She looked down at Nora, whose eyes slowly fluttered open and closed, and she loved her youngest sister with an affection so fierce it frightened her. Was this an inkling of what the love of a real parent felt like? She glanced back at Caesar. "She's a handful, to be sure. But we're sisters, so I'm guessin' I'm stuck with her."

The comment drew soft laughter. But Catriona thought she detected the faintest shadow clouding Tempy's features, and she felt a pang of remorse at her own careless choice of words, even humorously intended. Tempy had had a sister. And a brother. But they'd been sold. Taken away. As had been the life Tempy and their mother would have shared with those siblings had their family been born into a different circumstance.

As difficult as life was now—and had been in recent months—Catriona did not want to imagine life without Nora. Or Ryan. She only hoped the Almighty wouldn't put her to the test in that regard.

"Cattie . . . me arm hurts," Nora whimpered.

Catriona leaned down and pressed kisses to her forehead. "I know it does, dearest. But thanks to Caesar here"—she indicated the man with a nod in case the concoction Tempy had brewed rendered Nora's memory useless—"you're goin' to be good as new soon enough."

Nora managed a smile, then her eyes slipped closed again.

Wade took that opportunity to approach the bed, a somewhat satisfied look in his features. "Miss O'Toole," he began softly, "if you're still open to my previous offer, which I hope you are, I would be happy to speak with the McGavocks about you and Nora staying in the cottage. Especially now that this has—"

"She got no need of the overseer's cottage,

Mister Cunningham." Once again, Tempy's tone bordered on strident. Catriona wondered at the formidable expression on the woman's face.

"She and Nora gonna be stayin' here with me, sir. In the bedroom right next door. That way I can see after 'em both. So you can stay on in that cottage just like you and the colonel done agreed to."

Wade's smile came slowly. "That's mighty kind of you, Tempy. But are you certain the colonel will—"

"I done checked with him, sir—and the missus too—when I went to make the tea earlier. I'm mindful of what broken bones call for in the healin', so I took to askin', and everything's all settled."

Tempy smiled widely, and Catriona was certain she saw victory lighting the woman's countenance. Even more baffling was the hint of amusement in Wade's.

"Excuse me, Mister Cunningham." Caesar approached Wade, his demeanor even more timid than before. "Mister Pender here just told me who you are, sir. My pardon for not keepin' mind of your name earlier. You only said you needed a bonesetter. You never said you was Carnton's new overseer."

"That's because that was of secondary importance at the moment." With a self-deprecating smile, Wade extended a hand, and Caesar accepted. "I look forward to working with you, Caesar. Allow me to offer my thanks as well for what you've done for the younger Miss O'Toole. I've seen bones set before, many times, and Tempy is right. You have a gift for it."

Caesar dipped his head. "Thank you, Mister Cunningham. I look forward to knowin' you better too, sir."

"Same for me, Mister Cunningham," Pender added.

Catriona immediately looked at Wade to see his reaction. But Wade only smiled in return and glanced away, which confirmed nothing. Yet her instincts insisted she was right in believing the two men knew each other better than they let on. So why were they pretending otherwise?

After a midafternoon ride to town with Catriona to retrieve her hidden trunk—and that only after Tempy swore to her she'd never leave Nora's side—Wade grabbed the report he'd written for the chief. It was still in the cast-iron skillet inside the cold oven where he'd left it. He tucked the portfolio inside his shirt, then headed out the door of the cottage, eager to get his hands on whatever information had been left for him. The dinner hour wasn't for a while yet, so he had time.

He glanced about, and not seeing anyone, he ducked into the woods behind the barn. Soon he happened upon the remnants of an old rock wall, precisely as the note he'd discovered in his room earlier indicated he would.

He followed the wall for a good four hundred

yards until he reached the edge of a clearing. There, the layers of dry-stacked limestone—the stone plentiful in this part of Tennessee—all but disappeared beneath an ancient oak. The oak's lower limbs, as thick as a man's waist and twisted with time, bent so low as to nearly touch the ground in some places, and Wade had to either duck under or climb over them to keep moving forward.

Sunlight filtered through the canopy overhead, the leaves only just now budded, and an earthy, dank smell sharpened the cool air. He'd walked a few more steps, his eyes quickly adjusting to the shadows, when he saw it—a rectangular-shaped rock buried at the foundation near where the wall ended. He looked around, then back across the field, making certain for a second time that no one had followed him. The woods were quiet, the only sounds an occasional birdcall or the squeak of an ornery squirrel as it rustled a path through wintered leaves and twigs. He stooped down and ran a hand over the rectangular-cut stone.

At a glance, the rock looked as though it had been buried deep beneath the foundation, leaving only the top to protrude from the soil. But with a little prying, the stone came loose and proved to be only a couple of inches thick. Beneath it lay a worn leather pouch that looked almost as ancient as the enormous oak itself. The pouch was bound by a leather cord, and Wade unwrapped it and withdrew a single sheet of paper.

He leaned against the wall, his gaze moving swiftly over the handwriting, eagerly devouring the update from a superior—until a single name stopped him short. Seeing the name dispelled the air from his lungs. He backed up and reread the last sentence, then slowly lifted his eyes. His gaze rested on the field ahead, but all he could see was Catriona's face. He squinted, as if that might make what he'd just read come into clearer focus. But it didn't.

He looked back down at the page and read the words in a hushed voice, thinking perhaps if he said them aloud, they would somehow make more sense. " 'Thursday morning, an operative interrogated a young Irish woman named Catriona O'Toole.' " Wade shook his head. She'd been questioned by an agency operative? Yet she had made no mention of it to him. Not even when he'd known something was wrong and had pressed her to tell him what it was. Then again, being interrogated wasn't exactly a topic someone desired to work into casual conversation. He continued, reading silently.

We have strong reason to believe that the woman's brother, whom she names as Ryan O'Toole, is part of the counterfeiting ring that moved from New York into this area back in early '65. The suspect claims her brother immigrated to the United States from Ireland in spring of '62 and was conscripted into the Confederate Army. That claim is currently being investigated. She stood by her story that the brother sent the money back to Ireland for the family to immigrate to the States as well. Records verify Miss O'Toole traveled from Ireland and entered the country via New York, then traveled directly to Nashville. She is accompanied by a young girl she asserts to be her sister. Authorities in Ireland are being contacted to confirm. The suspect deposited $656 with the bank two days ago—all counterfeit, which our contact at the bank intercepted. All bills are near exact replicas and match the currency confiscated in both Nashville and New York a year ago before the trail went cold. The suspect insists she is in Franklin to locate her brother, but strong suspicions point to an association with Peter McCartney. She has also made contact with Carnton's owner, as you are likely already aware. Investigate and advise.

Wade turned the page over but found the back side blank. That was it? He read the note through again, more slowly. This time comparing what he knew about Catriona and her activities over the past few days with the facts in this report. And they simply didn't line up. He was a fairly good judge of character, and his gut told him she wasn't involved with counterfeiting. Much less with a man like Peter McCartney. And yet . . .

He, along with everyone else in the agency, had been caught off guard a while back when a young woman about Catriona's age had succumbed to Peter McCartney's charms and joined him in his illegal endeavors. But Catriona? No. The pieces didn't fit. She wouldn't do such a thing. But as she'd told him earlier that day, she was out of money. So that part lined up. And what else had she said? " 'I thought I had more than I did,' " Wade said aloud, recalling their conversation and how she'd given him that little shrug. She'd told him she had sixteen cents left—and a dozen chickens. He sighed, half smiling. Yet he wondered . . .

Had his attraction to her blinded him to something he should have seen? Something that—if she was indeed guilty—would have tipped him off earlier? A voice inside his head answered no. But he'd studied human nature long enough to know that voice could be biased. So he painstakingly combed back through every moment he'd spent in her company from the time she'd walked into Carnton demanding to see McGavock up until today, looking for any evidence that might suggest—

His thoughts snagged on a particular memory. The note slid beneath his door at the hotel. She easily could have managed that. Her room had been right across the hall from his. And when he'd come out of the washroom that night, he'd found her having fallen coming up the stairs. Who fell coming *up* the stairs? Then there was her connection to John McGavock. Wade hadn't fully figured that one out. They shared a common ancestral homeland in County Antrim, Ireland— he knew that much. And that day when Catriona was in the colonel's office, she'd inquired about someone. A *he,* whom Wade had to believe, based on everything he knew, was her brother. Then she'd accused McGavock of something. But what, he still didn't know.

He sighed, recalling the personal exchange between Catriona and Nora and Tempy in the kitchen. *That* had been real. Nothing fake about it. And one thing he knew with absolute certainty— the pain and dread in Catriona's expression when she'd learned the details about the Battle of Franklin had been real too. For him as well, knowing what the 104th Ohio had done to her brother's division. He slowly shook his head. He'd interrogated enough people to know when someone was guilty. She wasn't. Still . . .

The thought *had* occurred to him that she wasn't being fully open with him. Even so, that didn't make her a counterfeiter. And no question in his mind, Catriona and Nora were sisters. He exhaled a slow breath, his thoughts turning to her brother. But first, he needed to walk. He always thought more clearly when he moved.

He pulled a metal container of matches he'd

bought at the dry goods store from his pocket. He broke one of the twelve sticks off the brick, then struck it on the side of a rock. A flame leapt to life. After giving the brief note one last scan, committing the details to memory, he held the single sheet of paper by the corner and lit the opposite end. The fire licked up the edges of the page. Seconds later, the paper all but consumed, he laid the burning remnant on top of the wall and waited for it to burn itself out.

He pulled the portfolio from beneath his shirt and slid it inside the leather pouch, then returned the pouch to its hiding place. He continued in the direction he'd been walking, not wanting to risk running into anyone, plus curious to see what this part of the Carnton land looked like. Not a hundred yards away, he came upon a creek and decided to follow it.

Sifting back through his memory, he recounted every detail Catriona had shared about her twin brother, and he lined up the facts, one by one, against the report. Per the fellow operative, Catriona claimed Ryan had sent the money back home so his family could come to America. That rang true. She'd been most forthcoming with him and the McGavocks about Ryan's last letter dated the twenty-ninth of November 1864, and she'd made no attempt to hide that she was looking for him.

If she were a counterfeiter, the very *last* thing she'd want would be to draw attention to herself or to anyone she was in cahoots with. So he saw little room for culpability there. And yet something still bothered him, niggled at the back of his mind before it scampered away again. Something Catriona had said about Ryan, perhaps? Yet no matter how he tried to remember, it remained just out of reach. But one thing he did recall. When John McGavock questioned her about not having heard from her brother since Ryan's last letter dated the twenty-ninth of November—Wade slowed his steps—she had hesitated. He remembered it clearly because it had made an impression. When a typical person was about to lie, they almost always hesitated. He'd learned that back in the war when questioning captured Confederates. However, for someone accustomed to lying or practiced in deceit, the words rolled off their lips like honey from the comb.

Seeing the sun begin to sink in the west, he turned around and started back, letting his thoughts roam where they would. But in the end, they kept returning to the same conclusion. Catriona O'Toole was no counterfeiter. But her brother . . .

He'd seen many a man do many a desperate thing to care for the people he loved, and Catriona had made no secret that she and her brother had been—or were—very close. Just as she and Nora were, despite the sparks that flew between them fairly often.

The top of the barn came into view just as the sun sank behind the hills, and its golden rays

411

bathed the overseer's cottage and the main house beyond in a wash of amber glow. A lump rose in his throat, and Wade swallowed back unexpected emotion. He missed Wesley and his parents. He and Evelyn had never been especially close, but they exchanged letters on occasion, and in a recent missive, she'd invited him to visit her in Chicago. He needed to do that. And he would as soon as he solved this case.

He headed for the kitchen, hoping to catch Catriona and Nora at dinner. Tempy, too, despite the woman's obvious dislike of him. He also hoped Nora was doing all right. But he figured she was. She was a tough little thing. Nearly to the main house, Wade glanced down and noticed the mud and grass caking the soles of his boots. Frowning, he made a quick detour back to the cottage to grab his second pair, not wanting to give Tempy any more ammunition against him.

No sooner had he opened his front door than a savory scent greeted him. He instinctively looked toward the stove, then caught sight of the plate loaded with food and the glass of milk on the table, an oil lamp burning low beside them. So far, breakfast, lunch, and dinner had been delivered to the cottage at the appointed times. And while he was grateful for the food, he didn't have to get hit over the head to take the hint.

He sat down at the table, draped the napkin across his left leg, and began to eat. The thick-sliced ham was delicious and had a sweetness to

412

it that reminded him of his mother's recipe. Same for the potatoes and the green beans cooked with chunks of bacon. He suddenly paused mid-chew, a feeling he hadn't experienced in quite a while coming over him. He swallowed the bite in his mouth, then laid aside his fork and bowed his head, picturing being back in his childhood home at the table with Papa, Mama, Wesley, and Evelyn.

"Father God," he prayed aloud just as his own father had taught him to do. *"Don't you whisper all quiet-like to God the Father,"* Papa had said. *"You come right out and talk to him straight on, like a man. You're a sinner just like me, son. Just like we all are. But the Lord Jesus bought your way into the throne room and told you in his Word to come boldly. So that's the way you should come. Just always remember who you're talking to—and that he's Almighty God and you . . . are not."*

"Thank you for this fine meal, Lord," he continued, still comforted by the echo of his earthly father's voice. "For a warm bed, and for this fine cottage to live in while I'm here. Give me discernment and wisdom to see the truth of matters and the courage to stand in the right." Catriona's face came to mind, as did Nora's, and he didn't so much say a specific prayer for them as he committed them both to the Lord's care and guidance. "Always for your glory and cross, O Lord. Amen."

He sat for a moment in the silence, eyes still closed, and again thought about the dinner table

413

from his childhood—his father, mother, brother, and sister—all but Evelyn gathered together in the afterlife now. A yearning for family and home tugged at him. Knowing better than to give those thoughts free rein, he shook off the melancholy and sank his teeth into the muffin Tempy, or someone, had perched on the side of his plate. He didn't know what kind it was, but after finishing the one, he could have eaten another. Still, the bowl of still-warm apple cobbler topped the meal off nicely enough.

He drained the last of his milk and wiped his mouth, then went to sit on the front porch in one of the two rockers, not ready for sleep just yet but not wanting to be alone inside the cottage either. At the main house, the warmth of lamplight issued from the kitchen windows as well as from windows on the second floor. Winder had told him the kitchen along with the bedrooms on the second floor were part of the original homestead built by his grandfather, Randal McGavock, and it was the house John McGavock grew up in. Years later, Randal added the larger portion to the homestead that made up the main house today, and it was a handsome home. Stately without being ostentatious.

And built completely by slaves. That truth never left his mind. Nor did the hope that those who'd owned slaves would come to bear the just consequences of that decision.

A thought occurred, a brighter one, and he ducked

back inside the cottage and retrieved his father's pipe from his satchel, along with his matches and a fresh bag of tobacco, another purchase from the dry goods store. Seated again in the rocker, he packed the pipe like his father had taught him, then struck a match and circulated the flame evenly over the fragrant leaves, taking a firm, steady puff as he did. The "charring light," Papa had called it, and after a minute or so, the charring light went out. Wade tamped the tobacco and relit it, then leaned back and took a draw on the stem.

He'd tried to choose a tobacco that most reminded him of what his father used to smoke, and the subtle hints of cherry and vanilla wafting around his face told him he'd done well. Movement in one of the windows in the hallway above the kitchen drew his attention, and he spotted Catriona. She walked to the far end of the hall to the bedroom closest to the smokehouse, then paused as though speaking to someone already inside. Nora, perhaps.

He watched her—until he realized his thoughts were leading him down a path best left untrod. With effort, he looked away, contenting himself with the fact that she and Nora were well cared for and weren't out in the middle of some field. When he'd seen the condition of that trunk . . .

He closed his eyes, and much as he'd done earlier that day, he gave his thoughts the lead in regard to Ryan O'Toole. They took him in several directions. An immigrant male coming to a new country, arriving relatively penniless, Wade felt sure. He was familiar with Ireland's recent political and social state. The young man would be intent on earning enough money to bring his family over as quickly as possible so they could all share a better life. A common and well-understood theme rooted in the very origin of these United—

Wade sat up, that niggling thought from a while ago returning, dancing at the edge of his thoughts. He could almost grasp it. It was something Catriona had said the day of the chicken debacle, as she referred to it, as they'd left the mercantile. Then it came to him. Her response to his question as to whether she could handle the rig. *"In me sleep. I used to deliver orders for our family's print shop."*

Wade grimaced. *"Our family's print shop."*

For the longest moment, he stared at the pipe in his grip, almost wishing he hadn't remembered how she'd answered, wishing he could forget. But, of course, he couldn't. He could, however—and would—write his superior in the morning and tell him that he was all but certain Catriona O'Toole was innocent. He'd bet his life the woman wasn't a counterfeiter but that her brother most assuredly was.

CHAPTER 26

Lying in bed beside Nora, Catriona found herself wide awake, her body exhausted, her mind whirring, and her pride and sense of self-sufficiency thoroughly battered yet her heart undeniably grateful. Nora was well fed, safe, and being cared for, and they had a place to stay even if it wasn't by her own provision.

She caught the aroma of smoked pork from the smokehouse adjacent to their bedroom and breathed deeply. Earlier, at Tempy's insistence, she'd accepted Wade's offer to take her into town to retrieve her trunk. Even though she'd hated leaving Nora, she couldn't bear to leave the trunk there for another night, hidden though it was. But the look Wade had given her when he saw the side of the trunk bashed in . . . Well, it wasn't a look she'd be forgetting anytime soon. The anger in his features hadn't been aimed at her, she knew full well, and she hadn't feared Wade in that moment. Not at all. Still, his demeanor had reminded her a bit of Da, which was disconcerting to say the least.

She turned onto her side, careful not to jostle Nora and not wishing to think about Wade in the same breath as her father. And not wishing to think about her father at all.

She rubbed her hands together, her palms rough after washing her and Nora's soiled clothes from the trunk. Thankfully, all the stains had come clean. Now if she could only wipe away the memory.

After a good night's rest, surely the various options available to her would become more evident. Mam was right—things were always clearer come morning. This part of the house was quiet, and Catriona closed her eyes, intent on falling asleep. Tempy, whose bedroom was the closest to the kitchen stairs, had just retired, the lamplight beneath her closed door extinguished only moments earlier.

A breeze stirred, and moonlight streaming through the trees cast mottled shadows across the ceiling. Tempy told her earlier that this bedroom had been occupied during the war by a young widow and her son. The widow had been in the family way. Such tenderness filled Tempy's tone when she'd spoken about the bedroom's former occupants. Catriona wondered what had happened to them.

The second bedroom, in between theirs and Tempy's, was occupied by Mary, the young servant girl Catriona had seen on occasion. Per Tempy, Mary's father had hired out his fourteen-year-old daughter to the McGavocks for the entire year with the agreement that she would be well clothed and cared for. Mary seemed happy enough, and not only was she swift to offer Tempy help in the kitchen, but she freely joined in the conversation.

Still . . . Catriona couldn't imagine hiring out her own daughter—or Nora, for that matter—to another family for an entire year.

Nora's breath came softly, and Catriona focused on its rhythm, hoping to entice slumber. Following dinner, Tempy had made Nora a second cup of her special tea, and Nora slipped off to sleep shortly thereafter. Catriona focused on the patch of moonlight tracing a patient silver path across the far wall. She'd hoped Wade might join them for dinner, but Tempy said he'd been taking his meals in the cottage.

Try as she might to relax, something lingered at the edge of her thoughts. Something about Isham Pender's earlier comment. The man had never actually *stated* that he and Wade hadn't met before. Pender had only said he'd been recently introduced to the new overseer. Clever. Very clever. Then later, he said he looked forward to getting to know Wade better. Wade hadn't contradicted him.

Strictly speaking, she realized, Pender's statements could be true. But she was still convinced that their connection to each other extended back before Wade had come to Carnton a week ago. The only question was *why* the men would lie about knowing each other.

The hoot of an owl sounded surprisingly close to the open window and brought her head off the pillow. She hoped the bird wouldn't decide to go exploring inside the house during the night. Knowing that was highly unlikely, she settled back into the bed—even while she kept one eye on the window.

Dear Braxie's sweet face came to mind, and she wished she could do something for the girl. Show her a kindness like was being shown to her here. Wade's willingness to approach the McGavocks about her staying in his little cottage was generous, and she was grateful. But she much preferred being closer to Tempy, who knew so much about doctoring. And, if she were honest with herself, she also preferred not being so closely tied to Wade Cunningham. Not that she believed he held unsavory motives toward her. Far from it.

Nay, it was more the noble way he seemed to want to take care of her and Nora that sounded an alarm inside her. That, and the way she felt when, on occasion, she caught him looking at her longer than a friend should. Then there was the way his mouth would tip in that wry smile, making even her thoughts blush with heat. The mere memory caused a stirring inside her, and she blew out a breath. She gently nudged back the bedsheets, welcoming the breeze from the open window on her bare legs.

Her stomach rumbled, and she pictured again what they'd had for dinner. Slices of ham with potatoes and green beans that tasted so good. And the apple cobbler too. Oh, and the cinnamon oatmeal muffins Tempy served all slathered in butter and honey. Her mouth watered just thinking about them again. She'd wanted seconds but hadn't dared ask, especially after Nora had eagerly helped herself to such.

To say she was having to resign herself to being here at Carnton for a few days wouldn't be putting it fairly. She was grateful to be here and not back in that field by the church or somewhere like it. Yet in the same breath, she was eager to be on their way again, once Nora was able. But what she could not—and would not—resign herself to was doing nothing to earn her keep while they were here.

First thing in the morning, she intended to discuss the topic with Colonel or Mrs. McGavock. She'd make certain they knew she was a person who repaid her debts. She also had a keen idea as to what she would offer in return for room and board for a handful of days—if only she could convince them to agree.

A wave of fatigue swept through her, and she closed her eyes again, willing her body to yield to it. Sometime later, in the mist between wakefulness and dreaming, she could almost make out the tearstained faces of a young slave boy and girl as they clung to each other, desperate hands gripping skinny arms tight. The children heartlessly torn from their mother and older sister. She awakened to darkness, loneliness crouching in every dark corner, and she slept fitfully the rest of the night.

When she next opened her eyes, pale sunlight reached through the curtains, and she turned beside her to see Nora still sleeping soundly, her face tranquil and innocent in slumber. But as she stared, she imagined Nora's sweet face superimposed on that of the slave girl in her dream, and an ache thudded heavily inside her chest. As often as death had visited her life, she could not imagine Nora—or Bridget or Alma—being *sold* to someone and taken away, never to be seen or heard from again. And taken into a life where they had no say whatsoever in their destiny, no freedom. Given a choice, death seemed a much kinder alternative.

She closed her eyes and drifted. Then a while later, the aromas of coffee and bacon wafted up the stairs from the kitchen, and she pictured Tempy standing at the stove, already deep into her work. How did a woman who had lost so much give so generously? Not to the McGavocks, necessarily. Tempy was in their employ, after all. But to a total stranger like her. And Nora. How had the bitterness of life not taken root and spread inside her like a noxious weed?

Catriona reached over and traced a feather-soft trail along the curve of her sister's cheek, wondering if Tempy's siblings were still alive. Tempy said she'd been at Carnton for sixty-seven years and had been brought there when she was just a girl. That meant the woman must be around seventy—or a little older. Which, in turn, meant her brother and sister, if they were still living, were likely only a handful of years younger than that. Up in age, no doubt, and likely bearing the weight of the life of slavery they'd been forced to live. But it was possible Tempy's siblings were still among the living, and that possibility sent a rush through her like a lightning bolt across a night sky.

She quickly rose, then made use of the chamber pot before dressing in the skirt and shirtwaist from the previous day, all while doing her best not to awaken Nora. If she could write to the War Department about Ryan, surely there was someplace or someone she could write to about former slaves and where and to whom they'd been sold. And she intended to do just that.

"Beggin' your pardon, Mrs. McGavock, but I'll not be takin' charity. I aim to be earnin' whatever 'tis given me, ma'am." Ashamed at being destitute and at needing to have this conversation in the first place, Catriona found that this exchange was not unfolding as she had rehearsed it during the predawn hours. Nor was the exchange to her hostess's liking, judging by the tiny lines crinkling the bridge of Mrs. McGavock's nose.

It didn't help that they were seated across from each other in the fancy parlor opposite the farm office. Aye, the room was lovely. But all its fanciness and folderol only served to make Catriona more uncomfortable, as did the placating smile slowly curving Carrie McGavock's mouth.

"*Charity* sounds like a harsh word when only kindness is meant, Miss O'Toole. And what's more, your suggestion, while sincerely appreciated, I assure you, is most *un*conventional."

"Unconventional?" Catriona stared. "For a woman to be plantin' flowers?"

"No, not to plant flowers. Many women do that, of course. But to manage the entire garden, all the plots, the tilling of the soil. To lay out the beds and plant vegetables. To tend them. To *be* a gardener." She shook her head. "I'm afraid it's simply not done."

Catriona tried not to appear as flummoxed as she felt. "Who else is goin' to be doin' it for you, then? April's almost upon us, ma'am, and the beds are still covered in winter. The soil should've already been turned a month ago so it can be breathin'. The winter weeds, twigs, and such need to be cleared away. And you've got plenty of cows; some of their deposits should be carried in to—"

Mrs. McGavock lifted a hand. "I am quite aware of all that needs to be accomplished. The colonel and I have been searching for a replacement for Mr. Lamb, our former gardener, for weeks now. I've spoken with neighbors, I've advertised the position in the Franklin newspaper, and still not a single formal inquiry."

Catriona lifted a brow. "So what if *I* were to be makin' a formal inquiry? Would you allow me to be doin' it then?"

Mrs. McGavock stared for a moment, her expression inscrutable, and Catriona began to think she'd overstepped her bounds.

Then the woman laughed. "I guess a young woman being a gardener would be no more unconventional than a woman heavy with child building a nativity for Christmas."

Catriona looked at her, sifting through the comment yet coming up empty. "I'm afraid I'm not understandin' your meanin', ma'am."

"No worries." Mrs. McGavock waved a hand. "What I'm saying is that yes, *for the time being,* you may work the garden in exchange for staying here. Although I wish to be clear that I am *not* mandating that duty upon you. It is my earnest desire that you would see yourself as a guest here at Carnton while your sister recuperates. After all, my husband's family and yours have more than a little shared history."

Catriona smiled, feeling triumphant and more than a little hopeful. "I'm grateful to you, ma'am, for hearin' me out, and for allowin' me to start the garden, at least. I want to do something that benefits you. I wouldn't feel right about stayin' here otherwise."

"You've made that abundantly clear, and I appreciate your industrious nature."

Mrs. McGavock relayed what the former gardener had done in terms of design, then with no little enthusiasm shared some of her own desires for her garden. The more Catriona listened, the more excited she became. She offered a few ideas of her own, heartened when Mrs. McGavock nodded in agreement. A flame of hope unlike any she'd felt in a long time began to flicker inside her. Perhaps being here at Carnton, for however long, would be a better experience than she'd imagined. It would for certain allow her to stay informed about the burial team's progress while also maintaining a much-desired distance. She was grateful they were seeing it done. Within that field might lie the answer she was seeking, even though she prayed it didn't. Stepping back and looking at her current situation . . .

Could it be that the Almighty had heard her prayer at the church that night? The night she and Nora had hidden from that man. Could it be that he was making a way for Nora? And even making a way for her too? It sounded absurd, but perhaps he wasn't going to be forever against her after all. The thought was such an unexpected one that she had trouble wrapping her mind around it. But her heart responded with an enthusiasm that revealed far more, especially to him, than she would have wanted. Because while she was grateful for the reprieve from his harsh hand, she was once bitten, twice shy when it came to trusting him.

After a moment, Mrs. McGavock paused in the conversation and angled her head. "By chance has the colonel had an opportunity to speak with you about the War Department?"

"The War Department?" Catriona repeated, her worst fears swiftly rising. "I wrote them, like you encouraged me to do. But I haven't received any word back. And nay, the colonel hasn't spoken to me about it. Did the War Department contact *you?* About Ryan? Is there news?"

"No, no, I'm sorry. It's not that they've contacted us. And to my knowledge, there's no news to tell. Perhaps I should wait and let the colonel tell you himself, but . . ." Her expression softened. "The colonel contacted *them*. On your behalf. The War Department is still inundated with letters, and he knows how long it can take for correspondence to be researched and answered. So he sent a telegram to a colleague there, inquiring about any information they might have about your brother."

Catriona's eyes watered. "That was most kind of him, Mrs. McGavock. And of you."

"Oh, I did nothing in that regard. It was all John's idea." She paused. "He is a kind man, Miss O'Toole. I count myself most blessed to be his wife."

With painful clarity, Catriona recalled how she'd accused John McGavock of taking pleasure in the fact that his family had acted in honor and hers had not. And she'd done it in this very room, no less. While she still didn't think she knew enough to make a firm judgment on the man, she managed a nod. "Aye, ma'am. I am comin' to see that very thing."

"I count myself most blessed to be his wife." As the words replayed inside her, she wished her mother could have said those words about being married to Da, wished she'd been happier in her choice of whom she'd wed. It wasn't that there were no good marriages in the world, Catriona knew that. John and Carrie McGavock's apparently

being one of them. But choosing the wrong man could lead to a lifetime of regret and misery. So all things weighed together, in her estimation the safest choice was still to remain unmarried. Only, she had to find a way to provide for her and Nora.

"I'm praying you receive word about your brother soon, Miss O'Toole. And that it's good news."

"Aye," Catriona whispered, gathering her scattered thoughts. "Thank you, ma'am."

A knock sounded on the door.

"Come in," Mrs. McGavock bade.

The door opened, and Mary peered inside. "Sorry to be interruptin', Missus McGavock. But one of them burial team men—the oldest brother, I think—is here to see you. Says he needs to speak with you right quick 'bout somethin' important on what they's all doin' out there."

Considering the responsibilities awaiting the burial team made Catriona cringe. If forced to, she could endure many things not of her own choosing. She'd learned that. But what these men were doing? She didn't have the strength for it.

"Please send the gentleman in, Mary."

Catriona rose. "I'll be excusin' meself then, ma'am, so the two of you can—"

"No, please stay. This won't take long. Then you and I can discuss what to plant this year. I must admit, spring is swiftly upon us, and I'm weary of seeing the garden in such disarray."

Nodding, Catriona seated herself again.

A man stepped through the open doorway, hat in hand. "Mrs. McGavock, thank you for seeing me, ma'am."

The man was tall and lean and spoke with an accent similar to others in Franklin, yet the inflection was slightly different. He looked familiar to Catriona, too, and his quizzical expression suggested that he was having the same thought about her.

"It's Mr. Cuppett, isn't it?" Mrs. McGavock gestured for him to sit in the chair next to Catriona.

He looked back, nodding. "Yes, ma'am, that's right. But I'll politely decline on sitting." He glanced down at his trousers. "My brothers and me, we've already started working this morning, and I don't wish to mar your fine furniture."

Mrs. McGavock offered a conciliatory nod, her expression inviting him to continue.

"I got a favor to ask of you, ma'am. Something I didn't perceive needing until after we got underway." He fingered the hat in his grip. "We could use someone to come alongside us and keep tally of the names of the soldiers we're exhuming, along with their rank and units, if noted, and whatever personal items we find buried with them. I thought one of us could do it, but"—he shook his head—"to put it delicately, we need someone who isn't in the middle of doing all the digging and transferring. And to keep on the schedule we promised the colonel, I need all of us continuing with the work." He smiled briefly. "I heard you have a young servant girl working for you who might be able to help. And if she were to have a neat hand, that would be appreciated, too, ma'am. Not like our chicken scratch."

Mrs. McGavock inclined her head. "Yes, Mr. Cuppett, I do have a servant girl. Her name is Mary. But I'm afraid she won't be able to help. She doesn't know how to read or write. Perhaps you could place a notice in the post office or an advertisement in the newspaper."

"I've already done both, ma'am. And both places warned me we wouldn't get any takers. So far, their estimations are proving right."

Mrs. McGavock offered a commiserating look, and Catriona mirrored it, feeling sorry for the man but understanding all too well why no one had responded to his request. Deciding to let them deal with the issue, she looked out the front window. She couldn't see the garden, but that didn't prevent her from laying out the beds and the plants in her mind's eye. She didn't know precisely what Mrs. McGavock wanted in the way of flowers and vegetables, but she'd already decided to plant a small corner of Spring Squill in some spare space. She wouldn't plant all the bulbs she'd brought from home, of course. Only a few. But how encouraging it would be to see that resilient little flower whose pale-blue petals reminded her so much of home and of—

"Miss O'Toole?"

Catriona looked back to find herself the object

of Mrs. McGavock's attention. Mr. Cuppett's too. "Aye?" she said, looking back and forth between them.

"As I was saying," Mrs. McGavock continued, "I realize it's not an easy task, but you would be doing a great service by assisting Mr. Cuppett."

As Mrs. McGavock's request came into clearer, harsher focus, Catriona felt the blood drain from her face. She swallowed. "Nay, I-I'm sorry. B-but I cannot. I—" She shook her head, reaching for a reason to refuse their request, any reason *other* than an utter fear of death she couldn't begin to describe and would be ashamed to admit. Especially after learning what took place on that field and then within the walls of Carnton following the battle. "I'll be workin' in the garden, ma'am." She turned to Mr. Cuppett, the disappointment in his eyes not helping her case. "Sir, if you haven't seen the garden yet, when you do, you'll be knowin' it'll take me from sunup to sundown to get the beds prepared and ready for plantin'." The words spilled out so quickly she could scarcely draw breath. "The beds are still covered in winter and neglect, and I—"

"Miss O'Toole."

The patient calm in Mrs. McGavock's tone expelled every thought from her head, and Catriona could only stare, the beat of her own heart drumming in her ears.

"I realize what I'm asking constitutes a great sacrifice. Not of time so much, but of sensibilities,

431

and it *will* take great courage." The woman's gaze deepened. "I also realize at what personal cost this task might come to you should the news about your dear brother be contrary to what we're all praying. But even having known you so short a time, I believe you possess that kind of courage."

Catriona fisted her hands in her lap so neither of them could see her trembling. It was a selfish thought, but if the woman felt so strongly about seeing the task done, why did she not do it herself? If it had been anyone else, Catriona would have said as much. But to Mrs. John McGavock? The woman under whose roof she was taking shelter while Nora recuperated? Nay, it was not to be done.

"If this aids your decision at all," Mrs. McGavock continued, "you will most certainly be doing something that will make a lasting difference. Far more than you or I might realize at the present. And most importantly, you will be honoring every soldier who died in that battle."

Hearing what the woman wasn't saying, Catriona briefly closed her eyes and pictured Ryan's handsome face. If he'd been here that November night, if he'd faced the onslaught of the 104th Ohio with General Cleburne and the rest of his men, which Ryan's last letter seemed to indicate, then the least she could do was help keep record of the bodies of those soldiers who'd given their lives. Soldiers whom perhaps Ryan had fought alongside. She squeezed her eyes tight.

432

"Aye," she finally managed, a shudder passing through her. "I'll be helpin' you, Mr. Cuppett."

"Oh, *thank you,* Miss O'Toole." Gratitude swept his expression. "And there shouldn't be occasion for you to have to come out to the field by town, ma'am. Only to the cemetery just yonder behind the house. We'll need your services after we've moved the bodies but before we lay them to rest again here. We'll commence in just a few days."

Mrs. McGavock rose from her seat, and Catriona followed suit, surprised her legs held.

"Oh, and I've already purchased a journal in which to mark the names." Mr. Cuppett pulled a small leather book from his inner coat pocket and handed it to Catriona.

She fingered the supple brown leather, knowing two things. That if it came to it, writing Ryan's name in this book would be one of the most difficult things she'd ever done—and that she was an utter fool to have thought the Almighty had granted her a reprieve.

CHAPTER 27

"Are you for certain, Miss Bartel?" Catriona eyed the governess—a woman about her own age—and tried to gauge the sincerity in her expression. "Even with a broken arm, me sister can be a handful," she added softly, glancing at Nora still seated at the breakfast table, only to find Nora glaring back.

"I'm not a *handful,* Cattie! And I can mind meself!" Nora huffed. "I'm tired of bein' still all the time. And I'm tired of havin' me arm all wrapped up like a sausage!"

"Nora Emmaline, it's scarcely been three full days since you fell from that ladder! Havin' your arm wrapped up like a sausage is what's keepin' it from hurtin' so badly. That, and Tempy's magic tea." Catriona threw a grateful glance at Tempy, who stood stirring a pot on the stove. "You *must* take care of yeself, child, and rest. And that means no scamperin' about."

Nora made a face, and Catriona looked back at the governess with an expression intended to say, *Are you certain you know what you're gettin' yeself into?*

Miss Bartel smiled. "I assure you, Miss O'Toole, that I welcome Nora's presence in our schoolroom, and I'll make certain there is *no* scampering."

Catriona found the offer tempting. Tempy and Mary had taken turns watching Nora for her over the past couple of days so she could make progress on the garden. Saturday she'd actually started weeding and cleaning up the beds. Yesterday she'd spoken with Mrs. McGavock and gained approval for all she'd planned. But Nora wasn't Tempy and Mary's responsibility, and she couldn't expect them to continue helping in that way. Their duties were already daunting enough. However, she didn't want to overstep any bounds. "Perhaps I should be checkin' with Mrs. McGavock first? Just to be certain it's all right with her?"

The young woman shook her head. "It was Mrs. McGavock's idea to include Nora to begin with, and I readily agreed. Besides, Hattie and Winder are already counting on her attending school with them while you and your sister are here." With a knowing look, Miss Bartel cast a glance behind her at the short staircase that led up to the main house. Sure enough, Winder and his older sister, Hattie, stood peeking around the corner, all smiles.

Catriona sighed. "All right, then, if you're certain."

With simultaneous squeals, the McGavock children made a beeline for Nora, Winder covering the brief distance at a faster clip. But Miss Bartel stepped forward, effectively forming a barrier between them and Nora, and the children skidded to a halt.

436

"*Easy* now, Winder," the young governess warned. "Remember what we spoke about earlier. Nora has a broken arm, so we must treat her gently. No running and *no* boisterous playing, do you understand?"

"Yes, ma'am." The boy nodded, his excitement never waning. He peered around Miss Bartel. "You get to go to school with me, Nora!"

"And with me too!" Hattie chimed in. "You can sit next to me, Nora. Since we're both girls."

"She can sit next to me too!" Winder frowned up at his sister. "I was her friend *first!*"

"She may sit next to *both* of you, children," Miss Bartel interjected, placing a hand on each of their shoulders. "Now, I'd like for you both to accompany Nora to the stairs, then I'll join you and we'll escort her to our classroom. I expect you *all* to walk at a slow and reasonable pace, please," she accentuated, giving the threesome a rather stern look.

So stern, in fact, that Catriona hoped it might have a sobering effect on Nora. But alas, her sister, suddenly all sugar and sweetness, peered up at the governess with a most endearing smile, which Miss Bartel readily returned. But Catriona could see the hint of mischief in Nora's eyes and sent her sister a silent warning.

Nora simply lifted her chin in response and slid out of her chair, dragging Virginia with her. Somehow the doll had "broken" her right arm in recent days as well, and thanks to Tempy's ministrations, her damaged limb was wrapped up like a sausage too. Why Nora still insisted on carrying around that faceless little plaything, Catriona didn't know.

She only hoped Miss Bartel really did know what she was getting herself into and that Nora would have the sense to behave and be careful. The child's impetuous nature was making it difficult to keep her subdued. What if she fell and reinjured that arm? Catriona cringed just thinking about it. On second thought, perhaps Nora joining the other children in the schoolroom wasn't the wisest idea. And yet even entertaining the thought that Nora would sit still on a blanket outside while she worked the garden beds was absurd. The girl would be off in a flash and into who-knew-what. No, this was by far the better choice.

She hoped Nora would apply herself in the classroom. The girl had a quick mind and soaked up knowledge like a sponge. But they'd not been faithful to their studies for months now. Yet one more thing she could feel guilty about.

With Hattie on one side and Winder on the other, Nora made her way toward the stairs, moving at a far feebler pace than she had when she'd come down for breakfast. Catriona shook her head, loving her younger sister but also wishing she could wring her dramatic little neck. Hearing a chuckle, she turned to see Miss Bartel shaking her head right along with her.

The governess leaned close. "Never you fear,

Miss O'Toole. I am quite accustomed to dealing with high-spirited, theatrical children." She gave a little wink. "Because I *was* one! None of your sister's shenanigans will get by me."

Relief washing through her, Catriona found her opinion of the woman increasing a hundredfold. "I can't tell you how happy hearin' that makes me. I was beginnin' to feel sorry for you before you'd even left the room!"

Tossing her a smile, the governess headed for the stairs, then turned back. "In case you need us, the schoolroom is on the second floor of the main house. You'll see the family bedrooms on either side of the gallery, and the schoolroom will be straight ahead toward the front of the house. And you're welcome anytime!" She turned again. "Now, children . . . Let's be very careful as we climb the stairs and . . ."

Watching Nora grab hold of the stair rail with her left hand and start up, Catriona winced, willing her sister not to trip and fall. Nora looked so small and fragile next to Winder and Hattie, who were considerably taller. And Winder's exuberance . . . He was the kind of active, rough-and-tumble boy Nora always tried to keep up with. Catriona swallowed hard, an affection for her youngest sister sweeping through that nearly took her breath away.

Mam once told her that raising children was similar to agreeing to have a portion of your heart walk around in someone else's body. At the time, Catriona hadn't realized how frightening a prospect that could be. But she was beginning to, and it wasn't the least comforting. Especially when Nora's welfare and safety depended solely on her.

"She be all right, Miss O'Toole."

Catriona glanced over to see Tempy watching her.

"That Miss Bartel . . ." Tempy motioned. "She ain't been teachin' the McGavock children that long a time, but she's good with them. Strict too. But that's what a child needs. Lots of love and lots of fencin' in when they's young. If'n they don't get it then, they head out into the world not ready for what's waitin' for 'em."

"How long has Miss Bartel been here?"

"Nigh onto four months, I guess. The last governess, Miss Elizabeth Clouston, was here for years. Now, you talk 'bout a good woman. Mmm-hmm." Endearment softened her voice and her features. "She the one who taught me to read."

Catriona stared, wondering if she'd heard the woman correctly.

Tempy's brow rose. "Back 'fore my people was free, ma'am, it were against the Southern law to teach us to read and write. But Miss Clouston, whose name be *Missus* Roland Ward Jones now, she done taught me anyway. And taught me good too. I'm teachin' two of the sharecroppers' wives their letters right now."

The radiance in Tempy's face made it impossible for Catriona not to smile. But she felt a sadness

440

too. "That's wonderful, Tempy. But . . . I'm sorry life was so hard—no, so *unimaginable*—for you for so long."

Tempy nodded, her eyes glistening with emotion. "It was that, ma'am. And I had it better than so many others I knew. But the world, it's changin'. Right here, today, in front of our eyes." A serious expression swept her face. "That's what Miss Lizzie always used to say. She and Captain Roland, they met after the battle here and done got married in the fancy parlor just 'fore this past Christmas. They livin' over yonder in Mississippi on his family land. I's waitin' to hear anytime 'bout her bein' with child. She told me they weren't gonna waste no time." She laughed. "I told her I weren't figurin' they would!"

Tempy began clearing the breakfast dishes from the table, and Catriona joined her, grateful again that her path had crossed that of this woman, even if it meant coming to Carnton.

Sunshine streamed in through the window, and Catriona found herself eager to get outside and continue ridding the garden of dead leaves and winter debris. She was making good progress. But the endeavor was far greater than she first imagined, and the strain in her shoulders and back was proof of it. Yet seeing the progress gave her a sense of satisfaction she'd not experienced in some time, and the pungent aroma of freshly turned earth provided a strange sense of comfort and belonging. A breeze wafted in through the open kitchen windows facing the back of the house and carried with it traces of sunshine and honeysuckle.

Yesterday after the McGavocks returned from church, George Cuppett had called on the house to inform them that he and his team had finished the design layout for the cemetery and that the reinterring would begin in the next couple of days. He'd invited everyone to come and view their work in the cemetery thus far. Catriona had politely declined, and she still wondered how she was going to fulfill her pledge to assist them. Still, she'd given her word, so she would do it.

The McGavocks had invited her to attend church services with them, telling her that Tempy or Mary could watch Nora in her stead. And as it turned out, the church the McGavocks attended was none other than Franklin Presbyterian, the church Catriona had vowed never to step foot in and where she and Nora had hidden the night they went camping. She'd thanked the couple, then kindly explained that she felt an obligation to stay behind and keep watch on Nora in case—

Movement through one of the windows caught Catriona's eye, and she turned.

Wade was leading a horse from the barn. A pretty little mare, her reddish coat shining coppery gold in the morning sun. She'd seen Wade a few times over the past couple of days but only from a distance. Once, she'd thought he was headed to her in the garden, but he'd kept on walking.

The mare suddenly tugged on the lead rope,

442

and Wade paused long enough to give the animal a quick rub on the nose, then continued on. The horse followed begrudgingly, then suddenly nudged him hard in the arm. The momentum sent Wade sideways, and he nearly lost his balance. Hand flying to her mouth, Catriona couldn't help but laugh. Apparently the mare wanted more than a wee bit of his attention.

"What's so funny out that window, Miss O'Toole?"

She hadn't realized Tempy was standing beside her. Catriona gestured. "It's Mr. Cunningham. That horse is givin' him what-for. Nearly knocked him flat on the ground."

Tempy gave a humorless laugh. "I reckon that horse got the right idea, then."

Catriona sneaked a look at her, already having formed a strong impression that Tempy was none too fond of Wade. The question was why. Catriona cleared her throat. "May I be askin' you somethin', Tempy?"

The older woman looked over. "Sure you can, ma'am."

"Have you been knowin' Mr. Cunningham before he came to Carnton?"

" 'Course not. I ain't never met him 'fore he come to speak to the colonel 'bout the overseer's job."

"So . . ." Catriona returned her gaze out the window to see Wade rubbing the horse's neck in long, smooth strokes. The mare stepped closer to

443

him, nuzzling his chest, and Catriona saw Wade's mouth moving. The horse's tail swished from side to side, and she wondered what he was whispering to her. "What is it about the man that turned your opinion against him so quickly?"

Half expecting the woman to deny that such was the case, Tempy's smile came slowly. "I like a female who speaks her mind. Who just puts her thoughts right out there."

"Well then, you should be especially fond of me sister Nora!"

Tempy laughed. "I *am* right fond of that little miss. But surely you know who she learnt all that from."

Friendly sarcasm lit Tempy's voice, but Catriona pretended not to notice.

"Nay, I do not. I've no idea where she gets that ornery temper! Or the way she looks at you as though her very eyes could set you to flame!" Catriona waited, then slowly slid her gaze back to Tempy's, and they both laughed.

Tempy patted her arm, then her smile slowly faded. She looked back outside, and Catriona didn't have to follow her gaze to know who she was looking at.

"I been livin' a long time, Miss O'Toole, and I seen all sorts of people in my life. Some good, some bad. Most a blendin' of both, still tryin' to figure out where they's gonna land. But through all that seein', the good Lord's taught me somethin'. He's put a kind of . . . knowin' inside me, I guess.

444

A feelin' I get when I study on a person." She turned back to face Catriona. "I ain't one to go talkin' 'bout others, so this ain't somethin' I'm sayin' lightly. But you's a right handsome woman, which means you gonna get attention you may not be wantin'. And you been through a lot o' hard in recent days, too, which can dull a body to seein' as clearly as they usually do." She lifted a shoulder. "I just figure if I know somethin' bad is down the road ahead of you, I wouldn't think much of you if I didn't say somethin'. And I *do* think much of you, ma'am. You and Miss Nora both. You's special people. I knew that right off."

Catriona smiled, her eyes misting a little. Yet she sensed that she wouldn't like what Tempy was about to share.

"The first time Mister Cunningham come to Carnton was the same day you did. I found him standin' out there in the front hall." Tempy gestured toward the staircase leading up to the main house. "He was standin' right by the door to the farm office, tryin' to listen in on what you and the colonel was sayin'."

Catriona frowned.

"But soon as he come to know I's there"—the older woman huffed—"he starts talkin' smooth as lard meltin' in a skillet! I let him know right off that I knew for sure he weren't part of that mess o' men who done met with the colonel 'bout the buryin' business. And Mister Cunningham, he comes right back at me with, 'No, ma'am, I met

445

with him after that. 'Bout the position of overseer.' Then he says he got a question to ask the colonel. Wantin' to make me think that's why he's standin' there." She made a *pfft* sound with her lips. "So I say, 'I get him back for you, sir.' 'Fore I can even reach for the door, he says, 'Colonel McGavock is meetin' with a Missus O'Toole.' "

Catriona exhaled. "*Mrs.* O'Toole?"

"Mmm-hmm." Tempy nodded. "But that ain't all of it. Miss Nora, her and Winder start goin' at it. Well, I ain't even knowin' who she is yet, so we gotta work that through first. Then get her and Winder's little tiff ironed out. Meantime, in all that back-and-forth, the little miss says somethin' 'bout how her *sister* is meetin' in that room with the colonel. And plain as day, I see a dawnin' come over Mister Cunningham's face. 'Cause he's done learned you *ain't* married." Tempy's eyes narrowed. "And I can tell by the look on the man's face that he's favorin' that idea. A whole lot."

Tempted to smile at that discovery, Catriona knew better than to do so in front of Tempy.

"So a few minutes later," Tempy continued, "I finally grab the chance and let him *know* I think he was snoopin', and you know what he says to me?"

Catriona waited.

Tempy crossed her arms. "He acts all shy like and says he got hisself a *good reason* for standin' by that door. He says he's waitin' there 'cause he wants to see if you might let him walk you back to town."

Catriona shook her head. "Walk me back to town?"

"Mmm-hmm. Which seems right mannerly on the top of things." Tempy leaned closer. "But you gotta remember, ma'am, he done said *Missus* O'Toole back there at the first. So he was standin' there even *after* he thought you was married. And since then, I seen the way he looks at you. I may be old as dirt, but I still know the look of a man when he sees somethin' he wants."

Catriona briefly looked away, her pulse edging up a notch at Tempy's implication. But as the facts quickly shook into place, truth rose to the surface, and the earlier temptation to smile vanished completely.

Tempy's gaze held hers. "No matter how you look at it, ma'am, you can't get away from two things—either the man was downright lyin' 'bout him not listenin' in on your conversation with the colonel, or he's a man who thinks nothin' 'bout askin' a *married* woman if he can see her back to town. Whichever way you come at it, it don't say nothin' good 'bout him. So you's askin' me what it is that turned my thinkin' agin' him so quick like? That's the whole of it right there." Tempy sighed. "I just can't get a good readin' on him, Miss O'Toole. And that ain't never happened before but what it ain't ended that the person wasn't what they seemed."

In a breath, every warning Catriona had experienced since first meeting Wade Cunningham resounded inside her. But why would Wade have been trying to eavesdrop on her conversation with the colonel? It made no sense. He hadn't even known her at that point. What interest could there have been on his part? So the latter possibility had to be the right one. Yes, being noticed by a handsome man might have flattered some married women, but not a woman who'd been raised by a father who'd had a wandering eye. Nothing about a man who would desire to pursue a married woman was flattering to her, no matter how handsome or charming he might be.

Catriona looked back out the window, but Wade was gone. "What did Wa—" She caught herself. "What did Mr. Cunningham do when you made it plain you knew he was lyin'?"

"He went real still like. You could see it in his face that he knew he'd been found out." Tempy looked beyond her, as though searching her memory. "He just gave me that handsome ol' smile of his and made like he was tippin' a hat. Then walked out the door like he owned all of Franklin."

Catriona had no problem imagining Wade acting as Tempy described. He *did* have an arrogant side to him. She'd noticed that early on. And despite a small part of her still not wanting to believe it, she found herself weighing everything she knew about the man—and believing Tempy.

"Thank you, Tempy, for tellin' me all that." She shook her head. "Early on, when first meetin' him, I had me doubts. *Strong* ones. But then afterward,

I set them aside. Foolishly so, 'twould seem now."

Understanding swept Tempy's face. "Here now, don't you go blamin' yourself, ma'am. There ain't a woman livin' who ain't been tempted by the sweet makin's of some smooth-talkin' man. 'Specially when there's so few men left among us." She sighed deeply. "But a good one'll come along for you soon, Miss O'Toole. You just wait for him. Trust the good Lord. He'll show him to you at the perfect, right time."

Catriona laughed. "I'm neither waitin' for a good man to come along nor trustin' the *good Lord* to bring one. In case you haven't noticed, the Lord hasn't exactly been on me side for these last few—" She stopped short, remembering who she was talking to.

A flicker of surprise touched Tempy's expression, and Catriona wished she could take back the words. Even having known the woman so short a time, she knew Tempy was a woman of faith. And she didn't begrudge her that. Not at all. The Almighty did work in people's lives. Catriona didn't doubt that. Trouble was, he apparently had his favorites while choosing to leave others to their own devices. She was proof of that, was she not?

Not wanting to risk further offending the woman, Catriona offered a thin smile. "What I meant to say is—"

"Child . . ." Tempy gently patted her arm. "You ain't never gotta worry 'bout bein' honest with me. Or with the Lord. He already know what you

449

thinkin' anyway. He know it before you even got the words laid out on your tongue."

Catriona blew out a breath. "Which isn't very comfortin', considerin' some of me thoughts of late."

Tempy laughed. "With all the peoples who done lived and died 'fore us, don't you think the Almighty's heard just 'bout everything there is to hear? People been railin' at him since the beginnin' of time. But he *still* loved this ol' world enough to send his only Son to bring us back to him. Don't that say a lot about him? 'Bout how much he loves us? How much he wants to take care of us?"

Catriona tried to smile but couldn't. "Aye, it does. Until I think about what he did to that only Son while he was here."

Tempy's expression sobered. She searched Catriona's gaze, her own filling with what Catriona could only define as loving compassion, and seeing it brought tears to her own eyes yet again.

After a squeeze of her hand, Tempy resumed her work, and Catriona did the same. She scraped the remaining bits of pancake and maple syrup into the compost bin, then dunked the dishes into the tepid water in the wash bucket. A thought occurred.

She glanced over, keeping her voice low. "Did you tell the colonel what you discovered about Mr. Cunningham? Before the colonel hired him?"

Tempy paused, hands on hips. "The day a white man starts askin' me what I think is the day this world gone plumb outta whack." She gave a quick laugh. "So no, ma'am, I didn't go tellin' him nothin'. Way I figure it, one way or the other, give it enough time, and the truth always has its say. Same as it'll do this time. Just wait and see."

Tempy added hot water from a Dutch oven warm from the stove to the wash bucket, and Catriona scrubbed the dishes clean. Over the past two days, they'd formed a rhythm of her washing and Tempy drying. As Catriona worked, she combed through what she knew—or *thought* she knew—about Wade. How was it that a wee part of her wanted to believe that what Tempy shared with her wasn't true? Yet try as she might, and she *did,* she kept stumbling over the fact that she herself thought Wade and Isham Pender were hiding something. She had just turned to ask Tempy about that when Mary joined them, bringing a tray laden with breakfast dishes down from the family dining room.

Together, the three of them worked to quickly put the kitchen to rights. When Mary stepped out to fetch some ingredients for lunch from the springhouse, Catriona seized the opportunity.

She kept her voice soft. "I think Mr. Cunningham and Isham Pender might be hidin' somethin'. Together." She gauged Tempy's expression and clearly read surprise in her features.

"Why you be thinkin' that, ma'am? 'Bout Mister Pender, I mean. Mister Cunningham, I be sayin' yes without blinkin'. But not Isham. I know him. He a good man. He been here for a while now.

451

Done proved hisself to be a kind sort o' person and honest. What he says he gonna do, he do."

"I'm not sayin' Pender isn't a kind man or that he's dishonest. All I'm sayin' is that when Nora fell the other day, I saw him and Mr. Cunningham exchange a look."

Tempy eyed her. "What sort o' look?"

Catriona paused from wiping down the last worktable, wondering how to describe it. "A look that one friend would give another friend. A look that holds a passel full of words without havin' to say any of them."

Tempy said nothing, but she seemed to be weighing that possibility.

"I simply get the feelin'," Catriona continued, "that he and Mr. Cunningham are already knowin' each other. *Well.* And reasonin' that through, they had to know each other *before* they came to Carnton. Yet they're actin' like they've just now met."

Tempy finally shook her head, the firm set of her jaw saying she wasn't having any part of the idea, at least in regard to Isham. "I just ain't seen that at all in Isham. He ain't nothin' like Mister Cunningham, Miss O'Toole. He's as good a person as they come."

Realizing she'd made a misstep in broaching the subject, Catriona nodded. "I'm bettin' you're right and I'm mistaken. You've known Isham much longer than I have." Eager to change the subject, she added a smile for good measure. "Do you

452

happen to know where Mrs. McGavock typically is this time of the mornin'? I'm needin' to ask her about how and where I'm to be orderin' the garden supplies. I made a list of all we're needin', but I want to be sure I've included everythin' Mrs. McGavock wants to—"

"Did I hear my name?" A voice carried down from the same stairwell Nora and the others had ascended a while earlier, and seconds later Mrs. McGavock appeared.

"Yes, ma'am, you did." Catriona approached her. "I've got me list here of all we're needin' for the garden based on the conversation we had yesterday. And I'm wonderin' how you want me to go about gettin' the supplies. I'm eager to get started." She reached into her pocket, then handed Mrs. McGavock her list.

As Mrs. McGavock read through the requested items, Tempy poured a fresh cup of hot coffee from a pot on the stove that never seemed to run dry, and Mrs. McGavock accepted it with thanks.

"Well done, Miss O'Toole. On quick perusal, I believe this contains everything you'll need. *And* you remembered every item I mentioned. Thank you." She handed the list back. "Simply give this to Mr. Cunningham, and he'll see that everything you need is purchased."

Catriona hesitated. "To Mr. Cunningham?" She sensed Tempy's attention but didn't look at her.

"Yes, that's right," Mrs. McGavock responded. "He's in charge of purchasing."

Catriona smoothed her hands down the front of her apron. "Is there a way, perhaps, ma'am, that I might simply go to town and fetch these items meself? So I wouldn't have to wait on him," she added. "I'm sure Mr. Cunningham is quite a busy man."

Mrs. McGavock took another sip of coffee, then returned the china cup to its saucer with a soft *clink*. "While that is true, Mr. Cunningham is the overseer. And one of his responsibilities is to oversee all ordering. So busy or not, he will make the time to obtain the garden supplies for you. I've already spoken to him this morning, so he's aware that the garden is a priority. *And* that he'll be supervising the project."

Catriona cocked her head. Surely she hadn't heard the woman correctly. "That he'll be supervisin' the project? The burial project, you mean?"

"Yes, that too. But the garden as well. The colonel likes for the overseer to have his eye on the entire property. That way, Mr. Cunningham can relay any and all concerns that may arise. So should you have any issues, please see Mr. Cunningham. He'll be checking in with you on occasion too. The man is quite knowledgeable about plants and farming. I feel sure he'd be more than willing to share his wealth of knowledge with you."

This time Catriona *did* chance a look at Tempy, who wore an implacable expression, which precisely described her own emotions at the moment. Catriona summoned what she hoped was a pleasant

454

expression. "Aye, ma'am, I've no doubt about Mr. Cunningham's willingness to be sharin' his knowledge. Wealth of it that there is."

Mrs. McGavock and Tempy began discussing the menu for the week, and Catriona excused herself from the kitchen, eager to get this done and over with.

CHAPTER 28

Annoyed at having to go through Wade to order what she needed, Catriona looked for him first in the barn. He wasn't there. Then she searched the fields around the house. No sign of him there either. She walked as far as the rise in the hill to peer over the pastureland. Only cows on one side of the fence and horses on the other. Growing more resentful by the minute, she headed for the overseer's cottage.

"The man is quite knowledgeable about plants and farmin'," she said aloud, trying her best to mimic a Southern accent. "I feel sure he'd be more than willin' to share his wealth of knowledge with you." She laughed under her breath. *Wealth of knowledge, me eye.* She'd wager she knew more about gardening than Wade Cunningham ever did. Granted, he did know how to catch chickens, but that didn't mean he knew everything there was to know under the sun.

Clearly, though, Mrs. McGavock was under Wade's spell. But Tempy wasn't. And neither was she. Not anymore.

She passed the chicken coop and spotted a few of the chickens with the paint-tipped feathers. Some of them *her* chickens. If not for Nora's injury, she would have already made the trip into town to sell them. Leaving Nora in the care of Tempy or Mary while she was working a short distance away in the garden was one thing. And aye, she'd made a quick trip into town with Wade to get her trunk the other day. But being gone for several hours to sell chickens was out of the question. Still, if Nora's attending class with the McGavock children proved successful, she would feel more comfortable with being gone for that amount of time.

Their lack of money continued to weigh heavily. The Irish were already viewed as thieves and beggars by most, and to think that she'd contributed to that misperception galled her. She not only intended to pay Caesar for his part in caring for Nora, but she still owed the debt at Mr. Pritchard's mercantile in addition to the other stores in town where she'd purchased goods.

Her face burned when she thought of revisiting each proprietor and offering an apology, then promising she'd pay in full. Especially when the promise felt as flimsy as the lining in her pockets. But hopefully the sale of the dozen chickens would bring enough money that she could pay each merchant at least a portion of what she owed. Not that doing so would change their opinion of her.

A counterfeiter. That's what the government operative, Frank Bonner, had implied she was, or at the very least had implied she was involved with one. A charge that would have been laughable if not for the fact that Ryan *had* sent that money.

458

Where had he gotten it? She'd assumed he'd saved it from his soldier's pay. Which would've been just like him to do. Only four Christmases ago, or had it been five now, he'd scrimped and saved for months to buy each of his four sisters winter stockings. Catriona remembered the wry smile on his face as she'd opened her package. He'd included a small sketch of a Celtic cross, special for her, the same cross he had tattooed on his arm. He'd known she would like it. She'd slipped it into the pages of Mam's Bible for safekeeping before she and Nora left Ireland.

But where Ryan had obtained that money he'd sent the family was a mystery. Another was how Bonner had known all those details about her! When she'd arrived in this country. All the places she'd been. And although he never stated it outright, she'd gotten the feeling he'd even known about her being here at Carnton. But how?

Her gaze rose to the heavily wooded edge of the field a short distance ahead, then to the shadows beyond, and a shiver passed through her. She glanced behind her toward the main house, then back to the barn, unable to shake the feeling she was being watched.

She quickened her stride, telling herself she was being foolish, yet her inner counsel didn't prove nearly as convincing as the memory of Bonner's steely stare. But surely her and Nora's being guests of Carnton provided an added measure of protection. And even anonymity.

Telling herself that was the case, she climbed the front porch steps to the overseer's cottage and knocked twice on the door, then stepped back to wait. Realizing she hadn't given any thought to what she was going to say to Wade, she tugged the list of supplies from her pocket and attempted to gather her thoughts. Mrs. McGavock had specific varieties of flowers she wanted planted, and fairly familiar with the stock items at the local shops, Catriona had an inkling that some of these seeds would need to be ordered. Which would take time. As it was, the weather was warming up nicely, and she would have the garden beds ready for planting in the next few days.

With a sigh, she knocked on the door again, harder this time, then bent slightly to peer through the upper-paned portion of the door. No sign of him inside either.

Just inside the door was a kitchen with a cast-iron stove nestled between a worktable and a lovely blue-painted pie safe. By the window sat a kitchen table with two chairs, and beyond that lay a sitting area with an upholstered settee and matching chair. A tiny round wooden table claimed the space between them, marrying them nicely, while hosting the only oil lamp in the room. Her gaze roamed a few feet more to a door that, she assumed, led to a bedroom. Simple furnishings. Nothing like those in the McGavocks' home but still very comfortable.

Then she spotted a stack of cut paper and pen

on the table and got an idea. But did she dare? She looked around, then back at the table, and tentatively tried the doorknob. It turned easily in her grip.

She stepped inside and quickly shut the door behind her. Lingering aromas of maple syrup, pancakes, and coffee greeted her—as did the strong sense that she did not belong here. She crossed to the table, tore a sheet of paper from the pad, and grabbed the pen. Starting with his name, she wrote Wade a brief note referencing the list of supplies, then added that she would appreciate it if he could have the items ready for her by tomorrow morning.

Satisfied with what she'd written, she signed her name and placed the note near the edge of the table along with the list. That's when she saw them. Two oblong wooden boxes stacked one atop the other on the floor beneath the kitchen table and a portfolio leaned against them. She cocked her head to read the wording on the sides of the boxes.

Farm Receipts and Ledgers (1859–1865)
Farm Correspondence (1857–1865)

What was Wade doing with Colonel McGavock's personal files? And in this kitchen? Then again, as Mrs. McGavock had reminded her earlier, Wade *was* Carnton's overseer, so he was responsible for all ordering. Perhaps the colonel had requested that Wade review expenses, or maybe Wade was perusing past correspondence to gain a better understanding of McGavock's preferred manner in his business dealings. Catriona frowned. She had to admit, whatever reason the boxes were here, it wasn't out of line for Wade to have them. Still, she didn't trust him.

She walked to the door and peered outside. No one within view. She could dash out right now and no one would see her. She turned the knob, then paused. She mentally shook her head, knowing better than to give in to curiosity. But when would she ever have the chance to be in here again? She glanced behind her. She could look around, just a wee bit, and see if she came across something—anything—that would explain her misgivings about Wade. As though on cue, her earlier conversation with Tempy replayed through her mind. Tempy disagreed about Wade and Pender knowing each other, aye. But despite that, the woman basically said herself that Wade was either a liar or a scoundrel. Still, that gave her no right to go rifling through—

She was back to the kitchen table in a flash.

She knelt, opened the portfolio, and felt a rush of anticipation as she saw pages of notes within. She scanned them quickly, one after the other. Assuming they were in Wade's handwriting, she found them neat and tidy—and completely absent of anything interesting. His notes summarized amounts spent on feed, saddlery, seed, and an endless litany of other farming supplies, then listed which ledgers corresponded to which receipts.

Nothing the least bit scandalous or revealing.

With a sigh, she closed the portfolio and returned it to its place, then quickly peered out the side window. Still no one.

The kitchen worktable bore only breakfast dishes, an empty coffee cup, and a crumpled cloth napkin. A heavy coat she recognized as one Wade had recently worn hung on a hook by the door. Beneath it, a pair of boots. No knickknacks or books adorned the space.

Her gaze trailed to what had to be the bedroom door.

"No, Cattie, don't!" She could hear the echo of Ryan's dear voice on the countless occasions when, as children, he'd egged her on to do something, only to finally warn her off once he realized that she indeed possessed the nerve to follow through on the dare. Which was precisely what she needed to do now. Because if Wade really was someone other than who he pretended to be—and didn't every bit of evidence point to that as truth?—didn't she need to know? And wouldn't she be doing the McGavocks a substantial service if she revealed that fact?

Hearing a resounding, if silent, *Aye* within her, she purposefully silenced her other far-less-than-altruistic motives and crossed the room. But no sooner had she started to open the bedroom door than she froze. What if Wade was on the other side?

The thought all but shut down her lungs. She

grimaced. How would she explain herself to him? Perhaps she should leave now and not look back. Seconds passed. Then slowly, inch by inch, her bravery came skulking back. If Wade *was* on the other side of this door, he would have said something by now.

Relaxing a little, she thought briefly about knocking, then realized how absurd that would be under the circumstances. She gently pushed the door open the rest of the way, and her nerves settled back into place. Definitely a bedroom, and definitely empty. A wardrobe, an unmade bed, and a side table. That was all the tiny room held. Except for the open leather satchel beneath the window. Struggling to ignore the not-so-distant warning sounding inside her, she walked to the window, knelt, and made a mental image of the state of the bag. Then she carefully rummaged through the few pieces of clothing within. But it was only clothing. Still . . .

She caught the scents of bay rum spice, fresh sunshine, and something else distinctly male. She fingered the black chambray shirt on top, then told herself that her pulse edging up a notch had nothing to do with the shirt's owner and everything to do with where she was and what she was doing.

Knowing she'd been in the cottage longer than she'd anticipated—her conscience beginning to eat away at those *altruistic* motives—she returned the satchel to its disheveled state and hoped her memory could be trusted in that regard.

She searched the wardrobe next, finding more clothing and the photograph of a dog nestled in the bottom drawer between two pairs of pants. And not just a dog, but one seated on a fancy chair. The name HARVEY was on the front of the image, but it wasn't handwritten. The photographer had propped up a sign with the name HARVEY on it, then intentionally included it in the portrait for all posterity. She turned the picture over. Nothing written on the back. Why would Wade have a picture of a dog? Whatever the answer, she decided it would have to remain a mystery. But one thing was undeniable. Wade Cunningham had very few items of a personal nature in his possession, which seemed odd. Her and Nora's bedroom was full of personal items—books, letters, a few treasured photographs, Mam's Bible—and they'd only packed what they considered essential when they left Ireland.

Could it be that Wade Cunningham was who he said he was? Was it possible that she had simply imagined seeing a knowing look pass between Wade and Pender? And here she was standing in Wade's bedroom, invading the man's privacy. Guilt tore a chunk out of her confidence. But Tempy had caught him in a lie. She mustn't forget that. And Tempy did not seem the type to misjudge a person.

Catriona closed the wardrobe drawer and headed for the kitchen, then saw what appeared to be a rolled-up document shoved to the back of the bottom shelf of the bedside table. She glanced out the bedroom window again, then seeing no one anywhere near the cottage nor around the house or barn, she retrieved the document and, with care, unfurled the wrinkled and stained piece of paper. Only, it wasn't a document. It was an illustration. Or more rightly, illustrations.

At the top of the page was the word *EMANCIPATION* printed in all capital letters. Catriona looked at the largest, most prominent vignette in the middle and felt the slow curve of a smile. It was an illustration of a Negro family. Only, this family lived in a very nice house, with a modern woodstove and nice furniture, and they all wore stylish clothes identical to those any white family might wear. No tattered shirts or ragged hems. The da was bouncing a wee child on his knee, and both of their smiles—along with those of older children looking on—were carefree and happy, so full of hope. An older woman in a headscarf seated by the stove looked a little like Tempy.

Catriona's gaze moved to the right-hand side of the page, to images that portrayed Negro children leaving their house to attend school, books tucked under arms, smiles lighting their faces, a puppy bouncing alongside them. Next was a Negro man being paid for his work, the man's posture communicating the humble pride of accomplishment. But when her gaze moved to the left side of the poster, her smile faded.

A black woman, stripped to the waist, was

tied up and being beaten, and a black man was being tortured. One of the drawings depicted a Negro being chased by vicious dogs and another being branded. In the next, a white man was on horseback, his whip raised high above his head, as a black man raised his arms as though to ward off the blow. But it was the image of a Negro family being sold off one by one at a slave auction that caused Catriona's throat to close. The father was on the auction block, the mother on her knees begging the auctioneer. Utter dread and panic lined her face and those of her precious children.

Catriona's thoughts flew to Tempy and the woman's younger siblings who'd been sold away at so young an age and so long ago. An entire lifetime had passed since then. Her eyes watered, and she pressed a fist to her mouth. There had to be a way to track down slaves who'd been sold. An office located somewhere, perhaps, that she could write and make an inquiry. She should have already acted on that by now, and she vowed again that she would.

Scanning each image again, she noticed detail in the uppermost corners that she'd missed. On the left, the artist had rendered what looked to be demons loosed from hell. While on the right, storm clouds were clearing, a new day was dawning, and a woman Catriona assumed represented liberty, or maybe justice, held a set of balanced scales in her left hand while lifting an olive branch in her right.

The artist had drawn each illustration in such

detail and clearly with the intent of shaming those who supported slavery and honoring those who opposed it. She lifted her gaze. So why did Wade Cunningham have something like *this* in his possession? Wade, a Confederate, like John McGavock. A man who, by his own admission, had fought for the Southern states. It made no sense.

She searched the poster for any other identifying information and found the artist's scribbled signature in the lower right-hand corner. But she couldn't decipher the name. Her gaze fell to a faded line of tiny print that ran along the bottom. THE EMANCIPATION OF THE NEGROES—THE PAST AND THE FUTURE—DRAWN BY MR. THOMAS NAST, *HARPER'S WEEKLY*, JANUARY 24, 1863.

She'd never heard of Thomas Nast nor *Harper's Weekly*. But the real question for her, again, was why would Wade, a man who'd fought for the South, have such a thing in his possession? Unless . . . She looked up. Unless he *hadn't* really fought for the—

"Sure, come inside here and we'll get the details down on paper."

Catriona spun to see Wade walking right by the bedroom window. She dropped to the floor, heart thudding. Crouching, she briefly squeezed her eyes closed. How was she going to get out of here? With trembling hands, she rolled up the poster and shoved it back where she'd found it, then slowly rose and moved to hide behind the bedroom door.

The squeak of hinges announced the opening

of the door, and she wished the wood floor would open up and swallow her whole.

"Come on in," Wade offered, his deep voice carrying throughout the small cottage. "Let me write down exactly what you need, and I'll get it for you the next time I go to town."

Catriona pressed her back against the bedroom wall, afraid that at any moment he'd open the door and find her. She instinctively felt for the dagger nestled in the left sleeve of her shirtwaist, then was struck by the absurdity of the gesture. It was *Wade* in the other room, not some miscreant! For pity's sake, it wasn't as though she would have to defend herself. But if caught, she *would* have to give a defense. She grimaced. Best she not be caught.

"I 'preciate you doin' this for me, Mister Cunningham. I put in an ask to the man who had this overseein' job 'fore you, but he ain't never got it bought."

Catriona didn't recognize the other man's voice but hoped they wouldn't be long. As the two men discussed the purchase of some piece of equipment for the farm, her mind raced. She glanced at the bedroom window and gauged the height. It wasn't that far off the ground. And she could still climb a tree, so she could certainly climb out from that window with no problem. But it faced the barn. If anyone saw her . . .

Nay, it made the most sense to wait until Wade and the other man left, then she'd slip out the front door same as she came in. She briefly closed her eyes, wishing again she'd had the sense never to enter the cottage in the first place. Keeping her eyes closed, she listened, and she was heartened when their conversation sounded as if it was winding down.

"On second thought, I should have this for you tonight if you want to come back and get it. I think I'll head into town shortly. First, though, I need to load up a few things in the barn."

She perked up at Wade's comment. Not only were they leaving, but Wade was going into town. *Saint Peter be praised!* Not two minutes later, the front door closed, and she took her first full breath in what felt like ages. Anticipating Wade passing by the bedroom window, she ducked down a little just in case he happened to look over. But he didn't. He strode toward the barn, his long legs eating up the distance.

Guilt still nipping her heels, she slowly opened the bedroom door and peered through the crack, making sure both men were gone. They were. She left the bedroom and noiselessly closed the door behind her, then hurried toward the front porch. She paused briefly to peer through the upper glass-paned portion of the door. She looked first one way, then the other. Not a soul in sight.

She'd exited the cottage and started down the front steps when a creaking noise drew her attention. She looked back. Wade was seated in one of the rocking chairs, a far-too-appraising look on his handsome face. Heart in her throat, she missed the step and grabbed for the banister, narrowly finding it. How on earth had the man—

"Good day, Catriona." His mouth curved, but the underlying seriousness in his tone sent a shiver through her.

"Wade, I—"

He lifted a hand. "Whatever you're about to say to me, make sure it's the truth."

CHAPTER 29

Even with the evidence standing right in front of him—the stark pallor of guilt lining Catriona's face, her hands knotted tight at her waist—Wade still had trouble believing that what appeared to be the truth actually *was*.

He would have staked his reputation on the belief that she wasn't involved in any way with the local counterfeiting ring. And he had basically done just that in his last report to the chief. Watching her now, he hoped—no, he *prayed*—she wasn't. But what other reason would she have for snooping around in his cottage? And he found her behavior especially suspicious since it followed on the heels of the interrogation by a fellow Secret Service operative.

Catriona opened her mouth as though to say something, then hesitated, apparently heeding his advice to choose her words carefully. He'd witnessed this scene countless times before— the guilty caught in the act—and he'd even enjoyed it on occasion. Suspects scrambling to think of a way to explain their behavior even if it meant lying. Most of them kept that skill at the ready. Yet with every second spent mentally spinning their yarn, the guiltier they appeared, so they usually rushed to their own defense.

It just never occurred to him that he would ever have to watch Catriona O'Toole playing out this role. And watching it twisted his gut. Then he saw it, clear as day. That telling flicker in her eyes.

She cast a fleeting glance back at the door of the cottage. "I was leavin' you a note," she said quickly, her voice overly cheerful. "A list of supplies I'm needin' for the garden. I left it on the kitchen table there for you." She attempted a smile, but it would seem her conscience wouldn't abide the further falsehood.

Wade tried to take heart in that fact, even as disappointment settled like a stone in the pit of his stomach. "Do you mean this note here?" Coming to his feet, he pulled the piece of paper from his pocket, the old rocker creaking back and forth behind him, filling the heavy silence.

He closed the distance to the steps, and her chin lowered bit by bit the closer he came. He held up the note.

She blinked, obviously recognizing her own handwriting as well as the full measure of her culpability. "So all that time, you were knowin' I was—"

"Hiding in the bedroom. Yes, I did. What I don't know is why."

She pressed her lips together. Her breath came quickly. "Wade, I can explain. But first let me say—"

"What were you doing in the cottage, Catriona? And in my *bedroom.*"

Her face flushed a deep crimson, and she bowed her head. "When I first stepped inside, I truly meant to only leave a note. But then I looked around and—"

"The *truth,* Catriona. And I would appreciate it if you'd look me in the eye when you're speaking." He intentionally said the latter as though addressing someone Nora's age, fully expecting it to rile her temper. Anger could be useful. It loosened a person's tongue and encouraged them to say things they otherwise wouldn't.

Slowly, she lifted her gaze. Guilt still tainted her expression. But sure enough, his comment must have nicked her pride, too, because a subtle fire lit her eyes. "Aye, I'll look at you, Wade Cunningham," she said evenly. "And I'll tell you the truth—if you'll stop jumpin' in on me every other word."

Despite the defiance he saw in them, her beautiful blue eyes threatened to draw him in. Reminding him of why he was here at Carnton, he determined, yet again, to maintain his objectivity where this woman was concerned. He gave a single nod, and her chin lifted ever so slightly.

"I *was* leavin' that note, precisely as I said. Only then, I—" She glanced away, then must have remembered his request and, with visible effort, locked her gaze again on his. "I saw the crates with all the receipts and letters. And frankly, I began wonderin' why you were havin' all the colonel's *personal* files right there in your very own kitchen."

"I have them, Catriona, because I'm the—"

"The overseer, aye. I'm aware. But you have to be knowin' that"—she blew out a breath, then closed her eyes tight—"ever since I've come to Carnton, I've been seein' things that—"

"Look at me, Catriona."

"*Och!* Would you stop sayin' me name? It's makin' me nerves jump. Same as havin' to look at you the whole time. You with those eyes that see straight through a person."

"I see only what's plainly in front of me. Like I saw you walk out of my cottage a few minutes ago." He glanced back at the door.

"Oh nay, you see *far* more than that, *Mr.* Cunningham. I've watched you watchin' others, and watchin' *me* when you think I don't know." She gave a pert little nod, her accent growing even more pronounced. "You're always takin' everything into account, writin' every detail down in that head of yours. I'm not sayin' there's a law against it, but it's not what a normal person does, I'll tell you that much!"

Wade stared, a slight wind of warning blowing through him. Was this her subtle way of threatening him? Of telling him she knew who he was? He examined every nuance of her expression and demeanor, relying on training and past experience to help him interpret whether she was telling the

476

truth. Everything within him said she was, yet every scrap of evidence said she was *not*. And realizing how he felt about her—how even in that moment he wanted to take her in his arms and kiss her long and slow until she melted into him, until she could scarcely breathe, until a soft moan of pleasure rose in her throat—Wade swallowed, knowing with absolute certainty that he could not trust his instincts regarding this woman. He could trust only what he'd seen.

"Let me tell you, Miss O'Toole, what *I* think is making your nerves *jump*. It's that you're not telling me the truth."

She narrowed her eyes. "You want to be knowin' exactly why I went lookin' in your cottage?"

He gave a harsh laugh. "That's precisely why we're having this conversation."

She leveled a stare. "I went lookin' because I don't believe you are who you say you are. I think you're hidin' somethin'. And furthermore, I think I know what it is!"

Wade maintained a calm demeanor even as his pulse ratcheted up a notch. He gave her a doubtful look. "You think I'm hiding something?"

"Oh aye. I know you are." A confident little smile tipped her mouth.

He more than matched it. "Then please, enlighten me."

She leaned in, challenge in the act. "For one, I saw the looks passin' between you and Isham Pender the other day. You're actin' like you don't know each other a'tall, but I think you do. In fact, I think you're knowin' each other well. And that's not all. I—"

She halted as though weighing the wisdom of saying whatever was coming next. Knowing she needed a nudge, Wade goaded her with a slightly raised brow.

"I've learned from Tempy," she continued, squaring off in front of him, "that you lied to her the first day you came to Carnton. Oh aye, she told me all about it. She says you're either a liar or a scoundrel. So which one are you, Wade?" Hands on hips, she stared up. "A liar? Or a scoundrel?"

The brush of warning he'd felt a moment earlier gave his confidence a firm tug. Catriona had picked up on the connection between him and Pender? Interesting. He'd thought she'd been fully focused on her sister. And Tempy holding that opinion about him wasn't surprising. After all, liar and scoundrel were the only two options his actions had given the older woman in the entrance hall that day. What he *did* find surprising was that Tempy had warned Catriona about it. About him. Already, a bond had formed between the two women. But even that he could use to his advantage, once he got to the bottom of this.

He started to speak, but she beat him to it.

"And there's something else. I found that poster of yours too. The one hidden in back of the lower shelf of your bedside table."

Wade frowned. "A poster?"

478

"Aye." She had no trouble meeting his gaze now, obviously sensing the scales had tipped in her favor. "The one with the word *Emancipation* written across the top. And don't be gettin' me wrong, I like the poster very much. But I had to ask meself, why would a *good* Confederate man such as yeself be havin' something like that? It made no sense a'tall. Until I thought about it, then suddenly it did. Because what that poster's sayin' goes right along with you wantin' to stand up for me, an Irishwoman, at the mercantile that day. And even though Tempy doesn't care a lick for you, I've seen the way you treat her. With respect. Not like she's invisible. Not like the way so many white men treat her. Same goes for the way you speak to Pender and ol' Caesar. So . . . would you like to know what I'm thinkin', Wade Cunningham?"

In the space of a blink, before she could even answer her own question, Wade saw exactly where she was headed and quickly weighed his options. Convinced now more than ever that she wasn't involved with counterfeiters, that discovery pleased him more than he could let on. But he still needed to tread carefully. Her quarrel with him was *personal,* and that could prove far more revealing for him than he wanted. Impressed at her intuitiveness, he was equally frustrated with himself for not having considered how his interactions with freed men and women might spur her suspicions. He'd been careful around the McGavocks, but he'd figured Catriona's unfamiliarity with life in the South would give him some leeway in that regard. What would he do if forced to admit to her that he'd fought for the North? First, it would mean he'd lose his position here at Carnton. McGavock would waste no time in sending him packing once he learned the truth, and the man would undoubtedly make the news public. That would end any hope of continuing his investigation of McGavock's colleagues without drawing attention. And then second, and equally as important to him, was Catriona herself.

Her brother—a counterfeiter, all but certain—likely died here in the battle at Franklin and at the hands of the 104th Ohio. Without question, Wade knew that whether he or someone else had fired the bullet that killed Ryan O'Toole, Catriona would see her brother's blood on his hands. How could she not? He did too. And what was worse, they would never know the truth.

Her unanswered question still hanging between them, he knew the choices open to him and what he had to do if she forced the issue of where his true loyalties lay. But confident he could sway her from that, he smiled down. "What *are* you thinking, Catriona O'Toole?"

"I'm thinkin' you didn't fight for the South at all. You fought against all this." She glanced back toward the main house. "You don't like it any more than I do, what life used to be like here in this part of your country. Stealin' people's lives away and treatin' them as though they meant nothin'." Her

480

expression turned more earnest than triumphant. "I know some of what that's like, havin' everything taken from you. Havin' someone march in and tell you what you can and cannot do. Takin' the very food you've planted and grown in your fields and then leavin' you with nothin'. Leavin' a whole country to starve. It's not right. People oughtn't be allowed to do that to each other!"

The personal turn in the conversation caught Wade slightly off guard, and judging by the realization dawning on her face, she'd surprised herself by it too. She stared up at him, a good deal of the fight having drained from her. In its place was a vulnerability that softened her features and stirred him more than he could have imagined.

"But what I'm not understandin', Wade, is why you're claimin' to be something you're not."

Wishing they'd met under different circumstances and that he could be more honest with her, he spoke with condescension he didn't feel. "And here I thought your little sister was the one with the good imagination. Now I see where she gets it."

In a flash, the vulnerability vanished, challenge returned, and she slowly shook her head. "I'm seein' that apparently Tempy's *first* guess about you was the right one. You're a liar. Only thing is, I think you're lyin' to me still."

"Catriona—"

A stable hand rounded the corner of the cottage.

Wade paused and nodded to him. "Afternoon, Jeb."

"Mister Cunningham." The man nodded to him, then to Catriona. "Ma'am."

"Afternoon, sir," she said, her voice sounding almost normal.

Seeing another worker coming up the road in a wagon, Wade knew he needed to end this discussion quickly.

"Catriona, I—"

"If you're a Confederate, how do you explain the poster? I saw that with me own eyes."

Wade frowned. "Where did you say you found it?"

"On the lower shelf of the bedside table. Hidden in the back."

Sighing, he rubbed his jaw and tried for a more conciliatory tone. "You *do* know that others have lived in this cottage before me, don't you?"

A glint of disbelief flashed in her eyes, and Wade instinctively knew he had one more chance to convince her.

"And while you," he continued, "are free to like whatever poster or picture you wish to, I would appreciate you *not* assuming that I share your opinion. I guarantee you that Colonel and Mrs. McGavock would agree with me on that count, and they would likely take great offense if they knew you held their beliefs in contempt. Especially with you being a guest in their home."

Her brow furrowed. "I never said I held their beliefs in contempt. I was sayin'—"

"As for Pender," he went on, speaking over her,

"I guess you could say I know him." He shifted his stance, feigning a measure of discomfort. He was willing to lie to protect his cover and the agency's investigation, but only as a last resort. Especially with her. So he chose to walk a very thin line. "The first day I was here at Carnton, I saw Pender. And you're right, our paths crossed some years back. Before the North won the war. Before the slaves were given their freedom."

Her eyes narrowed the slightest bit. "So you're sayin' he was your slave?"

"No, I didn't own him. My family was never wealthy enough to own slaves," he answered honestly. "But he *was* given to me for a time, and I was responsible for making sure he did as he was told."

She studied him, still not fully convinced, he could tell. But he sensed her confidence finally beginning to wane.

"As for Tempy, she may be just the cook. But at a place like Carnton, the cook knows everything about everyone, and that information can be helpful. Especially to a new overseer. So while I usually don't kowtow to the likes of her kind, I'm willing to for a while, to learn what I need to about the other workers here." He shook his head. "But I got off on the wrong foot with her from the start, so that plan hasn't served me well."

Catriona searched his gaze, and Wade could hardly believe it when he saw understanding dawn in her features. She smiled. "And let me be tellin'

483

you what else hasn't served you well. Lyin' to me."

He blinked.

"I'm givin' you to the count of three, then I'm walkin' back into the main house, and I'm tellin' the colonel what I believe is the truth about you. Then we'll be seein' which one of us is *enlightened*. One . . . two . . ."—she arched an eyebrow—"*three.*"

With a look that said she would follow through, she turned on her heel to go. And with the choice made for him, Wade gently but firmly took hold of her upper arm.

CHAPTER 30

She knew it! Catriona turned back to face him, feeling not so much a sense of victory—although there was that—but more one of immense relief. Despite the caution she'd felt within her about this man, not to mention Tempy's warning about him, she liked Wade, far more than was likely wise given how little she really knew about him. And yet, thinking about it, she knew more about him than some people knew about acquaintances they'd had for a lifetime. She knew he was kind to strangers. He treated a plantation owner and a freed man, or woman, with the same respect and courtesy. Same for the Irish. Intuition had told her he'd been hiding something. And to discover she'd guessed correctly about him, that he hadn't fought for the South and all it had stood for, only deepened her feelings for him and made him even more attractive to her. But along with the relief came a trace of dread.

Because from what she recalled about his behavior in the parlor that day the McGavocks described the battle in Franklin, she suspected he might have also fought here, which meant he'd stood against Hood's army—and possibly against General Patrick Cleburne's division. But what were the odds of that? That with twenty thousand Federal soldiers present, he would have been numbered among the 104th Ohio. And him being from Kentucky, as he'd told her recently. It simply couldn't be. It was too far a stretch even for the imagination. And yet doubt lingered.

"Catriona," he said softly, then glanced beyond her, quickly letting go of her arm.

She turned to see Mrs. McGavock walking from the back door with a neighbor friend, a woman she'd seen before but hadn't formally met.

"If you have time," he continued, "why don't you ride with me into town? We can purchase your supplies for the garden and . . . talk." He attempted a smile that didn't hold.

Understandable, given how she'd just threatened him. And it hadn't been an idle threat. She would have followed through, even while not fully wanting to. "I'd be welcomin' a ride into town with you, Wade."

He nodded. "I'll go hitch up the wagon. Meet me in front of the barn in about twenty minutes?"

"Aye." She started for the house.

"And, Catriona?"

She looked back, and the seriousness in his features prodded the dread at the edge of her thoughts.

"Would you give me your word that you won't tell the colonel or anyone else about this until after we've spoken?"

So *that* was it. He was worried she might still go

486

tattle on him to the McGavocks. "I won't be tellin' anyone. I give you me solemn word."

With a final nod, he strode toward the barn, and she hurried inside the kitchen, wanting to check on Nora before they left. The comforting aromas of yeast and coffee greeted her, and Tempy looked up from where she stood kneading a wad of dough at one of the worktables.

"There you is, ma'am." Tempy's smile reached her eyes. "You said you's wantin' me to teach you how to make them yeasty rolls you and Nora like so much. I done mixed up the dough, but I can teach you how to knead it right fast and then knot 'em up to rise, if you want. This be 'bout the most important part anyway, workin' the flour and the water together, gettin' it all good and springy. Makes your bread come out so light and fluffy!"

Catriona hoped her expression conveyed gratitude. "I'd love nothin' more, Tempy. But I'm needin' to get to town to purchase the supplies for the garden."

Tempy paused. "I thought the missus done said Mister Cunningham's supposed to do that for you."

"She did, and I gave him the list, but he's askin' me to go with him. I guess he's wantin' to make sure he buys the right things."

Tempy held her gaze, then slowly nodded. "Yes, ma'am," she said evenly, and Catriona would have to have been deaf not to hear the disapproval in her voice.

Wishing she could tell her more, Catriona hurried up the stairs, eager to be out from under the woman's appraising gaze—and feeling plenty guilty about it. She found the schoolroom on the second floor without issue. And even without Miss Bartel's earlier directions, she could have trailed the eager voices. Nora's above them all.

"Oh, I'm knowin' that one, Miss Bartel. Please, *please* be callin' on me again!"

"Nora, *thank you* for staying seated this time. And since you did stay seated, yes, you may answer the question."

Not wanting to interrupt, Catriona stayed to one side of the door. Then she peered around the corner until she could see the children. Miss Bartel was still out of her line of sight, but true to the governess's earlier promise, Nora was seated at a desk between Winder and Hattie.

"It's called the Atlantic Ocean, Miss Bartel! Cattie and me, we sailed over it in a ship."

"*Very* good, Nora. Atlantic is correct. You know your geography quite well."

Catriona smiled. Perhaps the little scamp had been listening during some of their past lessons after all.

"But it was a nasty, stinkin' ship, ma'am," Nora continued. "We both got sick and had to be usin' the chamber pot most every hour. When it got full, Cattie would take it upstairs and dump it over the side of the ship."

Catriona cringed.

"Did it storm real bad?" Winder asked.

"Did waves crash over the boat?" Hattie chimed in.

"It wasn't a *boat,* Hattie!" Winder corrected. "And I want to hear more about the stinkin' ship."

Laughter followed, Nora's and Winder's loudest of all.

"Children!" Authority accentuated Miss Bartel's voice, and the room quieted. "Nora, I'm sorry you and your sister were unwell on the voyage to America. But please, let's attempt to keep our comments . . ."

Hearing a sound behind her, Catriona turned to see Mrs. McGavock tiptoeing toward her. Readying an apology, Catriona paused when her hostess quickly held up a hand.

"I do this quite often myself, Miss O'Toole," she whispered. "I sneak up here and eavesdrop. It's a treasure, isn't it? Listening to children learn."

Catriona nodded, keeping her voice hushed. "Thank you for your kind understandin', ma'am. And for allowin' Nora to take part in the classes. I mainly came up here to be makin' sure me sister wasn't interferin' too much."

Mrs. McGavock waved away the comment. "Nora is a dear, sweet child. Spirited, yes, but I have one of those myself."

"But, Miss Bartel!" Nora's voice rose. "I have one more story I'm wantin' to share."

Mrs. McGavock laughed softly, and Catriona only shook her head.

"*One* more story about the voyage, Nora, then we must return to our lessons."

"One night, after Cattie went to dump a chamber pot, she was gone a *long* time. So I went lookin' for her. I got lost on that stinkin' ship, and then—"

Catriona felt the blood drain from her face. *No, no, no . . . Not* that *story.*

"—these two men come up and start tellin' me they'll help me find her. But they're takin' me the wrong way. They're takin' me down to the belly of the ship, the know-nothin' oafs! That's not where Cattie went, I tell 'em. But they're not listenin'."

Half frozen, Catriona didn't know whether to apologize to Mrs. McGavock again or race into the classroom and escort her sister out. But hearing Nora recount the events from that particular night on the ship—something the child had never done— stirred the memory vividly inside her, along with the fear of what *could* have happened. Catriona started for the door of the schoolroom, but a gentle hand on her shoulder drew her back. She turned to see Mrs. McGavock slowly shaking her head, tears in her eyes. She grasped Catriona's hand in hers, and only then did Catriona feel herself shaking.

"So I start screamin' for Cattie and try to get away. But they keep draggin' me between 'em down the hall! That's when Cattie comes round the corner with that knife of hers."

"A *knife?*" Wonderment filled Winder's voice.

"Aye, 'tis a fancy one me brother, Ryan, gave her. I get to hold it whenever I want."

490

"Nora," Miss Bartel's voice cut in. "Perhaps we should wait and finish this story at a later—"

"But I'm comin' to the best part! Cattie screams at 'em to let me go. One of 'em says he won't be doin' it. So Cattie, she comes straight for him and *cuts* him right on the cheek!"

Catriona bowed her head, and Mrs. McGavock's grip tightened around hers.

"He lets me go, then Cattie shows the other man the blade. He turns and runs, and Cattie and me, we do the same, all the way back to our cabin, where Cattie, me daft sister"—Nora accentuated the comment with a sigh—"she gets sick in the chamber pot all over again."

Catriona's breath came hard. She turned back. "I-I'm so sorry, Mrs. McGavock," she whispered. "I never dreamed she would—"

Mrs. McGavock took Catriona's face in her hands, her own features strained with emotion. "You brave, *brave* young woman."

"Nay . . ." Catriona drew a breath. "I wasn't brave. I was scared out of me wits. Comin' back to the cabin and findin' her gone . . ." She exhaled. "All I could think about was what if somethin' horrible had happened to her. And here I'd given Mam me word. I'd promised to take care of Nora. To come to America and find Ryan. The three of us were supposed to be makin' a new life here." Tears strangled the words. "But now I fear he's dead, and I'm not knowin' what the future—"

Mrs. McGavock's arms came around her.

"Shhhh . . . Try not to dwell on the future, my dear. As difficult as that is at times, I realize. Here, let's get you a handkerchief."

Mrs. McGavock led the way into a bedroom. Hers and the colonel's, Catriona soon realized. She followed the woman to a bureau by the window, then glanced outside, the warm sunshine beckoning. She hadn't realized what an unhindered view of the barn and surrounding fields this vantage point offered with the draperies drawn aside. She glanced down to see if Wade was waiting for her yet, but she saw no wagon in front of the barn. He *had* said he needed to load some items first.

Catriona accepted the handkerchief and dried her eyes and cheeks, then attempted a smile. "I'm sorry for gettin' so blubbery on you, as Nora would say."

"Don't you dare apologize for that. Especially tears that stem from the love of a devoted sister."

Catriona sniffed. "I do love the child, more than me own life. Even when I might wish I could wallop her." Laughing softly, she glanced to a portrait in an oval frame hanging above the fireplace mantel. The sweet faces of three young girls, beautiful, all of them. One resembled Hattie so much—the girl's precious little button nose— that Catriona was certain the image had to be her likeness. But the other two . . .

"Those are our three precious daughters." Mrs. McGavock's voice held a hushed reverence.

"Sweet Hattie's there on the right. My beautiful Martha is in the center. She was twelve when she passed into heaven. Then there's my precious Mary Elizabeth, who was seven when the Lord took her from this world and ushered her home."

Her voice faltered, and Catriona looked at her.

"Not a day goes by—or on some days, like this one, not an hour—that I don't long to see them again. To hold them, to hear their voices and their laughter."

"I'm so sorry, ma'am, for such terrible losses." Catriona stared at the two girls. One brunette, the other blonde, their cheeks rosy with youth, their expressions containing such joy and contentment.

"I bore John a son as well, before Winder. We named him John Randal. He died as an infant."

Catriona felt the tug of her own grief that always resided just below the surface. "How long ago was that?"

"John Randal passed in '54. So twelve years ago."

Catriona stared at the portrait. Martha had been Alma's age, and Mary Elizabeth was Nora's. And an infant son gone too.

Why are you so cruel?

The question, so pronounced, took her by surprise, and she panicked, wondering if she'd spoken it aloud. She sneaked a look at Mrs. McGavock, and the woman's calm countenance, her attention still focused on her daughters, assured her she hadn't heard it. But the Almighty most certainly had. Not wanting to pick at that thread, or give *him* a chance to either, she turned.

"Thank you again, Mrs. McGavock, for your understandin'. And for this." Offering a smile, she returned the handkerchief, then glanced out the window again to see if Wade was—

He stood by a wagon below, staring up at her, looking none too happy. Even at this distance, Catriona could read the question in his eyes. Nay, not so much a question as the look of a man who thought he was being betrayed.

CHAPTER 31

Catriona thanked Mrs. McGavock again and descended the stairs to the first floor as quickly as she could. She dashed through the family dining room and down to the kitchen, grateful to find Tempy elsewhere, then retrieved her reticule upstairs from her bedroom. Out of breath, she hurried back down the stairs and outside to the wagon.

"Wade, I'm sorry I'm a wee bit late." As she closed the distance between them, she realized how severe his expression really was.

Saying nothing, he held out his hand to assist her into the wagon.

She accepted, and his fingers closed tightly around hers—much as, she imagined, he was envisioning them closing around her throat about now. She sneaked a quick look at him and realized he must have gotten a haircut and shave recently. It suited him. Of course, the way he'd looked before had too.

She scooted over on the bench and peered up to the second-story porch. Sure enough, with the slant of the sun, she could see straight into the McGavocks' bedroom window. "Wade, I wasn't speakin' to Mrs. McGavock about you. I gave you me word about not sayin' anything to anyone before we spoke, and I meant it."

He climbed up beside her, tension radiating from him. He gathered the reins in his hands, then paused and looked down at her. He studied her features as though trying to decipher a mystery, and she didn't turn away even though somewhat uneasy beneath his scrutiny. Under the circumstances, she felt she owed him that much.

Gradually, the stress in his own features lessened. "I believe you," he said simply, then released the brake. He snapped the reins, and the wagon lurched forward.

Catriona shook her head, speaking loudly enough to be heard over the clomp of hooves and the creak of wagon wheels. "So, you're believin' me now. But you didn't at first."

He kept his gaze forward. "Would *you* so easily believe *me* if you'd seen what I saw?"

She didn't even have to think about it. "Nay. I would have assumed you'd be sellin' me out as soon as lookin' at me." She said it with all the seriousness she could muster, and only when he finally looked over did she let her smile come.

He shook his head, but she could sense the tension between them lessening. All was not forgiven and certainly not forgotten, but it was a step in that direction.

"May I be askin' you a question, Wade?"

He didn't respond at first, then looked over. "Just one?"

"Aye."

He nodded.

"How did you know I'd been in your cottage?"

His eyes narrowed slightly. "I'm not sure I want to tell you."

She frowned. "And why is that?"

He faced forward again. "How can I be certain you won't go sneaking back in there again?"

She blew out a breath. "Oh, I give you me word on that. You scared me half to death! I'm surprised you didn't hear me heart all but knockin' out of me chest."

"And who says I didn't?"

Hearing a subtle olive branch in his tone, she waited. "So?"

After a moment, he cast her a sideways glance. "A tiny piece of paper slipped in by the latch as you close the door. Not very sophisticated, but also usually not even seen."

She nodded slowly. "Very clever. And I can attest to it not bein' seen. But what cause do you have for doin' that in the first place? Carnton is safe enough, don't you think?"

"I believe we agreed to *one* question, did we not?"

She stared up at him. "Aye, that we did."

Seconds passed.

"But in the hope of satisfying that ever-curious mind of yours . . ."

She smiled. "Somethin' I think we have in common, aye?"

He merely stared ahead. "Others have trespassed in my quarters before. It's not a good feeling, to know someone's been rifling through your personal belongings. Much less when you realize something's missing and that you've been robbed. So I take precautions when I can."

Hearing the matter-of-factness in his voice, she didn't think he was intentionally trying to make her feel even worse about what she'd done. But she did.

As the wagon bumped and rumbled down the dirt road leading from Carnton to Lewisburg Pike and into town, she became increasingly aware of their bodies touching. Shoulders, arms, hips, thighs. And the more she tried not to think about it, the more she did. She took a steadying breath, keenly aware of the man beside her. But unlike the last time she'd ridden into town with him, the feeling wasn't uncomfortable. In fact, she made no effort to move away. Not that her effort would have been rewarded on such a narrow bench seat.

"Oh . . ." He reached into the front pocket of his shirt. "Seems those chickens of yours have been laying eggs more regularly than the McGavocks' birds have. And larger ones too. So the decision's been made to keep them." He held out a wad of bills.

She looked at the money. "They're wantin' to buy me chickens? But I was plannin' on takin' them to town to sell."

He shrugged. "What does it matter whether you

sell the birds to Carnton or to people in town? As long as you sell them."

"Aye, I guess you're right on that count." She took the money. "I'm not even sure how much money a chicken can bring."

"Usually at least two dollars, if not three and some change."

"That much?" She quickly counted the bills. "Blimey!"

He looked over. "Is it a fair amount?"

Relief bubbled up inside her. "Aye, I'll say it is! They're payin' me four dollars per bird!"

He whistled low. "I guess the price of poultry is higher than I thought."

"I'll be sure to be thankin' the colonel when I see him next."

"No need to thank him. This is a business transaction. Carnton will profit on those chickens in the long run while you profit in the short."

"Short profit or long, I'm grateful just the same." She tucked the wad of bills safely in her reticule, already thinking of how far the money would go in paying off her debts to proprietors in town. She would get the money to them this week, while holding back a small portion for living expenses, which were minuscule considering room and board at Carnton were provided. Still, she and Nora couldn't stay here forever. Nor did she want to.

They rode in silence for a few moments, her mind whirring with what-ifs when he turned to her.

"Do you mind me asking what the two of you

were discussing? You and Mrs. McGavock. From what I could see, it seemed serious."

She looked beside her. "Are you sayin' you're still not trustin' me, Wade?"

"This from the woman I just caught snooping around in my cottage," he said flatly.

She nodded. "Fair enough. I was askin' her about a portrait I saw in their bedroom, and—" Visualizing the portrait again from her memory, she instinctively softened her tone. "She was tellin' me about the children she and the colonel have laid to rest."

Wade's brow furrowed, but he kept his attention straight ahead.

"Two girls, ages twelve and seven. Then a son, an infant."

She spotted two workers a short distance ahead walking toward them on the side of the road. She thought she recognized them as sharecroppers who worked the colonel's land. One of them was tall, muscular, and wore a slouch hat. The other was lighter-skinned and boasted more of a stocky build.

"Mister Cunningham," the men said as the wagon passed, including her in their nod. The taller man tugged at the brim of his hat.

"McConnico." Wade nodded. "Judson."

So few words exchanged, but still Catriona sensed the respect passing between them. How much deeper the respect those men would have for Wade if they knew he'd fought to free them.

"So the two of you speak often?" Wade asked.

It took her a moment to pick up the dangling thread of their conversation. "Oh, nay. The only reason Mrs. McGavock and I got to talkin' today was because I went upstairs to check on Nora before we left. She's attendin' classes with Hattie and Winder now. It was Mrs. McGavock's idea. Anyway, she found me lurkin' in the hallway upstairs, listenin' in on the lesson."

"Is she doing well? Nora, I mean."

"Aye, she is. The girl loves to learn. Or used to, before . . . everything happened in recent months. I haven't been faithful with her lessons, so I'm grateful to Miss Bartel for lettin' her take part."

"Nora's a smart girl."

"Aye, she is. And she's got herself a wee smart mouth to match."

Wade only smiled, his gaze ever forward.

As the silence lengthened, the tension between them crept back in, and Catriona sensed he was sifting through his thoughts, gathering what he wanted to say to her. So she decided to mind her own, which went straight to Nora. Her sister telling that story in class . . .

The recounting of details, especially from Nora's point of view, stirred memories that she wished could be long forgotten. But it *had* made one thing clear to her. Nora had not understood the intent of those two men, and for that she was grateful beyond—

Wade suddenly reined in and brought the wagon to a stop.

Catriona waited as they sat side by side, bodies touching, neither speaking. Yet she knew better than to prompt the conversation. That was for him to do, not her. But he'd chosen a good place for a private discussion, she'd give him that.

She'd not realized before now how secluded this part of the road leading from Carnton to Lewisburg Pike could be. To their left a stand of stately oaks stood shoulder to shoulder as though lined up according to rank, and on their right, a thick grove of newly leafed walnut trees stretched as high as they did wide. Lewisburg Pike still lay a fair distance ahead, and Carnton was far behind. If Wade hadn't already proven himself an honorable man, she might have been worried.

So why was it that when he finally turned to her—his blue eyes deepened to near steel gray—all she could think about was running her hand along his clean-shaven jawline and wishing she knew what it felt like for those lips to be on hers. To be held in his arms and sheltered there. For him to kiss her until she could scarcely think straight. Her gaze dropped to his mouth and lingered, enticing her thoughts down a path such that, if Wade were privy to them, the man might have been a wee bit worried about himself.

She told herself to look away, and finally did, but not before a shadow of foreboding swept across his features and took every ounce of her desire with it.

• • •

"Catriona . . . I appreciate your willingness to give me a chance to explain." Wade sought her gaze, but she suddenly wouldn't look at him.

He prayed again that the still, small voice he'd heard earlier while he'd loaded the wagon was indeed the wisdom he'd been seeking, not some foolhearted notion of his own making. But he never would have chosen this particular course of action himself, which made him certain it was from the Almighty. Still, even though he was determined to do the right thing—to not lie or mislead her about this any further—he feared the truth would come at a high cost. His training with the Secret Service had drilled into him that presenting a false front was oftentimes necessary for the greater good. Namely that of apprehending criminals. But Catriona O'Toole was no criminal. She wasn't even a suspect. Not anymore. At least not in his eyes.

He knew his intended course likely ran counter to what Chief Wood would order him to do. But he also knew without question that hearing even the slightest whisper from heaven's gates far outweighed any directive from the Secret Service.

"Catriona . . ." He struggled to get the words out, grateful now that she *wasn't* looking at him. "You guessed correctly about me. I did fight for the Federal Army. But . . . that's not all."

"*Don't* be sayin' it," she whispered. "*Please* don't be sayin' it."

The pain in her voice, her silent admission, twisted his gut. She already knew what he was going to say.

"I'm so sorry, Catriona. But I fought in the 104th Ohio Infantry. One of the regiments that stood against General Cleburne's men."

The quiet around them grew deafening. Slowly, she lifted her head and searched his eyes even as the light in her own faded.

His chest ached. "That day in the McGavocks' parlor, when you told us about your brother—" He struggled to speak past the knot in his throat. "I couldn't believe it. And every time I've thought of it since then, I—"

"I've been tellin' meself it couldn't be true. That—" Her voice faltered. "That out of all those soldiers, surely you couldn't have been in the 104th Ohio."

"I'm sorry," he said again, the words feeling so weak.

Her hand went to her midsection. "I can't breathe . . ."

"Here, let me help you."

He took hold of her hand, but she only stared at it, then at him, betrayal and hurt thick in her expression.

She gently tugged her hand free. "I can't be near you right now."

Wade instinctively reached for her again, but she drew back, choking on a sob.

Reticule on her arm, she climbed down on her

504

own accord. He quickly set the brake and jumped down, yet he knew better than to approach her.

"Catriona, I know the colonel has contacted the War Department on your behalf, trying to find information on Ryan. But I want you to know that the US Government has resources as well, and I've already reached out to people I know who may be able to help. They've agreed to see if—"

"You were *there* that night," she managed through tears. "On that battlefield."

Hurt riddled her expression, and the weight of it all but forced his gaze elsewhere.

"Catriona, I wish I could tell you that I'm certain your brother and I didn't meet on that battlefield, but I can't."

She nodded. "I'm knowin' that."

He started toward her again, but she shook her head, then put a hand over her mouth as though to keep from being sick. She turned and made her way through the waist-high winter grass toward the grove of walnut trees, then stopped, her back to him, her arms wrapped around herself. A sob rose from her that tore at everything in him. He'd heard the cries of countless soldiers as they'd lain dying on the battlefield, crying for their mothers, their wives, their loved ones. But this . . .

And knowing that he could well have been the one who had taken Ryan's life, she blurred in his vision. "Catriona," he whispered, wondering if she'd even heard him.

She didn't turn. She gave no acknowledgment.

After several moments, he climbed back up into the wagon, hoping he'd done the right thing in telling her the truth. Because in this moment, he felt as if he'd torn both their worlds apart.

CHAPTER 32

"Are you certain you have an appointment with Mr. Cockrill, Mr. Cunningham?"

"Yes, I am. The last time he and I spoke, we agreed to meet here at his office at noon today. A lunch meeting, I believe he called it. To discuss the latest quarterly reports for Colonel John McGavock."

"Oh, this is for Colonel *McGavock*," the secretary asserted, then appeared to search the schedule for Wade's name with greater fervor. But she wouldn't find it. Wade also knew Woodrow Cockrill wasn't in and wouldn't return for at least another hour and a half. He glanced at the clock on the secretary's desk. Twenty till twelve. Her reticule lay atop the desk. She and the other two secretaries seated nearby also took their lunch around this time.

Over the past week, he'd confirmed the comings and goings at the office of Cockrill and Associates. Woodrow Cockrill and his two associates routinely left the office at half past eleven and returned at half past one. The three accountants walked four short blocks to Burkey's, the nicest restaurant in Franklin, where they enjoyed a leisurely lunch with a local judge, all four of them Confederate war buddies. Twice Wade had sat at a nearby table eating lunch and eavesdropping on their conversations, and twice he'd learned nothing other than the men enjoyed slowly sipping brandy and recounting past accolades with an inflated sense of pride and accomplishment. He'd also learned that Burkey's had nothing on Tempy's cooking.

"I'm so sorry, Mr. Cunningham, but I don't see your name on his calendar today. He does have an opening on Friday, four days from now. Will that accommodate your schedule, sir?"

Wade frowned. "No, I'm afraid it will not. I'm meeting with the colonel this afternoon. It's the second of April, and my employer is expecting a review of the entire first quarter." He sighed. "I can't believe Cockrill is doing this to the colonel again. An accountant who doesn't keep his appointments and can't supply reports on a timely basis. That's not good for anybody's business."

The young woman glanced at the other two secretaries, who both stared back wide-eyed, reticules in hand, before turning back. "Mr. Cunningham, Colonel McGavock's business *and* his trust are very important to Cockrill and Associates Accounting Services, I assure you. If you come back at half past one, Mr. Cockrill may be able to provide you with the details from—"

"My meeting with the colonel is at two o'clock, Miss"—already knowing her name, Wade made a point of looking at the nameplate on her desk— "Davison. So unless you can provide me with those final quarterly reports right now, I'm afraid

I'll have to inform the colonel that Cockrill simply didn't have them ready as promised."

Her face fell, and she looked again at the other two young women as though asking for a solution. One of them gave a quick motion with her head. Miss Davison's eyes narrowed the slightest bit, then lit again. "If it would help you, sir, I can provide the details on all the colonel's accounts for the first three months of this year. I believe Mr. Cockrill has already completed the figures for March. That way, at least you'd have the—"

"Information I need, yes," Wade finished for her. "But that still leaves me doing all the compilation work Mr. Cockrill is paid to do."

She briefly looked down at her desk. "I'm certain this is all my fault, Mr. Cunningham. Mr. Cockrill is very precise in his work and wouldn't make a mistake like this, I guarantee you. So please don't lay the blame for an error clearly mine at his feet."

Wade sighed. "Tell you what . . . Give me the most recent numbers for March, then I'll take those back to Carnton and do the compiling myself. *This* time."

A smile of relief crossed her face. "Thank you, Mr. Cunningham. I'll get those numbers right away and then copy them for you."

Wade held up a hand. "No offense meant, ma'am. But I'd prefer to copy those numbers myself. That will give me a chance to catch anything that seems amiss. And I'd appreciate a quiet corner in which to do so. With no interruptions."

"Of course. We have a conference table in another room, sir." With subtle regret, she gestured for the other two secretaries to take their leave.

The two women closed the front door behind them while Miss Davison retrieved a key ring from her top desk drawer. She hurried into Cockrill's office. Wade heard the distinct sound of a key slipping into a lock, then the opening of a drawer. He peered around the corner to see which drawer she thumbed through from a line of ornate wooden cabinets, then quickly stepped back.

He checked his pocket watch, eager to get back to Carnton. Catriona was supposed to start planting flowers and small trees today, not to mention George Cuppett had let him know this morning that the first reburial of the exhumation process would take place this afternoon. Heavy rains in recent days had delayed the reburials for the past week. But Saturday, two days past, the skies had finally cleared, giving way to cloudless blue and a radiant April sun that gradually dried the rain-soaked ground.

He wanted to be close by in case Catriona needed anything. Not that she would let him or even welcome his presence. She'd scarcely spoken to him since that day on the wagon when he'd told her the truth about himself. Or some of the truth. He'd visited her in the garden and had offered his help—or tried. Since the ground had been too wet for planting, she'd taken on the task of replacing the rotten timbers that outlined the flower and vegetable beds. But that work was too strenuous for a woman. The least she could do was let him carry the timbers and set them in place. Yet every time she saw him, she either walked the other way or answered his questions with the politest of refusals. Usually, *"I'm thankin' you for your offer of help, but I can handle it on me own."* She apparently didn't mind Marcellus Cuppett helping her, though. Wade had seen the man out there in the garden numerous times. And always, he and Catriona were talking and laughing.

He checked the time again. Catriona would be with Tempy in the kitchen by now, eating lunch with the children. She'd assured him she wouldn't tell anyone about his having fought for the North, but that had been *before* she knew about the 104th Ohio. So every time he heard John McGavock calling for him or saw the man walking his way, Wade braced himself for a swift and blunt dismissal. But that dismissal hadn't come. Apparently she was keeping her promise. Now for him to keep *his* about finding her brother. Any day now he expected to receive an answer from Chief Wood.

"Here you are, sir." Miss Davison accompanied him to the conference table in an adjacent room and provided extra pens and a stack of cut paper. "I'll be at my desk. But before I go, would you care for anything to drink? Coffee? Hot tea?"

Wade feigned irritation. "I take it the *lunch*

511

portion of my meeting with Mr. Cockrill also went unplanned?"

She winced. "Once again, I'm sorry, Mr. Cunningham. But I'd be happy to go get you something."

"That would be much appreciated." He glanced beyond her. "I believe the three of you were going to lunch when I arrived." He raised a brow.

She ducked her head. "Yes, sir, but I'm most happy to go and bring something right back for you."

"I work best in quiet, Miss Davison. So go on to lunch with your colleagues, but please bring me a sandwich when you return. And take your time. I'll relish the silence."

"Yes, sir. Thank you, sir. I'll do that. And I'll lock the front door to make certain you're not disturbed."

He watched her return to her desk for her reticule, then, key ring in hand, depart through the front door, locking it behind her.

Wade waited a moment in case she returned for something forgotten, then quickly perused the March numbers for McGavock's financial statement and found nothing out of the ordinary. So far, to his consternation, McGavock looked clean. Wade crossed to the front window in time to see Miss Davison disappearing around the corner.

He entered Cockrill's office and pulled the shades, then withdrew the hand pick from his jacket pocket. In a few seconds, he had the drawer with McGavock's records open. In another three, he had access to every file in Cockrill's long line of cabinets. Already having reviewed McGavock's records back at Carnton, he quickly scanned the duplicate files in Cockrill's possession to make certain the accountant wasn't keeping a double set of books. But everything lined up.

Going in alphabetical order, he searched the files next for his four remaining suspects, starting with Leonard Bishop, the owner of the local haberdashery who had experienced an exceptionally profitable year, especially considering he operated his business in a town with seven hundred and fifty residents, scarcely a quarter of them men. Wade had no idea whether Bishop even used Cockrill's accounting services, so he was aware he might be looking for a needle in a—

Bishop, Leonard, a file toward the back read.

Starting with the oldest financials in the folder—August 1851—Wade scanned the documents until he ran across a sizable increase in income that commenced in April 1865 and continued on a monthly basis to date. The very increase that first sparked the Secret Service's interest. Not recognizing the name of the company beside the entries, he withdrew a small leather journal and pen from his pocket and wrote down the name. *Brummel Enterprises.*

Finding nothing else of import in the file, he returned it to its place, then searched for Woodrow Cockrill. But, of course, he found nothing. He glanced back at Cockrill's desk, guessing where the man might keep his personal records. Either there or at his residence.

Whitley Jacobs came next, but Wade found no information on the farmer in Cockrill's files. Finally, he searched for Laban Pritchard, the mercantile owner. Even though he no longer considered Pritchard a suspect in counterfeiting, if he could find anything else on the man to help the agency's investigation, he wanted to. But he came up short on that name as well.

He closed and locked all the file drawers again, then peered into the front office, then to the street. Miss Davison and her colleagues should be returning in roughly twenty minutes, and he determined to make the most of the time.

All the drawers but one in Cockrill's desk were locked, which told him the man was either overly suspicious by nature or had something to hide. The locks on the smaller drawers opened with little resistance, and one of them held Cockrill's billing records. Reading through the entries, Wade frowned. Cockrill was billing McGavock for *forty-five hours* of work in the past month? Wade shook his head. He himself had spent numerous late evenings reviewing McGavock's books yet hadn't clocked even a third of that time. So Cockrill was overbilling, and based on these entries, McGavock wasn't the only client being defrauded.

Wade made some quick notes, then returned the billing journal to its drawer and moved to the last and largest drawer, which proved to be the most secure, the lock bearing the emblem *S&G*. He smiled to himself, familiar with Sargent and Greenleaf. In advertisements, the company boasted that they used the latest metallurgy processes, best tools, and most durable lock components in the industry. Hence providing the safest locks in the world. Virtually "crack proof."

"We'll see about that," Wade whispered, welcoming the challenge.

He checked the time again. Fifteen minutes remained, but he knew it could be less. Eyeing the lock again, he pulled a tiny tension wrench from his pocket, the instrument about the length of his pinkie, then slid the wrench into the bottom of the keyhole. Applying slight pressure on the wrench, he inserted the hand pick at the top of the lock. Concentrating, he carefully raked the pick back and forth in a vibrating motion, moving the pins up and down in the lock until he got the gap between the key pin and—

The jiggle of a door handle brought his head up. He froze, listening. There it was again. He moved to the door of the office and slowly peered around the corner. A man stood outside, frustration lining his features. The man checked his pocket watch, then gave the door handle another firm tug. Wade returned to his task, his heart beating a little faster.

He reinserted the tension rod, then the hand pick, and felt a trickle of sweat edge down his temple. Ignoring it, he closed his eyes, concentrating as he worked to get the pins lined up. There it was, the first *click*. He worked the pick up and down, up and down. Then a second. The third quickly followed, and the lock turned. Wade released his breath.

But far from relaxed, he hurriedly opened the drawer. At first, he was disappointed at its lack of contents. It contained only one file. Then his focus fell on the name. *Pritchard, Laban.* His pulse picked up. He flipped through pages and pages of entries. Money being sent back and forth. Large sums of it too. Records of purchases of supplies including rope, wood, chains, ammunition. *Secret society,* indeed. Of which Woodrow Cockrill appeared to be an *esteemed* member. Wishing he had a way to memorize all the information instantly, Wade wrote down what he could, then committed the rest to memory.

He checked the time. Two minutes.

No sooner had he placed the file back in the drawer than he heard the jiggle of the door handle again. But this time the sound of feminine con-versation and laughter accompanied it. A rush of energy coursing through him, he slipped the tension wrench and hand pick back into the keyhole and worked furiously until he felt the pins slip into place. He pulled up the window shades, then moved to peer around the corner of the office door.

The secretaries walked in, chatting with one another, Miss Davison carrying a cloth-covered plate. Wade took a step back into the office, scrounging for a reason he would be in here. Then he heard the front door open again.

"I had an appointment with Mr. Cockrill *ten* minutes ago, and *no one* was here to greet me!"

Wade chanced another look. The man he'd seen earlier trying to open the front door now stood in the entrance, face flushed and neck veins bulging. The secretaries turned in unison, and Wade saw his chance.

He ducked out of Cockrill's office and into the conference room. He tore two pieces of paper from the pad, then folded them and grabbed the folder Miss Davison originally handed to him before heading for the door.

"Miss Davison . . ."

She turned, a panicked look on her face.

"I appreciate your help earlier, ma'am. I got what I needed." Wade held up the folded pieces of paper, then traded her the folder for the cloth-covered tin plate. "And I appreciate the lunch. So much so"—he dropped his voice to a whisper—"that I won't say anything to Mr. Cockrill or the colonel if you don't."

Relief flooded her features. "Oh, *thank you,* Mr. Cunningham! If I can ever do anything for you . . ."

Wade made a quick exit, but no sooner did he round the corner than he spotted Cockrill and the man's two associates crossing the street toward him. He did a quick about-face and headed in the opposite direction, but not before recognizing one of the associates as the man he'd seen coming from McGavock's office the morning the colonel had invited him back for a second meeting about the overseer's position. With that mystery solved, Wade shoved the pieces of paper into his coat pocket and made his way back to the wagon, the rush of energy coursing through him gradually settling. This case certainly wasn't coming together as quickly as he'd thought it would. But at least he'd made headway today.

After negotiating the traffic in town, Wade guided the wagon onto Lewisburg Pike. The overseer position at Carnton, while providing excellent cover for him, was taking more of his time than he'd anticipated. Of course, some of that was his own fault.

Beyond reviewing McGavock's financial files, he'd reviewed the man's personal files, looking for any scrap of evidence that pointed to counterfeiting, past or present. McGavock's records reached back for several years and included those kept by his father, Randal, who'd died in '43. But most recently, in the attic, Wade had stumbled upon boxes of records dating back into the eighteenth century. Records from John McGavock's grandfather, James, who was from County Antrim, same as Catriona.

Strange how after all these years the McGavock and O'Toole families had intersected again so far from Northern Ireland. Though not by chance, he knew, from having overheard Catriona's conversation with the colonel more than two weeks ago. He'd pieced together enough to know that she'd come to Carnton expecting that her brother had visited here. Why, Wade didn't know yet. But maybe those files would turn up something.

CHAPTER 33

"Miss O'Toole, we appreciate you recording the information on these soldiers, ma'am. Me and my brothers, we're awfully grateful. So is Robert over there. And Charley, coming yonder with the wagon."

Gripping the leather-bound journal, her nerves in a bundle, Catriona managed a nod to George Cuppett and the other three men. But she did her best not to look at the oilcloth-covered wagon Charley brought to a stop by the edge of the cemetery. Under the oilcloth, she knew, were the first caskets containing the remains of exhumed soldiers to be reburied in the McGavock Cemetery, as George Cuppett and his team had taken to calling it.

She cleared her throat, struggling to appear more at ease than she felt. "Me contribution is small when comparin' it to what you're all doin'. So it's me who's grateful to each of you."

George turned and spoke in low tones to his brothers and Robert Sloan, gesturing toward the cemetery, while Charley Baugh, the youngest among them—fifteen, she'd learned, and tall for his age—hopped down from the wagon and came to stand beside her. She nodded to him as well.

The boy whipped the worn cap from his head. "Finally got the rains behind us, Miss O'Toole, and God gave us some clear blue skies. Now we can get to moving these fine men. Give them a better resting place."

"Indeed," Catriona said softly, seeing Ryan's face so clearly in her mind and praying he wouldn't be counted among this number.

With the rain-soaked ground of recent days, she'd been unable to do any planting until today. So she'd undertaken to replace some of the rotten timbers edging the beds and had done her best to smooth the uneven bricks in the herringbone walkways. Both tasks greatly taxed her strength, but she found it exhilarating to see the transformation taking place right before her eyes.

The Cuppett brothers and Mr. Sloan moved to unload the back of the wagon. It was grinding work, the task these men were performing, as evidenced in the somber set of their faces. Marcellus, the middle Cuppett brother and the closest to her own age, had taken to visiting her in the garden in spare moments here and there. Which surprised her at first, seeing how shy he was. But he'd quickly warmed up to her, and she enjoyed their conversations. A kind, soft-spoken man, Marcellus possessed an innocence that made him seem considerably younger than his twenty-five years.

At Tempy's insistence, the burial team had started taking their noon meal outside the kitchen on the brick patio behind the house. And every day at lunch, Marcellus would tell the children a story. His tales always centered around animals. The little bunny that couldn't hop. The little pig that couldn't oink. The little bird that couldn't sing. Nora, Winder, and Hattie had taken an instant liking to the man and his tenderhearted tales.

Catriona watched him as he walked, head slightly bent, shoulders stooped, alongside his younger brother, Polk. It hadn't taken much ruminating on her part to recognize that the seed of Marcellus's stories stemmed from his own lack of self-certainty. Yet he was so gentle and had so much to offer in the way of decency, generosity, and human kindness. Slight of build himself, he was surprisingly strong and insisted on helping her carry the large timbers and pushing the wheelbarrow with additional bricks.

Without warning, Wade intruded on her thoughts. And as she did at least a hundred times a day, she tried to wrestle those thoughts into submission and place him firmly outside of them. *"I fought in the 104th Ohio Infantry."* She closed her eyes, unwillingly snatched back to that horrible moment beside him in the wagon. Her lungs had failed her. She couldn't draw breath. She'd had to move away from him, thinking she was going to be ill. She still couldn't see him without thinking about the part he might have played in Ryan's death. Even now, the possibility of that truth soured in the pit of her stomach. Wade had offered to help her in the garden in recent days as well, but she couldn't abide being in his company. Not with knowing that it was *his* regiment that had cut short the lives of the majority of General Cleburne's men. And likely her dear Ryan's as well.

So why, even now, even after knowing what he'd done, did a small part of her miss him? It made no sense. Then again, with all that Da had done to Mam through the years, Mam had still cared for him in some way, Catriona knew. Though she'd never understood it. How could someone who inflicted so deep a wound on your heart still manage to possess a piece of it?

Determined to corral her thoughts, she looked back to see the Cuppett brothers and Robert Sloan removing the tarp from the back of the wagon.

"Marcellus, you and Polk carry the first one," George instructed. "Me and Robert will come behind you."

Marcellus had told her that young Charley's primary responsibility was to build the caskets. The boy's father was a carpenter by trade, and apparently he'd taught his son well. But as she watched Marcellus and Polk pull the first casket from the wagon, she stared, unable to make sense of what she was seeing. The caskets were scarcely three feet in length. Far too small to hold a man's body. A wee babe, aye. But not a grown man.

She turned to Charley. "The caskets. They're so small. I . . . I don't understand."

His brow creased, then understanding beyond his years moved into his eyes. "Yes, ma'am, they're

524

small because"—he briefly looked away—"it's been so long. Nigh onto fifteen months now since these men were buried. Most of the body is gone back to the earth by this time, and there's mostly just bones left. So Mr. Cuppett, he told me to build the boxes so they could fit a man's femur. He says the femur is—"

"The longest bone in the body," Catriona whispered, her voice faltering. Why had this never occurred to her when thinking about the reburials? In all her dread and worry about assisting with this task, she'd never once imagined this. And somehow, seeing the stark reality of the aftermath of war—nay, not just of war but of this earthly life—rattled her to her core. In the end, so little was left to say you were here. To say you had lived and breathed and spent a life.

Charley gave her a shy look, then ducked his head. "If you'll excuse me, ma'am . . ." He made his way on to the cemetery.

Catriona knew she needed to join the men, to help them as she'd agreed, but she couldn't move. She could feel the sun's warmth on her face, could feel the cool breeze lift her hair from her shoulders, yet she could not make her body obey. She watched as Marcellus and Polk carried the first casket between them in the same manner they would have if it were of normal size. Same as George and Robert did. And instinctively she knew they were doing it out of respect and reverence for what remained of the soldier who'd given his life on that battlefield.

Realization hit, and she sucked in a breath. She lifted her gaze beyond the cemetery in the direction of the Harpeth Valley. *Don't you be in that field, Ryan O'Toole. Don't you be doin' that to me, do you hear? You come back to me, brother. To Nora and me. Come build a home with us like you promised you would.*

Movement ahead drew her eye, and she blinked to clear her vision. George was waving to her. Forcing one foot in front of the other, she joined the team by the first row of freshly dug graves.

"As we discussed, Miss O'Toole," George said quietly, his tone solemn, "and all agree among us"—he looked to the others, who nodded in turn—"we want, at all costs, to protect your sensibilities. So if you would, please take your place over here on this side."

Obliging, Catriona moved to stand opposite him.

"Then I'll open the caskets one by one. The entries need to be numbered, and I'll give you all the information we were able to find on each body. Thus far, for *most* of the forty bodies we've exhumed, we've managed to determine name, rank, and which unit the soldier was in. It helps that members of their own units buried them and that they buried them where they fell on the battlefield the day before. Buried side by side with their Confederate brothers. We'll be burying them by state as well." He paused. "And, Miss O'Toole, on behalf of us all, I want to tell you that we sincerely pray we *don't* find your brother's body among those buried out there. But if we do, we'll be sure to tell you straightaway, ma'am."

Emotion threatening her fragile composure, Catriona looked at Marcellus, knowing he must have shared with them what she'd told him about Ryan. Not minding in the least, but appreciating him for it, she nodded and mouthed a silent "Thank you."

Marcellus wordlessly pointed to the sky, his quiet way of telling her, yet again, that he was praying for her, for Ryan, and that he wished she would trust in God Almighty for the outcome—something she'd done previously in her life. But that was before he'd proven himself untrustworthy. At least in her own affairs.

"Well . . ." George looked at each of them. "Let us commence, shall we?"

Catriona opened the journal, her pen poised and ready.

"Father God . . ."

She looked up to see George's head bowed and quickly did likewise, aware of the others already looking down, hats in hand.

"We thank you, Lord, for these men we're burying here today. Men who willingly gave their lives for the Confederacy. And we ask that you guide our work as we . . ."

Her head still bowed, Catriona heard the sound of a wagon coming up the drive. She discreetly peered up. But seeing Wade glance in her direction, she just as quickly bent her head again, the frustration

527

she'd felt moments earlier returning. She hoped he wouldn't stop by. But then, why would he? To help reinter men he'd helped kill? She tasted the crassness of the thought, but she couldn't bring herself to recant it. After all, it was true.

At certain moments in recent days, her anger with him had all but gotten the best of her, and she'd been tempted to march straight into the colonel's office and tell him the truth about the new overseer he and his wife seemed so pleased with. But every time she considered following through with it, she heard Nora's voice—*"You're lyin', Cattie. Just like Da used to do! You're just like him!"*—and the thought of being anything like her father kept her mouth firmly closed on the matter.

George Cuppett turned and said something to Charley, and Catriona lifted her head, realizing the prayer must have ended. She glanced back toward the road leading to Carnton but saw no sign of Wade or the wagon.

As the men spoke, she eyed the journal open in her hands and ran her fingers over the blank lined pages, thinking of all the mothers, sisters, wives, daughters, grandmothers, and aunts who had wept for the men whose names she was about to write in this book. A book of death. Aye, these men had given their lives, but in a way, so had the families they'd left behind. Everyone suffered, everyone lost. She thought of Braxie and wanted to get back to town to check on the girl. Yet she was none too eager to meet up with the likes of that Frank

Bonner again. She could go her whole life without interacting with him—or any other *government operative*—and die happy. But Braxie was her friend. A friend who needed help. And Catriona knew only too well what that felt like.

Charley, Robert, Marcellus, and Polk started back toward the wagon, and George knelt by the first casket. The wee caskets were made of oak, the workmanship simple but neat. Every corner matching. Every line straight as an arrow. Charley had done well.

Recalling what George had said a moment earlier, she quickly penned the words *Number*, *Name*, *Rank*, and *Unit* on the top line, leaving some space between each, intent on keeping the details straight.

"Miss O'Toole, would you write section number one, Texas, at the very top of the first page, please?"

She did as he requested, aware that he and his brothers hailed from Texas. Had they known any of these men? Had they fought alongside them? Imagining the even greater heartache that would accompany their task with such a discovery, she chose not to inquire.

George carefully lifted the lid of the casket toward her, so its contents remained hidden from her sight. "Number one. His name was J. H. Robertson. He was a private and with the Third Texas Cavalry."

Catriona wrote as neatly as she could, imagining

529

that Private Robertson's loved ones might one day be viewing his name in this book, and she wanted it to be legible. She wanted his family to know just by looking at his name that it had been recorded with care.

George replaced the lid and moved to the next casket beside which several others now rested, Marcellus and the other men wordlessly emptying the wagon.

"Number two," George said, lifting the lid before promptly closing it. "Unknown," he added somberly, then laid a hand atop the oak box for a brief moment before moving on.

Catriona recorded the information on the second line, then wiped away tears. In that moment she felt the burdening weight of the overwhelming probability that she might never know what happened to the one person she'd known from the very second her heart was formed and started to beat inside their mother's womb. Same as his.

CHAPTER 34

"But why can't I be goin' with you on a walk, Wade? It's Saturday, so we're not havin' any classes, and I've got me lots of time."

The earnestness in Nora's blue eyes tugged at Wade's heartstrings. But he knew better than to say yes to the child. Not with where he needed to go, for one, and certainly not with how things stood between him and Catriona. If Catriona were here, she would have scolded her sister for using his Christian name, but he didn't have the heart to.

He sat down on the top step of the cottage porch to be at eye level with the girl. "Because, little one, it's a rough walk through the woods, and I don't think you would enjoy it. Besides, we can't risk you getting hurt all over again." He gently touched her arm that was still wrapped snuggly in a sling, same as the arm of her bedraggled, faceless little doll. Virginia, he thought Nora called her.

Nora's bottom lip pudged for a second, then her eyes lit. "You could be carryin' me, Wade! Ryan, me brother, used to do that on his big, strappin' shoulders." She puffed out her little chest and made a fierce-looking face. Or tried.

Wade laughed. "You're a funny little thing, you know that?"

Her smile dimmed a mite. "Ryan used to call me a *wee corker.*"

"A wee corker," Wade repeated softly. "I can see that." He could also see from the yearning in her expression that she missed her brother terribly, and for the umpteenth time, he prayed he hadn't been responsible for Ryan O'Toole's death. Just living with that possibility—and knowing Catriona was living with it now too—ate away at him.

He glanced toward the woods, eager to check the rock wall to see if the courier had left anything for him today. He'd checked every day for the past five days, and nothing. In Chief Wood's last correspondence, the man had confirmed Ryan's conscription into the Confederate Army, which Wade had never questioned. The chief had also confirmed that Catriona and Nora were sisters. Again, not something Wade questioned. He'd submitted his own findings from Cockrill's office in a report, and he hadn't received any word back on that. But he'd thought surely by now the chief would have responded about whether the military records listed Ryan O'Toole as present at the Battle of Franklin. Even if the records were inconclusive, the agency could let him know.

Seeing Nora clutch the doll tighter to her chest made him remember. "When I was in town this morning at the dry goods store, I got you a little something." He pulled the candy from his shirt pocket, and her eyes went wide.

"You got me *three lollipops?*"

He held up a hand. "I got you *one*. The other two are for Hattie and Winder."

After plopping Virginia down on the step, she grabbed for all of them, but he pulled them back. "Miss Nora O'Toole, I want you to give me your word that you will give both Hattie and Winder a lollipop."

She lowered her chin a little, eyeing him. She looked at the candy, then back at him as though weighing the cost. Finally, she nodded. "Aye, I will." She promptly spit into the palm of her left hand and held it out. As though reading the surprise on his face, she shrugged. "Winder says this is what you have to be doin' when you make a promise. Only, I have to be shakin' with me left hand for now. But he says that doesn't matter much. He says shakin' hands this way binds the promise forever."

Wade frowned. "And just what *promise* did the two of you make that needs binding forever?"

She quirked her mouth to one side, keeping an eye on the candy in his grip. "I'll be tellin' you, but you have to promise not to go tellin' anyone else. 'Specially Cattie!"

Wade pretended to spit into his left hand and held it out, which earned him a wide grin. Nora shook on the deal, and he held out the lollipops for her to choose one. She did, then began unwrapping it, a bit of a challenge with her injured arm, but she managed without help and popped the candy into her mouth.

Wade gestured for her to sit down beside him on the step, then furtively wiped his damp hand on his pant leg. He handed her the other two lollipops, which she slipped into her skirt pocket.

"Now . . ." He gently nudged her. "That promise you two made."

"Well," she began, speaking around the stick she twirled between her lips, "me and Winder, we were talkin' 'bout how when we grow up, if we're not findin' anyone to marry us, then we'll be marryin' each other." She ended on a high note, peering over at him.

Wade suppressed a grin. "You'll marry each other. That's certainly planning ahead."

"Aye, 'tis." Her red curls bobbed. "But Winder, he says that with the war, there won't be any men for me to marry. So I'd best be choosin' now, and he says he's a right good catch."

"Does he now?"

"Aye. He says whoever's marryin' him will be gettin' all this." She looked around, then leaned close. "But mostly," she whispered, "I want to be marryin' him because then Tempy can be me grandmother!" Her face lit with a joy that reached all the way inside him.

"You *are* a wee corker, Nora O'Toole, you know that?"

She nodded, sucking hard on the candy, then proceeded to tell him in great detail everything that had happened in the schoolroom that day. Although he needed to be on his way, Wade lingered a little longer, enjoying their visit and hoping that perhaps Catriona might come looking for her little sister. Eventually, when Nora took a breath, he saw his opportunity.

"So how's your sister doing these days?"

Nora shrugged. "She's tired a lot. And she was *mean* to me this mornin'."

Wade raised a brow.

She pulled the lollipop from her mouth. "She told me straight out that God gave me red hair 'cause he knew I needed to come with a warnin'!"

Wade tried not to laugh, but he couldn't help it. At first he thought Nora was going to slug him with her good arm, but then she just giggled. Mindful of her injury, he put his arm around her slender shoulders and gave her a little hug. She scooted closer to him, and he thought his heart was going to melt. Still . . . Thinking about *"coming with a warning,"* he wondered if Catriona was on to something. For her sister, yes, but also for herself. These two were quite the pair.

The screen door off the back of the kitchen slammed shut, and they looked over to see Winder walking toward the barn. But as soon as the boy looked in their direction, he made a beeline straight for them. Or straight for Nora.

"I'm heading to check on Little Nora . . . *Nora.*" Winder grinned. "Want to go with me?"

She looked up at Wade as though asking for his permission.

"Sure, you two go on." He stood. "But let ol'

Thomas know you're there, and *don't* go inside that stall, do you hear me? Penelope is still awfully protective of her new calf."

Both children nodded and headed in the direction of the cattle barn. Wade watched them as they went, waiting. And sure enough, though he couldn't hear what Nora was saying, she pulled a lollipop from her pocket and held it out to Winder.

"Good girl," Wade whispered, smiling to himself. He turned to leave and spotted Nora's doll lying on the porch step right where she'd left her. He picked it up and started to call out for Nora, then paused and studied the sad little thing. An idea came to him, and he juggled the possibilities, then stashed the doll inside the cottage for safekeeping and headed for the woods.

A short while later, Wade lifted the rectangular-shaped stone from the foundation at the base of the rock wall and withdrew the familiar, worn leather pouch hidden beneath it. He untied the leather fastener, hoping that Chief Wood had surely—

He felt a piece of paper inside! He pulled it out, hopes rising. But when he read the first line, every hope within him gave way.

Military records confirm that your suspect, Ryan Tomás O'Toole, immigrant from County Antrim, Ireland, was indeed present at the battle in Franklin and marched with his regiment in General Patrick Cleburne's division.

Gut sick, Wade stopped reading. He couldn't have continued if he'd wanted to. The words blurred on the page. He drew in a breath and bowed his head, feeling the weight of blood he'd spilled during the war all over again. He leaned back against the rock wall and closed his eyes, the sense of loss reaching down deep inside him. "Oh Jesus," he whispered, other words failing him. He raked a hand through his hair.

As long as there had been a chance that Ryan O'Toole hadn't been in that battle, he'd held out hope for Catriona. Slim as it was. But the fact that her brother *had* been on the battlefield that night, and that she hadn't heard from him since . . .

Wade slowly lifted his head. As difficult as it had been to live with the haunting memories of mutilated bodies, the sickeningly sour smell of blood-soaked earth, and the scream of cannon fire followed by the screams of men . . . those horrors etched into his memory, brutal as they were, somehow seemed less so compared to this news. He'd ventured beyond the breastworks that night after the firing had ceased, and through the smoke and haze, he'd seen what remained of Cleburne's division. He'd seen the ditches strewn with corpses and bodies of men so . . . Well, they hadn't even looked like men anymore. *"But it was war. And men die in war!"* he'd heard said so many times, and he'd even said it to himself when demons— late at night, when sleep wouldn't come—dredged up sights and smells and sounds he'd begged God to banish from his memory forever. But war *was* war. And he knew human nature well enough to know that sometimes, for some men, brute force was all they understood. It was the language they dealt in. But now . . .

He glanced back at the report gripped in his hand. Those words—*It was war. And men die in war!*—felt so trite, so anemic when knowing that one of the lives snuffed out on the other side of the breastworks upon which he'd stood and fought had belonged to Catriona O'Toole's brother.

After a moment, he straightened, and ever mindful of his duty, he wiped his eyes and continued reading.

> As you know, Cleburne's division suffered substantial losses in that battle. Few men were left, and most of those were so badly injured they succumbed to death in days following. But according to Confederate records recently acquired—

Wade's pulse spiked, and he stared hard at the next sentence as crushed hope dared to draw breath. " '—a handful of Cleburne's men' "—he read in a hushed whisper, as though speaking the words would make them more real—" 'wounded but still able to fight, moved on with Hood's army to Nashville.' " He gave a sharp exhale. " 'Ryan O'Toole was one of those soldiers.' "

He glanced back in the direction of the main house, his thoughts firing at rapid speed. This news, welcomed by him, still did not bode well for Ryan being alive. Quite the opposite. Ryan had most likely met his fate at the battle in Nashville only two weeks following the defeat of Hood's army here. Hood's battered men arrived in Nashville only to find themselves outnumbered almost four to one. And in the end, after enduring days of freezing temperatures—hunkering beneath trees, logs, or whatever shelter they could find—those barefoot, half-starved Rebel soldiers finally faced their unflinching defeat and retreated as fast as they could back down south.

Wade didn't know if all this would make any difference to Catriona, but at least *he* knew now, and he could tell her that her brother had *not* died here in Franklin. Not at the hand of the 104th Ohio—he looked down at his outstretched palm—and not by *his* hand.

He quickly read the last of the report.

Repeated efforts to discover the suspect's whereabouts following the battle in Nashville have revealed nothing. Inquiries to the War Department and their records of the Confederate dead have also proven fruitless in that regard. Will exhaust all resources. Suspicions remain regarding the suspect's sister and her likely ties with Peter McCartney, whose whereabouts are still unknown. The findings in your recent search proved helpful. More to follow.

From habit, Wade turned the page over. But that was all. He read through the note again, committing the important details to memory. As though he could forget them. He pulled the metal box of matches from his pocket, then broke off a stick and struck it on a rock. Flame leapt to life. He held the single piece of paper by an edge as fire licked it up like kindling. He dropped the burning remains on the wall and watched them burn to nothing, wondering what had happened to Ryan O'Toole and whether the man had lived through—

A twig snapped in the dense woods somewhere beyond the wall to his right, and Wade ducked behind the rock wall. He kept absolutely still, listening, just as whatever—or whoever—was doing right now. Because suddenly the woods had gone silent. Even the warble of birds in the canopy above had fallen away.

He cocked his head, hearing the sound again. Only this time it wasn't just a twig snapping. It was the sound of footsteps. Someone was headed straight for him.

CHAPTER 35

The sound of footsteps stopped briefly, then started again, and Wade reached for the revolver holstered at his hip. He carefully pulled back the hammer and listened, thinking of Bern and hoping again he'd get the chance to avenge his partner and friend. But not a snap of a twig nor a crunch of wintered leaves braided the sudden silence. Slowly, he peered over the wall, but the dense foliage beyond kept its secrets well. Yet no sooner did he duck down than the footsteps resumed. Only, they weren't moving toward him anymore. They were moving off to his left. Trying to throw him off, perhaps? Regardless, it lent him an advantage.

He quietly released the hammer, then, pausing to listen, he carefully made his way to the end of the wall, only moving when he heard movement. He eased himself over and slipped into the woods. Welcoming its shadows, he pressed his back against a large, high-limbed pine and let the forest envelop him. Whoever it was, was being cautious. This wasn't just a Saturday afternoon stroll in the—

The crack of a branch sent a bolt of lightning through him. Whoever was out there was only feet away now. On the other side of the tree! He could hear them breathing. Gripping his gun, he slowly panned to his left and could see the barest outline of a shadow, thanks to the faint slivers of sunlight finding their way through the branches overhead. If the man knew he was here, he would have already called him out. Wade thumbed the hammer on the revolver, debating. Then he quickly decided surprise would be his first option. The Colt, a close second.

He took a deep breath, watching, waiting for the right moment. Then, seeing his chance, he stepped from hiding and plowed into the guy. Wade delivered the first punch, a hard right beneath the fellow's rib cage. But the man didn't go down. Instead, he came back like a locomotive, and Wade braced himself for—

Suddenly the world stopped.

"Wade?"

Wade blinked, lightning still coursing through his veins, his body braced for the impact. Then he let out a breath. *"Isham?"*

They both stared for a moment. Wade read confusion in Isham's expression just as something Chief Wood had said to him weeks ago, before he'd left to come to Franklin, washed up from his memory. And he smiled, the pieces falling into place. " 'You can trust this man without reservation.' That's what Chief Wood said to me about my courier this time."

Isham frowned. "You mean you're—"

542

Wade held out his hand. "Welcome to the Secret Service, Isham. How long have you been in?"

It took a few seconds, but Isham's smile slowly dawned. "About four months. Just before I came to Carnton."

Wade grabbed his friend around the neck, and they hugged. Wade stepped back. "I knew you were lying to me the other day, by the way. In the cattle barn. I just didn't know why."

"And I could tell you knew. You had that look about you."

Wade shook his head. "I don't have a look."

Isham exhaled. "Oh yeah, you do. At least to me. Then again . . ." His expression sobered. "We've been through a lot together."

Wade nodded. "We sure have, my friend. And it looks like we're not done quite yet."

Isham made a show of glancing around, then reached into his pocket. "Seeing as we're both here . . ." He handed Wade a folded piece of paper.

Wade opened it, read the brief report from Chief Wood, then looked up to see Isham's slow nod. And the crushed hope that had dared to take another breath just moments earlier came to its feet, ready to fight.

Kneeling by the daffodil bed, Catriona glanced through the white picket fence and spotted Wade headed for the garden, purpose in his stride. Earlier that afternoon, when she'd seen Nora chewing on that lollipop stick, she'd had a good idea, even before asking, of who had given it to her. But it was the sweet inflection in Nora's tone when she'd told her it was Wade that bothered Catriona most of all—in addition to her little sister calling him Wade.

"Do you need this, Miss Catriona?"

She turned to see Marcellus holding out a garden spade.

"Aye, I am that. Thank you." With a smile, she took the tool from him, noticing that he held her gaze considerably longer than necessary. He usually stopped by to see her in the garden just before lunch, then again after he and the other men finished their work each day. She enjoyed their visits, even when he was overly quiet, like he was today. She was very fond of Marcellus, but she'd begun sensing that his feelings for her were somewhat different from her feelings for him. Yet he was so kind, so gentle, that she hadn't been able to bring herself to say anything. Then again, perhaps she was flattering herself to misconstrue his kind attention.

Since the burial team had begun, Marcellus and the others had exhumed and reinterred nearly one hundred and fifty remains of the nearly two thousand soldiers buried in Harpeth Valley. And each afternoon, today included, she'd done her best to record in the weathered journal each soldier's name and what few details were known about them. She kept the book by her bed and had even read back through the names on several occasions, wondering if any of those men had known Ryan. Or if he had known them. And while she was determined to keep her word and continue assisting the burial team, she honestly didn't know if her constitution was up to it.

Every time she looked at one of those caskets, something deep inside her seemed to shift, and she felt as though she were standing on the edge of a precipice, looking down into a ravine. Her heart could not fathom that all that might be left of her dear Ryan could fit into one of those boxes. And to know that Wade Cunningham could be responsible for it.

From her peripheral vision, she spotted him nearing the garden gate closest to the house. She felt her defenses rise. Somehow she had to get across to him that it physically hurt her to be in his company now. Surely he could understand that.

"Here you go." Marcellus scooted the bucket of fertilizer closer to her, always seeming to anticipate her next move. "The garden's looking really nice. I'm grateful to you for letting me help you with it."

"Thank you, Marcellus. And it's me who's grateful to *you* for helpin'." She slipped on a pair of old gardening gloves and scooped a portion of fertilizer from the bucket. Mrs. McGavock had insisted this "special fertilizer" ordered from a catalog be used on her flower beds instead of manure. Which suited Catriona fine, for obvious reasons. She gently worked the mixture into the soil, determined to focus on her task instead of

545

Wade's ever-increasing proximity to her. She knew how important these daffodils were to Mrs. McGavock.

More than once, the woman had mentioned that "the vibrant yellow daffodils" were her favorites and that the original bulbs had come from an estate called the Hermitage some forty miles northwest of Carnton. Later, Catriona had asked Tempy if there was anything special about that place, and Tempy had herself a good laugh. "Why, it's only the home of a man who used to be president of the whole United States, Miss O'Toole. President Jackson and his wife, Miss Rachel, was awfully good friends of the colonel's parents, Mister Randal and Miss Sarah. Miss Rachel done shared a bushel of her flowers with Miss Sarah a whole bunch o' years back. Them daffodils are some of 'em."

Tempy knew everything there was to know about Carnton, and as they worked together in the kitchen, the woman told story after story about all that happened in the home through the years. Catriona relished those times more than Tempy would ever know. But hearing those stories about the McGavocks and their extended family only carved a deeper remorse within her. Because Tempy had missed an entire lifetime of knowing her own brother and sister.

Catriona moved down the daffodil bed a ways and worked another spade full of fertilizer into the soil. She heard the unmistakable squeak of the gate, then footsteps behind her, and the dull ache inside her grew sharper.

"Pardon me, Miss O'Toole. May I have a word with you?"

Not looking back, Catriona shook her head. "As you can be seein' for yeself, Mr. Cunningham, now is not a good time." She shoved her spade into the bucket.

"I wouldn't bother you if it wasn't important . . . Catriona."

At his use of her Christian name, her throat tightened. But not with tears. She rose and turned to face him, aware of Marcellus watching them. "I've been askin' you repeatedly not to—"

"I need to speak with you *privately*." The seriousness in Wade's features both unnerved her and sparked her temper. *"Please,"* he said quietly but firmly, then looked at Marcellus. "Would you please excuse us, Mr. Cuppett?"

Marcellus looked at Wade, then at Catriona as though uncertain what to do next.

Catriona finally sighed and removed her gloves. "It's all right, Marcellus. I'll be seein' you on the morrow?"

"Yes, ma'am. I'd like that very much. Good evening, then." He ducked his head, then looked at Wade. "Evening, Mr. Cunningham."

Catriona attempted a smile. "Good evenin', Marcellus."

"Evening, Mr. Cuppett." Wade nodded.

"Oh, and, Miss Catriona?" With the purest smile,

547

Marcellus wordlessly pointed to the sky, then walked on.

Catriona waited until he was out of earshot, the frustration and pain building inside her with each passing second. "Wade, I don't know how else to be sayin' this to you. But bein' with you, even *seein'* you, causes me insides to—"

"Ryan *did* fight in the battle here, Catriona. And he was wounded. But he didn't die here."

She heard what Wade said, but the only portion her mind grabbed hold of was *"But he didn't die here."* She tried to speak, yet the words wouldn't come.

"Remember I told you that the US Government had resources?" he continued.

She nodded, hope and fear warring inside her.

"I heard back from them just a while ago, and I had to come tell you."

She looked around. "Someone was here? Who was it? What did they say?"

He hesitated. "A person delivered the message, and according to Confederate records that recently came into their possession, a handful of General Cleburne's soldiers who were wounded but still able to fight pushed on to Nashville with Hood's army. Your brother was one of those soldiers."

That news sinking in, Catriona grappled for something solid to steady her. Wade gently grasped her arm. She didn't pull away. Because no matter what else he was—or wasn't—to her, right now he was her best chance of finding Ryan. She crossed to the nearby bench beneath the large Osage orange tree and sank down. Wade joined her, resting his forearms on his knees.

Her thoughts stumbled one over the other as the afternoon light quickly faded over the hills and evening crept closer with its dusky hues, painting the deep-blue sky in a wash of purple and pink. A breeze stirred and carried with it the pungent scents of pine and freshly turned earth.

Wade looked back. "And to be clear, Catriona, while they know he did march with Hood's army to Nashville, they weren't able to find out what happened to him afterward. So there's still no way of knowing—"

"Whether me brother's dead or alive," she finished for him, leaning forward, gripping the bench beneath her. "Aye, I'm knowin' that full well."

"They also said they would continue to exhaust every resource they have."

"And you're believin' them for that vow?"

"Without a doubt. If anyone can find out about him, it's them."

Finding reassurance in his certainty, she also found herself curious. "And exactly who is *them?*"

"The US Government," he said simply, then lowered his voice. "Which includes connections I made while in the Federal Army."

She weighed that information, then shook her head, recalling her "conversation" with Frank Bonner, which cast its own glaring light on Wade's response. "The US Government," she repeated softly. "Your government, Wade, is a mighty powerful thing. And not just a little frightenin', I'm tellin' you."

He looked back at her. "A person who's done nothing wrong has nothing to be afraid of."

She studied him, wondering if she'd imagined the subtle accusation in his voice. But reading only kindness in his eyes, she decided to give him the benefit of her doubts. "Were you there, Wade? In Nashville, I mean. For the battle you're sayin' Ryan was in after the one here?"

"I was." He bowed his head. "I was stationed at Fort Negley, but my unit didn't take part in the fighting."

"And why was that?"

He stared out across the garden. "Because we weren't needed in that battle. The Federal Army had the Confederates outnumbered almost four to one."

"And what else?"

He glanced back. "What do you mean?"

"What else are you not tellin' me that you know I would want to know?"

He rubbed a hand along his stubbled jaw. "Catriona, I really don't want to—"

"I'm wantin' to know the truth, Wade. Whatever it is." She studied his profile. "And I've come a long way to get it."

His breath left him slowly. "It was bitter cold those couple of weeks after we left Franklin. Snow

550

and ice. Everything was frozen for the longest time. And most of the Confederates . . . they didn't have shoes or food. They were out there freezing to death, and we knew it. It was brutal. For both sides. In different ways, but . . . it was especially brutal for the South."

For the longest time, they sat in silence. Him leaning forward, elbows on his knees, head bowed, his thoughts a mystery to her. Her with her arms wrapped around herself, all while thinking of all the caskets Charley had yet to build and the men they had yet to bury. And of all the names she had yet to write, including the scores of Unknowns. Would one of the dead in Nashville be Ryan, and she might never know?

Finally, Wade stood as if to leave, then turned back and looked down at her. "I know what I've told you just now, learning that your brother didn't die here in Franklin, doesn't make any difference to you. Because Ryan could still be dead."

"And most likely is," she said, her voice shaky. "I'm knowin' that well enough, even though I'm still not wantin' to."

"But what I want *you* to know"—his voice caught, and he swallowed, the sound detectable in the silence—"is that it makes a difference to *me*. To at least know that I wasn't responsible for your brother's death. Because"—he took a breath—"I could live with a lot of things. And I will for the rest of my life. But . . . I couldn't live with that."

Teeth clenched, she trembled, fighting to control

her emotions. He finally turned to go, and it was all she could do to muster a breath, much less find her voice.

"Wade," she whispered, wondering if he would even hear her.

But he stopped midstride and turned back.

She rose and went to him. "You're wrong. When you're sayin' it makes no difference to me. Because it does." A tear threatened to slip down her cheek. "And I'm indebted to you for contactin' whoever you did and helpin' me in the way you are." She bowed her head so he wouldn't see her cry.

"I would do anything within my power to help you, Catriona. I hope you know that."

She nodded but didn't look up. He tenderly cradled her cheek and encouraged her to lift her gaze. His own glistened with emotion.

"You can always come to me. No matter what."

She nodded, unable to speak. He took a step closer, then with a tenderness that threatened to scale all her defenses, he drew her into his arms and cradled her head against his chest. She wept, holding on to him as though she had nowhere—and no one—else to turn to.

Moments passed—how many, she didn't know. But when she opened her eyes, twilight had settled over the garden, and through the windows of the main house, warm arcs of lamplight illuminated the darkness. Suddenly feeling self-conscious, she took a step back, and though he seemed reluctant to release her, he did. She looked up at him, seeing both friend and foe. But more friend now, admittedly, than the latter. "Thank you again, Wade."

"Anything," he said succinctly, his voice as deep as the night. "All you have to do is ask."

She nodded, then stilled. "Wait. *Anything?*"

He cocked his head. "I would hope you know I mean what I say by now." His tone hinted at a smile, but the shadows hid his features.

"Aye, I'm knowin' that. But *you're* not knowin' what it is I'm about to ask."

"Which, I will admit, scares me to a certain degree."

His frankness tempted a smile from her. But just as swiftly, the thought of her request dispelled it. "I need you to be findin' someone else for me. *Two* other someones."

CHAPTER 36

"Should we not be feelin' a wee bit guilty, our scourin' through all the colonel's personal files this way?"

Wade looked at Catriona across the table between them in the McGavocks' attic, her focus intent on the crate of files in front of her, and he found her question both revealing and amusing. Especially considering this was their second time in two days to meet up here. Hoping to coax a smile from her, something he hadn't seen lately, he feigned a superior tone. "I'm his overseer. So the colonel's already given me permission to look at anything. It's *you* who should feel bad."

She looked up, mouth slightly agape. Contrition clouded her expression.

Ever so slowly, he let his smile show, hoping to bridge the gap between them.

"*Och* . . ." She leveled a stare. "I was bein' serious."

He lifted his hands in truce. "And I was only kidding."

A trace of mirth crossed her expression.

"So do you really feel bad?"

She quirked her mouth. "Nay, I don't. Well, maybe a *scant* wee bit. But to me thinkin', the wrong done to Tempy far outweighs what we're doin' here."

"Ah . . . so the end justifies the means?"

That earned him a bland look. "*Nay,* I'm not sayin' that. Not necessarily, anyway. But I do think when someone's done wrong, they open themselves and their lives to be scrutinized more closely. And rightly so. Because they've proven themselves unworthy of bein' trusted. And besides"—a spark of humor touched her blue eyes—"this lookin' for a bill of sale was your idea. So I'm figurin' if there's blame to be had, it's goin' to you, Overseer Cunningham." Not waiting for his response, she returned to her search.

Wade smiled to himself, grateful for the opportunity to study her and appreciating what she wanted to do for Tempy, although he wasn't at all hopeful about their prospect for success.

He thought again about the report Isham had given him the other day. Peter McCartney had been spotted again, and in Nashville of all places. If Wade could choose only one counterfeiter on the agency's apprehend list to take into custody, it would be McCartney—for a second time. Only, next time he wouldn't let the man out of his sight.

Catriona still hadn't even hinted to him about the counterfeit money she'd had or about her meeting with a government operative—which Isham had discovered was none other than Frank Bonner. But Wade felt certain she still clung to the belief that her brother had nothing to do with the money being fake. Just as his gut told him she was innocent, though—and he'd assured Isham of that—it told him Ryan was guilty. Now all he needed was proof.

Yet in the same breath, part of him wished he could find evidence that would declare Ryan innocent, even if that wish countered all logic. He knew how much Ryan's guilt would burden his sister. But she was stronger than she likely knew.

He returned to thumbing through the files. The image of her and Frank Bonner going back and forth was a scene he would like to have witnessed. Bonner was legendary for his intimidation tactics. Even some of the men in the Secret Service feared him. So learning that Catriona had been interrogated by the man and had apparently stood her ground—according to what Isham had learned from their contact at the bank—was impressive, although not surprising. Catriona O'Toole was a formidable woman, and she was beautiful to boot. The memory of holding her close in the garden two nights ago returned. He'd never felt anything so right in his life. But when she'd slipped her arms around him, and he'd pulled her closer . . . That feeling still hadn't left him.

Her soft gasp brought his head up.

"I've found another bill of sale for a slave. The date on this one is lookin' like . . ." She brought the piece of paper closer to her face. "October twenty-seventh, eighteen hundred and twenty-two. And it's from Alabama, which is where Tempy said the colonel's father bought her and her mother. But the ink's so faded. I'm havin' trouble readin' it."

Wade moved around to her side of the table. "Let's take it closer to the window. Better light over there."

She followed him and held the receipt closer to the window, at a slant. "I still can't make it out. Can you?"

"Here, let's see if I can find something that'll help us." He quickly scanned the attic, and his gaze snagged on some fabric folded on a shelf. A table-cloth, maybe, or an old sheet. But it was the right color. He retrieved it and placed it on a box by the window. "If you put a faded document on top of something yellow, it helps the ink show through better."

Catriona eyed him. "You're knowin' some of the strangest bits and pieces of things I've ever heard from a man." She peered down at the bill of sale, and Wade caught a whiff of lilac and rose water. He inhaled deeply, grateful for her prolonged interest in the note.

"Well, I'll be . . . You're right!"

"Thank you for sounding so surprised."

She waved a hand at him. "It's sayin', 'Received of Randal McGavock . . . three hundred and fifty dollars in full payment for a Negro girl by the name of' "—she squinted—" 'Hany, about . . . *three* years of age'?" She paused, the muscles in her jaw tightening. With a sharp exhale, she continued, squinting as she went. " 'I also warrant in this title that . . . said Negro is sound both in body and mind.' " She straightened, and for the longest time simply stared down at the receipt. Then she looked at him. "I'm so glad your side won that war, Wade," she whispered.

"I am too."

Standing there together in the seclusion of the attic, their bodies all but touching, her nearness and the softness in her eyes sent a rush coursing through him. He dared to reach up and finger an auburn curl at her temple, knowing he should not—and could not—act on his desires. Not in his position. Not knowing what he knew. Already regretting it, he took a step back, and a shimmer of disappointment—or relief?—clouded her expression before she looked down again.

She picked up the bill of sale. "This one's obviously not what we're lookin' for." A tightness slipped into her voice. "The name is wrong, for one. There's little way to be gettin' Tempy from Hany."

"But you have to take into account that the names of slaves were often changed."

She frowned. "Changed?"

"After purchasing slaves, owners would often change their names to something more personally pleasing to them. So it's best to go by the age and gender listed on the bill of sale."

The frustration in her features spoke volumes. "Well, this girl, Hany, was the age Tempy said she was."

"True. But look at the date the girl was purchased. Eighteen hundred and twenty-two. That would mean Tempy would be . . . around forty-seven years of age."

She stared at the paper, her lips moving silently, and he could tell she was confirming his arithmetic. Did the woman not even trust him to calculate correctly?

"Besides," he continued, "Tempy said she and her mother were sold together. When families or members of families were purchased, most often the bill of sale reflected that."

Resignation slowly settled over her features, and her gaze moved toward the window. "What time is it gettin' to be?"

Wade pulled out his pocket watch. "Almost half past two."

She made a low growl. "I'm late to be helpin' the burial crew. I'm sorry, but I've got to be goin'."

"That's all right. We have only one more box to go through anyway. I'll finish."

"And what if we're not findin' the answer we're lookin' for in there?"

He wished he could offer her more hope. "Then we pray that the telegram I sent to the government yesterday will turn up something. But if past experience proves true, record keeping on slaves was often minimal at best—and sometimes downright sloppy."

"And if they find nothin'?"

"Then we may have to accept that we won't be

560

able to find Tempy's siblings. *If* they're even still alive to be found."

The determination in her expression said she was clearly unwilling to accept that option. And if she couldn't accept that fate for Tempy, how on earth would she begin to accept it for herself with her brother?

Catriona's footsteps faded as she descended the staircase. Wade returned to the crate of files he'd been working on. Finding nothing in those, he moved to the last crate. An especially heavy one.

Even before he and Catriona started this yesterday, he'd already been through the past twenty years or so of McGavock's files and several of his father's as well. So he'd specifically not gone through those boxes again. Considering Tempy's age and how long she said she'd been here at Carnton, he figured the bill of sale had to be in the crates dating before or around the turn of the century. So they'd focused their attentions on those.

An hour or so later, Wade turned over the final piece of paper in the last crate. Nothing. After returning the files to their place, he holstered his revolver, then picked up the oil lamp he'd brought with them from downstairs. He started for the staircase before remembering he'd laid his hat aside on the table. Turning to retrieve it, he noticed a crate sitting off to one side of the stairs. It was half hidden behind a larger box as though someone had ascended as far as the landing, then had simply shoved the crate aside for safekeeping. An aging leather notebook protruded from the collection of files. Again, as though it had been viewed, then hastily returned to its place.

He carried the crate to the table and withdrew the book. Reclaiming his chair, he opened the notebook with care, the binding overstuffed with what appeared to be old receipts, bills, and odd pieces of legal documents. The book was a ledger of some sort, an old one judging by the worn leather edges. Wade turned to the front, and as he'd guessed he would, he read the name James McGavock, the colonel's grandfather. Beside his name, *County Antrim, Ireland.* Then beneath James's name was the colonel's father's, Randal McGavock . . . *Carnton, Franklin, Tennessee.*

Knowing that if a record of Tempy and her mother's purchase was in this notebook it would likely be *after* James McGavock's entries, Wade flipped to the last page and started working his way back toward the front. Sure enough, the last third of the book comprised Randal's entries made here at Carnton. But nowhere in the ledger had the man recorded the purchase of a Negro mother and young daughter. Wade found receipts confirming the purchase of other slaves, but none fell into the window of dates needed to match Tempy's age.

Discouraged, he continued into James's portion of the book, skimming the ledger entries as well as each piece of paper stuffed between. Roughly

562

halfway through, a cigar band caught his eye and stirred a half-forgotten memory. His own father had used a similar-looking cigar band to mark his place in their family Bible after reading it aloud at the dinner table each night. And remembering the playfully scolding look about the cigar band his mother cast his father's way framed the memory for him. That, and the twinkle in both his parents' eyes. Warmed by the recollection, he turned the page, then paused.

Staring back at him was a deed. An official-looking deed, thanks to the illustrative work embellishing the top and sides and, at the bottom, a skillfully drawn family crest. But it was the name that brought him upright in his chair. Tomás O'Toole.

Wade's gaze devoured the page. *Deed for O'Toole land, with exception of homestead . . .* His eyes widened. "Two thousand dollars?" he whispered, skimming on down. *Loan to be repaid within ten years. No interest demanded.* He lifted his head, his focus moving far beyond the confines of the McGavocks' attic, across an ocean, to the lush green hills and valleys of County Antrim, Ireland.

He turned the document over, instinctively knowing in that moment that Catriona had seen this deed and read the very words on the back of it. And, searching his memory, he would've bet all the green in Kentucky that she'd seen it that day he'd first driven her and Nora back to town.

Catriona had been so angry over something. More than merely at him, anyway. So could *this* be what brought her here to Carnton? She came to Franklin to find Ryan. He already knew that much. But had she come to Carnton because of the history behind this deed as well?

He tugged at a thread of memory, something he'd overheard in her exchange with McGavock in the farm office. *"But he wrote sayin' he was comin' here."*

Wade closed his eyes as he sifted fact from assumption, then let the final result marinate inside him. Finally, he continued working his way to the beginning of the ledger. Finding nothing pertaining to Tempy, he set it aside. He rubbed his eyes, weary of reading, then dove into the remaining collection of files, which proved to be a mishmash of James's and Randal's farming records. Both men were meticulous record keepers and had passed that trait down to the colonel, which Wade, in his line of work, greatly appreciated.

The final stack of papers thinning, same as his hope for finding anything helpful, Wade flipped through receipt after receipt for grain, feed, and farm implements purchased in County Antrim over a century ago. Then a piece of paper about the size of a handbill, stuck to the underside of one of the receipts, caught his attention. He carefully worked it loose.

The words *Alabama* and *Montgomery* were the first to draw his focus, then the date—October

14, 1794. Contrary to the faded ink on the bill of sale Catriona found earlier, the ink on this piece of paper was still legible. Due mostly, Wade assumed, to the thickness of the paper itself. He turned it over, and the disgust he already harbored for slave owners only deepened. This bill of sale had been recorded on the back of an old flyer hawking some sort of tonic claiming a miracle cure that would set a person free from aches and pains.

With a deep sigh, he turned the paper back over and read . . .

State of Alabama
City of Montgomery

Notice is hereby given that I, Justice Hubert, do receive four hundred and fifty dollars from Randal McGavock of Franklin, Tennessee, in exchange for Nutt, a Negro woman about thirty years of age, and her female child, Lacy, about six or seven years old. Both are of sound body and mind. Randal McGavock has satisfied the balance in full and therefore may duly claim all rights afforded to him by the state of Alabama and . . .

Wade read the remainder of the note, then stared at the signature, concentrating finally on the seller's first name and asking the Almighty to deliver that very thing—justice—for Tempy and her siblings, *if* her brother and sister were still living. *And use me, Father, in any way you desire to see this through.*

Now, to tell Catriona the news.

"Section eighty-one. Georgia. Number sixty-two. Captain William T. Cochran of the 37th Georgia regiment."

Fatigue accentuated George Cuppett's voice. Catriona knew the weight of the task was wearing on him and the other men, dealing in death all day, as they were, and surely having it invade their dreams at night, as it sometimes did hers. Yet the men were determined to see their job done swiftly and well, and she vowed to be more cognizant of the time and not be late again. Especially since her and Wade's fairly intrusive search of the colonel's files had revealed nothing.

Beside the number sixty-two she'd just written in the left-hand column on the page, she carefully penned the name William T. Cochran, followed by his rank and unit. While she was no more at ease with this task than when they'd started, she and George had fallen into a rhythm together. They spoke only rarely as he announced the names and information, then she recorded it all in the leather-bound journal.

Marcellus, Polk, Robert, and Charley worked tirelessly carrying the caskets from the wagon to the cemetery, then digging the graves and burying each casket in its numbered spot. The work was done in reverent silence, and she found herself in awe of their fortitude.

"What number are we on in this section, please, Miss O'Toole?" George asked quietly, moving to the next casket even as Marcellus and Robert claimed the one they'd just recorded.

Catriona checked to be sure. "We just recorded number sixty-two."

"Very good. Please move to a new page and write section eighty-seven. South Carolina. And remember, since it's a new section we'll start with number one again."

She did as requested, and George lifted the lid.

"Private Brody Walsh of the South Carolina Fifth Regiment."

The pen in Catriona's hand began to shake. *Brody* . . . One of Ryan's mates. Brody's face, boyishly handsome, rose in her sight, and she clutched the book to her chest.

"Miss O'Toole?" George asked. "What's wrong, ma'am?"

It took her a moment, but she finally found her voice. "I-I knew him. We grew up together in Ireland. Brody was one of . . . me brother's friends."

George bowed his head. "I'm so sorry, ma'am."

Catriona nodded, then brought the pen to the page. She had to wait for her hands to stop shaking, then she wrote the number one followed by the name and details with painstaking care. She dried her eyes, then nodded for George to continue. He hesitated as though not wanting to, then gingerly lifted the lid of the next casket.

"Private Liam Kelly," he said softly, then lifted his gaze to hers.

Catriona shook her head, feeling a reprisal of tears.

"We found these two bodies buried together, ma'am." George's own eyes misted with emotion. "I'm sorry as I can be."

She nodded, and only then did it occur to her . . . Surely Ryan had been the one to bury his two friends, same as the three of them had buried young Ferris Murphy, as Ryan had written her early in the war. So when Ryan left Franklin for Nashville, he'd left his last two mates behind. What desperation he must have felt. What heartache.

She opened the book and wrote the number two, then Liam's name, rank, and unit, thinking of his dear mam and da who'd died years ago from sickness. She looked heavenward, hoping they were all together again and that the Almighty wasn't making them wait in some dark, lonely place like the priest had told her was happening to Mam, Bridget, and Alma. *God, don't be doin' that. To any of them. Please . . .*

Hearing footsteps behind her, she turned to see Wade coming toward her. The hopeful look on his face quickly dimmed. She wished she could walk into his arms as she'd done the other night. Or that he would draw her to him. But she couldn't. And, of course, he didn't.

568

He gently touched her arm. "What's wrong?"

The tenderness in his voice was nearly her undoing. She glanced down at the caskets. "Two of Ryan's friends." She took a breath. "I knew young Ferris was killed shortly after they were conscripted. But I wasn't knowin' about Brody and Liam . . . until now."

"I'm so sorry, Catriona."

She nodded, then caught sight of the piece of paper in his hand and felt herself beginning to hope—until she saw it was a printed advertisement of some sort. Then he turned it over, and she saw the writing. She had trouble reading it at first, but she finally managed, then couldn't contain her smile, shaky though it was. *Nutt.* And *Lacy?* The name didn't seem to fit Tempy at all, but she remembered what he'd said about slave owners changing names. Despite her disgust at the practice, she had to admit the McGavocks might have sensed the little girl's true spirit.

He gestured behind him. "Would you like to ride into town with me? I want to send another telegram, telling my contact about this."

She looked beyond him expecting to see a wagon but saw that pretty little reddish mare instead.

"Or I'd be happy to go back and get a wagon, if you'd prefer."

She searched his expression, not seeing any hint of a dare but definitely sensing one. A trip into town meant she could check on dear Braxie and see how she was doing. But it also meant risking another run-in with Frank Bonner—*if* the man was even still around. It had been weeks since he'd questioned her. He was likely long gone by now. Wanting to believe that more than actually believing it, she weighed her options and nodded. "Aye, I'd be likin' a trip to town very much. And nay, no wagon is needed. But we have a few more caskets to—"

"Take your time, Catriona. I'll wait for you." He took the bill of sale from her, his hand briefly covering hers. A tingling warmth traveled up her arm. "No matter how long it takes," he added in a voice so soft she almost didn't catch it.

For a moment she thought he might have meant something more by the statement. And when she looked into his eyes, she was certain of it.

CHAPTER 37

Holding the reins, Wade assisted Catriona to sit sidesaddle on the mare, then swung up behind her, grateful she'd agreed to go into town with him. At the cemetery, he'd planned to tell her only about finding the bill of sale. But then she'd told him about her brother's two friends, and he thought a trip into town—and maybe dinner at one of the few local eateries, if she would allow him that much—might help take her mind off that loss, at least for a while.

She sat quietly in front of him, her posture and ease with Sassy indicating she was accustomed to riding. Why did that not surprise him? And while she didn't sit ramrod straight, she did keep a respectable distance between them—or tried. But by the time they reached Lewisburg Pike, she'd relaxed a bit and leaned back into him. Every move made him increasingly aware of each shapely curve of her body, and his thoughts started meandering down a road he knew was best not traveled, no matter how pleasing. A little conversation would help.

"Did you find Nora when you went back inside?"

"Aye, but the children were still in the school-room. So I told Tempy where we were goin' in case Nora comes lookin' for me. Not that she will. The little urchin doesn't seem to be likin' me much these days."

"Why do you say that?"

"Mainly because she told me so, again, last night 'fore we were goin' to bed."

The dry tone in which she said it made him laugh, and from her profile he was pretty sure she was smiling.

"I'm sure she didn't mean it, Catriona."

"And I'm sure she did." She shook her head. "The girl blames me for our mam's death."

Wade frowned. "Why would she do that?"

"Because she overheard me talkin' to a friend, tellin' her that if God wasn't goin' to heal Mam, I wished he would go ahead and take her. That he wouldn't let her suffer."

"Hmm." Wade nodded. "And she misunderstood."

"Aye. I tried to explain, but 'twas no use."

"She'll come around soon enough, I bet."

Catriona's silence told him she thought otherwise.

They rode without speaking for a while. Spring was settling in, and the days were getting longer. He figured they had a couple of hours before sunset, maybe a little more. For several of the past few evenings, he'd spent time nursing beers at taverns and talking to locals. Franklin had its fair share of alcoholics, prostitution, and petty crime, but he'd uncovered not a shred of evidence that supported counterfeiting. He was beginning to question the intelligence the agency had received about a counterfeit ring operating out of this area.

As much as he didn't like Woodrow Cockrill, the accountant—guilty of overbilling numerous clients—the man looked clean on counterfeiting. A recent report from the chief also cleared Leonard Bishop, the haberdashery owner. It seemed he had expanded his market to include a haberdashery in England. Hence, Brummel Enterprises and the sizable deposits being made to Bishop's account. Those Europeans apparently liked their fancy suits. As for John McGavock, he was simply an astute businessman who leveraged Carnton's reputation to his best financial advantage. No breaking the law there. Yet John McGavock couldn't have done what he'd done without the benefit of slavery. And Wade took some comfort, at least, in knowing that Carnton and other enormous estates like it would, in time, disappear from the Southern landscape, as well they should.

Catriona shifted a little to look back at him.

"When I saw Tempy earlier, I started to tell her about what you found today."

Wade raised a brow, hoping she hadn't, thinking it best to wait and see what came from it first. "But?"

"But then I decided 'twas best not to get her hopes up only to have them dashed. Best wait until we know somethin' a little more sure."

"I agree," he said softly, wondering if she was referring to him telling her about Ryan. Yet he didn't hear any bitterness in her statement.

"I've tried to picture what that would be like." Wonder filled her voice. "Findin' out after all these years that you still have a brother and sister. Only, they'd be like strangers to you."

"Still, being alone like Tempy has been for so long, then to learn you have family left . . . Think of how that would change her life."

She nodded. "Aye, family is precious."

"That they are. Even after they're gone."

She took a breath as though to say something else, but she didn't.

They passed by the field where George Cuppett and his men were again exhuming bodies, but she didn't look in that direction, and neither did he.

A local reporter from the *Weekly Review* had recently visited Carnton to speak with George Cuppett about the burial team's progress, then had asked for the names of the soldiers reinterred thus far. Catriona had provided the man with a list. And sure enough, the names were printed in the newspaper with a note that more names would be published as the project continued.

"Wade?" she asked softly after a moment.

"Yeah?"

"Would you mind takin' me to where the fightin' took place? With Cleburne's men, I mean. And the 104th Ohio."

A cold wind blew through him, and he didn't

answer immediately. "Catriona, I'm not sure that's for the best."

She turned to the side again, and he could see her profile. "Before I knew Ryan had lived through it, I wouldn't have wanted to see it. But now that I'm knowin' he didn't die there, I'd like to see where he fought. Where what you and the colonel described took place. And where dear Brody and Liam died."

Wade didn't respond. How could he tell her he wasn't concerned only about her but about himself as well? That going back to the Carters' house and the surrounding acreage, to where the Federal breastworks had stood, would feel like he was losing Wesley all over again. Even now, he could hear the distant shriek of rifle fire in his memory and feel the earth shake from the repeated explosions of the Napoleon guns. He couldn't tell her all this without appearing weak, and that was something he never wanted to be in her eyes.

"I give you me word," she continued. "I won't be holdin' you to blame for anything. Not anymore."

Wade briefly closed his eyes. He'd spent so long trying to forget all that happened there that night, and he feared going back would only encourage the demons he'd fought so hard to keep at bay. Then he felt her hand cover his on the reins.

"Please?" she asked softly.

He reined in. "Catriona, I—" But he couldn't find the words.

She shifted in the saddle and turned back to

575

see him, her face so close to his he could see the flecks of green in her blue eyes. He tried to mask the turmoil inside him, but he could tell by the understanding in her expression that it was too late. Her gaze compassionate, she reached up and touched his face as though to comfort him. But her touch had a far more powerful effect. Desire for her bolted through him, and he caressed the curve of her waist and pulled her closer. He watched for the least sign of resistance, but none came. Instead, she tilted her head back, her lips parting, and he took her mouth with his. He told himself to kiss her slowly, gently, but when her hand came around his neck, pulling him closer, he deepened the kiss. She relaxed her full weight against him, melting into him, and a soft sigh rose in her throat. Reason strong-arming desire, Wade finally broke the kiss, his breath coming hard, as was hers.

Her eyes were still closed, and he was certain, as he'd been since the moment he saw her, that she was the most beautiful woman he'd ever seen. Slowly, she opened her eyes and looked up at him. The tiniest smile touched her lips, and he was tempted to kiss her again.

But before he could, she whispered, "So should I be takin' that as an *aye?*"

Even though a voice inside screamed for him not to, he nodded. "Aye," he whispered, his voice husky. "I'll take you there." As he leaned forward to gather the reins, his left arm brushed hers, and he felt something solid beneath her sleeve. "What do you have in there? A bowie knife?" He smiled, but she didn't.

"Actually, aye, of sorts. It's a dagger me brother gave me before he left for America. He made me promise to keep it with me." She unbuttoned the buttons on her cuff and removed the dagger, then pulled it from the scabbard and handed it to him.

"It's beautiful. Did he teach you how to use it?"

"Aye. I was nervous at first, but not anymore."

"I'll remember that the next time you're angry with me."

With a gentle smile, she turned back around, and he prodded Sassy toward the one place he'd promised himself he'd never visit again.

The closer they got to Fountain Branch Carter's homestead, the more he recognized the terrain and the more everything within him resisted going forward. When the house, still some distance away, came into view, he reined in, wondering if he should call on the family and let them know why the two of them were here. Then again, he decided not to risk that Fountain Branch Carter's memory might be better today than it was weeks ago when they saw each other in McGavock's entrance hall.

Wade dismounted. No matter how much he enjoyed being close to Catriona, he had to get some distance between them to do this. He helped her down, grateful to see that only the barest traces of the Federal breastworks remained. And those only because he knew where to look for them.

"This is the place?" A shade of surprise colored her voice.

He nodded, then, holding the reins in one hand, offered her his other. She slipped her hand into his. His heart pounding against his ribs, he walked over the ground that had haunted his dreams for so long. When they crested the gentle rise, he tied Sassy's reins to a tree, then sat on the ground. Catriona sat down beside him. He swallowed and hoped his voice would hold.

"I'll never forget the sight of the Confederate Army that afternoon. It was about this time of day, sunset not far off." He leaned closer to her and pointed. "Look out across the valley about two miles or so from where we are now. That's where the Confederate line formed. And what a sight it was. That line of butternut and gray moved forward steady as a clock. The Federal Army—we'd arrived early that morning—sneaked by Hood's men during the night. They were camped in Spring Hill, about ten miles from here. And as you already know, that gave us time to build breastworks. My unit was lined up about ten feet back from where we are now"—he looked around to be sure, the memories from that day crowding dangerously close—"and as the Rebels wheeled into formation, able to see us waiting for them clear as day, their precision and military bearing was as beautiful a sight as ever witnessed in war.

"We all stood spellbound as each division unfolded itself into a single line of battle with as much steadiness as if they were forming for a dress parade." He shook his head. "And not a sound jarred the quiet. It felt like the world just held its breath and watched right along with us. As long as I live, Catriona, I'll never forget that."

She took a quick breath, and he looked over to see tears spilling down her cheeks.

His chest wrenched tight. "I'm sorry. I shouldn't have—"

"Nay. Don't be," she whispered. "Please keep tellin' me what it was like. It's makin' me feel like I was here. With Ryan."

Knowing he would never tell her everything—some things he would take to his grave—he leaned close and drew a line across the fields in the distance. "For about two miles wide, the Confederate divisions moved into line, at least a hundred battle flags of the different regiments fluttering in the breeze. The day started out warm. An Indian Summer day, we call it. And then around four o'clock—" He blinked and could see those next few seconds unfolding as though he had traveled back in time. "The first Federal cannon fired, then another, and another, and soon the whole valley was a haze of fire and smoke. But still the Confederates pushed forward." He chose his words carefully and shared only the barest of details with her. What was more, he could tell she knew that. Yet she didn't call him on it.

They sat in silence for a moment, the sun sinking closer to the hills in the west.

"Where were Cleburne's men before they charged the Federal line?"

He stood and offered her his hand to help her up, then promptly gave her release. They walked a short distance down a slight incline, and he paused for a second, searching the lay of the land. Then he continued on until he came to the spot that matched the one in his memory. "This is where General Cleburne and his men were. And over there, about ten feet away, is where Cleburne died."

She stared up at him. "How are you knowin' that for sure?"

"Because later that night, after the firing finally stopped, some of us came out to see if any Federal troops might have been injured in the fighting and couldn't get back behind the line. And though it pains me to say it, I saw some of our own men stripping General Cleburne's body down to his shirt and trousers, and then stealing his boots and other personal items. I ordered them to stop, and they did. But . . ." He shook his head, searching the shadows of his memory again to see if he recalled seeing any young Irishmen wounded and bleeding, maybe begging for help, as so many men had done that night. But he didn't. Had Wesley cried out like that? Had his own brother called out for him before he died?

Telling himself not to, Wade looked back in the direction where Wesley's division had been, on the far end of the field, and his chest ached with love for his brother—as well as with regret over not having told him he loved him after their argument about the war and before Wesley left to join the Rebels. If only he'd known that would be his last chance.

"So this is where Ryan would have been? With General Cleburne and the other men?"

He looked back and saw a question in her eyes that had nothing to do with the question she'd just asked. "Yes," he said quietly. "This is where Ryan would have been."

She walked over the area for a moment, then stopped and knelt. She looked back up in the direction where the Federal line had been. "It took such courage . . . to do what it is you're sayin' they did. To come at that line from such a disadvantage."

"I've rarely seen such bravery as I did from Cleburne's men that night."

She bowed her head for the longest time, and Wade did the same, praying for her, praying for himself. And praying that the blood that had soaked this ground would somehow continue to mend the wounds in this country. That all who suffered and died here would not have done so in vain.

She rose and came to stand beside him again. "Thank you," she whispered. "For bringin' me here."

"You're welcome." He turned to leave.

"Wade?"

He looked back, and the discernment in her eyes all but made him turn away again.

She closed the distance between them and searched his gaze, then briefly looked beyond him as if saying she knew something else had happened here. She laid a hand to his chest, and Wade shook his head, his emotions threatening to get the best of him.

She slipped her hand into his, tears rising to her eyes. "Why do you keep lookin' in that direction? What else happened here that you're not tellin' me?"

He took a deep breath, a voice inside screaming not to tell her, that keeping the hurt buried deep would help contain it. But another voice, one far gentler yet insistent, encouraged him to tell her the truth. He squeezed her hand tight. "I lost a brother here too."

Pain moved into her expression, and she looked back toward the Federal line.

"No," he whispered. "Wesley fought for the South. Like Ryan did."

She briefly bowed her head. "Show me."

As they walked hand in hand to the far end of the field, Wade told her about the last time he saw Wesley, and the harsh, even hateful words they'd exchanged. Then the conversation turned to their families and childhoods.

"Were you and Wesley close to each other growin' up? Like me and Ryan?"

"We were inseparable. We did everything together. It used to make Evelyn, our younger sister, so angry. She could pout for days."

"Oh, I'm knowin' a thing or two about a younger sister poutin'."

He laughed softly. "Yes, you do. But she's a keeper, that Nora."

"Aye, that she is. Ryan was her favorite by far."

"She talked about him the other day."

Catriona stopped midstride. "Did she now? What was she sayin'?"

Wade recounted their conversation on the front porch of the cottage. "So I've taken to calling her a wee corker. She seems to like it. I hope you don't mind."

"Nay . . ." Her eyes glistened. "I don't mind a'tall."

Conversation came easily, and even when she said nothing, her gentle smile said everything.

Wade paused to look across the valley, not nearly as familiar with the terrain on this end of the battlefield. But he'd seen a sketch of where the Confederate troops had been stationed. "He died somewhere in this area. I don't know where exactly."

Moments passed, and she finally looked up at him. "Thank you for sharin' this with me. It makes me feel"—she shrugged—"less alone, somehow."

They stood silent, staring out across the valley. But Wade sensed that, like him, she was seeing so much more than what lay before them. Wrapped in his own thoughts and memories, he felt a burden slowly lift inside him. It was by no means gone—

and he knew it likely would never be this side of heaven—but he thanked God for his grace and peace in the moment. And holding Catriona's hand, he brought it to his lips and kissed it, praying that she, too, would know that grace and peace, if she didn't already.

On their way back to Sassy, Catriona pointed toward the Carters' house. "That buildin' there." She looked up at him. "Are those from the fightin' that night?"

Wade nodded, looking at the scores of bullet holes that marred the walls of the corncrib, kitchen, smokehouse, and office. "The battle lasted only four or five hours, but the fighting was intense. On both sides."

They'd continued on when someone called out after them.

"Good day to you!"

Wade turned to see Fountain Branch Carter walking straight for them. Cringing, he desperately hoped that meeting here, on Carter's land, wouldn't jog his memory of the Federal regiment that had taken control of his house the morning of the battle. Wade also hoped Catriona wouldn't say anything to give him away. He stretched out a hand. "Hello, sir. How are you today?"

Carter's grip was firm. "I'm good, young man. I believe we saw each other over at Carnton a while back."

"Yes, sir, we did. I'm Wade Cunningham. And may I present Miss O'Toole, a guest of the

584

McGavocks'. Miss O'Toole, this is Fountain Branch Carter, the gentleman who owns this land."

Carter tilted his head. "Pleasure to meet you, ma'am."

"And you as well, Mr. Carter. I'm hopin' you're not mindin' this, but Mr. Cunningham was showin' me where the battle here took place."

Carter nodded, either studying her or appreciating her beauty. Maybe both. "You had someone you knew in this fight, ma'am?"

Wade's pulse surged, and he quickly jumped in with the hope of guiding the conversation. "She did, sir. Her brother was part of Cleburne's division. But he survived the battle and went on to Nashville."

Surprise showed on Carter's face.

"But Mr. Cunningham's brother wasn't so fortunate," she added, empathy softening her voice.

Wade felt a trickle of sweat down his back.

"Which division was he in, Mr. Cunningham?"

"In Tucker's division, sir."

He shook his head. "Our boys in that group took an awful beatin'."

Wade briefly looked away. "Yes, sir, they did. They fought bravely, though."

Carter stared. "If I remember right, you were up fighting with Lee's men."

Wade felt Catriona look over at him, and he placed his hand on the small of her back and gently squeezed, hoping she'd follow his lead. "Yes, sir, that's right."

Carter eyed him. "So you and your brother, you didn't fight in the same division."

It wasn't a question, and Wade definitely sensed the man fishing. "No, sir. We signed up at different times. My brother left to fight before I did."

"But you weren't here?"

Wade shook his head, guilt nipping at him. "No, sir."

"Hmmph . . . I would've sworn I'd seen you before. Had that same feeling back in McGavock's hallway that day."

Catriona gave a soft laugh. "I had much the same thought, sir. When Mr. Cunningham and I first met. I think he's just havin' that kind of face. Common and homely as it is."

Carter laughed along with her, and Wade did, too, surprised at how easily she added to the lie and feeling guilty for having put her in a position where she had to.

"Well—" Wade offered his hand again. "We won't keep you any longer, sir. Thank you for allowing us to look around."

"Aye, it's helped to settle a wee bit of the pain inside me, Mr. Carter. Bein' here where me brother was."

Carter shook Wade's hand, then looked out across the land. "I honestly don't know if any of the pain inside me will ever go away." He cleared his throat. "I lost my youngest boy, Tod, over there." He pointed in the direction from where they'd come. "Hadn't seen him in over two years when someone came running up after the battle and told us he was shot up bad." He sniffed and wiped at his eyes. "But at least my boy got to die here at home, with all his family gathered round him."

"Aye," Catriona whispered, her voice thin. "When each of our time comes, isn't that where we're all hopin' to be?"

"Yes, ma'am, it sure is. But as I told myself so many times during the war when young Tod was gone, if he did die away from me, he wouldn't die alone. Not with the Lord looking out over him."

Thinking again of Wesley, Wade took that statement to heart. "Thank you again, sir," he said quietly, then took hold of Catriona's arm and led her away, knowing he had some explaining to do.

CHAPTER 38

Wade helped Catriona into the saddle, then swung up behind her and guided Sassy toward town, eager to put some distance between him and this place. He covered her hand. "I'm sorry for lying back there, and for making you feel as if you had to do the same."

She shook her head. "At first I wasn't followin' what you were doin', but then it made sense. You can't exactly be tellin' the colonel and everyone else one thing and then be tellin' his neighbor another."

Wade hesitated, wishing he could tell her the whole truth. But with her brother being a prime suspect in their investigation . . . "Still, I'm sorry for putting you in a situation where you had to do that for me."

"I didn't mind doin' it." She gave a breathy laugh. "Whatever that says of me, right or wrong. Because I know you're not doin' it with a mean intent or to hurt anyone. And truth be told, at times, though I'm proud of me heritage, if I could hide bein' Irish to some people, I would. Before they can even be knowin' me, they've already made up their minds." She paused. "I found a book in Mrs. McGavock's library. She told me I could be readin' any book I wanted to from there, mind you."

Wade smiled.

"It's called *Means and Ends, Or, Self-Trainin'* by a Catharine Maria Sedgwick. Fancy bones kind of name that is! The book was written some years back, but do you know what she's writin' about Irish women like me? And about children like Nora?"

Wade's smile faded. "No, I don't."

"She calls us ignorant, dirty, rude, and repulsive." She exhaled. "And she says that it's up to 'native Americans to be trainin' up these future citizens of *your* country in order to avoid a great *scourge.*'" She said it as though quoting. "And the way she writes, it's as though she thinks she's bein' sympathetic to *our kind,* when really her words say just the opposite. She thinks we're a threat to society." She huffed. "I'd like to have me a talk or two with Miss Catharine Maria Sedgwick. I'd show her scourge!"

Wade didn't even try not to laugh. "For her sake, I hope she never crosses your path."

She chuckled. "I'm just sharin' all that so you'll know *I* know what it's like to feel as though you have to hide somethin' about yeself."

Wade heard what she said—and also what she didn't. The operative in him wanted to ask a question, wanted to lead the conversation in a way that encouraged her to delve deeper into that subject so he could gain more information. But

590

he couldn't in good conscience, and he wouldn't given the way he felt about her.

By the time they reached town, several of the shops were closing, and they barely made it to the post office in time for him to send the telegram pertaining to Tempy to his contact in the Freedmen's Bureau. With intention, Wade approached the older of the two mail clerks behind the counter, having encouraged Catriona to wait for him outside.

"I'd like to send a telegram, please"—Wade glanced politely at the nameplate on the counter—"Mr. Pressley."

Pressley nodded. "Very good, sir."

Wade handed him the slip of paper containing the information, and the man moved to a desk off to the side and succinctly tapped out the message, then returned.

"Will there be anything else, sir?"

Wade shook his head. "How much do I owe you?"

Pressley told him, and Wade handed him a dollar bill. Pressley made change from the till, then dropped the coins into Wade's palm. But no accompanying message this time. Which meant no more counterfeit money had passed through the post office since the various bills Catriona spent had been removed from circulation. That went for the bank, too, or Grissom, the manager, would have sent word. Wade had hoped for at least *some* lead from these two contacts. More and more, he questioned if whoever was running the counterfeiting ring in this area had left Franklin. Either that or they were lying low for a while.

Pushing aside his frustration, Wade met Catriona back outside, noting the look of question on her face.

"Would you mind goin' one more place before we head back?"

He shook his head, having already decided that their dinner out would need to wait.

He was surprised when she told him where she wanted to go, especially after how Laban Pritchard treated her the last time she was in the mercantile. But he guessed she had her reasons.

The mercantile was only two streets over from the telegraph office, so they walked. Passersby on the streets were few, the day winding down into evening. As they passed the livery, Wade stopped by a trough to water Sassy. He rubbed behind her ears, and she whinnied in response.

Catriona stroked her neck. "She's a pretty thing."

"And spirited."

"Aye. I saw her nearly knock you down one day a while back."

He laughed along with her. "It wasn't the first time, I'm sure. And it won't be the last. She likes to have her way. And if she doesn't get it . . . beware."

Smiling, Catriona looked up at him, then away, then finally met his gaze again. Only, her smile was gone. "Wade, I . . . I want to be tellin' you somethin'. But at the same time, I don't, for fear of what you'll be thinkin' of me. And of me brother."

He appreciated the sincerity in her expression, the honesty in her tone. The way the blue of her eyes deepened whenever she spoke in earnest. And the way one little, rebellious curl at her temple always worked its way free of the others. He loved so many things about her. He loved *her.* He didn't quite know when it had happened. He only knew he did. He also knew he needed to move slowly where she was concerned. It was clear she didn't trust easily. And if he ever had a hope of her someday reciprocating his feelings, the way he handled this moment right now would color that moment then. Because he already knew what she was going to say, and she would know that looking back.

"Catriona, if you fear telling me something because you think you might regret it later, for whatever reason, then maybe you should give it more consideration before you do."

She nodded and bowed her head, but he gently lifted her chin.

"But if you fear that telling me something is going to change my opinion of you, then you have nothing to fear. Because the way I feel about you . . ." He reached up and fingered the auburn curl he'd admired a moment earlier. "Let's just say my feelings for you can't be easily swayed. If they can be swayed at all."

Warmth moved into her expression, followed by

a smile he knew he'd carry inside him for a very long time.

Sensing she was having trouble finding the words, he gestured. "Shall we walk?"

Nodding, she fell into step beside him. "Do you remember the day Nora and I went campin'?" she asked after a moment.

He nodded.

"I didn't just decide to leave the hotel. We were asked to leave because the manager from the bank called me into the hotel manager's office, where a man from the government, an operative, he called himself, was waitin'."

She stopped, and he did likewise.

"He started tellin' me that the money I'd put in the bank wasn't real. That it was counterfeit—" She shook her head. "But I'm not tellin' this in the right order."

Wade wished he could make this easier for her. Tell her he already knew it all. But if by chance she told him something new, something in addition to what she'd told Frank Bonner and what was included in detail in a recent report, he needed to know that. He only hoped that, when the time came and she learned he worked for the Secret Service, she would understand and forgive him for not telling her the truth sooner.

"Ryan sent us money. The whole family. Back in Ireland . . ."

She continued in the direction of the mercantile, and Wade matched her pace, listening as she

594

described the events all the way from receiving the money from Ryan to her meeting with Frank Bonner. Every detail matched what he knew perfectly. He spotted the mercantile ahead and slowed.

She took a deep breath and turned to him. "So that's why Nora and I are at Carnton, why we have no place else to go, and why I'm wantin' so much to find me brother. I'm not knowin' anymore what to think." She shook her head. "When I look at this from one direction, I say there's no way Ryan would do such a thing. But when I look at it from another, knowin' how gifted he is at drawin' and how much he loved"—she firmed her lips—"*loves* us, and I think of what I wouldn't do to keep food in Nora's mouth, to keep her safe . . ." She choked on a sob. "I start thinkin' that maybe he did do it. For *us*."

Wade drew her to him, and her arms came around him. He pressed a kiss to the top of her head, grateful she'd confided in him but feeling an even greater burden to find Ryan O'Toole. "We'll find the truth, Catriona. And one way or another, we'll find your brother. I promise you that."

Head against his chest, she nodded. "Aye, I hope we will."

"And for the record," he whispered, waiting until she looked up, "not swayed in the least."

She gave him a fragile smile.

When they reached the mercantile, through the window he spotted the young girl he'd seen

Catriona conversing with before and realized why she'd wanted to come here.

The Closed sign hung in the front door, but Catriona knocked softly. The girl looked up and saw her, then quickly glanced behind her as though worried someone else might have heard. She hesitated, then hurried to open the door.

"Catriona," she said in a hushed tone, then gave Wade a shy look, sweeping her brown hair toward one side of her face.

"Braxie, how are you? I've been meanin' to come by. But I haven't been back to town for quite a while."

"I'm fine. How are you? And how is Nora?"

"I'm well enough, but dear Nora fell and broke her arm, and she's . . ."

As they spoke, Wade couldn't be sure, but it seemed to him that the girl was doing her best to keep to the shadows. And she kept tugging her hair toward her face. As soon as a break in the conversation came, Braxie glanced behind her again.

"I'd best get back to work now. You know how Uncle Laban can be. If he catches me—"

"Braxie, who are you talking to out there?"

The pounding of boot steps on stairs followed, and panic spread across the girl's face. That's when Wade saw it—the dark bruise across her cheek.

"Oh, Braxie . . ." Catriona reached out to her, apparently seeing it as well. "What happened to you? Is that from—"

"Catriona, *please,* you have to go. Both of you!" Braxie tried to close the door, but Wade prevented it, seeing Laban Pritchard round the corner.

"The mercantile is closed!"

Already knowing what he did about the man, and knowing Catriona well enough, too, Wade's decision came without hesitation. "Catriona, get Braxie on Sassy. Now."

With little argument, Braxie followed at Catriona's urging, leaving only Wade when Pritchard finally made it to the door. The sour smell of whiskey preceded him.

"Braxie!" Pritchard yelled, trying to push past him. "Get your backside back in this store right now!"

Wade held his ground. "The girl's going with us, Pritchard. We'll talk once you're sobered up."

"Sobered up," the man repeated, then squinted and muttered a profanity. "Who are *you?*"

"Someone who doesn't let a man like you take a harsh hand to a young girl. Or freed men and women," Wade added, knowing the agency was already building a case against him and his brothers in their secret society.

"Why, you sorry piece of—"

Wade easily avoided the drunken swing, but when Pritchard came at him again, he laid him out flat with a right hook to the jaw. Pritchard went down hard, and Wade thought he heard Braxie crying behind him. Grabbing Pritchard beneath the arms, Wade dragged him back into the mercantile and left him lying on the floor, then closed the door behind him.

Tempy met them at the back door of the kitchen, and Catriona read unmistakable irritation in her expression. Tempy had been none too thrilled—and that was putting it lightly—when Catriona told her she was going to town with Wade. But seeing sweet Braxie now, Tempy's irritation faded, and she wrapped loving arms around the girl.

"Come here, child. I'm Tempy, and I'll see to you, if you'll let me."

Braxie nodded, still crying a little, just as she'd done all the way back to Carnton. Catriona watched Tempy with a measure of awe as the nurturing side of her poured so freely onto those around her. Well, all except Wade Cunningham. That thought made Catriona smile. If only Tempy knew who he really was, and that he wasn't at all who she thought him to be.

"Is she going to be all right, you think?" Wade whispered, coming alongside her.

Catriona nodded. "She's frightened right now. And has been, I'm thinkin', for some time. I just wasn't seein' it because of me own grief and fear."

His hand came to the small of her back, and she leaned into him, so grateful she'd gone into town with him and for all that had happened between them. She believed him, too, when he said they'd find the truth . . . and Ryan. Her throat tightened.

Something had happened to her on that ridge as they'd stood staring across that valley. Parts of her life had risen before her eyes like sketches fluttering by, some so swiftly it had all but taken her breath away. And like a blind man given sight, she'd seen the past few months and years through a different set of lenses. She couldn't explain it, and even now she wasn't sure what had happened or what it meant. But something deep inside her had . . . shifted. She couldn't deny it. And she didn't want to.

Hearing a familiar *clomp clomp* coming down the stairs from the main house, Catriona turned to see Nora making a beeline straight for her. Maybe the child had come looking for her after all. Catriona smiled at her sister, and the reciprocating smile that lit Nora's face did her heart such good. She bent and started to hold out her arms to—

"Wade!" Nora yelled as she half walked, half ran into his outstretched arms.

Straightening, Catriona watched the two of them and caught Wade's unmistakable look at her. The man could say so much with a single glance. She tried to do the same, and he nodded and winked. Still disappointed, Catriona found herself hoping— Nay, it wasn't merely a hope. She found herself praying that God would open Nora's heart to her again. She blinked away the tears before anyone could see. Well, anyone except Wade. He slipped his arm around her and gave her a quick hug. But not quick enough. The look Tempy gave them could have fried corn in a cast-iron skillet.

"You might need to do some *wee* campaigning for me on that front," Wade whispered.

Catriona shook her head. "I think it's goin' to take a lot more than a wee bit."

A knock sounded on the back door, and Catriona saw George Cuppett through the paned glass. She opened the door, but before she could even greet him, George stepped inside.

"We need help. Marcellus is sick. His stomach is hurting him something awful, and he can't keep down any food."

Catriona nodded. "I'll be comin' with you right away."

"Me too," Wade echoed.

"Does he have fever, Mister Cuppett?" Tempy called from across the room.

"No, ma'am. Not yet, anyway." George briefly looked down. "He keeps asking for you, Miss O'Toole. He wants to see you."

Hearing that caused her heart to squeeze tight. But her real worry was that, based on what George had said, she'd seen the likes of such an illness before, and it had taken three of the people she'd loved most in the world.

Nora pushed in between them. "I'm wantin' to come too!"

"No!" Catriona and Wade cried in unison.

Catriona gripped his arm. "Stay here with her,

600

please? At least until Tempy is finished with Braxie?"

As if only then seeing Braxie seated at the kitchen table across the room, Nora made a beeline for her.

"And then bring yeself as soon as you can," Catriona continued. "And whatever Tempy says we might be needin'."

Wade nodded. "I won't be long. And be careful. We don't know what—"

"I know." She left out the back door with George, who was already several paces ahead of her.

"Do you know any sickness like this, Miss O'Toole?"

"Aye." She hurried to catch up to him. "I can't be sure, of course, but it's soundin' a lot like dysentery."

She'd seen the men coming and going, so she knew the burial team was staying in one of the old slave cabins closest to the main house. But she'd never been inside before now. The stark contrast to her own quarters above the kitchen, much less the McGavocks' home, took her aback. The stench of sick filled the room, and she resisted the urge to cover her nose. She spotted Polk, Charley, and Robert standing off to the side, but it was the sight of Marcellus curled on his side on a cot, eyes clenched tight, gripping his abdomen, that sent a shudder of fear through her.

She knelt beside him. "Marcellus," she whispered, laying a hand to his head. He flinched, yet his skin felt cool to the touch.

"Catriona?" He sucked in a breath, his eyes fluttering open. "Thank you." He gasped. "Thank you for coming."

"I'm right here." She wished she could tell him he was going to be all right. But she'd learned not to make promises she couldn't keep. So she made the ones she could. "I'll be here with you for as long as you need me. Tell me what you need, and I'll do me best to get it for you."

"I don't want nothing but for the pain to stop."

Hoping to help him relax, she gently rubbed his shoulder, but he cried out in pain.

"That *hurts*." His breath came hard. "P-please don't touch me again."

Catriona stared, then looked up at George. "This isn't dysentery, Mr. Cuppett."

His face paled. "What is it, then?"

"I'm not knowin' for sure. Maybe Tempy will. But I know the signs of dysentery. And this . . ." She shook her head. "I barely touched him just now."

The door opened, and Tempy hurried inside. Wade followed closely behind carrying a crate containing a collection of bottles Catriona recognized from one of Tempy's kitchen cupboards.

Tempy leaned over the bed. "Tell me what you know, Miss O'Toole."

"The slightest touch is painin' him greatly.

And there's no fever. I was thinkin' it might be dysentery, but it doesn't act like it."

Tempy looked at George. "Bloody bowel?"

George shook his head.

"Show me what his stomach sent back up."

George pointed to a bucket near the cot.

Tempy peered inside, then shook her head. "It ain't the dysentery."

George stepped closer. "Then what is it, Tempy? Can you do something for him?"

"I can try, but we best send for the colonel's doctor."

"I'll ride for him." Wade was already to the door. "Anything else you need, Tempy?"

"Prayers, Mister Cunningham. If you're a prayin' man."

Shortly before daybreak, Marcellus fell into delirium. When he spoke, his words no longer made sense. He no longer recognized anyone. He reached into the air as though trying to grab something that wasn't there. George encouraged her to go get some rest, but Catriona couldn't leave Marcellus's side. What if he awakened only to find she wasn't there as she'd promised to be?

She looked across the small cabin and saw the colonel's personal physician lay a hand on George's shoulder, their conversation in hushed tones. After watching the doctor through the night, she knew that, for all his training and knowledge, he was at as much a loss as they were to know what to do. But one thing he did say . . . Whatever this was, instinct told him it wasn't contagious. The other men who'd been with Marcellus the whole time, eating and drinking the very same things, hadn't taken ill. But still, he admitted, he couldn't be sure.

The door opened, and Wade quietly entered. He came to stand behind her chair and rested his hands on her shoulders. She reached for his left hand and held on tight.

He leaned close. "Nora is crying back at the house. She wants to see him."

She shook her head. "Nay. I'm not wantin' her to see him like this."

Wade's breath was warm on her cheek, his hands strong and comforting. "It's your decision, of course. But think about how you would feel if you weren't given the chance to say good-bye to someone you loved."

Her throat all but closed, and she bowed her head.

"We'll just stand in the doorway. We won't come inside."

Worn and weary, Catriona finally nodded.

Minutes later, the door opened, and Catriona rose, having done her best to hide the marks of grief. Wade held Nora in his arms.

"Good mornin', wee one." Tempted to brush back a curl from Nora's temple, she resisted, in case the doctor's instinct proved to be wrong.

But Nora looked at Wade. "What's wrong with him?"

"Mr. Marcellus is very sick, like we talked about on the way here." Wade spoke softly, and Nora's left arm wove its way around his neck.

"Is he goin' to be gettin' well?"

Wade looked at Catriona, then shook his head. "No, sweetheart. We don't think he is."

Nora's lower lip began to quiver, and Catriona recognized the look of fear in her sister's eyes. She'd seen it in Nora's face as the wee girl had watched their mam and two sisters slowly, painfully slip away. And Catriona knew then that her gut instinct had been right all along. Nora didn't belong here, and she opened her mouth to say just that.

But Marcellus cried out, "It hurts me! Don't touch me. It *hurts!*"

Nora shrank back, and Catriona motioned to Wade for them to leave. But Wade only drew the girl closer to him.

"Marcellus is in pain, Nora," he whispered. "And the very most we can do for him right now is to pray. Can you do that?"

Nora nodded, tears slipping down her cheeks. "But he's me friend. I'm not wantin' him to die."

Wade pressed a kiss against her hair. "I know. I'm not wanting that either. But would you rather him stay here like this? In pain? Or go to a wonderful, big house that Jesus has built for him, and where lots of friends and family who love him are waiting for him? And where he won't be in pain ever again?"

Nora looked at him, her gaze guileless and pure—and unrelenting. "I'm wantin' him to stay here with me and be gettin' well."

Wade's eyes watered. "I would choose that, too, little one, if I could. But sometimes we don't get to choose. And *this* is one of those times." He took hold of her little hand. "You love Mr. Marcellus, don't you?"

Nora nodded, her chin trembling.

"Then the best thing we can do for Mr. Marcellus right now is to pray that, if he isn't going to get well, the Lord will take him to heaven quickly—so he won't be in pain anymore."

Wade looked at Catriona, and only then did she realize what he was doing. Not just for Nora but for her too.

CHAPTER 39

"Dear friends and loved ones of the deceased . . ."

As the preacher spoke, Wade looked at the draped tombstone, surprised they'd managed to have a marker prepared so quickly. Marcellus had died only yesterday, four days after taking ill. Then again, they'd all feared this outcome from the start. Then, too, the physician attending Marcellus said he thought the sickness might have come from the work the burial team was doing, and Wade figured the colonel had used his considerable influence to bring together whatever needed to be done to help ease the burden for Marcellus's brothers. George Cuppett had also asked the colonel if his brother could be buried in the Texas section of the new cemetery, where the very men Marcellus had exhumed and reinterred were resting in peace. The colonel and Mrs. McGavock had readily agreed.

George and Polk stood side by side next to the oak casket, Charley Baugh and Robert Sloan beside them, hats in hand. The gathering at the cemetery was small. Only a dozen or so, Wade counted. Catriona stood close by his side, Nora by her, then Braxie. The girl had opened up a bit more about her uncle Laban. Nothing Wade didn't know, or suspect, already. And he wasn't sure, only time

607

would tell, but he sensed that Catriona might have just gained another sister.

To a person, everyone assembled had known Marcellus and could attest to the man's kind and gentle nature. Even now, Wade could picture Marcellus's good-natured smile and him pointing his forefinger toward the sky.

"Now I will read some of Marcellus's favorite passages from the Word of God . . ."

Wade found himself nodding, realizing he and Marcellus shared an affinity for some of the same scriptures. As Wade looked out over the cemetery, he realized how much work had been done yet how much was left to do. Not only for George and his team but for him as well.

Yesterday he'd made a call on Whitley Jacobs, the suspect whose farm had not only doubled in size late last summer but who had doubled the number of cattle he was running. Under the guise of buying a couple of the farmer's bulls for Carnton, Wade had managed to get a layout of the place. Then he'd returned around midnight last night for a more private inspection. And while what he'd found didn't help him with his investigation in the least, what he'd discovered would be of great interest to a revenue agent he knew. While the government was fine with people running stills, revenue agents frowned on running secret stills and not paying the mandated taxes on that liquor. With a telegram already sent that morning, Wade had no doubt the revenue agent would be making a call on Whitley Jacobs right soon.

But while it was good to have answers about these suspects, they in no way helped his own investigation. He had to be missing something, an important detail he wasn't seeing. Sensing someone's attention, he peered down to see Catriona watching him. A tiny frown creased her brow, and he gave her a look saying he was fine, then discreetly reached over and took her hand in his to confirm it.

"Rock of ages, cleft for me," the preacher sang, and everyone joined in.

The words of the hymn took Wade back to his childhood. The song had been one of his father's favorites, and he could still hear his strong tenor voice ringing so pure and clear in church—and from the back of the barn. "Let the water and the blood, from thy riven side which flowed," Wade sang, "be of sin the double cure, cleanse me from its guilt and power."

Catriona sang beside him, so softly he almost couldn't hear her. He looked down to see unshed tears in her eyes. But she was smiling. Without peering up, she gave his hand a tight squeeze, and in that moment, Wade knew that no matter what his future held, he wanted it to include her and Nora. And young Braxie, too, if that was part of the Almighty's plan.

Nora chose that moment to reach up, not for him, but for Catriona, and it did his heart a world of good. He'd talked to Nora again as the two of them had walked back to the main house the night Nora saw Marcellus for the last time. He'd tried to impress upon her that what they'd just prayed for Marcellus—for God to mercifully call him home—was exactly what Catriona had prayed for their mam. He wasn't certain the meaning had really stuck, until now.

Catriona lifted her sister, and Nora's arms came around her neck. As though sensing his attention, Catriona looked over, still singing. But she paused long enough to mouth "Thank you." If she only knew how much more he wanted to do for her. How much more involved in their lives he wanted to be.

At the song's conclusion, the preacher walked to the headstone. "Marcellus Cuppett," he said, his voice carrying in the warmth of the spring sun filtering through the mighty oak trees canopying overhead, "may you rest in peace in the bosom of the Father for all eternity. We will see you again soon one day." The preacher removed the drape, and soft murmurs of approval rippled through the crowd. Wade felt his own chest clench. Etched at the top of the headstone was a hand with a forefinger pointed to the sky.

Catriona finished weeding the tomato beds, then stood back to admire her work. Especially the plots thick with brilliant yellow daffodils. The flowers had started blooming the morning after they'd buried Marcellus, which had seemed fitting to her considering how the flowers stood proud and tall, reaching for the sun. But it was the patch of lilac-blue Spring Squill blooming in a corner of one of the beds—the flower petals so delicate, yet so resilient—that she cherished most.

Hearing the telling squeak of the gate behind her, she glanced back to see Wade making his way toward her through the maze of the garden. Sometimes when he looked at her, she could all but read his thoughts—and reading them now made her both blush and smile. How, in such a short time, could a complete stranger—and not one she had cared to know any better—come to mean so much to her?

These past weeks had seen May ushered in with its warmer days yet still cool nights. She never thought she and Nora would be at Carnton this long, but it had taken Nora's arm longer to fully heal, and the McGavocks insisted the two of them were no bother. In fact, Mrs. McGavock raved that the garden was the most beautiful it had ever been. And Catriona had to admit, it did look lovely. The McGavocks had also been complimentary of the Irish beef stew and butterscotch pie she'd made recently for dinner as well. But Wade's praise had meant the most.

She stood and tugged the gardening gloves from her hands, the enthusiasm in his handsome face causing her own thoughts to scatter in a hundred different directions. "I thought you said you were goin' into town."

"I did. But when I got this"—he held up what looked like a telegram—"I had to come right back."

She stilled. "You've finally heard somethin'?"

"Yes, ma'am."

She tried to read his expression, wondering if it was news about Ryan or Tempy. Instinct told her it was the latter, and though a part of her heart ached, another part soared. "It's about Tempy."

He nodded, then seemed to hedge a bit before answering. "And actually, I first heard something back about this almost two weeks ago. But it wasn't conclusive, so I waited to say anything until I knew for sure."

She batted him with a glove, but she was too hopeful and in love with this man to be cross with him. "So it's good news, then?"

"Very good news that, frankly, I'd hoped for but wasn't expecting." He handed her the telegram.

She read it quickly, her own excitement building. "So this means they're *here?* Close by?"

He nodded. "In Nashville, all this time. And yes, according to all the leads, that's where they still are."

She laid her gloves aside. "When can we leave?"

He smiled. "So you *do* want to go with me, then?"

"Of course I'm wantin' to go. How could you be thinkin' otherwise, you daft man!"

Still smiling, he gestured toward the barn. "I need to get some things settled here, but I could leave in a couple of days. McGavock has been wanting me to check on some farming equipment in Nashville, so I should be able to arrange the trip easily enough. But best prepare yourself. Tempy is likely to take a shotgun to us both when she learns you're accompanying me."

She waved the comment away, more than ready for him to give her permission to tell Tempy the truth about him. "She simply doesn't know you yet. Not like *I* do."

A flicker of emotion she couldn't describe briefly clouded his face. "And if she asks why you're going?"

Catriona thought for a moment. "I'll tell her it's got somethin' to do with the hope of findin' Ryan. I don't think she'll be questionin' me on that count."

He briefly looked away. "I'm sorry we haven't made more progress on finding him, Catriona. But nothing's turned up. We know he made it to Nashville with Hood's army, but after that . . ."

Seeing the disappointment in his eyes made it difficult for her to speak. "I know you're still tryin', Wade, doin' all you can. And I'm grateful for it."

He nodded, but frustration clearly lined his features. "We shouldn't be gone but a day. We'll get an early start, then should be back by nightfall. Since you already told me Braxie knows what we're up to with Tempy, maybe you could ask her to help with Nora while we're gone."

Catriona nodded. "I'll ask Braxie to help with assistin' the burial team, too, in me absence. She came to the cemetery with me the other day, wantin' to know what it was I did. She handled it well. Better than I did me first day."

Wade studied her. "Braxie's fitting in quite well around here. And with you and Nora."

She heard more in the comment than was stated and followed his thread. She knew Wade cared about her, yet she had no idea if he'd thought about the future. Much less a future together. If he had, he'd kept those thoughts to himself. But when faced with Braxie's situation and future, she'd found it an easy decision to make. After all, the girl had quickly become like a sister to her. What she didn't know for certain was if the decision she'd made would impact Wade's.

"Aye, she *is* fittin' in well," she finally answered. "I'm grateful to Mrs. McGavock for agreein' to Braxie stayin' here. The three of us sharin' a bedroom is workin' out just fine. Except when those two go runnin' their mouths late into the night." She smiled to let him know she was kidding. "Braxie will be here with me and Nora until I can find a way to provide a home for the three of us." Once the words were out, she realized how they might sound to him, as though she were hinting at something or another, so she hurried on. "Braxie told me she penned a note to Pritchard shortly after she arrived tellin' him she wouldn't be comin' back, but that she appreciated what he and his wife did for her."

"What little that was," he interjected dryly.

She met the comment with a look. "While I'm agreein' with you on the one hand, Braxie did tell me that her uncle and aunt didn't *have* to be takin' her in a'tall after her parents died. That they simply could have cast her off in some orphans' home. So she's grateful they spared her that fate, at least. Her aunt sent her clothes and the few keepsakes the girl has from her parents, which was decent of her. And there's somethin' else." It angered her all over again, recalling what Braxie had described. "She says her uncle is part of a *secret* society, they call themselves. One bent on hurtin' and scarin' freed men and women. She says the group holds meetin's late at night out in the woods east of town, and that her uncle is one of the higher-ups. I asked her if I could be tellin' you about it, and she said I could. I thought that with all the people you know, you might know someone who could put a stop to it."

Wade nodded, not looking nearly as surprised as she'd been herself when Braxie told her about her uncle's clandestine meetings. "Tell Braxie thank you for confiding in me, and I'll look into that for sure." He paused, then reached for her hand and held it briefly between both of his, the uncertainty in his manner telling her that whatever he was about to say wasn't coming easily. Then just as swiftly his expression changed. "Well, I'd better get back to work. I'll be looking forward to Nashville."

Watching him walk away, she felt her former suspicions about him tugging at old doubts trying to resurrect themselves. But she *knew* him. He'd been honest with her. She had no reason to question him. Not anymore. So why did she?

Catriona awakened before sunrise, not having slept much during the night. The possibility of meeting Tempy's siblings today had kept her thoughts whirring. She quietly lit the oil lamp on the bedside table, Nora and Braxie still fast asleep. Nora on the bed, Braxie on the cot the McGavocks had brought down from the attic for her.

Yesterday Wade had suggested she bring along a change of clothes in case they needed to spend the night, so she made a neat pile of clothing on the bed and added other items she would need for the brief trip. She looked around the room for anything she might have missed. Her gaze fell on Mam's Bible lying on the bedside table.

She picked it up and turned to the page marked by the sketch of the Celtic cross Ryan had drawn for her years earlier. The same cross he'd had tattooed on his arm. "Where are you, dear brother?" she whispered, smoothing a hand down the page until she came to the verses Tempy had shown her recently, after one of their nightly readings.

At Tempy's suggestion, the five of them— including Mary, Braxie, and Nora—had taken to reading small sections of the Bible together before they went to bed. She loved listening to Tempy read, the woman's voice so full of hope, her cadence strong and sure.

" 'For we know' "—she started softly, her own voice paling in comparison—" 'that if our earthly house of this tabernacle were dissolved, we have a building of God, a house not made with hands, eternal in the heavens. For in this we—' " She paused, then glanced toward the bedroom door. She heard Tempy downstairs fixing breakfast, so she knew the woman's bedroom would be empty. Tempy had given her permission to read from the journal before but . . .

Catriona still felt a little sneaky slipping down the hall and into Tempy's room. She opened the treasured journal atop Tempy's Bible. It took a moment, but she found the page Tempy had read from the other night. And though she hoped the Almighty wouldn't take offense, she far preferred Tempy's thoughtful rewording of the verses to the fancier words from this King James fellow. She read silently . . .

For we know that when this earthly tent we live in is taken down, meaning that, when we die and leave this old, worn-out earthly body behind, we will have a house in heaven. A body that will last forever, made for us by God hisself and not by any man or woman's hands.

She read on, looking for the phrase she'd thought about so often since hearing Tempy read it. She only wished she'd learned these truths earlier in life. How much pain and angst that would have saved her. Finally, she found it, and she smiled.

While we live in these earthly bodies of ours, we groan and we sigh. O Lord, don't we groan and sigh. It ain't so much that we wanna die and get rid of these earthly bodies. Instead, it's that we want to put on our new bodies from you so that these dying bodies will be swallowed up by life.

That was the phrase. " 'Swallowed up by life,' " Catriona repeated. Tempy told her people who trusted Jesus went to be with him when they died, and then she'd turned to this very scripture in her own Bible, along with several others that said the same thing. Catriona had made note of where to find them because the verses gave her such hope. They changed how she viewed death and the afterlife—and how she pictured where Mam, Bridget, and Alma were. And especially how she looked upon the nearly eleven hundred bodies of soldiers buried thus far in the cemetery. The grave wasn't the end of life. For those who trusted Jesus, it was only the beginning.

The creak of a wagon drew her attention, and she crossed to the window in the hallway to see Wade hitching a team to the rig, the sun just beginning to peer up over the horizon. She returned Tempy's journal to the bedside table and hurried back to finish packing. She placed Mam's Bible on top of her belongings, then, using her cloak, she wrapped the bundle and headed downstairs.

Her excitement at the possibility of having found Tempy's brother and sister was overshadowed only by the possibility that she might never learn what happened to Ryan. As heartbreaking as that would be, at least she could try to see Tempy's story come full circle—even if her own never did.

CHAPTER 40

Wade reined in and brought the wagon to a stop a short distance down the street from a finely appointed house in one of the nicer areas of Nashville. Catriona sat close beside him on the bench seat, and he sensed her cautious excitement, same as his own.

He turned to her. "Whatever happens today, I want you to know that you've done everything you could."

"Nay, *you've* been doin' everything. You found the bill of sale, you contacted the Freedmen's Bureau, you—"

He took hold of her hand. "Catriona, I wouldn't have even thought to do any of that without you. I was there in the kitchen that day, same as you, when Tempy mentioned a brother and sister. Yet to my shame, never once did I think about trying to find them. Until you brought it up."

"But as soon as I did, you started movin' heaven and earth to find them. Same as you've been doin' to help me try to find Ryan."

Knowing it wasn't her intention, her words brought a stab of disappointment. "I'm sorry for having failed you in that regard. I'm not giving up, but I also don't hold out much hope that we'll find—"

"Havin' failed me? Failin' me is the *last* thing you've done, Wade Cunningham." She reached up and touched his face. "I don't know what Nora and I would have done or where we'd be without you. But aye, I know hope's growin' slim for findin' Ryan, and yet—" She drew in a breath, a sheen of emotion in her eyes. "The Almighty knows where he is. And even though I wish he would be lettin' us know, too, even if he doesn't, I'm finally comin' to trust him again."

Grateful the street was empty of traffic, he leaned over and kissed her, only intending a quick peck. Then she pressed closer, responding to him with an eagerness he'd only dreamed about, and a jolt of desire shot through him. Not wanting to, he pulled back slightly, and she opened her eyes. He saw within them a desire that mirrored his own, and yet he knew he didn't deserve it. Because while she thought she knew him, she didn't. Not completely.

He'd come close to telling her about working for the Secret Service yesterday, but he'd told himself that until Ryan O'Toole was found, until the young man was either cleared or convicted of counterfeiting charges, he wasn't at liberty to. Still, he realized that wasn't the full truth. The real reason he hadn't told her yet was because he feared losing her once she found out.

He set the brake and climbed down, then assisted her descent. He offered his arm, and she slipped her hand through. Though the late morning sun blazed brightly overhead, rain had fallen during the night, and the trees and shrubs lining the street shone an emerald green. He glanced at her, again sensing her excitement.

Side by side, they walked the short distance to the house, and when they reached the door, he didn't have to ask if she was ready. He cleared his throat and knocked. A moment passed before a woman answered.

"Good afternoon, ma'am. My name is Wade Cunningham, and this is Miss Catriona O'Toole. We'd like to speak with Delphia Carrington, if she's home."

The woman, about as round as she was tall, didn't look a thing like Tempy. But then she eyed them both in a manner that felt all too familiar, and Wade's hopes lifted.

"I'm Delphia, but I don't think I'm knowin' you, sir. Or you either, ma'am," she added with a touch more politeness.

Wade gestured. "Miss O'Toole and I have come from Franklin to speak with you, if you'd allow us a few moments."

She seemed to stew on that, then stepped to one side. "Come on in, then. But my mistress and her husband are gonna be back anytime. So we need to get this done right quick. Mister Ledbetter, he don't like strangers in his house. 'Specially when he ain't home." She hurriedly ushered them into a parlor off the front hall.

Wade exchanged a look with Catriona, and he could tell she shared his same thoughts. He decided he best get right to it. "Miss O'Toole and I are friends with a woman named Tempy who works at Carnton." He waited for a flicker of recognition but saw nothing. "We've done some research, and we believe you and Tempy may be related. In fact, we believe you *and* your brother are related to her by blood."

The woman looked at him as if he'd grown a third eye. "I ain't got no brother, sir. Leastwise, not that's alive. And what's this . . . *research* you say you been doin'?"

Wade reached into his pocket and pulled out the telegram, thinking that showing her something official might aid their cause. "This telegram confirms that you and your brother were sold as very young children by a judge in Montgomery, Alabama, to a man who used to live here. A Mr. Carrington. The names of the children on that bill of sale were Rufus and Jinsey." Wade saw a spark of recognition—or was it fear?—in the woman's eyes. "We understand that Mr. Carrington died a few years back, but—"

"You both gots to go. And you gots to go *now!*"

"But, Delphia—" Catriona started.

The woman raised her hand. "I'm tellin' you, I don't know no Rufus and Jinsey. And I'm not pullin' your leg when I say you need to leave. And don't be askin' 'bout my brother, Demetrius. He's dead. Got hisself killed out there on Danby Road, late one night in January of '61. Beaten to death by a no-good—" She motioned them toward the front door, starting in that direction herself.

"Delphia," Catriona tried again, pausing in the lobby, "Tempy is a dear friend, and both Mr. Cunningham and I are truly wantin' to—"

Delphia opened the door. "Good day to you both."

Catriona looked back at Wade as if asking what else they could do. Then the sound of barking preceded a dog running around the corner and straight for the open door. Wade could only stare, feeling as though he were seeing a ghost. Only in canine form.

"Oh no, Mister Harvey, you can't be in here when Mister Ledbetter come back." Delphia tried to grab the dog, but it slid right by her—and ran straight to Wade.

Wade knelt, and the dog licked his neck and face. He pulled the animal close, rubbing his neck and scratching him behind the ears like he used to do. Back in the war. Wade looked closer. The dog still wore the same collar he'd worn during the war with the name Harvey engraved on a little metal tag.

"Wait . . ." Catriona looked up at him. "I'm knowin' this dog. You have a picture of—"

"Meet Harvey." Wade looked up at her. "Who used to be the mascot for our regiment. He went missing after the war, and we never knew what happened to him." He slowly stood. "How did you come to have this dog, ma'am?"

Delphia rolled her eyes. "I'm tellin' you both, you need to be leavin'. Mister Ledbetter, he ain't a kindly man, and that's puttin' it nicely."

"How did you come to have this dog?" Wade asked again, this time with more authority. He already suspected the woman was lying about her brother. The way she rattled off where and when he'd been killed sounded like something she'd rehearsed. Like she'd been asked for that information before. When posed with troubling questions, especially about the death of a loved one, people usually gave short, clipped responses, not wanting to dwell in that memory any longer than they had to. But not her. And despite her assertion to the contrary, she'd definitely recognized the names Rufus and Jinsey.

Delphia firmed her lips. "After the battle here in Nashville, we all done our part takin' in the Confederate wounded, carin' for 'em. And one of them boys came with this dog. Said he found it, and it started followin' him everywhere. So he brought it here with him."

"Where is this soldier now? And why didn't he take his dog?"

Delphia glanced out the door. "Sir, you and this lady is gonna get me into a mess o' trouble if—"

"Then you'd best answer our questions, ma'am. *Please,*" he added more politely.

She heaved an exasperated sigh. "I don't know, sir. All I know is that he got hisself a job and was workin' for somebody in town. He was savin' up money, he said. He wasn't here for more than a month, probably less. Stayed out yonder in one of them ol' slave cabins. 'Cause the Federals, they came around every now and then collectin' any Confederates left. Then one day he just didn't come back."

Wade felt Catriona looking at him, but he kept his focus on Delphia.

"Left me with this sorry little excuse for an animal," the woman continued. But even as she said it, she peered down at Harvey with scarcely masked affection. "And like I said, I ain't knowin' the soldier's name. But"—Delphia looked at Catriona—"he talked just like you, ma'am. Looked a lot like you too."

Catriona gave a soft gasp, and Wade looked at her. Then he reached for the door and closed it, only too familiar with the piercing look Delphia leveled in his direction. He'd seen it countless times in her older sister's eyes.

CHAPTER 41

No sooner had Wade closed the door than he heard the rumble of a carriage on the street in front of the house.

Delphia stepped to a window and peered through the curtain. Her eyes went wide. "Oh Lord, it's Mister and Missus Ledbetter! They's home!" She turned back. "I'm beggin' you both, you gots to go!"

Wade recognized genuine fear when he saw it and though he had no intention of bringing her harm, how could he leave here without—

"That soldier." Catriona grabbed Delphia's hand. "The one you're sayin' stayed in the slave cabin. I'm thinkin' that could be me brother. We've been lookin' for him. Is the name Ryan soundin' familiar to you?"

Sweat broke out on the woman's brow. "I didn't swap names with any of them soldiers, ma'am. Was safer not to. Now *please* . . ."

Wade spotted a couple exiting the carriage, and they made their way to the front door. "We'll leave out the back right now, Delphia—but will you promise to meet us at the slave cabins and answer our questions? *Please.*"

Delphia's jaw hardened, then she pointed. "Go

through there. That's the kitchen. Take the back door and head on around behind the shed so the Ledbetters won't be seein' you through the parlor window. Keep to the edge o' the woods and walk for a piece until you come to some ol' cabins. I'll meet you there soon as I can. And take Mister Harvey with you!"

Harvey followed them without even being told, and as Wade closed the kitchen door behind them, he heard Delphia greeting the Ledbetters. He grabbed Catriona's hand, and they followed Delphia's instructions until they came upon a cluster of what appeared to be abandoned slave cabins. Weeds left too long to themselves reached up past the windows, and partially open plank wood doors sagged on rusted hinges.

"It has to be Ryan, don't you think?" Catriona finally said, breaking the silence.

The cautious hope in her voice mirrored his own feelings, yet he didn't want to encourage false hope. "I sure want to think it is. Let's check out the cabins while we're waiting. See if we can find anything."

He pushed open the door and stepped inside, Harvey close on his heels. Wade reached down and petted him, unable to shake the feeling that this dog that had helped see his regiment through a war was about to help him again.

Catriona followed. "What are we lookin' for?"

"Anything. But step carefully. Some of these boards feel like they're nearly rotted clean through."

The one-room structure was empty save for vermin droppings left by its most recent occupants. Usually he would search for items hidden beneath the floorboards, but he could clearly see the ground through the widely spaced planks.

"I'm not believin' Delphia, are you?"

He shook his head. "Not a bit." He crouched by the hearth and peered up the chimney, then reached inside and felt around. Nothing.

"I'm thinkin' I caught a look in her eye when you said the names Rufus and Jinsey."

"I saw the same thing. She's definitely not telling us something. Now to find out what."

They'd headed for the second cabin when Harvey started barking. They turned to see Delphia hurrying toward them, and the dog ran to greet her.

"That ain't the cabin the soldier was stayin' in." Delphia pointed, never breaking her pace. "It was that last one down there on the end."

"About what we asked you earlier—" Wade began.

But the woman shook her head and glanced behind her. "You can see these cabins from some of them upper rooms in the main house. Best let's go inside."

Wade and Catriona followed her into the last cabin. Unlike the first cabin they'd searched, this one had furniture, rudimentary though it was. A table and chair in one corner and an old rope bed with a stained ticking mattress in the other. He saw no personal effects. Ryan must have taken whatever he had with him.

Delphia turned abruptly. "I toted meals down here to him every day. Mornin' and night." She spoke quickly as though eager to see this done— and them gone. "Sometimes I saw him and Mister Harvey, but most times they wasn't here. But I'd find the tin I'd piled high with food clean as a whistle, so I knowed they'd come and gone. But one day he was waitin' for me, and he asked me if he was to get me some money, would I buy food for them freed men and women starvin' in the shantytown he passed every day on his way to work and back."

"The shantytown?" Catriona asked.

"Yes, ma'am. It ain't too far from here. Near the heart of town. Or what used to be the heart."

Wade nodded for her to continue.

"So I said I'd do it, and he give me some money." She blew out a breath. "More money than I ever knew was in the world."

Wade exchanged a look with Catriona, whose pained expression reflected everything he was thinking. She slowly bowed her head.

"I bought boxes and boxes of food and then, with some help, carted it on over there. The next day I come back to this cabin to pass along the thanks all them people give to me for him, but he was gone. And he never came back again. Leastwise that I saw him." She gazed down at Harvey. "Couple o' days later, this pesky ol' dog shows up at the kitchen door and won't leave for nothin'. So I start feedin' him again. And on cold nights, I sneak him into my room by the kitchen so he can stay warm by the fire." Her attention moved to Catriona. "You say you been lookin' for your brother, ma'am. If this soldier *was* your brother, I hope you find him. He struck me as a kind soul, and not just 'cause o' what he done with all that money. There was just somethin' about him that made you want to like him even before you knew why you should."

Catriona slowly lifted her head, her cheeks wet with tears.

Almost imperceptibly, Delphia's expression changed. "Y'all got the same eyes," she whispered, her own glistening with unshed emotion.

Wade sensed something pass between the two women, similar to what he remembered that day in the kitchen when Tempy told Catriona about her siblings. Seeing his opportunity . . .

"Delphia, about you and your brother—"

"I done told you my brother's dead, sir. Now I gots to get back to—"

"I know you told me that, but I don't believe you. I also don't believe you're telling the truth about the names Rufus and Jinsey."

"We saw it in your eyes," Catriona offered, compassion in her gaze. "Both of us."

Delphia started to speak, then looked toward the door as though weighing her option to run. When she looked back at Wade, a fierceness sharpened her eyes. "I ain't never laid eyes on you before

633

today, sir. How am I knowin' I can trust you?"

"Because I do," Catriona answered before he could. "And because as hard as it is to face the truth, it's even harder to live with a lie."

A short time later, Wade escorted Catriona back to the wagon, a plan already forming in his mind. But he couldn't act on the first phase, briefly visiting the shantytown with her today, without first telling her the truth. Not after what she'd just said. Not knowing *she* was the reason Delphia had finally trusted him.

Spotting a park bench just off the road, he gestured. "Would you sit with me for a minute?"

She looked up at him. "Don't even think you're goin' to talk me out of goin' with you."

"No." He tried for a smile and fell short. "But I do need to talk to you before we head there."

Her expression sobered.

They sat down on the bench, and Wade turned to her, feeling as if everything he cared about hung in the balance. "Do you remember the afternoon you told me you needed to tell me something, but you feared it would change the way I thought about you?"

Her brow furrowed. "Aye. I'd be a wee bit daft if I didn't remember that."

He might have smiled under different circumstances, but he found that impossible to do at the moment. "Well, I'm feeling the very same way right now."

She reached for his hand. "Wade, there's nothin' you could tell me that—"

He stood, needing to put some distance between them. "You don't know what I'm about to say."

"Nay, I don't. But—"

"Catriona, I'm a government operative for the United States Secret Service. My job is to track down counterfeiters and bring them to justice. My position as overseer at Carnton is merely a ruse, a way for me to investigate certain men in town without drawing suspicion. The McGavocks, of course, don't know that." He paused, trying to gauge her reaction.

She stared for a long moment, then her brow furrowed. "Track down counterfeiters. You mean, like Frank Bonner does?"

"Yes. I started working for the agency last summer. My primary goal is—"

She held up a hand, then slowly stood. "Are you . . . investigatin' me?"

He exhaled. "No. I've never thought you were involved."

Her eyes narrowed. "*Never* sounds like a long time. How long have you been thinkin' I wasn't involved?"

He kept his gaze on hers, wanting her to know he had nothing to hide. Not anymore. "I've known about the counterfeit money Ryan sent to your family since the day you and I went back into town and got your trunk."

Her jaw slipped open. "And you never said anything?"

"I couldn't."

"And just why is that?"

Wade felt his gut twist tight. "Because I'm in charge of the investigation against your brother."

A soft rush of air threaded her lips, and she sank down on the bench. He sat down by her, but her posture—and the look she gave him—held warning. So he still kept his distance.

Finally, she turned to him. "He's guilty, isn't he?" she whispered, her voice barely audible.

"The agency doesn't have the proper evidence yet to say conclusively whether—"

"I'm not askin' about the agency, Wade. I'm askin' about you. Do *you* think me brother is guilty?"

The hurt in her eyes tore through him, but the truth he read in them, same as he'd seen back in the cabin, all but broke his heart. "Yes . . . I do."

She sucked in a breath and leaned forward, holding tight to the bench seat.

"Catriona, I—"

Once more she held up a hand, and it took a moment before she met his gaze again. Tears in her eyes, she nodded. "God forgive me, but I do too. How can he not be? Knowin' what we know."

Wade took her in his arms and held her as she cried, struggling to contain his own emotions and failing to. They sat there for a while. He couldn't say how long, other than he'd silently prayed for her, for himself, and for Ryan until he'd run out of words.

Finally, she straightened, then wiped her cheeks. "I'm thinkin' you're mighty good at what you do, aren't you?"

He looked away, then shrugged. "I was well trained."

She gave a little laugh, but the way she searched his expression said she wanted more than that brief response. So he told her about some of the cases the agency had solved, the criminals they'd arrested. He told her about Anson Bern, how they'd been partners and how Bern had been killed in the line of duty. And he told her about the note left under his door at the hotel.

Disbelief colored her features. "So whoever it was, he was right there in the hotel?"

He nodded. "But he's still holding his cards close to the vest."

"And you're not the least worried?"

"I'm careful. And cautious. That's better than worried any day."

She studied him, and he began to wonder if he'd shared more with her than he should have. Or perhaps she'd further considered his role in her brother's investigation and her feelings toward him had changed. Then she covered his hand with hers, and he was grateful he was seated. Because he felt his entire world hung on whatever she said next.

"Thank you for tellin' me all that. And for the

record"—she leaned close and kissed him on the cheek—"not swayed in the least."

As Wade guided the wagon through the maze of streets toward the shantytown, Catriona imagined Ryan walking these very paths to and from work. From *work*. Her chest tightened till it ached. From wherever it was he'd been helping to print counterfeit money. All doubt removed now, she knew he'd done it. And while she felt an undeniable weight of guilt, she also felt the precious weight of her brother's love and longing to protect. Similar to the depth of love and protection she'd witnessed earlier from Delphia.

She stole a glance at Wade seated beside her. *A government operative*. That explained so much, while also sparking even more questions. But those would have to wait.

His grip tightened on the reins. "We don't have long before we'll need to be heading back. But at least we'll drive through the area, see if anything stands out. Then I'll bring another agent with me when I come back."

"I'll come back with you too."

He looked at her, his expression noncommittal but his eyes saying that was out of the question. She decided not to force the issue for now. But if he thought that, after all this, she was simply going to sit by and—

Distant barking drew their attention, and they turned to see Harvey running after the wagon for all he was worth. Wade stopped the rig and whistled, and the dog took a running leap and landed right at his feet. Harvey scampered up to Wade's lap, and Wade hugged him close, his affection for the animal apparent. Harvey's backside shook with absolute delight. Catriona made as much room as possible on the seat, and the dog settled in between them.

"I really was tempted to take him back to Carnton, but we'll drop him back by the Ledbetter house on our way home." Wade slapped the reins. "I think Delphia needs him."

Minutes later, they turned a corner, and Catriona looked out across an endless sea of lean-tos and makeshift shelters. She sensed Wade doing the same. The shantytown. It didn't take long for her to realize why Ryan had done what he'd done. Given the opportunity, she might have done it too, the scene so reminiscent of years past back home in Ireland where hunger and want had been so plentiful. Clusters of women and children with bodies far too thin sat hunched on overturned crates outside the various dwellings. Men, too, but they gathered in separate groups. To a person, they all turned and stared as the wagon passed. And in their faces, Catriona saw a definition of freedom that defied the meaning of the word. At least how she defined it.

"Even after winning a war," Wade said beside her, his voice flat, "they're still not free."

As his words sank in, one child in particular

caught Catriona's attention. The little girl, no more than two years old, stood close to the edge of the road, her stark blue eyes telling a story all their own. Catriona wondered if part of Ryan's motivation behind buying all that food for these people was to atone in some small way for having fought on the wrong side of the war. The choice hadn't been his. But where was it written that people only ever bore the consequences of their own wrongdoing?

A few streets over, Wade brought the wagon to a stop and set the brake. Brick and clapboard buildings lined the thoroughfare, at least half of them closed and boarded up. The other half appeared to be open for business. But if the disrepair of the buildings was any indicator, those businesses were not prospering.

He turned to her. "I'm going to walk the area real quick. See what I can see. I'd appreciate it if you'd stay here in the wagon, Catriona. And keep Harvey with you."

She started to offer protest, then allowed the earnestness in his eyes to persuade her otherwise. *This* time. He disappeared around the corner, and the dog whined as though it wanted to follow him.

She grasped hold of Harvey's collar. "You're stayin' here with me, boy. He'll be back soon enough." She stroked the dog's head, imagining that Ryan had done that very thing. He'd always loved animals.

The sun overhead was warm, and she leaned her

640

head back a little. Anticipating today's journey, she hadn't slept too soundly last night, and she closed her eyes, imagining herself and Ryan as children again, all piled into the old hammock stretched between two pinion pines out back of Miss Maeve's cottage. *Dearest Ryan, no matter what you—*

Harvey gave a sharp bark and bolted free.

Catriona came wide awake and turned around in time to see the dog headed for a door where a man was just entering one of the buildings. The dog managed to slip through just before the door closed.

"*Och!* You ornery little sneak!" Catriona climbed down from the wagon and followed, not about to lose that dog. Not after seeing how much it meant to Wade. And apparently to Ryan, as well as to Delphia, even if she wouldn't admit it. Catriona looked up at the two-story brick building but couldn't make out the faded name of the company once painted on the side.

She started to knock on the door, then reasoned it was a business and thought better of it. She stepped inside. It took a moment for her eyes to adjust. A long, dark hallway lined with shelves lay ahead, and best she could tell, reams of fabric filled each one. Solid wooden doors led off to her right, but they were all closed. All except for a door at the far end of the hallway that appeared to open into a much larger and well-lit room. Just where a dog would head. So she did likewise.

"Harvey?" she called as she went, figuring who-ever might have found the dog would appreciate her retrieving the little rascal. "Harvey, come here, you wee—"

"May I help you, ma'am?"

Catriona startled at the voice behind her and spun around, hand on her chest. A man, about her height, maybe a little taller, stood behind her. She thought he was the same man she saw come into this building. Where he'd come from just now, she didn't know. All the doors were still closed. She gave a breathy laugh. "Aye, you can. I'm lookin' for me dog. He ran in here just now, and I'm wantin' to get him before he causes more mischief than either of us can account for." She added a smile for good measure, but regardless of the poor lighting, she was relatively certain the man didn't return it.

"A dog, you say. Named Harvey."

"Aye. White all over except for markings of black on his ears and round his eyes."

"And what did you say *your* name was?"

Maybe it was the false tone of his voice or the way he eyed her, but instinct screamed at her not to trust him. As much as she didn't want to leave without Harvey, she knew she could come back again. With Wade.

"Perhaps I got it wrong, sir. Maybe the wee dog didn't come this way after all. I'll check around outside instead." She tried to skirt past him toward the exit, but he grabbed hold of her upper arm.

Catriona jerked away, but his grip was like a vise.

"I don't think you should leave just quite yet, ma'am."

"And I'm believin' I should." She delivered a hard kick to his shin and tried to wrangle free, but he shoved her against the wall. The back of her head met the brick with a dull thud, and the hallway swam in her vision.

CHAPTER 42

Catriona blinked, trying to get the hallway to stop spinning. The weight of the dagger in her sleeve all but called out to her, but how to get to it with this man watching her?

He said something vulgar beneath his breath, then laughed. "Don't ever start a fight you can't finish, sweetheart."

The door where she'd entered suddenly opened, and sunlight briefly illuminated the hallway. She recognized Wade's silhouette but not her attacker's face. She'd never seen the man before. But she did see her opportunity.

She shoved the man hard in the chest, then had just started running for Wade when a sharp pain exploded at the base of her neck. Her attacker hauled her back by the hair. Struggling against him, she saw Wade running toward them—then heard the unmistakable cocking of a gun by her head. Heart pounding, she went absolutely still.

"Hold it right there!" the man shouted, his breath hot against her ear.

Wade stopped midstride, hands outstretched. "This is between you and me. She has nothing to do with this."

A door opened somewhere beyond Wade, and light filtered into the hallway. Another man stepped out. "What do we have here, Gunnar?"

The man tightened his grip on her arm. "She came in calling after a dog, Harvey. Probably the one that belonged to that Irishman. And *he* came in after her."

"And just who is *he?*" The man took a closer look at Wade, then began laughing, the sound as smooth and gentlemanly as his voice. "Agent Cunningham! We meet again, and so soon. And let me guess, ma'am. Since you're with the dog—and seeing as you have the *Irish* written all over you—you must be related to the young Irishman. Who ended up costing me a fair amount of money, I must say. But then, I'm betting we *all* know about that already, don't we? No need to rehash past grievances."

Catriona looked from him to Wade, feeling as though she'd walked into the middle of a conversation. Wade started to turn around.

"Stay exactly as you are, Agent Cunningham," the man continued. "Or the harm that comes to her will be laid at your feet. Now slowly, and I mean *very* slowly, remove that beloved Colt, a gun my left temple remembers only too well, from beneath your coat and lay it on the floor, then kick it away. And remember, Miss O'Toole will pay for any foolishness."

Catriona could only watch as Wade did precisely as the man asked, his eyes locked on hers. She sensed he was trying to tell her something, but she didn't know what it was.

The man stepped closer. "Now, that wasn't so hard, was it?" In a blink, he punched Wade in the lower back. Wade grimaced and staggered forward but managed to stay standing.

"That was for the left temple, Cunningham. And this"—the man punched him in the back again, and Wade went down on one knee before struggling back to his feet—"is for all the money I lost when you arrested me and put me on that train."

Pain registered on Wade's face, and Catriona clenched her jaw to keep from screaming as anger and fear warred inside her. Faces flashed in front of her—Mam's, Bridget's, Alma's. *Ryan's.* But mostly Nora's. She wished she'd taken the few extra seconds to press a kiss to her sister's forehead before she'd left that morning. Same for Braxie. She promised herself she'd do it tomorrow morning and held tightly to that pledge. But the fragile hope she'd clung to for months, that Ryan was still alive . . . She felt that hope being ripped away.

Wade's breath came heavy. "What do you mean . . . money you *lost?* You jumped from that train before we could even get you locked up."

"Yes, that is quite true. And the jump while still being handcuffed was none too pleasant." He circled to stand in front of Wade but maintained his distance. "But do you realize how difficult it is to buy loyalty these days? As soon as the newspapers printed that I had been captured, all the people so loyal to Peter McCartney suddenly . . . weren't. They took all the money owed me and ran."

The man's attention shifted to Catriona just as the gun pointed at her head shifted to Wade.

"Pardon my manners, Miss O'Toole. It *is* Miss O'Toole, isn't it?"

Catriona only stared.

"Answer him!" The man dug his fingers into her arm.

"Aye, 'tis."

"Very good. Allow me to introduce myself. I'm Peter McCartney." The man bowed at the waist as though they were attending a formal gathering. "I already know a little something about you. A little birdie told me you and one of my favorite Treasury agents, Frank Bonner, had a most enjoyable conversation a while back."

If Catriona had met this man on the street, if they'd exchanged pleasantries, she would have considered him charming. But seeing his charm in this situation sent a chill up her spine. She glanced past him to Wade, who gave her an almost imperceptible shake of his head. *That,* she understood, and she kept silent.

McCartney finally shook his head. "Apparently the little birdie got it wrong, then. Either that or the cat got your tongue." He laughed at his own joke, then extended his arm to her. "Accompany me down the hall, please, Miss O'Toole."

She glanced again at Wade, who clearly looked

down to her left arm as she accepted McCartney's offer with her right. The man holding the gun on Wade picked up the Colt and motioned for Wade to precede him down the corridor. As they walked, Catriona carefully worked the dagger in her left sleeve down to the edge of her buttoned cuff. But that was as far as she could get it. She would have to unbutton the cuff to remove the knife.

"Please, Miss O'Toole"—McCartney smiled at her—"don't be alarmed. I have no intention of hurting you. Though I am none too certain of Agent Cunningham's commitment to good behavior. He does have a stubborn streak, that man. He will simply not give up! I've even offered him a cut of the spoils, but he flatly refused."

Itching to respond, she didn't. She heard Wade's steps behind her. At least they were keeping them together.

The room at the end of the hallway was smaller than she'd imagined, but windows situated along the tops of two walls provided an abundance of light.

"So you've already broken everything down?" Wade asked. "You're moving the operation again?"

"Yes," McCartney answered, seemingly unbothered. "I'm afraid you caught us on our last day here. We use this location from time to time, but we're moving everything tonight. It's this constant game we play, my colleagues and me. If only you and yours would grow tired of it."

"Never." Wade smiled.

McCartney showed Catriona to a chair, and she sat down, demurely placing her hands in her lap—left over right. Then she ever so carefully began to work at the row of tiny buttons on the left cuff of her shirtwaist.

"Tie him up," McCartney said simply. "Her too."

Exchanging glances with Wade, who sat opposite her looking completely calm, Catriona began working more hurriedly. As McCartney held the gun on Wade, the other man frisked him. He removed a knife from Wade's left boot and grinned.

"Check his right boot as well. He always keeps one there too."

Following McCartney's orders, the man extracted a second knife and smiled. "These are nice ones!" He searched Wade's coat pockets and withdrew a set of handcuffs with keys. "I'm keepin' these!"

Wade's expression never changed—except for a quick frown Catriona almost missed. Was she understanding him correctly? She wasn't sure.

The man tied him up, first his wrists, then his ankles, then moved to her.

Hoping she understood Wade's meaning, she clutched at the man's sleeve. "Please, sir," she said quickly, the fear in her voice coming honestly. "*Please* don't be tyin' me up. I give you me word I'll—"

"Shut up and put your arms behind the chair."

"But I won't be givin' you any—"

"I said put your arms behind the chair!"

With all the buttons loosened on her cuff, Catriona did as he said, mindful of holding her sleeve closed. He pulled the rope tight around her wrists, then paused, and Catriona held her breath.

The man laughed. "What do we have here?"

He pulled the dagger from her sleeve and handed it to McCartney.

"Oh, Miss O'Toole, I am so impressed! And it's such a lovely piece of work too. For a very lovely woman, of course. But alas, I'm afraid I must keep it." McCartney tucked it into one of his coat pockets.

Wade bowed his head. And as the man bound Catriona's ankles to the chair, she felt a cold seed of fear and regret in her stomach. Her last gift from Ryan. And their last hope of getting out of this mess.

Having a good mind what McCartney was up to, Wade wished he could have gotten Catriona out of here. The man possessed a cruel sense of humor, and Wade's greatest fear at the moment was that he would aim that dark and twisted trait at Catriona.

Wade caught her eye, and she gave him the tiniest nod. But the disappointment in her expression over losing the dagger from Ryan cut him to the quick.

McCartney relinquished the gun to his underling. "Go on and get the last of everything loaded, then wait for me outside."

Gunnar left the room, smiling back at Wade

and holding up the knives he'd taken from him.

McCartney pulled up a chair. "While I have you here, Cunningham, I would like to lodge a formal complaint against the Treasury Department. All of these little improvements you boys in Washington insist on, all in an effort to make the money more difficult to copy, are simply making my life more arduous. It's high time you accept that you will never be able to outwit a coney man. You're simply a bunch of government schoolboys playing at a losing game."

The man prattled on for a few moments, his ego unable to let him do otherwise, then Wade finally shook his head. "Don't you have a train or something to catch?"

McCartney slowly smiled. "In fact, I do. Now, if you'll both excuse me, I must be on my way. I'm sure someone will be along in a day or two, or maybe three, to check on the building. It will help if you scream. Loudly." He flashed a smile. "That worked for me when I broke my ankle jumping from that train." He bowed to Catriona. "It's been a pleasure, Miss O'Toole."

McCartney paused, then his expression sobered, and Wade saw it in his eyes.

"Don't," Wade warned, fighting against his restraints.

McCartney offered a manufactured look of compassion. "Since fate and circumstances have seen fit to bring us together, ma'am, may I be the first to offer my condolences on the untimely death of your brother last year. That was, indeed, a shock to us all."

Catriona sucked in a breath, and Wade wanted to rip out the man's throat.

"Look at me, Catriona," Wade whispered, and she did, for a moment. "Try not to listen to a thing he's going to say."

"Your brother was quite an artist too." McCartney spoke louder. "The best I've had in my employ. But when I discovered that he'd stolen money from me, well, you can imagine I was not pleased. But when he told me the money was for his dear family back in Ireland, that made all the difference."

Tears welled up in Catriona's eyes, and Wade rocked from side to side in his chair, working to break free.

"McCartney, I'm asking you, if there's the least shred of decency left in you—"

"Oh, there's not. So no use in appealing to that. But what I do want you to know, Miss O'Toole, is that it was never my idea to kill your brother." A slow smile turned his mouth. "And in fact, I did not kill him. No, that happened at someone else's hand when that young, idealistic brother of yours informed us that not only was he no longer going to work for us, but he was determined to turn himself in for *crimes* he'd committed." McCartney shook his head. "Once one of these agents like Cunningham here gets ahold of someone, that someone tends to tell all, and we simply could not let that happen." He cocked his head. "I do hope you understand, ma'am."

Tears running down her cheeks, her chin trembling, Catriona slowly lifted her gaze. "What I'm understandin' is that despite your arrogance and lack of compassion, you have given me a gift that I'll be carryin' with me for the rest of me life. Even though I'm doubtin' you'll ever know or understand it yeself. But—" Her voice had started as a whisper but gained strength as she went. She drew in a breath. "Perhaps you *will* be findin' it one day. Before it's too late."

McCartney's expression went slack, and he looked at her with something akin to confusion, even frustration. But Wade felt only awe. How she had responded to such intentional cruelty and meanness with such love and patient kindness, he didn't know. And yet he did. He saw the evidence in her eyes.

Slowly, McCartney regained his composure and drew himself up. "Well, as I said, I must be off to the next grand adventure. Ah, but one last thing . . ." McCartney leaned down to Wade. "Your partner, Anson Bern," he whispered. "I should offer my condolences to you as well on another most unfortunate occurrence." But the pleasure in his voice said he felt quite the opposite.

Wade's anger burned. "Careful, McCartney. You're beginning to sound like an accomplice to murder."

"Oh no. My focus is always on the money. I have

others who take care of those messy details." He glanced toward the door through which Gunnar had left. "But I must admit, if only to you, that the note under the door, at the hotel? That was mine." Pride flushed his face. "I thought that was a particularly nice touch. Understated, yet poignant. It's a fine balance."

Just one punch to his face. That was all Wade wanted right now.

McCartney straightened, and Wade braced himself. "Agent Cunningham—" McCartney hauled back and punched him in the gut. "Until we meet again."

Wade gasped for breath, the residual ache in his kidneys now lessened by the pain in his abdomen. He had to give McCartney his due . . . the man knew where to land a blow. Wade forced his head up. "That meeting might come sooner"—he sucked in a breath—"than you think, McCartney."

McCartney paused, laughing, then took a step back toward him. "Why do you say that?"

"Well . . ." Wade grimaced as he sliced through the last piece of rope binding his wrists. "Because you're cocky, and you talk too much." He grabbed the man by the shirt, hauled him close, and punched him twice in the face. The cartilage in McCartney's nose buckled beneath the force, and he went down hard and didn't move.

"*Och!*" Catriona's mouth slipped open. "How did you manage that?"

Keeping close watch on his prisoner as well as

the door in case the underling returned, Wade made quick work of the ropes binding his own legs, then cut her loose as well. "McCartney's right. I carry a knife in each boot, but I also carry one in the back of my waistband. He doesn't know about that one. Yet."

His thoughts still centered on Bern, Wade searched McCartney for the Colt, found it, and tucked it back into his waistband. He grabbed the ropes and bound McCartney's wrists and ankles, then tied him to a cast-iron worktable for good measure. Finally, he reached for Catriona and drew her close. "Are you all right?"

She leaned into him and slid her arms around his waist. "I'm fine. Still a wee bit scared, and mad as a hornet. But I'm lovin' me brother more than I ever have." She looked up. "Ryan was goin' to turn himself in. He was goin' to do the right thing."

Wade kissed her forehead. "I'm just so sorry you had to find out this way. McCartney's a mean-spirited—"

She pressed her fingers to his mouth. "But he *did* give me a gift, even though he wasn't meanin' to." She frowned. "I want me dagger back!"

Wade smiled and dug through McCartney's coat pockets until he found it. Catriona held the scabbarded blade tightly, then slipped it back into her left sleeve and buttoned the cuff.

"I heard what he said about your partner. I'm so sorry, Wade."

"Me too." He brushed a stray curl from her

temple. "I wish I could have known your brother."

"And I yours. But who knows"—a light lit her eyes—"maybe they're knowin' each other by now."

"I think there's a very good chance of that. Especially if our mothers are involved."

Hearing McCartney coming to, Wade knelt beside him.

McCartney looked up and uttered a curse. "Are you planning to put me on another train, Cunningham? So I can jump off and break my other ankle?"

Wade smiled. "No. *This* time I'm taking you all the way to DC myself. I'm going to see to it that you're locked up nice and tight in a cell all your own."

"I'm deeply honored. And private quarters, no less."

Wade reached for his revolver. "And just so you know, this isn't retribution for anything. It's so I can go outside and apprehend your henchman without you attempting to escape." Wade raised the Colt, then paused. "Well, a little of it is for how you tried to hurt Miss O'Toole just now. And for what you did to my partner." Before McCartney could spout a smart response, Wade struck him on the right temple with the butt of the revolver, and McCartney sagged back to the floor.

$\mathscr{E}$PILOGUE

July 4, 1866
Formal Dedication of the McGavock Cemetery
Franklin, Tennessee

Catriona looked out across the McGavock Cemetery at the 1,481 whitewashed cedar markers that adorned the graves. But the small casket resting at her feet was the one that would take a portion of her heart to its grave. She knew her brother wasn't really dead, though. Despite what he'd done, Ryan O'Toole had been swallowed up by life. The Lord's grace and Ryan's trust in it confirmed that.

"Are you ready?" Wade asked softly beside her.

"Aye," she whispered. "As long as you're with me."

He pressed a kiss to her head. "Forever."

Wade nodded to George Cuppett, who along with Charley Baugh picked up the three-foot casket and slowly began walking the long, fourteen-foot-wide grassy corridor that divided the two columns of graves that seemed to stretch on forever. Fifteen graves in each row, and the sections laid out by state—every Southern state but Virginia—Catriona knew only too well. And she wouldn't have her brother's body to bury today if not for Wade.

As promised, he'd escorted Peter McCartney to Washington, DC, and all the way to his prison cell. Wade insisted McCartney be handcuffed to him the entire journey, not only so the counterfeiter couldn't escape, but so Wade could learn more about what happened to Ryan. Catriona took a measure of comfort in knowing that Ryan had died quickly—if what McCartney said was true—and she was grateful the man had finally revealed to Wade where Ryan's body had been buried.

Best they could piece together, Ryan had died early spring of last year, long before she and Nora ever left Ireland. All that time she'd spent wondering where he was, only to learn that he'd long been at peace and at home with the Lord. Her brother died knowing he was trying to do the right thing, which meant the world to her. But mostly her comfort came in trusting that the Almighty had been with him every step. Just as he'd been with her and Nora. Even when she couldn't see evidence of him anywhere around her, he was working. As Mam always said, *"God's help is nearer than the door."*

"I want you to hold me," Nora whispered none too quietly and tugged on Catriona's skirt.

"Come here, wee one." Catriona swept her up and pressed a kiss to her forehead, loving how her sister tucked her face into the crook of her neck like she used to do. In turn, Nora hugged Virginia close with her right arm all healed and whole thanks to ol' Caesar, and placed a kiss on the doll's new face. Wade had carved it from white pine, and Catriona had painted it. Finally, Virginia had a smile that not only Nora could see.

Wade looked down at them, and Catriona knew he was waiting for her to take the first step. She looked all the way down the grassy corridor to where Tempy, Braxie, ol' Caesar, Robert Sloan, Miles McConnico and his family, and a handful of other workers from Carnton waited by the empty plot of earth near the end. It seemed a long distance to cross from where they stood, yet they'd already come so far.

She spotted a wagon in the distance, on Lewisburg Pike, slowing to make the turn onto the drive up to Carnton. She glanced up at Wade to see him following the wagon's progress too.

"A little early," he whispered.

"Nay." She smiled. "Right on time."

Feeling his arm around her waist, she followed in George and Charley's footsteps, grateful again that the McGavocks had agreed that Ryan could be buried here. And considering whom she'd asked to conduct the funeral, she was also grateful that they'd issued their apologies for not being able to attend. They were preparing for the formal cemetery dedication that would take place later that day, where hundreds of guests were expected to be in attendance.

After the burial team had finished their work and she'd recorded the last name in the book, George Cuppett presented the leather-bound journal to

661

Colonel and Mrs. McGavock. And knowing what she knew now, Catriona no longer referred to it as the Book of the Dead. Formally, it was called the McGavock Cemetery Book. But to her, for so many of those men, it was a book of life.

"You both look beautiful," Wade whispered, his gaze taking her and Nora in.

Nora peered down at her new blue dress with tiny pink, blue, and purple flowers. "Grandma Tempy made it for me."

Catriona exchanged looks with Wade, already knowing he heartily approved of Nora's new name for the dear woman. And Tempy felt the same. "Aye, she did. And she helped make mine too." Catriona had never owned so fine a gown. And the color—a deep, vibrant lilac—was her favorite. Wade insisted on purchasing the fabric and notions for both her and Nora's dresses, and she and Tempy had spent many an evening in recent weeks sewing and planning for today.

Catriona mouthed a silent "Thank you" to him again, and he slipped her a wink.

Seeing the podium and line of chairs set up near the walnut grove for the cemetery dedication later, she leaned closer. "I'm still findin' it a wee bit hard to believe that, even knowin' the truth about you now, the colonel still wants you standin' with him today during the dedication. A Federal soldier!"

Wade smiled. "You're no more shocked than I am. But one thing he and I both agree on is that the North and South *must* start working together.

We don't have to agree on everything, and we never will. But we must find a way to live in peace together. To be neighbors and friends. Or we're going to find ourselves walking this particular path over and over and over again." He glanced back at her. "I do think I earned extra stars in my crown by revealing how much his accountant was overbilling him."

She nodded in agreement. "I'm lookin' forward to meetin' this Chief Wood you and Isham keep talkin' about. I'm glad he'll be comin' to the weddin'. But I'm most eager to hear more about the new position he's created for you, and about how you can work from Franklin."

"You and me both. I sure won't miss all that travel. Because being here with you three gals is where I want to be."

As she placed one foot in front of the other, she thought about the surprise they had for Tempy and could scarcely wait.

A few paces ahead of them, George and Charley lowered the casket into the earth, and Wade reached for Nora, who went willingly into his arms. Catriona picked up a handful of dirt and held it briefly in her hand—whispering a final, albeit temporary, good-bye to her brother—before letting it go. Then she looked at Tempy, who opened her journal and began to read. Catriona drank in the words.

" 'For we know that when this earthly tent we live in is taken down, meanin' that, when we die and leave this old, worn-out earthly body behind, we *will* have a house in heaven.' "

"Amen," ol' Caesar bellowed.

"Come on, heaven," George whispered, and Catriona could all but see Marcellus standing there pointing to the sky.

" 'A body that will last forever,' " Tempy continued, " 'made for us by God hisself and not by any man or woman's hands . . .' "

After Tempy closed her journal, Wade led them in prayer, and Catriona discreetly lifted her head and looked around the circle of friends—now family—giving thanks for each of them. When she came to Braxie, who stood beside her, she found the girl looking her way, and Catriona drew her close in a hug.

"And, Father," Wade continued, Nora's head now on his shoulder, "thank you for grace and for using every step of our walk with you to bring us closer home. And finally, thank you for swallowing us up in life when each of our time comes. Through Jesus we ask this, and all God's people said . . ."

A resounding "Amen" followed, and George and Charley quickly filled in the grave and smoothed out the dirt. Wade handed Nora the bag of rocks she'd been collecting for so long, many of them brought from their homeland in County Antrim, and Catriona helped her build a cairn atop the grave. With every stone Catriona placed, she thanked God for a different blessing, Nora, Wade, and Braxie at the top of the list. Then she laid a bouquet of dried Spring Squill beside it.

"Before I forget," Wade whispered, then pulled a piece of paper from his pocket. He handed it to her.

Catriona opened it, realized what it was, and hugged him tight. "How did you get this back?"

"Frank Bonner isn't so bad once you get to know him."

Catriona eyed him until one side of his mouth tipped.

"I told him if he didn't give Ryan's note back to you, I'd tell everyone in the agency that he'd been bested by a woman in an interrogation."

Loving the man more each day, Catriona read the note again, her gaze lingering on the last lines her brother had penned to her. *Come as soon as you can. So me heart can feel whole again.* She looked back at the grave, then lifted her gaze toward heaven and hoped the Lord would pass along the message in her heart.

Everyone visited for a few minutes, then made their way toward the house. Tempy leaned close to Nora, who was again in Wade's arms. "I got a good lunch ready for you, Miss Nora. And I done cooked up one special chicken. So I hope you's hungry."

"I'm always hungry!" Nora held out her arms to Tempy, and Wade made the transfer.

"I hope you's hungry too, Mister Cunningham," Tempy added, giving him a smile that said he was finally in her good graces after she'd learned the truth about him—but that she was still watching him.

Wade just laughed and tossed her a wink.

The wagon they'd spotted a while earlier was finally making its way up to the house, and Catriona and Wade exchanged a glance.

"Tempy . . ." Catriona came alongside her. "We have two special guests who'll be joining us in the kitchen for lunch today."

"Oh, that's fine," she responded. "We got us plenty of food. I'll just run and set another two places."

"No, I'll do that," Braxie offered, her mischievous smile set firmly in place. "You stay here."

"I want to go with Braxie!" Nora shouted, and Tempy granted the girl her freedom. Then she looked from Catriona to Wade and back again. "What you two got goin' on? You's actin' all sneaky. You done moved up your weddin' date? Can't wait another two weeks?"

Wade shook his head. "The wedding plans haven't changed. In fact, this has nothing to do with us, Tempy. It's about you, ma'am."

" 'Bout me?" Tempy slowed her steps. She followed Wade's gaze to the wagon Isham brought to a stop before the front gate, then her focus moved to the two people seated in the back. She squinted. "Who's that back in the wagon bed?"

Catriona linked arms with her. "Those are our special guests we want you to meet."

Isham helped Delphia and Demetrius down from

the wagon, and Harvey came bounding out with them. The dog made an immediate beeline for Wade, who knelt and gave him a good rubbing, then finally headed toward Nora and Winder as though instinctively knowing which people would be the most rambunctious.

Catriona had already met Demetrius once, but it hurt her all over again to see what had been done to him. He'd been beaten and left for dead by a man both Delphia and Demetrius refused to identify for fear he would come back to finish the job.

Demetrius walked hunched over with a cane and looked years older than his older sister—until he saw Tempy and a smile slowly spread across his face.

Catriona rushed to make the introductions. "Delphia, Demetrius," she said, greeting them. "May I present Tempy, who's the cook here at Carnton and who's been here most all her life. And, Tempy—" Unexpected tears rose to her eyes, and she turned to Wade as they'd agreed to beforehand, knowing this reunion wouldn't be happening without him. She would let Tempy know that full well.

"It's my honor, ma'am, to introduce you"— Wade paused, briefly firming his jaw—"to Rufus and Jinsey, your brother and sister."

Tempy stared, then reached out as though needing a support, and Wade steadied her as simultaneous disbelief and joy swept her face. She shook her head. "It can't be."

"Oh, but it can," Catriona whispered. "And it is!"

Delphia spread her arms wide, and Tempy rushed into her embrace. Demetrius gathered close, and the three of them laughed through tears and kissed one another all while talking at once.

Wade and Catriona stepped back, letting them have their moment. A moment that had been a lifetime in coming.

Finally, Demetrius drew back. "This can't really be our mama's *Sukey,* can it?"

Tempy frowned. *"Sukey?"* She looked from Delphia to Demetrius again. "That be the name our mama give me?"

"Sure is." Demetrius gently touched her cheek. "I'd done remembered it all these years and been prayin' God might bring us together 'fore he calls us all home. And sure 'nough, he did."

Tempy laughed through tears, then looked back at Catriona and Wade. "Sukey. My gracious. What kind o' name is that!"

As the siblings continued their reunion, Catriona felt a tug on her sleeve and looked down to see Nora, a bewildered look on the child's face. But before Catriona could pick her up, Wade did.

"What is it, sweet one?" he said in that voice that could scale every defense.

Nora shrugged and looked away.

He tugged a curl at her temple. "Did something happen? You can tell us."

"Nay," she whispered. "I'm just . . ."

"You're just what?"

She peered up at him and pressed a little hand against his cheek. "I'm just wonderin' why everyone else seems to be havin' a papa, and I have me a *Wade*."

Catriona's chest clenched tight, yet her own struggle seemed nothing at all compared to the emotion filling Wade's eyes. He looked at her as though asking for her permission, and Catriona nodded.

Wade took hold of Nora's hand. "Tell you what," he whispered, his voice a bit shaky. "What if you call me Papa, and I'll call you my sweet little girl. Would that be all right?"

Nora's chin quivered. "Aye, Papa. I'd be likin' that a lot."

He kissed her forehead, and Nora hugged him tight around the neck. Then just as quickly she wriggled free and ran back to join Braxie, who stood waiting with Winder and Hattie.

Wade blew out a breath. "If I'm not careful, your little sister is going to have me wrapped around her little finger."

"Is goin' to?" Catriona laughed.

"Excuse me, Mister Cunningham."

They turned to see Delphia approaching.

"I know this is gonna be a hardship to you, sir. But I'd be much obliged if you'd take Mister Harvey and keep him with you. I just can't abide that dog anymore. He's gettin' into everything!" She motioned behind her, and the more she spoke, the more her eyes watered and her voice shook. "So

I'm thinkin' good riddance to the little creature!"

Wade laid a gentle hand to her shoulder. "We all know you love that dog, Delphia. So you don't have to do this. Not for me."

She shook her head. "But I do. Y'all been through a lot together, you and him. Seems fittin' that you end up together. But I get to visit him anytime I want!"

Wade laughed. "It's a deal."

As Delphia rejoined her siblings, a fit of barking and squawking broke out, and they all turned to see Harvey chasing Brunhilde, who'd somehow escaped from the chicken coop. Again. Catriona had fully intended to serve up the little vixen today, but visiting the coop late yesterday afternoon, she'd experienced an unexpected wave of mercy. It hadn't hurt that the bird stood stock-still, staring at her as though reading her mind and already forming a plan of attack.

Wade shook his head. "Finally that chicken has met her match."

"We can only hope." Catriona laughed with him, then looked up. "A daughter *and* a dog. What more is a man needin'?"

"I need my wife," Wade whispered, then led her behind one of the tall evergreens lining the front walkway and drew her into his arms and kissed her. Not hurriedly as he had this morning, but slowly, as though wanting to memorize everything about her, just as she wanted to memorize everything about him.

Resting her head against his chest, Catriona heard the solid beat of his heart and thought about the confession they'd made to each other in recent days. Aye, they'd both suffered in ways they'd wish on no man or woman. But if God had never led them down those particular paths, they might never have found each other. And whatever he had in store for them—be it prosperity or hardship—they would face it together and look for the blessing in it. Her heart beyond full, she tried to find the words to tell her heavenly Father how grateful she was. Then a still, small voice inside her said he already knew.

AFTERWARD

Thank you for taking Wade and Catriona's journey (and spunky little Nora's too) with me in *Colors of Truth*. Post–Civil War history has long been of interest to me, so when I learned about the rampant counterfeiting in America during that era, I knew I wanted to write about it. Add to that the formation of the Secret Service agency in July 1865, along with my love for Irish history—my ancestors hailed from County Antrim, Ireland too—and the seed for *Colors of Truth* was planted!

Lies told to us. Lies we tell ourselves. Lies we tell others.

These themes run throughout this novel, and as is the case for every story I write, God met me on the page and drew me closer to him through the characters' struggles. Lying is wrong. Most of us learned that at a very young age, and I'd like to think that most adults today would still acknowledge that truth—and uphold it. And yet, falsehood and twisted narrative abound. Sometimes we don't see (or choose to see) the various ways we often abandon truth by downplaying it, twisting it "ever so slightly," or blatantly misleading someone. The latter is the most obvious, of course, and often the most destructive in relationships. But by no means is it the most insidious.

We've all told lies to ourselves and to others. But it's the lies told *to* us—lies whispered in the recesses of our hearts—that I believe can take the deepest hold. Lies that threaten to strangle our hope and damage relationships. The Word of God tells us that the devil is the father of lies. The Bible also describes him as a believer's adversary, who prowls around like a roaring lion seeking someone to devour. Care to guess one of the ways the father of lies does that? Through whispering lies. But through the power of God's Spirit living within us—who himself is only a whisper away—we can defeat that temptation to lie, both to ourselves and others, and we can live and walk in truth. We can take captive *every* thought to make it obedient to Christ (see 1 Peter 5:8 and 2 Corinthians 10:5).

I'm deeply indebted to the extraordinary folks at Carnton in Franklin, who are always ready to answer my endless questions about Carnton's history, the cemetery, and the former slaves who worked at Carnton, as well as a thousand other details. Special thanks to Joanna Stephens and Beth Trescott, who read the manuscript of *Colors of Truth* and offered much appreciated counsel for historical accuracy.

If you're interested in knowing more about the real history behind *Colors of Truth*, I invite you to visit the BONUS FEATURES page on my website www.TameraAlexander.com and click the icon titled TRUTH or FICTION. You'll access a page chock-full of "insider information" about Wade and Catriona's story, including an abundance of photographs featuring images of the real people portrayed in the novel (such as the McGavock family, the Cuppett brothers, and counterfeiter Peter McCartney), plus nineteenth-century counterfeit money, videos shot on location at Carnton, and much more.

The United States following the American Civil War was a country divided, a country on the brink of collapse both economically and relationally. Some might say that with current-day divisions in America, we are approaching that same brink again. Which makes it all the more important that we *remember* our history—unaltered, both the good and bad of it. An abundance of blood has been spilled for our freedom. Not only by fellow countrymen and -women on hallowed battlefields such as that of the Battle of Franklin at Carnton, but far more importantly, at the foot of the blood-soaked cross of Jesus Christ. As long as people inhabit the earth, we will have our differences. But as I stated at the outset in the author's note, we are *all* created in the image of God and are therefore his image-bearers. We are brothers and sisters. We should treat one another as such, bearing with one another in love, even when we disagree. Perhaps especially then.

Thank you again for sharing the precious gift of your time with me. I'm currently writing the third and final Carnton novel, which is Nora all grown up! The twists and turns of Nora's story have surprised even me (no shock there, knowing her, right?). The book releases Summer 2021. Be sure to connect with me via my eUpdates and I'll send you a reminder.

I'm so grateful for you, friend. Even as I write this note, I'm praying for you. I'm asking that God will draw you ever closer to him through the person and deity of Jesus, and that he'll deepen your love (and mine) for his living Word, the Bible. There's no better book to read than his!

Until next time,
Tamera

$\mathscr{A}$CKNOWLEDGMENTS

To Joe, Kelsey, and Kurt, I'm grateful for your love, humor, encouragement—and our never-ending family text thread.

To Deborah Raney, my dear friend and writing critique partner, I sincerely cannot imagine doing this without you. So don't even think about stopping!

To Angela Hunt, for helping me navigate the world of indie publishing. I will never not take your advice again.

To Kim Pressley, my wonderfully snarky friend, thank you for sharing that precious story about your young son "having a Jerry, but wishing he had a dad." And for allowing me to borrow it.

To the Coeur d'Alene Women, our five days of plotting, playing, and praying together every July is a taste of heaven for me—and a lifeline throughout the year.

To my friends at Carnton (especially Joanna Stephens and Beth Trescott, you lovely ladies), bless you for not only embracing my desire to share more of Carnton's real history but doing so with such enthusiasm. I'm forever grateful.

To Jean Bloom, thank you for coming alongside

me in the final edit and for so graciously helping me to see the forest for the trees.

To Natasha Kern, my agent, in a word (or three), *You absolutely rock!*

To my readers, you are among the greatest joys in this writer's life. How can I ever thank you for reading so faithfully and taking these journeys with me, and for sharing your lives. I hope our paths cross (again) soon!

To all who prayed for my precious dad, Doug Gattis Sr., as he walked the long road of dementia in recent years and was finally "swallowed up by life" in August 2019, thank you for praying for us and for your loving words of comfort. I wrote *Colors of Truth* during his last year here on earth, and you helped carry me (us) through those difficult—but blessing-filled—final weeks, days, and even moments. And I'm so grateful.

Finally, but always first, to Jesus, my beloved Rabbi, the anchor and Savior of my soul, whatever good there is in me is only because of you. Continue to break me, Lord, until I'm wholly yours.

$\mathscr{D}$ISCUSSION QUESTIONS

1. Before reading *Colors of Truth*, were you familiar with the discrimination of the Irish in nineteenth-century America? What was eye-opening for you about how Catriona and Nora were treated by certain townspeople or by the signs that, true to history, hung outside local businesses? Likewise, what did you know about the United States Secret Service and its history before reading Wade and Catriona's story?

2. Both Wade and Catriona suffered enormous losses. Sweet—and snarky—little Nora did too. The Word of God clearly states the truth that God is sovereign and that nothing touches our lives without first filtering through his loving hands. Why do you think God allows such pain and hardship to affect both believers and nonbelievers? (Read Romans 8:28; Genesis 50:20; Philippians 1:29; 2 Timothy 3:12.) Discuss the various trials faced by your favorite character in the story. How would you react if faced with a similar trial? How would you respond to Joni Eareckson Tada's statement, "God permits what he hates to achieve what he loves"?

3. The Bible teaches that the love of money is the root of all evil. Money plays a major part in this story—both the want of it and the lack. Discuss how Catriona's journey, in particular, is impacted by money. What struggles with money have you experienced? Could you relate to Catriona in this respect? If yes, how?

4. Catriona and Nora share a deep sisterly bond while also sharing a real love-hate relationship. Do you have a sister(s)? What relationships similar to this have you experienced? How did the widespread difference in the sisters' ages affect their relationship?

5. Wade and Catriona's love grows gradually throughout the story and takes several twists and turns along the way. It wasn't love at first sight. What are your favorite scenes in the novel pertaining to them as a couple? Do you prefer love stories where the characters slowly come to love each other—or "love at first sight" stories? And why?

6. Tempy, a beloved character in the Carnton novels, is based on the real woman who served as the McGavock family's cook for most of her life. Slavery is an abhorrent evil and strikes contrary to the truth that *all* people are image-bearers of thc living God. Africans bought and sold during the transatlantic slave trade were robbed not only of their dignity but of their lives and their families. Were you aware that owners of slaves often changed

a slave's name to better suit their personal likes? And that a slave searching for a family member after the Civil War stood little to no chance of ever finding them? Discuss Tempy's character and the outcome of her journey in this story.

7. The theme of lying runs throughout this novel. Lying is wrong. We learn that at a very young age. Why do you think we lie to each other? To ourselves? And even to God (although, good luck with this last one)? What lies have you told yourself? Do you ever hear whispered accusations, lies, in your heart? Read 1 Peter 5:8 and 2 Corinthians 10:5 (along with other scriptures group members may share) and discuss the temptation to lie versus the power a believer has to resist that temptation.

8. In the epilogue, we get a glimpse of the truths about God and the afterlife Catriona has learned in her journey. What are some of these truths? What do you believe about the afterlife? Read the various scriptures Tempy read (from 2 Corinthians 5) and discuss what you believe the Bible teaches.

$\mathcal{R}$ECIPES

MAM'S IRISH BUTTERSCOTCH PIE

Ingredients:
1 ½ cups packed light brown sugar
½ teaspoon salt
¼ cup cornstarch
3 cups whole milk
4 egg yolks from large eggs (discard the whites)
2 tablespoons butter
1 9-inch *baked* pie pastry

In a medium nonstick pan, whisk brown sugar, salt, and cornstarch. In a medium bowl, whisk milk and egg yolks (remember, not the whole egg, just the yolks). Pour this mixture into the pan with the brown sugar mixture and stir until combined.

Cook on medium heat, stirring gently, until the mixture begins to bubble and thicken (about 8 to 10 minutes—watch it closely so it doesn't scorch). When the mixture reaches pudding consistency, stir in butter until melted, then remove from heat. Pour into a baked pie shell and smooth to the edges. Chill for a couple of hours—or slice it right then and have more of a "warm pudding pie" like Tempy, Catriona, and Nora did. Either way, it's delicious! It's also wonderful with whipped cream. Enjoy!

Tempy's Cinnamon Oat Muffins

Ingredients:

1 cup all-purpose flour (or whole-wheat pastry flour)
¼ cup packed brown sugar
1 tablespoon baking powder
1 teaspoon ground cinnamon
½ teaspoon salt
1 cup whole (or 2%) milk
¼ cup oil
1 large egg
1 teaspoon pure vanilla extract
1 cup oats
½ cup raisins (if desired)

Topping:

2 tablespoons packed brown sugar
1 teaspoon ground cinnamon
2 tablespoons all-purpose flour
1 teaspoon melted butter

Preheat oven to 425 degrees. Spray a 12-cup muffin tin with baking spray (or use cupcake liners) and set aside. In a large bowl, mix flour, brown sugar, baking powder, cinnamon, and salt. In a separate bowl, whisk milk, oil, egg, and vanilla until combined. Add milk mixture to flour mixture, stirring until just moistened. Gently fold in oats and raisins (if using raisins, which make these muffins extra yummy and moist). Divide mixture evenly among prepared 12-cup muffin tin. Prepare the topping by combining brown sugar, cinnamon, flour, and butter in a small bowl until mixed well. Sprinkle over the top of each unbaked muffin. Bake for 11 to 13 minutes (your oven may vary) or until a toothpick inserted into the center comes out clean. Remove from oven and serve warm, slathered in butter. Enjoy!

For Catriona's Irish Beef Stew and more recipes from this novel, visit Tamera's website TameraAlexander.com and click on "Bonus Features," then click on "Novel Recipes."

About the Author

Tamera Alexander is a *USA TODAY* bestselling author and one of today's most popular writers of inspirational historical romance. Her books have earned her devoted readers worldwide, as well as multiple industry awards. Tamera and her husband make their home in Nashville, not far from Carnton and other Southern mansions that serve as the backdrop for many of her critically acclaimed novels.

Tamera invites you to visit her at:
Website: TameraAlexander.com
Twitter: @TameraAlexander
Facebook: Tamera.Alexander
Pinterest: TameraAuthor

Or if you prefer snail mail, please write her at:
Tamera Alexander
P.O. Box 871
Brentwood, TN 37024

Join Tamera on BOOKBUB and never miss a deal or new release!
bookbub.com/authors/tamera-alexander
Discussion questions for all of Tamera's novels are available at TameraAlexander.com, as are

details about Tamera joining your book club for a virtual visit.

Tamera hosts monthly giveaways on her website and invites you to sign up for her eUpdates and have your name tossed into the hat!

Center Point Large Print

600 Brooks Road / PO Box 1
Thorndike, ME 04986-0001 USA

(207) 568-3717

US & Canada:
1 800 929-9108
www.centerpointlargeprint.com